Praise for

The Forest Lord

continued . . .

"This is a book to treasure." —*The Best Reviews*

"A fascinating novel that combines mystical magic and enduring love. Those who enjoy out-of-the-ordinary stories will find this book intriguing." —*BookBrowser*

KINSMAN'S OATH

Susan Krinard

BERKLEY SENSATION, NEW YORK

KINSMAN'S OATH

A Berkley Sensation Book / published by arrangement with the author

PRINTING HISTORY
Berkley Sensation edition

ISBN: 0-7394-4420-4

BERKLEY SENSATION™
Berkley Sensation Books are published by The Berkley Publishing Group, a division of Penguin Group (USA) Inc., 375 Hudson Street, New York, New York 10014.
BERKLEY SENSATION and the "B" design are trademarks belonging to Penguin Group (USA) Inc.

PRINTED IN THE UNITED STATES OF AMERICA

This book is respectfully dedicated to the Science Fiction and Fantasy authors who have had the greatest impact on my life:

Madeleine L'Engle—whose *A Wrinkle in Time*, read to my fifth grade class, introduced me to the wonders of the genre;

Andre Norton—whose stories helped me live through the challenges of adolescence;

Marion Zimmer Bradley—whose work introduced me to lifelong friend Brett Carter;

C. J. Cherryh—my ideal world-builder, ultimately responsible for my wonderful marriage to fellow science fiction reader Serge Mailloux;

Sharon Lee and Steve Miller—who not only write wonderful romantic "space opera," but who, along with friends and mentors eluki bes shahar and Jennara Wenk and the television series *Beauty and the Beast*, can take full credit for setting me on the writing path.

Thank you all.

Prologue

The boy was young—young enough to be barred from the areas of the Persephonean corvette he most wanted to see, and to be assigned one of the Archon's own special agents during the voyage into shaauri space. Too young for wandering the corridors, where he might interfere with the duties of busy crew; too young to visit engineering with its vast sparkling pillars filled with dancing light like rainbows in a bottle, or to join his parents on the bridge.

All during the journey, he had spent most of his time in his small cabin or in the *Aphrodite*'s mess hall, where he played games on the holosim or cards with Agent Teklys. She laughed when he almost beat her at Nova and told him he was too young to be so good.

But he was not too young to know when something had gone terribly wrong.

The first warning came when the *Aphrodite* shook as if a great fist had slammed into its hull. Agent Teklys jumped out of her seat, hand flying to the gun at her belt, and stared up as if she could see through the overhead to the source of the explosion.

The boy followed her gaze. "What is it?" he asked. All of

a sudden he was very excited and very scared. "Is someone attacking the ship?"

Before she could answer, the first alarm shrieked over the intercom. Agent Teklys muttered something fierce under her breath. The boy felt her fear; he couldn't read thoughts, not yet, but he sometimes caught images, feelings. What he glimpsed in Teklys's mind made his stomach flip-flop like a spike-eel in a fishing net.

Agent Teklys ran to the bulkhead and punched the intercom. All that answered her call was static and the wail of the klaxon. She dashed back to the boy and knelt before him, grasping both his arms.

"Listen to me, young *ser.* I'm going out to see what's happening. I'll be right back, and I want you to stay here until I come for you. Is that understood?"

He nodded, swallowing the thickness in his throat. He wanted very badly to go with her, but he'd only get in the way. That was what his older brother Ambros told him constantly.

But Ambros was home on Persephone with Uncle Miklos, and *he,* the middle son, had been allowed to go with Mama and Papa on this most important of missions. He would *not* wish he'd been left at home as well.

"Very good," Agent Teklys said. "Don't be afraid. I will protect you." With a final tap on his shoulder, she ran through the mess door and sealed it behind her.

He waited. He was good at waiting, watching, and listening; Mama said he was very much like his father in that way. But he knew he was not nearly as brave as Papa, or as smart. The noises continued, explosions and bumps and thumps he could feel in the soles of his boots. He thought he smelled smoke. Stray emotions from the crew drifted around him like ghosts, adding to his fear.

Mama? he cast out wildly. *Papa?* There was no answer. He was not strong enough to make them hear. He ran to the door and placed his hand flat on the control grid. It vibrated against his palm. He stepped back just in time as Agent Teklys charged through, hair loose in her face and her gun raised to fire. The door closed behind her.

"We have very little time," she said in a clipped, tense

voice. "The *Aphrodite* has been boarded. You must get to the escape pods immediately."

Boarded? He knew what that meant; someone else had come onto the ship, someone who hadn't been invited.

"If ever the ship is boarded," Papa had told him, very seriously, on the day they left Concordat space, "I want you to go straight to the escape pods and do exactly what I've shown you. An automatic signal will go out to all of our nearby ships, and someone will come for you. Do you understand?"

He didn't understand nearly enough. But he took Agent Teklys's sweaty hand and let her pull him toward the door.

It slid open in a burst of bright light. Agent Teklys shoved him behind her, and then the tall figure in the doorway lifted his weapon and fired. She staggered and fell. The boy stood frozen where he was and looked up.

He knew what he was seeing. Mama and Papa had carefully shown him the holovids, answered all his questions, and tried to prepare him to meet his father's friends among the shaauri. But his mind compared the holovids to the huge shape before him and refused to make the connection.

Red fur. Red, black-striped fur covered the whole body, from long-nailed bare feet to the tips of pointed ears. He stood a head taller than even Papa, who was a big man. He wore short, loose trousers, many belts hung with tools and weapons across his chest, and metal decorations around his arms and throat. His face, wrinkled in anger or confusion, made the boy think of Uncle Miklos's cat on Persephone, but only a little. The shaauri were not cats.

Shaauri. Shaaurin—that was what you called one of them. And this shaaurin had just shot Agent Teklys.

"Boy?" the creature said. He grated out the word with effort, as if he couldn't quite make his mouth form the right shape. "What . . ." He flattened his ears and hissed out a stream of sounds the boy didn't understand.

"Why are you here?" the boy demanded, clenching his fists. "You aren't my father's friend. You hurt Agent Teklys."

The shaaurin's ears twitched back and forth, back and forth. He glanced down at Teklys.

"Not . . . dead," he rasped. "Sleep."

There was no reason to take the alien's word, even though Papa had told him that most shaauri didn't lie in the same way humans did. The boy dropped to his knees beside Teklys and put his ear against her chest. He could hear her heart beating, the air going in and out of her lungs.

She was still alive. The shaaurin had only stunned her. The boy sat up and rubbed his eyes with his hands.

"Why did you come here?" he asked, trying to keep his voice from shaking. "Where are my mother and father?"

A rush of emotion pushed inside the boy's head. It wasn't anything like what he felt from the crew, or Mama, or Papa, or his uncles. But it was just like what he'd seen on the alien's face: anger, uncertainty, confusion.

The shaaurin held out his hand with its bare-skinned palm and curved, claw-like nails. "Boy," he said, "come."

Come. Come where? *"Get to the escape pod."* That was what he had to do, and that meant getting past the shaaurin with his big weapon and his claws.

The boy stared at the small space between the shaaurin and the frame of the door. He had to move very, very fast. He met the reddish-gold eyes of the alien and lifted his hand. As the alien reached to take it, he darted sideways and dove through the gap.

In all the boy's life he had never run as hard as he did then. He caught a glimpse of other crew members lying in the corridor, heard bangs and loud voices behind him. But though he ran with everything that was in him, it was not enough. The shaaurin caught him. Nails hooked in his jacket and hauled him up like a sack of rockroots. He dangled there, terrified, and swung his fist at the face centimeters from his own.

The shaaurin shifted his grip, but not before the boy's fist connected with the alien's nose. The creature gave a grunt of surprise, just like a man. His long teeth bared in a grimace of rage.

Then something strange happened. One moment the boy hung between the shaaurin's powerful hands, and the next he was on the deck, free, and the alien was just standing there as if he had been shot.

But there was no one else in the corridor. And the boy's

head pounded and rang like the great bells of Hestia at the Harvest Feast. The shaaurin was *inside* him, with a thousand thoughts and feelings the boy could hardly begin to understand. He stared out of someone else's eyes from a dizzying height—down at himself, sprawled motionless on the deck.

You can do it, his father's voice seemed to urge.

He pushed up on his arms and tried to stand. Everything was wrong with his body—the shape, the size, the way it felt when he moved. But he took one step, and then another, and the shaaurin didn't follow. Slowly the alien mind inside his began to fade away. His arms and legs belonged to him again, and he was able to run without stumbling.

He did not look back. No one caught up with him or stopped him. He hid when he heard alien voices. He reached out for his parents with his mind, but they were gone—gone, as if a great wall had fallen between him and them.

Tears blinded him, but still he ran, along corridors and companionways, until he reached the nearest pod berth. All the pods were still in place, their lights glowing a steady green.

Papa had explained exactly what he had to do. He tapped out a sequence of numbers on the grid above the hatch. The hatch cycled open.

The inside of the escape pod was very large for a child of six, and he felt very small indeed. But he had to get away, for Agent Teklys and for his parents. He could get help and come back for them.

Pushing his way through the hatch, he settled into the webbing, strapped in, and studied the ranks of lights and controls overhead. It was easy to operate an escape pod; all he had to do was remember the sequence of operations. The pod did the rest.

He followed instructions and watched the lights change color from green to standby yellow. The hatch locked. There were several loud clicks as the pod disengaged from its berth, and then the sensation of motion, tumbling, weightlessness. The boy gripped the webbing and shut his eyes very tight.

I did what you told me, Agent Teklys. I got away. Mama, Papa, I'm coming back to get you.

He knew they couldn't hear him. Someday he might be

strong enough to push his thoughts across a big distance, but not yet. *"Be patient,"* Mama had told him. *"You have the gift. Ambros doesn't, and neither does little Damon. That's why we've brought you, so that you can learn."*

All he had learned was that there were bad shaauri, not like the ones who had adopted Papa. They had taken the ship. They were different from people, but not so different that he hadn't been able to feel one shaaurin's thoughts and know that it wanted to hate him for being human.

Just as he ought to hate it for what it had done. But he was suddenly very tired, and couldn't seem to think of much at all. He let himself drift and imagined the distress signal going out to all the Concordat ships on the border. Pressure increased as the pod's small engine propelled it on a course for the nearest wormhole to human space. He knew that the stasis field was about to put him into a deep sleep until someone found him.

He woke to the sound of something striking the hull of the pod. The display on the pod's small screen flashed a message: *Retrieval imminent. Prepare for docking.* The words were very big, but he knew they meant that someone had found him.

The clock said that it hadn't been very long. The *Aphrodite* had been deep into shaauri space; he didn't think there would be many other Concordat ships so close. He waited tensely while the pod was drawn into the ship's docking bay and the lights turned green again. Gravity sucked him down into the webbing.

He punched the hatch release. Strangely scented air rushed into the pod, but it was a minute before he recognized the smell.

It was exactly the same as that of the shaaurin who had tried to capture him.

Too late he tried to close the hatch. A sleek-furred hand reached in and caught at his harness, deftly undoing the clasps. There was no hope of struggle. He was grasped and carried and passed from one set of hands to another until he was set on his feet on an alien deck.

PART I

PEGASUS

Chapter 1

The shaauri striker was closing in, and Ronan knew that it was a matter of minutes before it either overtook his darter or blew him out of space.

He checked the flashing displays on his console, rows of shaauri numbers crowding the screen, and did a rapid calculation. Darter-class ships weren't meant to maintain this velocity for extended periods; they were like their namesakes, small, fierce predators efficient in a short pursuit but rapidly exhausted by a long chase.

And he was the prey, not the hunter. He'd counted on the darter to get him to the nearest wormhole. But the shaauri had intercepted him halfway there. Three times they'd demanded his surrender, and three times he'd managed to nurse one more burst of speed from his beleaguered ship.

No more. The engines had been pushed beyond their limits. His destination was still days away, the shaauri warship far closer.

If they caught him, it would all have been for nothing: the years of pretending, the careful observation, the waiting for just the right moment. He would be a prisoner again, and he wouldn't get a second chance.

Ronan rested his head against the seat and practiced the

Eightfold Way until his heartbeat slowed to a normal rhythm. His senses cast off the dullness of fear. One by one he brought his physical functions under control until he was as devoid of emotion as the ship around him.

His hands were steady as he activated the subroutine he had programmed after his escape. The shaauri might catch him, but they would not take satisfaction in their victory. If he was lucky, he would take the striker with him.

The countdown began, ticking out the last minutes of his life. So little time to be free. Twenty-three human years he had lived among aliens; twenty-three years he had been a captive, despised, outcast, struggling to make a place for himself among those who would never accept him. *Anki-ne'karo,* they'd taunted him, "body-without-fur," and *ne'lin,* "wraith," because he had no hope of finding his Path.

They were wrong. This was the Walkabout so long denied him. In these final moments, he was one of them at last.

The darter's sensors keened in warning. Ronan opened his eyes, expecting to see the striker, but the image on the monitor was that of a foreign ship dead ahead.

Ronan's comfortable detachment abandoned him. He leaned forward and trained all the darter's instruments on the bizarre construct.

The vessel had simply appeared as if it had emerged from a wormhole, but none existed at those coordinates. Nor would any shaauri shipwright design such a monstrosity. Ronan recalled the ancient myth of the *kio'n'uri,* a creature cobbled together of leftover parts and pieces rejected by the true beasts at the End of Void.

It was big enough for a modest freighter, with few visible gunports. But there was not the slightest elegance in its lines. Its midsection bristled with projections and flanges and blisters of no apparent function. Bow and stern were cleaner, built to strictly utilitarian standards. One gone mad might have conceived it in a *relka*-blind stupor.

It could only be a human vessel.

That was impossible. The blockade had held firm for over two decades, as humans reckoned the years, and any ship that slipped past shaauri defense survived by chance and extraordinary prudence. This one might as well have sung challenge

to any and all shaauri patrols within a hundred million kilometers.

Ronan weighed his chances. If he had detected the human
ship, it certainly knew about him. His shaauri pursuers would
not hesitate to destroy it without mercy, yet the ugly contrap-
tion held its position with blithe unconcern.

Pathless as children. But they were human, as he was, and
so he would perform one last act of defiance. He set the comlink for tightbeam communication and assembled the words
he'd thought he might never speak again.

"Human ship," he said, contorting his mouth around the
harsh sounds of his native tongue. "This is Ronan, called Vel-
Kalevi. I am a human fugitive from a shaauri warship. My
ship is set for self-destruct in approximately five of your
minutes. A striker warship is in close pursuit. Depart immediately if you wish to survive."

He waited while the darter hurtled toward the intruder,
prepared to alter course if its captain were foolish enough to
disregard his warning. But a voice filled the darter's tiny
cockpit. Human . . . and female.

"Unidentified shaauri vessel," the voice said. "Repeat. Do
you claim to be human?"

Ronan's ears twitched as if they might lie flat like any
shaauri's. "I am human, but my pursuers are not," he said.

"You are intruding in shaauri territory. This is your last
chance to escape destruction."

There was a long moment of silence, broken by the
crackle of static. "Shaauri vessel, we offer assistance," the female voice said. "Abort self-destruct and reduce velocity. We
will take you in tow."

Ronan hissed in laughter. "You can be of no assistance if
you are dead."

"The *Pegasus* can outrun any shaauri vessel. Will you
comply?"

The woman's claim was so outrageous, so confidently
stated, that Ronan almost accepted her word as truth before
he remembered that humans frequently deceived even their
closest kin. Yet why should this female lie, when her own
survival was at stake?

He was considering how to respond when the proximity

alarm alerted him to the imminent approach of his shaauri hunters. The human vessel *Pegasus* made no attempt to run, but he could buy them a little more time.

He spun the darter to face his pursuers. The self-destruct chimed its final warning. He composed himself for death, repeating the simple, calming chant Sihvaaro had taught him in boyhood.

The discipline worked so well that he was hardly disturbed by the sensors' impossible message: A ship was almost on top of him, its configuration identical to that of the human vessel. It was the *Pegasus*. The darter lay in its shadow like a small bird in the talons of a hovering *a'amia.*

"Abandon ship," the comlink spat in the human female's voice. "We will retrieve you. You have thirty seconds to comply."

Was human honor such that they would risk many lives for that of a stranger? If he did not obey instantly, the human vessel would be severely damaged when the darter detonated. The shaauri would have whatever scraps remained— as well as any survivors.

With a soft curse, Ronan gave the darter its final command. At once his seat contracted around him, binding him into a chrysalis of safety like a *ba'laik'i* in its nurturer's pouch. Clear shielding extruded from the deck to either side, forming an impervious bubble. Oxygen flowed in from the life support unit built into the seat.

Then the bottom dropped out from under him, and he was hurled free of the darter. The chrysalis tumbled several times and began to drift, giving him a clear view of the human ship.

Go, he willed it. But it swung away from the darter and maneuvered toward him with surprising grace. A moment later a cable shot out from a broad bay in its starboard flank. Ronan observed the cable's rapid approach and braced himself. The clamps closed with hardly a bump. The cable pulled him into the gaping mouth like the tentacles of a hungry cephalopod.

Just as the ship swallowed him up, he caught sight of the striker, slowing to approach the darter. But its prize was denied it. The darter exploded in a glorious plasma burst of

light and fire. The human ship's bay doors closed on the
hurtling debris of twisted metal.

The clamp released the chrysalis and the cable withdrew
to its source. Gravity pressed Ronan into his seat. Through
the shielding he could see at least two other vessels docked
in the bay, both larger than his darter. He judged them to be
shuttles designed to carry freight or passengers from ship to
planet.

The presence of breathable atmosphere began to dissolve
the chrysalis. A faint smell of lubricants filled the bay. Ronan
stepped cautiously from the chrysalis and listened for movement.

Silence. He located a porthole in the bulkhead near the
bay doors and ran to it, keeping his body low. The view of
space it accorded gave no sign of the darter's remains, but
Ronan could clearly see the striker closing fast.

Almost instantly the scene altered. In a span of seconds
the striker turned from ominous threat to a mere speck in the
distance, and then vanished entirely. The human ship was obviously moving—moving extremely fast—just as the captain
had boasted. But Ronan had not felt the crushing pressure of
rapid acceleration.

Somehow this vessel had escaped the striker, left it far behind. The humans were safe. So, it appeared, was he.

Shaauri did not believe in miracles. Ronan had thought
himself prepared, as a student of the Eightfold Way, to endure even the most sudden reversals of fortune. It was to his
shame that he felt a vast and overwhelming relief simply because he was alive.

Alive, and free. Free of his long captivity and on a human
ship. A ship that belied every one of his rash and overhasty
judgments. Ugly it might be, but it was fast enough to out-
pace a shaauri warship with astonishing ease.

And that meant the humans had developed technology
that might allow them to evade the patrols and robotic sen-
tinels that prevented their access to shaauri wormholes.

Ronan's eyes twitched in a shaauri smile. He should be
glad. These were his people. It was from them he had been
stolen as a child.

The humans of this ship would be coming for him at any

moment—the first non-Kinsmen he had seen in over twenty years.

They will not want me. I can never be one of them.

He made a blank slate of his mind and drew the Octagon upon it, contemplating each point as he whispered the ancient chant: *ba'ne, vali, vekki, kivi, riama, linei, anki, neva.* The human tongue only approximated the words' definitions: void, will, blood, reason, spirit, heart, body, nothingness.

Such was the Eightfold Way. Such were the elements of shaauri being, and of all sapient life, even humans. Upon the Eightfold Way, and only there, was he whole unto himself.

The bay's interior doors slid open. Three humans entered, wariness in the set of their stiff, unreadable bodies. The two males were clad in one-piece, belted shipsuits and carried heavy guns. After a moment of uncertainty, Ronan assumed that the shorter figure behind them must be female. Her wide body was as much metal as flesh, both her arms studded with interface jacks and instrumentation. Her dark, tilted eyes regarded Ronan with detached curiosity.

"I am Doctor Zheng, chief medic of the Alliance ship *Pegasus.*"

Chief medic. She was the ship's healer, and thus of the *li'laik'i,* but her cool demeanor was much more that of Reason. The fact that she had been sent to greet Ronan must mean that she had some status among the crew, yet she was not the one who had spoken to him before.

"I am Ronan," he said, bowing in neutral courtesy.

"Captain D'Accorso extends her welcome, *Ser* VelKalevi," she said. "She has asked me to evaluate your condition and escort you to the bridge. Are you injured in any way?"

"I am well, *Li*— I have suffered no injuries, Healer Zheng."

Zheng nodded in the human manner and touched a lighted panel embedded in the flesh of her forearm. Ronan's ears detected a faint hum, and as Zheng extended her hand, he jumped out of her reach.

Two weapons swung toward him. The taller of the guards moved with skillful grace, and Ronan quickly assessed the potential threat. The man was clearly of the Blood Path, *ve'laik'in,* a true warrior. His skin was weathered with much time spent in the sun, and he held the gun with easy confidence. Adult in age, but young enough to be reckless.

Formidable, perhaps, but not invulnerable. Humans seldom trained fighters as shaauri *ve'laik'i* did their own. The other guard Ronan dismissed as *an'laik'in,* Body, and so of little consequence. He allowed himself to relax.

"It's all right, Kord," Zheng said, waving at the males to lower their weapons. "*Ser* VelKalevi, I am attempting to scan for any injuries of which you may not be aware. I assure you that my instruments cannot harm you." Her dark eyes took Ronan apart piece by piece. "You have never seen a cyborg. Is there no enhancement among the shaauri?"

Irrational anger tightened his jaw. "The people of Aur do not mutilate their bodies with artificial components."

"Ah. In that case, they are little different from many human societies." She touched her arm again, and the interface hummed for several seconds. Zheng frowned. "You appear to be in excellent health. If, however, you feel the need to recover more fully, your meeting with the captain can be delayed."

"I am recovered," Ronan said. "I will meet with your First."

"First." Zheng tapped her fingers rapidly on her arm panel. "I believe that is a Voishaaur term for a leader of primary rank, is it not?"

"He should be confined to the brig until we know who and what he is, Mother Zheng," the warrior said, staring at Ronan from beneath his dark brows.

"I hardly think that he can do any damage under your watchful eye, O'Deira." Zheng entered a few notations and made a sound of satisfaction. "I will be most interested in discussing shaauri language and dialect with you at your convenience, *Ser* VelKalevi. But now Captain D'Accorso is waiting."

The young warrior shook his head, but he and the other guard stepped apart and positioned themselves on either side of Ronan. Zheng turned and the doors opened before her. She led the way through a hold stocked with containers of every size and shape.

The *Pegasus,* whatever the name might mean, was clearly

not an ordinary cargo vessel. She carried human goods through interdicted space and evaded the most advanced shaauri striker as if it were a ceremonial barge.

Ronan had never been on such a vessel before. He studied every detail of the hold and the design of the doors as they passed into a narrow corridor. The bulkheads and hatches were clean and utilitarian, lacking the bold color of Line banners or even the subtler murals painted by *ri'laik'i* artisans to simulate worlds left behind. He noted the armed guards who stood before a wide door marked with bars of red and yellow, and he guessed that it must lead into the very heart of the ship and the unfamiliar drive that propelled the *Pegasus* at such extraordinary velocities.

Armed warriors protected secrets. Human secrets. But did the captain guard those secrets from an OutLine stranger, or from her own crew?

"Keep moving," the young warrior said, prodding Ronan with the muzzle of his weapon. Ronan stopped and assumed the stance of Serene Preparation.

"It is not courteous to threaten one of undetermined Path," he said, testing the human's knowledge. "Do human *ve'laik'i* not learn such things before Selection?"

"*Ve'lai* is the warrior's way, isn't it?" Zheng asked, inserting herself between Ronan and the young guard. "What Path do you follow, *Ser* VelKalevi?"

"I will speak to your First, Healer Zheng. What she asks I will answer."

Zheng looked away, though she showed no indication of fear or offense. Ronan felt the young warrior's eyes burning into his back as they resumed their progress through the ship. The corridor widened and branched. A pair of crew members, male and female dressed in shipsuits much like those of the guards, stopped abruptly as Ronan approached. The male took a step back. The female's nostrils flared in alarm. Both humans' mingled fear and hostility set Ronan's hair on end.

They could see he was like them, but they did not trust him any more than did the young warrior.

He did not feel one of them. Like a wraith, he circled the outer gates of House and Hearth, taking whatever scraps they saw fit to leave for him. He was too proud to beg.

"Pride," Sihvaaro had said, "is your downfall, and it is nothing. There is no pride or shame. The Eightfold Way teaches that all Paths are One, as all Sentience is One."

Pride had won him nothing but pain among the shaauri, yet he could not abandon it even when he walked with those of his own species.

They reached another door and a lift that passed between decks. Four decks, to judge by the symbols on the lift's controls. The upper decks would contain crew quarters, life support, and the bridge. It was to the uppermost deck that the lift carried them.

The two guards pressed in on Ronan, and Zheng took the lead as the lift opened onto another short corridor. It ended in double-wide doors marked with the first decoration Ronan had seen on the ship, scrolls and spirals reaching from top to bottom.

Zheng touched a panel hidden among the spirals, tapping out a code with her surprisingly nimble fingers. The doors retracted. Beyond lay an expanse crammed with consoles, where a number of humans moved from one post to another with measured proficiency. A wide viewport framed by screens looked out on the starless void of a wormhole, represented as an opalescent sphere. There was no sign of shaauri presence.

In the center of the bridge a single seat overlooked the rest, and beside the seat stood a tall female. She wore a shipsuit as austere as that of her crew, fitting close to her slender body. Her only ornamentation was a set of golden rings on her long fingers, but her carriage was all Will from her booted feet to the mane of red hair at her crown.

Red. Among humans, even Kinsmen, the color of body hair was random, unmarked by bars of Path or rank. Even without such identifying signs, Ronan knew instantly that this female was the one who had spoken to him aboard the darter with such impatient authority. She was First and master of the *Pegasus*.

The woman studied him as he did her, one brow raised. He knew the gesture as a sign of inquiry or puzzlement, as he had observed during the annual Kinsman visits that were his sole previous contacts with humankind. Those occasions had provided him an imperfect mirror, for Kinsmen strove to suppress all that was not shaauri.

Yet he had grasped hungrily at each opportunity. He knew that this *aho'va* of *Pegasus* was attractive as humans reckoned such qualities. Her form was fit and muscular, her hips and breasts prominent, indications of female fertility and considered highly desirable among human males. Her facial features were even, lips full even by human standards, nose straight, eyes the vivid blue of a harvest sky over Ain'Kalevi-*ja*.

And her scent . . . it was unique and tantalizing, the natural odors of clean skin, pheromones, and elements beyond his ability to define.

"So," she said, her voice throaty and resolute and much more musical than it had been over the comlink. "You are human after all."

He'i, he was human. Why else would his body choose this moment to remember that it was male, and unselected—always ready for mating and very much aware that human females were receptive every day of the year?

He reined his hunger back under control. It wasn't as if he had never been with a female of his species. *Aho'Ain'Kalevi* had granted that he, too, had such needs, and there were Kinswomen willing to lie with him on their annual visits. No children came of such matings, of course; *he* was not Kinsman.

"I am human," he said carefully. "Ronan."

"I'm Captain Cynara D'Accorso, of Dharma and the Alliance ship *Pegasus*. You said you were a prisoner of the shaauri?"

"The only humans with shaauri are Kinsmen," the tall *ve'laik'i* guard said. "Be cautious, Little Mother."

D'Accorso cut the air with her hand. "Easy, Kord. He isn't armed, and he did try to warn us about his pursuers. We agreed to grant him our hospitality."

"For which I owe you thanks," Ronan said formally. "The shaauri would not have allowed me to live."

"And yet you said your name was VelKalevi," the captain said, cocking her head to one side. "Isn't that a Kinsman designation?"

"It is, Captain," said a dark-skinned man of medium height who stood just behind her. "I thought that 'Vel' was the Voishaaur prefix for 'adopted.'"

"I am not Kinsman," Ronan said. "I have been a prisoner of the Kalevi since the age of six human years."

"Yet you know Standard," the man remarked. "Surely you—"

D'Accorso held up her hand, and the golden rings on her fingers glittered in the dim light. "There will be plenty of time for questions later, Scholar-Commander." She stared into Ronan's eyes. "I presume you are willing to answer any questions we may have, and that you have many of your own."

"Yes, Captain." He searched for the proper phrase. "I am at your service."

"In that case," she said, "I think it best if you retire to the infirmary with Dr. Zheng for a complete examination and an interval of rest."

She smiled, and all at once Ronan understood why humans used the expression so freely. Captain D'Accorso's smile illuminated her face like a full moon reflected in the Sea of Ancestors.

"I am in good health," Ronan said, noting the sudden acceleration of his pulse. "My goal was to reach human space. Can you take me there?"

"Do you refer to the Concordat, or the Nine Worlds?" a new voice demanded. The man who entered the bridge was young and fit, dark-haired and of medium height, but it was not his physical attributes that triggered Ronan's body to battle readiness. The newcomer's carriage shouted both authority and hostility, though his shipsuit was as unadorned as the captain's.

Here was an enemy. Ronan pressed his lips firmly over his teeth and held the other man's gaze.

"Captain D'Accorso," the stranger said, "I only now received report of this man's boarding of the *Pegasus*. Why was I not informed?"

"*Ser* Janek," she said, "you are an observer aboard this ship. I am not obligated to inform you of every decision."

"But this—" Janek looked Ronan up and down, all the

muscles in his face tense with dislike. "This man claims to be a refugee from the shaauri. It's well known that the most powerful Kinsmen telepaths went over to the stripes when the Second War began. If he is one of them—"

The captain swung on Ronan. "Can you read my thoughts?"

Her question lodged in his gut like a bellyful of spoiled meat. "I am not Kinsman," he repeated, turning his stare on Janek. "When I was young, they stripped my mind of any such abilities."

"Then he was a telepath," Janek said. "It's vital that he be interrogated immediately. Your cooperation and assistance in this matter is essential, Captain."

Her expression had lost every trace of congeniality. "You have no authority to instigate such an interrogation, Ser Janek. I suggest that you adhere to your assignment."

"If you endanger Pegasus with your disregard for basic security . . ."

She turned on her heel to face him, legs braced. Janek responded in kind. Ronan stepped in front of Janek before he realized he was moving.

The warrior called Kord aimed his weapon at Ronan's chest. "Stand back," he ordered.

Ronan acted without thought. A casual slice of his hand caught the barrel of Kord's gun and pushed it toward the deck. Only the warrior's practiced grip on the weapon kept it from flying across the bridge. At the same time Ronan assumed the stance of Blood Waiting before Janek, prepared to strike.

Janek threw up his hands in an awkward attempt at self-defense. Kord recovered and slammed into Ronan, using his weight to throw Ronan off balance. Ronan kept his feet. He met Kord's gaze in the way of one acknowledging the worthiness of his foe, and saw the surprise and answering respect in the young warrior's eyes.

"Enough." The captain's voice rang with unquestioned command, and all eyes turned to her. Janek took advantage of the moment to back well out of Ronan's reach.

"They are animals, Captain," he said, brushing his shipsuit as if it had been contaminated by some foul purulence. "You've seen it for yourself. If he was raised among them—"

"I will give your opinion all the consideration it deserves." Captain D'Accorso set her back to him in the most brutal of insults. Janek spun sharply on his bootheel and strode from the bridge.

"I'll have no fisticuffs on my bridge, gentlemen," she said to Kord and Ronan. "Stand down, or I'll throw you both in the brig."

Kord slid back a few centimeters, his gaze never leaving Ronan's. He kept his weapon at his side as if he disdained to use it. Ronan straightened, his mind strangely heavy with thoughts and emotions he couldn't name.

"I regret, Captain D'Accorso," he said, turning his hands palm-up. "I was"—he sought the correct human word and could not find it—"unmindful."

Captain D'Accorso sat down in her chair, folding her arms across her chest. "At ease, *Ser* O'Deira." She addressed Ronan with a lifted brow. "If your ill-advised actions were on my behalf, *Ser* VelKalevi," she said, "I can assure you that they were unnecessary. Janek is prone to wild speeches with little intent behind them. There is a proverb on Dharma: 'The wave is loudest when it reaches its end.'"

"The shaauri have such a saying as well," Ronan said. "'One is a foolish wraith who paints on the stripes of Will.'"

Captain D'Accorso tapped her chin. "I think that something has been lost in translation," she said, "but that can be remedied in time. I trust that you understand I cannot permit any further displays of this kind, *Ser* VelKalevi?"

"Yes, Captain," Ronan said, turning his head down and to the side.

She relaxed, a slight dropping of shoulders and easing about the mouth. "I will take you at your word. And since you have met some of our crew under less than ideal circumstances, you should at least be introduced." Her sharp gaze swept over the guards and the black-haired cyborg. "Ronan VelKalevi—"

"Ronan," he corrected humbly. "Only Ronan."

"As you wish. I have already given you my name, and that of this ship. Our departed visitor was *Ser* Phineas Janek, civilian attaché representing the Concordat and the Archon of Persephone."

Ronan quickly revised his initial impressions of Janek. Persephone was First among the twenty worlds of the Concordat, the very heart of human space. Janek must be a man of some consequence, but the captain's words and stance made clear that she regarded him as an intruder and did not trust him.

She had referred to the *Pegasus* as an "Alliance" ship, and that alliance could only be the one between the Concordat and the distant star systems of the Nine Worlds.

Trade between the regions known as the Nine Worlds and the Concordat had endured during the century of peace brokered by the original Kinsmen. The formal Alliance had been created six years before the Second Shaauri War, only to be disrupted by the blockade.

Shaauri territory formed a vast, irregular bubble of colonies and uninhabited systems between the Concordat and the Nine Worlds. Shaauri wormholes provided the only means of crossing that territory, and any human ship that ventured to do so was captured or destroyed.

The very presence of this ship in shaauri space was proof that the Alliance had found a means of circumventing the blockade.

Who were these people, and what of all Paths was the *Pegasus*?

Ronan felt Captain D'Accorso's gaze and put aside his speculation. She gestured to the man at her shoulder. "This is my second-in-command, Scholar-Commander Taye Adumbe of Nemesis." The dark-skinned man nodded, his eyes bright with curiosity. D'Accorso indicated her two guards. "Weapons specialist Kord d'Rhian O'Deira of Sirocco, and gunner Bendik Toussaint of Dharma."

Healer Zheng stepped forward at the captain's nod. "You have already met our chief medic," D'Accorso said. "She'll be looking after you until she has completed a medical evaluation and releases you from the infirmary."

Ronan suppressed a flinch. He would have to learn to bear this altered female's touch if he was to be accepted among humans, but his shaauri upbringing rebelled.

You are not shaauri.

"You will have the opportunity to meet the rest of our crew at the appropriate time," the captain said. "Until then you may request, within reason, anything you need. The *Pegasus* will accommodate any specific dietary requirements."

Ronan's ears twitched. "I am human. I eat as you do."

"Then I presume you're hungry. If you'll accompany the doctor, we can begin making you comfortable."

"Am I to be a prisoner?"

"Not unless you make it necessary." Though the captain's voice was light with human whimsy, her gaze had lost none of its sharpness. "Kord will accompany you and Dr. Zheng to the infirmary."

He understood the warning. Captain D'Accorso would take no chances with him, in spite of her words to Janek and her easy manner. That was as it should be. She was a true First, committed to the safety of those under her command.

And that made him OutLine until proven otherwise. If he resisted Zheng's examination, as all his instincts demanded, he would give the captain reason to heed the warnings of Kord and Janek.

This was what he had wanted and never dared hope to achieve—escape and an escort to human space. Yet a deep unease pricked at his belly. He could not remember what he had intended once he evaded his pursuers. His mind was as empty of plans as a newborn *ba'laik'in.*

Empty save for the Eightfold Way. Discipline, and discipline alone, would restore his purpose.

He tilted his head in a gesture of profound respect and stepped between the two guards. "I will cooperate, Captain."

"Then I will see you again when time permits." She extended her hand. Ronan was prepared; even Kinsmen used some variation of the gesture. But the prospect of touching Cynara D'Accorso was a much greater disturbance than he had reckoned on.

Once he touched her, she would become something more than the first non-Kinsman female he had met in all the time he could remember. He would feel the warmth of her skin, her pulse, the vitality and strength so vivid to all his senses. Her seductive scent would enter his pores and flow in his blood. He would begin to admire in her the human qualities he had despised in himself.

"It is common in many human societies to offer one's hand in greeting," she said. "I realize that among shaauri—"

Ronan caught her hand as she began to withdraw it. The contact spiked through his body like the enervating bite of a venomous serpent, plunging into the center of his brain and driving his sexual awareness to an intolerable pitch.

Cynara D'Accorso dropped his hand, and he crumpled to the deck.

Chapter 2

The display on Cynara's wristcom glowed the steady amber of alert as she took her seat at the head of the briefing room's table. Her officers had already gathered, those whose skills were not immediately required at this time of crisis, and all of them looked to her with serious and troubled faces.

They had reason to be concerned. Though the *Pegasus* had made it through the wormhole, Chief Antiniou had reported that the slingshot drive had faltered again. They were stalled out in an unpopulated region of human space far from any assistance, and the ship would remain dead in the water until Charis and her team could jury-rig temporary repairs.

Cynara was confident that the shaauri striker hadn't taken a good scan of the *Pegasus;* the ship's shielding was built to resist even the most advanced scrutiny. Under normal circumstances the shaauri would remain on their side of the border . . . unless their prey was too valuable to let escape.

And that brought her to the most troubling subject of all. Ronan VelKalevi, who had collapsed on the bridge at the precise moment her mind had touched his.

Cynara's head still rang with that brief, blazing contact. She seldom found herself compelled to act as a telepath, and she certainly did not seek such experiences. On those rare occasions when she was forced to use Tyr's gift, she had done so only with extreme reluctance.

She hadn't opened her mind to receive, and yet she had tasted Ronan's emotions as if he were capable of projecting them. He'd claimed that any telepathic ability he might have possessed had been stripped from him in childhood, and nothing she sensed in him contradicted his story. He'd been as shocked as she was—shocked all the way into unconsciousness.

Ronan VelKalevi. Everything he did and said disturbed her, though certainly not in the way he ruffled Janek. Unless she had grossly misinterpreted Ronan's actions, he had confronted the Persephonean as if he defended her from an actual threat.

Ronan did not know her, owed her no allegiance, and yet he had behaved exactly as Kord might, a warrior sworn to his Watergiver for life.

And there was the way he'd moved . . . almost too fast for the eye to follow, swift and deadly, by every measure Kord's equal. She'd watched with a kind of bizarre fascination and far too much personal interest. That made no more sense than her peculiar willingness to accept him at face value.

Was this her personal weakness? Would Tyr have acted so in her place?

Something scraped the surface of the table, and she came back to the present and the urgent business at hand.

"Ladies and gentlemen," she said, "I doubt there is any need for preliminaries. The *Pegasus* is temporarily disabled while Chief Antoniou effects repairs sufficient to take us to the next wormhole. We remain a little too close to shaauri space for comfort."

There were several nods and a few uneasy glances. "No evidence of shaauri pursuit," Kord reported. "That doesn't mean they won't come through if they want their prey badly enough."

The suspicion in his voice told Cynara all that he didn't say. She hadn't had the chance to ask his impression of Ronan since their brief confrontation; she suspected that he was revising his initial judgment. But his unspoken question was the same as that of every man and woman present: Was Ronan VelKalevi what he claimed to be?

"I am well aware," she said, "of the implications of my decision to take VelKalevi aboard. Under no circumstances am I prepared to leave a fellow human to the mercies of shaauri warriors."

No one offered disagreement. Janek scowled, doubtless convinced that he was hiding his true feelings. "The question," he said, "is whether or not we were *intended* to rescue him."

Cynara smiled in a way she knew was sure to annoy him. "Of course. And we will expose any deception with all due efficiency—once we're safely home."

"Will you confine him to the brig, Captain D'Accorso-*fila*?" Cargomaster Basterra asked.

In spite of his apparent respect, Basterra always managed to remind her that she was still a Dharman woman, and unmarried at that. Cynara maintained her faint smile. "He is in the infirmary at the moment, Cargomaster, and will remain there until Doctor Zheng sees fit to release him." She turned to the woman seated on her left. "How is he, Bolts?"

Miya Zheng glanced at her with a typically bland expression. "He's clean. He lost consciousness for a few minutes, but I have discovered no indication of serious illness or other pathology to account for the syncope." She made a notation on her diagnostic scanner and consulted its display. "It may simply be exhaustion, but I should know more in a few hours."

"You said that you found it necessary to sedate him."

"Even when he was half-conscious, he put up vigorous resistance to my examination. It seemed more instinctive than deliberate. My full report will be ready shortly, Captain."

Cynara waved her hand. "I want your personal assessment, Zheng. You were the first to meet him."

"And you were the first to make a deep impression on our errant Kinsman," Zheng said dryly, "if that is what he is. He claims otherwise, and his cerebral scans indicate normal non-telepathic patterns. There are slight anomalies, however."

Anomalies, indeed. VelKalevi was an enigma—a human who claimed to have been raised among shaauri but was not

Kinsman. Shaauri might resemble seven-foot-tall, bipedal, tailless cats, but there any similarity with human-world fauna ended.

Once the human Kinsmen had been perfect go-betweens, negotiating treaties and trade agreements with the aliens, using their telepathic abilities to interpret the highly complex shaauri language. But the Second War had put an end to species loyalty; three-quarters of Kinsmen had chosen their adopted shaauri kin over humanity.

Ronan had said he'd been among the shaauri since the age of six—almost certainly near the time the war began.

"He claims he is not Kinsman," Janek said, "but not all Kinsmen are telepaths, or vice versa. You saw the way he behaved on the bridge. The very fact that he resisted Dr. Zheng's examination suggests that he has something to hide." He stared at Cynara. "You said you touched his mind, Captain. What did you observe?"

Cynara considered her answer. She could have told Janek that her gifts were not so precise or easily controlled as he might believe, but she had no intention of revealing anything he might perceive as weakness. The Persephonean frequently made the mistake in thinking that because she ran the ship with an egalitarian philosophy, she was soft—not woman-soft, but lacking in the discipline and training necessary for the command of such a unique and priceless vessel.

She'd become used to giving the impression that she took telepathy for granted, even if she seldom called upon it. The gift was common enough among the D'Accorsos. But few outsiders, even her fellow Dharman crew, realized how thoroughly a Dharman girl's abilities were suppressed by custom and training. Her own natural talents had never been great. Janek and the others couldn't know how much Tyr had contributed to any mental powers she now possessed.

Or how very much she hated and feared using them.

"I was able to learn very little," she said. "His brain shut down, which could be consistent with his claim that his mind was tampered with by shaauri-allied Kinsmen."

"I would advise caution in attempting further mental probing," Zheng put in. Her gaze met Cynara's with a conspiratorial glimmer.

"Certainly, Doctor. I will abide by your judgment." She glanced at Janek. "It is of far more importance to keep our guest in good health, both mental and physical, than to obtain by coercion whatever knowledge he possesses. As I'm sure you'd agree, Ser Janek."

"I must reiterate that this man cannot be left in a position where he may gain access to ship's manuals and schematics. If you will not confine him to the brig—"

"Our guest cabins are currently unoccupied," she said. "As they're located near my own quarters, I will take personal responsibility in seeing that Ser VelKalevi remains under control." Her gaze swept the table. "Every one of us has reason to be wary of any human associated with shaauri. I ask you to keep in mind that no Kinsman traitor has ever successfully eluded Concordat Intelligence. Those Kinsmen captured in human space have been conditioned to resist all questioning; if Ronan VelKalevi is one of them, his deception will be exposed.

"If there are no further reports at this time, I will be in the infirmary and my quarters for the next half-watch. Mes Montague," she said, addressing the quiet young woman at the end of the table, "lay in a course for the nearest wormhole in the event that our shaauri friends attempt further pursuit. Scholar-Commander Adumbe has the bridge. Ser O'Deira, maintain alert status."

She rose, and the rest followed. Only Kord remained seated. He waited until the others had left the briefing room and looked up at her with rebellion in his pale brown eyes.

"You're going to see the Kinsman, Little Mother?"

She chuckled and shook her head. Kord was as comfortably predictable as the tides of Calada. "You assume the worst, my friend. We have seen nothing to indicate that he is other than he says, and no evidence of telepathic ability."

"You underestimate the potential danger of this man."

"I witnessed what passed between you, Kord. He has the training of a warrior, doesn't he?"

"Yes." Kord touched the scar that ran from his cheekbone to chin. "He is a warrior."

"You respect him."

"As an enemy. Remember this: If he was raised by shaauri, he is one of them."

"Have you forgotten Sirocco, Kord?" she asked softly. "You came to Dharma at first manhood, but you have never lost the ways you were born to. Our fugitive was born human."

"The shaauri killed your cousin."

I killed him. She crushed the thought. "They killed Tyr in what they regarded as an act of defending their territory in time of war." She leaned on the table and met Kord's gaze. "I don't love the shaauri. They strangle the commerce we need to survive. But I will not judge this man according to his misfortune. And neither will you."

Kord rose from his seat, clearly unconvinced. "At least let me accompany you."

"I need you on the bridge. Toussaint may be competent, but he doesn't have your instincts." She smiled. "I'll carry a stunner, and Zheng will be with me. Not even a shaauri can match her where sheer brute strength is concerned."

"But a shaauri striker is more than a match for the *Pegasus.* If they do come through, we'll be outgunned. I strongly advise that we modify torpedoes with proximity sensors and lay them at the mouth of the wormhole. At the very least they'll slow the shaauri down. I can take the *Pontos* and have them in place within the next two hours."

"No shaauri has entered human space for years. I prefer to throw all our resources into getting the *Pegasus* spaceworthy again." She sighed at the look on his face. "I'll be all right, Kord. Stop worrying."

"As you say, Captain."

She gripped his shoulder and turned for the lift, wondering at the uneasy mixture of anticipation and apprehension lodged like a fist in her chest. She ought to heed Kord's advice and take at least one armed escort to the infirmary, but she felt no need of protection. She could defend herself very competently from most attacks, though Kord was her superior in that respect. He, like most Siroccan males, had been trained from birth to be a warrior. Her instruction had come late, but she'd pursued it with even greater determination because she was Dharman and female.

Whatever Ronan VelKalevi might be, he was unlikely to risk a blatantly stupid act. She well remembered his quiet dignity when she had questioned him on the bridge, the way he had faced Janek's hostility without alarm, his sincere apology. He had moved with spare grace and perfect balance. His face was striking, his eyes brilliant with intelligence.

Such a man seemed an unlikely prisoner among the shaauri. He was neither bent nor broken, neither fully indoctrinated into the shaauri culture nor clinging pathetically to the scraps of human custom. In a few brief minutes of observation, she had judged him a man of courage and purpose, not easily shaken by his precarious circumstances.

That might make him, as Kord said, all the more dangerous. But that brief and unexpected mental touch had failed to trigger any sense of warning. To the contrary—she had been left with the overwhelming desire to know this strange fugitive to the very depth of his soul.

Therein lay the truest hazard.

She reached third deck and entered the infirmary, greeting Zheng's assistant with a nod. Zheng stood just inside the door of the ward, studying the monitors suspended above the berth on which her patient lay. The screens indicated body functions within normal range: pulse, blood pressure, lung function, pupil response. Every attribute of an extremely fit and healthy young human male.

That made his appearance all the more shocking. Zheng had left VelKalevi unclothed save for a light blanket covering his lower body. He lay quietly with his back to the doctor, and as Cynara joined Zheng, she found herself gazing at a chronicle of horror.

On the bridge he had been wearing a shipsuit that covered him from neck to wrist and ankle. She hadn't seen the scars—layer upon layer over back and shoulders and hips, creating of his flesh a corrugated résumé of punishment and countless skirmishes with teeth and claws.

Shaauri teeth. Shaauri claws. No, not claws, but curved nails their warriors kept sharpened to dagger points as deadly weapons of close combat, just as they filed their teeth to resemble those of primitive ancestors.

If Ronan VelKalevi turned to face her, she knew she

would find similar records on his chest and arms. They continued the length of his legs and tattooed even his feet and hands.

Only his face was relatively clean, or so she remembered. Perhaps the shaauri had spared him obvious disfigurement. She knew nothing of shaauri notions of beauty. It might be that such scars were marks of honor.

Or perhaps he had merely suffered until he had learned to bear pain as other men bore the insignificant bites of sea-midges.

Barbarians, Janek called the shaauri. Natural killers who murdered any human caught intruding in the Shaauriat, who were raised communally and never knew their fathers, who chose their leaders and meted out justice through trials of physical violence.

But Kinsmen were allied to the shaauri. They were not treated so. The very truth of Ronan's story was imprinted on his flesh; he had been a prisoner, and he had known incalculable pain at the hands of humanity's greatest enemies.

"It isn't pretty, is it?" Zheng remarked. "I would have doubted that any unenhanced human could survive such an ordeal." She consulted the diagnostic screen and called up a holoscan of Ronan's body. All the organs were healthy, spine straight and muscles well developed, but nearly every major bone of his arms and legs had been broken in young adulthood. "Some shaauri physician did an excellent job of repairing the breaks so that no lasting deformation occurred."

Barbarians. Cynara fought the urge to stroke that ravaged back, as if she had the power to offer comfort with a gentle human touch. A typical, deeply conditioned Dharman female sentiment that she had never quite abandoned.

At least the shaauri regard males and females as equal in every facet of their society, unlike my own people. Who are the greater barbarians?

The answer eluded her, and even the question left her mind as Ronan VelKalevi groaned and rolled onto his back. The blanket slid across his waist and snagged under one knee. She had been right about the scars over the rest of his body, and about his face. His profile was unmarred save for a single line across his temple, ending at the dark edge of his hair.

Human. Utterly human. And most definitely male in a sense she could not ignore, no matter how much her family regarded her as tainted and forever ruined as a woman and childbearer.

"He's coming out of sedation," Zheng said. "He should be able to talk within a few minutes."

"There's no danger of relapse?"

"Not by my judgment, but I counsel restraint until we're sure." Zheng studied Cynara with narrowed eyes. "Are you all right?"

Trust Zheng to notice that her captain's skin had flushed and her pulse had jumped from walk to gallop. "A great deal rides on what we discover about our guest," Cynara said. "Leave me alone with him, Bolts. One way or another, he's lost in a strange land. He's going to need someone to trust, and I intend to be that person."

"I don't have to warn you to be careful. He's stronger than his muscle mass indicates. See for yourself." She tapped the monitor and pulled up a recording of her initial treatment.

In the recording VelKalevi had regained consciousness, but something was clearly wrong; he shouted in an alien tongue and flailed his arms and legs as if he were fighting off enemies. Zheng had to call her assistant to restrain him before she could administer the sedative.

"Our patient was suffering a delusional state and was unable to communicate coherently," Zheng said, stopping the recording. "He was extremely fast, just as he was on the bridge."

Cynara patted the stunner at her waist. "I'm prepared, Bolts. You can watch, of course—just stay out of sight."

Zheng nodded and left the ward. She would remain right behind the observation window, where she could note everything that occurred in the ward without being seen by her patient.

Cynara pulled up a stool beside the bed and waited for VelKalevi to regain full consciousness. Inevitably her eyes were drawn to the lines and planes of his body, as if to something alien and exotic but enticingly familiar.

She had seen unclothed men many times since she'd left the protection of her family's palace. From her first day of command aboard the *Pegasus,* she had treated her crew with no regard to gender, a fact that frequently distressed her Dharman contingent. She had lived in close quarters with males of every description and several cultures, some of whom regarded sex as a casual diversion.

She'd felt no interest in any of them. That part of her had been shut down like an obsolete drive coil, and not entirely because of Tyr, as her parents believed. Tyr's gender had given him all the opportunities denied her—until he'd bestowed his final, devastating gift.

Gift, and curse. All his knowledge was hers, all the skills she had hardly begun to absorb before her father had betrothed her to *Fico* Nyle Beneviste. She, a woman, had become captain of the *Pegasus.*

The price had been virtual rejection from Dharman society, horrified looks from every burgher-lord who considered her neither man nor woman but a grotesque combination of both, unfit for marriage or the position she held by virtue of Tyr's extraordinary death.

Their judgment was no more than convention, a terror of breaching the high wall between male and female. Once she *had* known what it felt like to want a man. Sexual need—unspoken by Dharman women except in hushed whispers—had vanished since the blending as if it had never existed.

But as she looked at Ronan VelKalevi, she realized with faint shock that those obsolete biological functions had come back to life. She recognized them in her response to Ronan's strong, scarred body, the steadiness of his gaze, the courage he must possess to have borne such pain.

Poseidon. She closed her eyes and let out a long, slow breath. Tyr was no part of what she felt now. Once she unbarred the gates to desire, she might never close them again.

How much do you know of human women, Ronan VelKalevi? Have you even been with one?

Ronan's arm dropped over the edge of the bed. Cynara had one second to bring her thoughts under control before he turned and opened his eyes.

"Cynara," he croaked.

He obviously remembered her, though she'd mentioned her given name only once. His breathing remained steady, but his pupils had constricted to mere pinpoints. The monitors showed a slight spike in his pulse.

"*Ser* VelKalevi," she said, "how are you feeling?"

His gaze shifted from her face to the monitors and medical equipment suspended from the overhead. Cynara could see the memories playing behind his eyes, the rapid acknowledgment of his situation. He tried to swing his legs over the bed, but Cynara stopped him with a firm touch on his knee.

He tensed as if he might resist and then relaxed his muscles. The tight ridges of his stomach had their own share of scars, and he seemed not to notice that the blanket had fallen to the floor.

Furred sentients with little sexual dimorphism had no real need for modesty. Ronan had evidently not learned the concept from his human parents. He looked into Cynara's eyes with open interest.

"I am well," he said, his words a little slurred.

"Do you remember where you are?"

"You are Captain Cynara D'Accorso, and I am aboard the Alliance ship *Pegasus.*"

"You blacked out on the bridge," Cynara said, watching his face. "Do you know what caused it?"

"No."

"His mental faculties read in the normal range, and he is obviously lucid," Zheng's voice spoke from the intercom. "Do you suffer from any medical conditions, *Ser* VelKalevi? Allergic reactions?"

Ronan looked toward the observation window. "Does the healer fear me?" he asked Cynara. "If I did harm, I regret."

Cynara bit back a laugh. She had never seen Zheng afraid of anyone, and her patient's face was so earnest and sincere that he might have been a child apologizing for stealing a sweetmeat. She found it oddly endearing.

But the body that moved under her hand was no child's. VelKalevi planted his feet firmly on the deck and stood, testing his balance. "Your scans must have confirmed my state of health, Healer Zheng," he said. "Where is my clothing?"

Cynara indicated a standard shipsuit folded on a nearby table. "Your own is being cleaned. Don't try to move too quickly, *Ser* VelKalevi."

He frowned, a faint crease between his brows. "This *'Ser'*—it is a title of rank?"

"It's the usual Persephonean male form of address," she said, "common among the worlds of the Concordat."

"But you humans do not make distinctions of Path."

You humans. Cynara's skin prickled. "You refer to the shaauri caste system? My knowledge of shaauri society is incomplete. How do you prefer to be addressed?"

He was silent for some time, gazing at nothing, but Cynara sensed that he was deep in thought. Far from pleasant thought, at that. She was sorely tempted to touch his mind again. She might not pick up anything but emotion or surface static, but to know what this man really was . . .

Command of the *Pegasus* accorded almost every challenge she could wish, fulfilling her ambitions and satisfying her need for adventure. There was always something to strive for, new experiences, new people. But Ronan VelKalevi presented a puzzle unlike any other, and her frankly sexual response was an added provocation she couldn't ignore.

This was no game. The stakes were astronomically high. If she failed to unravel this mystery, she might not only lose command of the *Pegasus,* but put the ship's mission at risk as well. Janek wouldn't hesitate to hasten her downfall.

And swift currents to him. Let them carry him right onto the reef. She was anyone's equal when it came to protecting the *Pegasus* and the Nine Worlds. When she was finished with him, Ronan VelKalevi would yield up his secrets and be none the wiser about his rescuers.

"I presume," she said cautiously, "that since you were a prisoner, you received no . . . Path designation. Yet you use the 'Vel' prefix."

He stared into her eyes. "I require no special form of address. Ronan is sufficient."

She required no telepathy to feel the sensitivity of that topic. "Perhaps, when you are ready to begin answering questions, you can remedy my ignorance of shaauri custom."

He tilted his head to the side. "I understand that you do

not trust me, and that you must ask questions. What do you wish to know?"

"I think you'd better dress first." She tossed him the shipsuit. "Doctor Zheng, is our guest fit to be released?"

"I see no reason to retain him, subject to review, of course."

Cynara nodded, half an eye on Ronan as he slipped into the shipsuit without a single awkward or wasted motion. Every one of his muscles was perfectly formed, balanced for supreme efficiency and strength. Only the most rigorous training could account for that body—training and the most brutal punishment for failure.

Zheng entered the ward, her heavy tread nearly shaking the deck. "I have prescribed a moderate bland diet for *Ser* Ronan until his nutritional needs have been evaluated. Shall I have his meal sent up to the guest cabin?"

"*Aho'Va* D'Accorso, I do not wish to further disrupt the operation of your ship," Ronan said, fastening the suit to the top of his neck. By your leave, I will take nourishment with your crew."

Cooperative, courteous . . . and remarkably fluent for a man raised by aliens. Cynara made a personal note on her wristcom to download the latest Voishaaur-Standard dictionary from the ship's databanks.

"Your offer is noted, *Ser* . . . Ronan, but most of the crew is on watch. It is necessary for you to eat. If you have no objection, I'll join you in your quarters and ask a few more questions before leaving you to rest."

His unreadable eyes cut through her like a razorback in a fisherman's net. "It is my honor, *Aho'Va*."

But you haven't dropped your guard, my friend—not for a moment. "If you're ready," she said, "I'll escort you to your quarters. You and I have a great deal to learn about each other."

Chapter 3

R onan *stepped forward, and Cynara half expected him to offer his arm in the manner of a Dharman gentleman.* But he paused a meter away, obviously waiting for her to take the lead.

She did so, gesturing Zheng back to her work. Ronan fell in behind her, padding as silently as Archimedes when he was given free rein of the ship.

That should be an interesting introduction. Archimedes was something of a ship's mascot, but no one presumed to own him. Ronan was certainly as much a curiosity as a domestic cat on a blockade runner. A pet he would never be. His calm demeanor was a mask. Underneath it he walked on the edge of violence, as unpredictable as a feline . . . or shaaurin.

Ronan seemed quite content to hold his tongue as they followed the corridor into crew quarters, but his eyes were never at rest. When he and Cynara encountered other crew members, he stood aside and let them pass with obliging constraint.

The crew was not so mannerly. If not for Cynara's presence, one or two of them might have confronted Ronan the same way Janek had done. Among those who hated the shaauri, no creature was more despised than a human loyal to the stripes. Even an unwilling prisoner might fare little better in their eyes.

All the more reason for her to determine the truth.

She led Ronan past her own quarters and to the guest cabins at the end of the corridor. She stopped at the first, where the lock awaited imprinting by a new occupant.

"Place your palm here," she said, indicating the lock, "and the door will open only to you and those who have override codes for this section—myself, Scholar-Commander Adumbe, and O'Deira. Your privacy will not be violated except in an emergency."

Ronan hesitated, studying the ID grid carefully before following Cynara's instructions. The door opened onto the small, spare cabin with its Spartan furnishings. Ronan's nostrils flared like an animal scenting the air for danger. He stepped inside and placed his back to the nearest bulkhead.

"The *Pegasus* was not designed as a passenger vessel," Cynara said. "I trust you will find these accommodations adequate for the time being."

"More than adequate, *Aho'Va.*"

She sat on the edge of the bunk. "You've called me that several times. What does it mean?"

He blinked slowly, just like Archimedes, and frowned. "I did not realize I had lapsed from your language. *Aho'Va* means First of Will."

"First, as in captain—that much I understand. But 'Will' . . ."

"You called the way of Paths a 'caste system,'" he said. "It is the foundation of shaauri culture. 'Will,' *vali,* is the Path of leaders and administrators—*va'laik'i.*"

She mouthed the word silently, testing the slight guttural break between each syllable of the alien term. "Then any captain would, by definition, be this . . . *va'laik'i.*"

"*Va'laik'in,* yes. Though sometimes *ve'laik'i,* those of the Blood Path, become Firsts of warships, and often Seconds or Thirds of Houses or even Lines. *Aho'Va* is a title of respect given in general to all *va'laik'i* Firsts." He gave the words "House," "Line," and "First" the kind of emphasis that suggested capitalization. "Each Path and vocational residence within a House-holding has its own First, Second, and Third as well. Crew of shaauri vessels are always of one Line, but—"

Cynara laughed and held up her hands. "Wait, my friend. I think cultural instruction will take more time than I have at the moment. Please, sit."

He obeyed, perched on the edge of the bunk with his feet planted for swift movement. He appeared as ready to fight as he had been with Zheng, and her mind called up the image of those terrible wounds over his body. Perhaps he expected constant abuse, even from humans.

"I want you to understand one thing, Ronan," she said. "You are safe aboard the *Pegasus.* No one will hurt you or force you to do anything you don't wish, as long as your intentions are peaceful."

"I understand."

Poseidon. Was that clear-eyed gravity the only emotion he was capable of? Even when he had threatened Janek and fought Zheng, his expression had hardly changed. What would make him react?

"I think you understand a remarkable amount for someone who has been a prisoner most of his life," she said, muting her smile. "How did that come about?"

She had not expected to achieve such swift results, but his vulnerability was so strong that it touched her mind without even the smallest effort on her part. "I have no memory of the time before my sixth year," he said. "I was raised in a shaauri House, and some of my adopted kin spoke your language. There were occasions . . . when other humans came to the House."

Humans. Kinsmen. Cynara discovered a tightness in her chest and knew that it was not merely sympathy for what he must have suffered. It came from Ronan, emotional leakage her shields were not designed to filter.

Loneliness. That was at the core of it, the pain that underlay his solemnity. So few men or women had the power to make her feel, unbidden, what they felt. He did.

No memory. Of parents, of human warmth. He might be lying, of course—everything he said might be a lie—but this had the ring of truth that echoed in her bones.

She sat on the bunk, keeping her distance. "You said

something to the effect that Kinsmen had stripped your mind
of any telepathic ability. How well did you know these people?"

"I know their history. They chose shaauri over their own
blood."

There. *That* was anger, contempt, invisible to anyone who
hadn't the skill to look for it. "But you did not choose, did
you?"

"No."

"What do you think of such men and women, Ronan?"

"N'akai Ne'li," he said, the words spat between his teeth
like acid. It was a curse and also a name. Cynara tapped her
wristcom and linked the Voishaaur-Standard dictionary to her
earpatch audiofeed.

"Ne'li, noun, plural of ne'lin," a flat female voice pro-
nounced.

*"Ne'lin, noun, singular. Definition one: shaaurin who re-
turns from Walkabout unselected and exists on the fringes of
shaauri society. Definition two: wraith or ghost. Definition
three: outcast. Usage: Ne'lin is frequently used as a deroga-
tory term of contempt."*

The only definition that seemed to apply in this case was
the last; Kinsmen certainly had a place in shaauri society. So
Ronan had no love for the only fellow humans he had seen
during his captivity. Or so he wished her to believe.

"This is a very important question," she said. "Some of
my officers are afraid that you may be Kinsman and a shaauri
agent, sent to us in the guise of a fugitive."

His head jerked up in very convincing shock, and a stream
of alien words, half growls and whistles, poured out of his
mouth. The single term Cynara recognized was *ne.* No. Em-
phatically no.

"Then I must ask why, as a prisoner, you were of such
value to the shaauri that they sent a striker after you."

She couldn't misinterpret the confusion in his eyes. "I . . .
know things," he said.

"About the shaauri? Things that might hurt them if humans knew?"

"I listened. I learned what I could. They feared what I
could tell."

"And now that you've come to us, you're prepared to share what you know for the benefit of humanity?"

His gaze cleared. "Yes."

Cynara leaned back against the bulkhead. "Kinsmen have been sent by shaauri to penetrate Concordat defenses. None of them have succeeded, but the danger is always there. That's why I must be sure of your loyalties and your background."

At first she thought the sound Ronan made was one of distress, perhaps some form of weeping, but it came to her that he was laughing. He puffed out a series of almost silent breaths drawn deep from his lungs, his eyes narrowed in unmistakable amusement.

"My loyalties," he said when he could speak again. "I will show you my loyalties, *Aho'Va* D'Accorso." He unfastened his sleeve at the wrist, peeled back the cloth to reveal the underside of his arm and rotated it slowly, displaying the bitter landscape of pale scars. Cynara opened her mind just enough to read the outer skin of his thoughts.

Loneliness, and now shame so deep that it amounted to self-loathing beyond what she had felt when Tyr died and she survived with his knowledge inside her. Ronan despised himself for these scars, for his weakness, for everything he was. All the waters of Mother Sea couldn't wash away such shame.

Cynara shrank behind her shields, and through the blur of her vision she saw Ronan roll down his sleeve and fasten it with calm indifference.

"Why?" She heard herself ask the question even as she knew it was a mistake. "Why did they hurt you?"

"They are shaauri."

Barbarians. Demons. "Was it Kinsmen who brought you to them?"

The muscles in his temples twitched. "I do not remember." He shifted, turning his body toward her. It was only a matter of centimeters, and yet she felt him draw closer as if the bunk had contracted beneath them. She dared to touch his hand.

He slumped against the bulkhead, eyes open and unseeing.

"Ronan?"

He didn't react. She raised him by the shoulders, cradled his head in her hand, and shook him.

"Ronan!"

No response. Clenching her teeth, she cuffed him lightly in the face.

He blinked. For a moment he seemed confused, unable to focus. He braced his hands on the bunk and shook his head.

Cynara kept a firm grip on his arms. "Do you know what just happened?"

"*Aho'Va?*" He pressed his palm to the center of his head. "Did you speak?"

"You've had another blackout. I'm taking you back to the infirmary."

He resisted her pull. "I am well."

"Do you remember what we were discussing?"

His hesitation was answer enough. "Scylla's teeth—"

"I have suffered no harm." As if to prove his contention, he sat up very straight and rested his hands on his thighs, palms up, in an attitude of complete serenity. "May I also ask a question?"

She laughed, spilling out her relief. "Forgive me. I am not laughing at you, my friend. Only at myself."

"Yes." He tilted his head again in that disturbingly charming gesture. "That is the second time you have called me 'my friend.' "

It occurred to her that he might regard such an address as being of greater significance than she intended. Papa had always accused her of being far too informal with inferiors and strangers, and the habit had only grown stronger with the vast changes in her life.

Her crew knew how to regard such little pleasantries. The word "friend" might have an entirely different definition in Voishaaur. It might indicate a lifelong bond, or the relationship between lovers.

All the awareness Cynara had felt in the infirmary returned like a well-placed blow to the solar plexus. She sat in a tiny cabin less than thirty centimeters from a man she found sexually attractive and intellectually fascinating. She thought about the generous bunk in her quarters, lights dimmed and Ronan VelKalevi naked in her arms.

Then her fingers would touch the scars.

She jerked herself back to reality. "Among humans, friendship is regarded as a way of expressing liking and trust. I want to be your friend, Ronan."

He gave her that hooded, catlike stare that reminded her so much of Archie. "I think I know what humans call 'friendship.' It is as important as kinship, is it not?"

"Sometimes. Kinship can be very important, but much depends upon culture, and friendship extends between members of different families, even different clans and worlds."

"It is like . . . *be'laik'i* on—" He hesitated, consulting some mental translator. " 'Walkabout.' When shaauri at first adulthood leave House and Line and wander at will until they reach Selection. There are no limits then. Companionship among *be'laik'i* occurs freely until the return of the selected ones to their Houses, but it is rare that such relationships endure across Paths. With mating it is much the same."

Cynara had heard some rumor of shaauri mating rituals— that they allowed their adolescents to experiment with sexual relationships and even bear young without regard to political boundaries or what most human societies would regard as moral restraint. Such freedom would be considered obscene on Dharma.

Her mouth went suddenly dry. "Have you been on this Walkabout?"

"I was a prisoner, and not permitted." He stared down at the bunk. "I remain unselected."

Selected—chosen for or by a Path, which would determine a shaaurin's future. Ronan meant that he had never crossed the threshold of shaauri adulthood. Was it possible that intelligent beings could look at such a man and consider him still a child? Was that why they had beaten him over and over again?

"You were alone among aliens. Were you . . ." *Maidenly modesty now, Cyn?* "Did you ever have the opportunity to take a mate?"

Ronan dared to look up again, for the pity he had expected to hear in her voice—the pity he had seen when he had revealed his scars—was entirely gone. Instead, what he sensed in her was the brightness, the boldness, the intensity she had shown at their meeting, when he had felt the first incongruous stirrings of desire.

He had not been permitted to satisfy the sexual needs of a *be'laik'in* like a normal shaaurin. Now they sprang upon him full-blown, years of restraint and deprivation shed like a winter coat at New Sun. Desire made him long to touch Cynara now as he had on the bridge.

But that contact had yielded unexpected consequences. He had collapsed, much to his shame, aware in the burning moment just before darkness that Cynara D'Accorso was no ordinary human female. Something of her very self had bled into him like candlelight through a paper screen, shadows just beyond his grasp.

She was like the Kinsmen—a telepath, a reader of minds. He did not know how he understood her nature so clearly when he was not of her breed. She did not make a show of her ability, yet if she chose, she could drain his thoughts from him as a *myl'vekk* sucked the lifeblood of its prey.

She had not, though she undoubtedly wished to learn all he could tell her of shaauri ways so that humans would have an advantage in the long battle. Perhaps she, like Kinsmen, held to unwritten laws against stealing thoughts.

Why should she steal? She believed she commanded him as any First might do one of lesser Path. Was he not *ne'lin,* and OutLine? Was his life not at her mercy?

Then why did that brief sharing of her being, her scent, and the silent signals of her body—even her question—tell him that she was ready and very willing to take him as her mate?

Kalevi-kai assist him—all she need do was command, and he would throw aside all propriety and join with her here and now. It was a deviant compulsion he had no will to resist.

"Is it not true," he asked, his voice rough and strange to his own ears, "that humans mate freely all their lives, regardless of Path?"

Her breath caught, and she smiled though her eyes held nothing of amusement. "You didn't answer my question."

"I have mated," he said, "but only when humans—Kinsmen—came to Ain'Kalevi."

"Kinsmen?"

After a moment he recognized the source of her confusion. "Females of the Kinsmen."

"There were no . . . children?"

"I was not permitted." His ears pulled back. "One without path has few privileges."

"And those of other Paths?"

"It is different for each. *Va'laik'i* may choose their own mates for offspring or pleasure, among other *va'laik'i, ve'laik'i,* or rarely those of other Paths."

"Indeed." Her gaze withdrew into some place he could not follow. "It's not always so, among humans."

Sorrow spoke in the small muscles about her eyes and the corners of her mouth. He wished to smooth those creases with his fingertips, as close kin might do, or mates. She was neither to him. He clenched his fist at his side and averted his gaze, permitting her the dignity of her rank.

"I'm sorry," she said. "You must be eager to understand human ways, and I haven't been very helpful."

He copied the human gesture of denial, shaking his head once. "You have saved my life, *Aho'Va* D'Accorso, and done me honor."

She smiled, and her hand came to rest on his knee. "If I am to be your first true human friend, you must call me Cynara."

Her delicate fingers with their blunt, inoffensive nails seemed to rake through his shipsuit into flesh, branding it as even the worst beatings had never done. The hair bristled along the back of his neck, and arousal tightened his *siv'alku* to the brink of pain. The deck and bulkheads spun as they had on the bridge.

Ronan caught at the one support available, the source of his confusion and the raging desire he could barely contain. Cynara's wrist felt surprisingly fragile in his grip.

"Cynara," he said, forcing the words out between his teeth. He turned his hand about and hers with it, so that her palm lay face-up. He bent to smell her inviting fragrance, the slight dampness and flush of surprise. He grazed her soft skin with the tip of his tongue. She flinched.

"This is not appropriate, Ronan," she said, breathing quickly. "Please release me."

He tasted her palm again, savoring the complex palette of flavors. The need to join with Cynara D'Accorso scattered all thought of race and rank like so much chaff. "Is it not your wish to mate?"

Chapter 4

Cynara's mouth dropped open, revealing a row of white, even teeth. She shut it firmly and became First again, the leader he had met on the bridge.

"I understand that you have been deprived of most human contact, Ronan, and that your circumstances are difficult," she said coldly. "Among humans, seizing another in this way is a hostile act. I advise you to release me immediately."

His hand opened in automatic obedience to her will. She snapped free, jumped up, and strode to the door, setting her back to it but disdaining its support. She seemed to draw upon some human breathing exercise to calm her agitation, just as Ronan chanted out the Eightfold Way to steady his racing pulse.

He should have looked away, acknowledging his error. He did not. He met her gaze in the challenge of equals, holding his body rigid against the need to seize her again.

"Ronan," she said, as if speaking to a child, "we have had a misunderstanding, which I regret. Humans may touch in friendship, to give comfort and for no reason beyond. That is one thing you should learn immediately if you are to live with us."

Sihvaaro had told him that among all sentient beings there

was a darkness that sometimes claimed the soul, overcoming all sense of rightness and tradition. Rejection was nothing new to Ronan, no more than shame. But that insidious darkness crept upon him now, sinking its needle-sharp teeth into the core of his reason.

"You are still my *friend,*" he said, "even though I am of no Path, and you are First of this fine ship? Even though this *ne'lin* dared to offer mating to one so great?" He exposed his throat in mock submission. "One is prepared to die for this offense, *Aho'Va.* It is your right under shaauri law."

She let out an explosive breath and laughed. "Your law permits one shaauri to kill another because—" She shook her head, loosening the red hair she kept confined in a knot at the base of her neck. "We truly don't understand each other. You speak as though you are nothing. You're wrong, Ronan. You—" She stopped, a new expression of deep concentration on her face, and touched the tiny receiver cradled in the hollow of her ear. Ronan listened. A faint human voice buzzed from the device, pitched in tones of alarm. When Cynara turned back to Ronan, her eyes were hard as skystones.

"I must return to the bridge," she said. "I said that I wouldn't make you a prisoner, but I require your word that you will remain in this cabin until I send for you."

His word. He did not know what humans regarded as keeping one's word. He only knew that if he gave a promise to this woman, he would hold to it at the cost of his life.

"Will you do as I ask, Ronan?"

"I will."

She gave him a brisk nod and left the cabin. Her scent lingered long after she had gone, and he knew, for all her protests, that she had desired him.

He had told Cynara that *va'laik'i* might choose their own mates for offspring or pleasure. Cynara's crew was made up of many unrelated Houses, forming a new House unto itself as happened when a *be'laik'in* on Walkabout selected as Will and attracted other *be'laik'i* to her.

If Cynara had little opportunity to mate except among her crew, she might look for partners outside it—even at one *ne'lin* and forbidden. So he dared to imagine. No discouragement from her could quell such conceits, nor shame. Only the Eightfold Way had the power to make him remember what he was.

He knelt upon the cool deck and closed his eyes, seeking the serenity that would not come.

D*amn you, Kord. Cynara slammed her fist against the* wall of the lift, cursing her friend in all the creative ways Tyr had taught her.

There was no time to make sense of what had happened with Ronan in his cabin, no time to think through her reaction to his astonishing invitation.

Poseidon. Was it so easy for shaauri to suggest mating with total strangers? What had made her believe that she could create an instant friendship with a man raised by aliens, and that her sexual attraction to him would have no consequences? How much of Ronan was human and how much beyond human understanding?

If not for the urgent message about Kord's reckless act, she might have learned the hard way. But the crisis only postponed what must eventually be faced.

Now that crisis demanded all her attention. She raced to the bridge and took her chair, staring at the image spread across the screens. Janek stood braced against a deck railing with a look of grim satisfaction on his face. The *Pegasus* rang with the klaxons of high alert.

"Status," she snapped.

"A shaauri darter has triggered the torpedoes O'Deira placed outside the wormhole," Adumbe said, stepping up behind her. "The *Pontos* was well clear of the explosions, but we estimate that it is only a matter of minutes before the striker follows through."

"And Kord isn't going to make it back before our friends arrive." The rudderless fool, disobeying her orders and taking it upon himself to rig the torpedoes at the risk of his own life. The shuttle was barely a blip on the monitor, much too near where the striker would emerge from the wormhole.

Kord had been wrong, but so was she in assuming that the shaauri wouldn't pursue Ronan into human space. She bore the blame. If she'd had the sense to question Ronan more thoroughly . . .

She called engineering. "Charis, what's the state of the drive?"

"Not ready, Captain," the older woman's voice answered, "Give me five minutes."

"Acknowledged. Montague, lay in a course for VAL03. Toussaint?"

"We have enough firepower to hold off a striker for a short time, Captain D'Accorso-*fila*," the Dharman said, "but only as a delaying tactic."

"That's exactly what I had in mind. Stand by." She turned to Adumbe. "Feasibility of the *Pontos* riding piggyback on the slingshot field?"

The Nemesian nodded his understanding. "I would estimate the chances of Kord's survival as even, Captain. In theory, it should be possible, but in practice the field's boundaries may fluctuate—"

"And dump Kord out. That's a risk we'll have to take. Balogh, patch me through to the *Pontos* . . . Kord, you'd better be listening. We'll delay the striker as long as we can, but I won't risk the ship. There won't be time for you to dock. You'll be riding piggyback, and that means you have to get inside our field before we run. Burn out the shuttle's engines if you have to, but get your *fenek* back here."

"Acknowledged, Captain."

No apology in Kord's voice, but she hadn't expected it. She and Taye followed the shuttle's trajectory as it flew at top speed toward the *Pegasus*. The mouth of the wormhole burned with sudden light, spewing forth the shaauri striker like the sea birthing a typhoon.

"Toussaint?"

"The striker will be within torpedo range in two minutes, Captain."

And the *Pontos* was stuck in between.

"Stand by. Balogh, open a channel to the striker. Let's hope their captain comprehends Standard." She made her voice into a flat, almost mechanical drone. "Shaauri vessel, this is the Alliance ship *Pegasus*. You have entered human space. Be advised that we will be compelled to fire if you continue on this course."

No answer. The striker forged on, closing the gap.

"They will not respond, Captain."

She heard the voice with a start of disbelief and turned toward the door. Ronan stood on the bridge as if he belonged there, gazing at the viewport.

He'd broken his word, but she'd been fool enough to accept it. There was a moment of stillness on the bridge as the crew became aware of the intruder, and then each went back to his or her duties.

All except Janek. He drew his sidearm—the one his observer status permitted him to carry—and aimed it at Ronan.

"Stand down, Janek," she commanded. "Hold him, but don't shoot unless you're attacked."

"I warned you—"

"I know the shaauri," Ronan said quietly, disregarding his danger. "Since they have entered human space, they will not be deterred by threats."

"They're after you," Janek accused. "If we give him up, Captain, there won't be any need for a fight."

"Enough. Ronan, is there any way to stall them?"

He met her gaze with that deep inner stillness. "They disdain long-range weapons, but they will not hesitate to attack with disruptors. It would be best if you do as *Ser* Janek suggests."

"Surrender you, in human territory?" She laughed. "Toussaint, prepare to fire as soon as the striker's within range."

The tension on the bridge was almost tangible. Ignoring Janek, Ronan had moved to stand just behind Cynara's chair. She could feel him with her body and her mind.

"In range," Toussaint said.

"Fire at will."

Silent and deadly, two of the *Pegasus*'s precious torpedoes streaked toward the shaauri ship, bypassing the *Pontos*. The striker's disruptors caught one of the torpedoes before it had gone half the remaining distance. The second torpedo hit and was brushed aside like a gnat on a seabull's tail.

"Damage?"

"Minor, Captain," Taye said. "The striker has decelerated fractionally, but the *Pontos* is nearly within range of their disruptors."

If the shaauri considered the shuttle a worthy target. Why should they, when their weapons could take out the *Pegasus* just as easily?

"It is *sh'ei-lostajoi*—the Reckoning," Ronan said, giving the human word a solemn emphasis. "They will show their contempt and approach within your range of fire before they attack. If you were shaauri, you would do the same or forfeit any chance of honorable victory."

"You mean it's a test," Cynara said. "A test of our courage."

"And of your willingness to die. In old days, one enemy would usually retreat before the shedding of blood."

"Very tidy," she said. "Why do they grant us this honor when they generally destroy human ships outright?"

"Because you are in human territory, not an intruder in theirs."

"They risk little by getting close to a ship one-tenth their size."

"That is why they will wait, reckoning you of small consequence."

"And perhaps forgetting that we are human. If we attack first—"

"They may destroy you with all honor." Cynara felt Ronan's weight rest upon the back of her chair. He leaned close to her shoulder, watching her monitor. "There is a way you may delay them until your warrior reaches your drive field. Do you have access to detailed images of striker-class ships?"

Quickly she called up the scant information Alliance ships had gathered over the years and displayed the most detailed visuals one after another. Ronan studied them and stopped her at the third image.

"There," he said, indicating a specific point on the striker's forward keel. "This is the location of their sensor array and the section most vulnerable to attack. If you fire your weapons at the last possible moment, the ship will be temporarily blinded."

Cynara breathed a prayer of thanks and sent the data to Toussaint's station. "Toussaint, lock in on these coordinates and prepare to fire torpedoes on my mark."

"You're taking a great risk," Janek said. "If—"

"If Ronan has betrayed us, you have my permission to shoot him. Taye, is Kord close enough?"

"Ten seconds, Captain."

"Montague, turn about and stand by to activate the drive."

"Captain," Toussaint cried, "the enemy is firing!"

The *Pegasus* shuddered as the disruptor beam struck the hull.

"Montague!"

"Turning, Captain." The *Pegasus* began to wheel about, away from the shaauri vessel.

"Five," Adumbe said. "Four . . . three . . ."

"Fire."

An intense shaft of white light illuminated the striker's image on the aft screen. A warm, strong hand gripped Cynara's shoulder.

"Shuttle in range, Captain," Adumbe said.

"Montague, go!"

The young woman's fingers flew over her console, and at once the *Pegasus* vibrated with the almost inaudible whine of the slingshot drive as it sprang to life. The striker disappeared from the ship's sensors, and the screens revealed a distorted view of stars, dancing like the mysterious lights Dharman sailors professed lay deep in the waters of the Indigo Sea.

"Kord?" she asked Adumbe.

"He's safe." The relief in his voice spoke for everyone on the bridge. Cynara allowed herself a moment to breathe and glanced at the hand still resting on her shoulder.

Ronan's hand, scarred from a hundred unequal battles far more personal than the one the *Pegasus* had so narrowly avoided.

"Thank you," she said, shifting from beneath his touch. He took the hint and moved back, deftly sidestepping Janek and his gun. A cold draft blew down Cynara's collar.

"Adumbe, damage report."

"The shuttle bay suffered a hit which has disabled the door mechanism. A repair crew is on its way."

"Charis, are the engines holding?"

"Just barely. She's running at half capacity and showing the strain. I advise deactivation at the earliest possible moment."

"Acknowledged. Montague, ETA to VAL03?"

"Ten minutes, Captain."

Now was the most critical moment of their escape. They had outrun the striker, but once the slingshot drive was deactivated, the *Pegasus* would revert to its prior velocity. The secondaries weren't powerful enough to keep it ahead of the shaauri vessel. If the *Pegasus* could hold out for another ten minutes, until they'd reached the wormhole . . .

"Captain!" Adumbe said. "We've lost Kord."

"Lost him? Poseidon's balls—"

"The drive field fluctuated and dumped him," Adumbe said, frowning over his console. "The *Pontos* is intact, but she won't be able to reach us unless we deactivate the drive."

Cynara punched her fist on the arm of her chair. If she turned off the drive and waited for Kord to catch up, the striker's engines might be powerful enough to close the distance before the *Pegasus* could enter the wormhole.

Once in the wormhole, the drive could not be used at all without dire consequences.

"Montague, shut it down."

She felt the subtle change in the ship as it switched to the secondary drive. At this speed, the *Pegasus* wouldn't reach the wormhole for nearly an hour.

"Kord? Copy that?"

"Yes, Captain."

"We've obviously got a problem. Once you get to us, you won't be able to dock."

"I'll find a way, Little Mother."

"You have one hour, and pray that the shaauri don't catch up."

He acknowledged, and Cynara visited each of the bridge stations, sharing a joke with one crew member and a bit of encouragement or praise with another. It was impossible to forget Ronan's presence, though his only movement was the turn of his head to follow her progress. How could anyone stand so blasted still?

The hour passed slowly, but it passed. Repairs on the shuttle bay doors continued. Lizbet Montague reported their imminent approach to VAL03, one of the three wormholes in the human Valhalla system. It wasn't until the last few minutes that the striker entered sensor range, and Cynara knew they were out of options.

Kord was out of time. "I have the *Pontos* on visual," Adumbe said.

"And it can't dock. Kord?"

"Captain?"

"You'll have to piggyback again and hope you don't fall off this time."

"You plan to use the drive in the wormhole?"

His question held as much alarm as she'd ever heard from him. "The striker's right on our tail. It'll catch us if we don't."

Capture was the one fate they couldn't risk. She didn't have to ask Adumbe their odds of survival. If the slingshot drive were activated within a wormhole, the interference between the two would cause the wormhole's collapse. It was only a question of how quickly, and if the *Pegasus,* and the shuttle, could make it out before the wormhole imploded.

"Adumbe?"

"Kord is within field range."

"Good water, my friend," she told Kord.

"To you also, Little Mother."

Cynara cut the link. "Montague, enter VAL03 and activate the drive."

The *Pegasus* plunged into the wormhole. Walls like molten glass closed around the ship in a spinning, writhing tunnel. Cynara watched the aft screens. The striker was a solid darkness against the chaos of color and light.

As the slingshot drive kicked in, the glass walls seemed to warp and collapse. A vast roaring, lamentation of death beyond imagination, erased every other sound. The ship's hull trembled, plates threatening to pull apart. Mere seconds stood between the *Pegasus* and obliteration.

With a final burst of reckless speed, the *Pegasus* shot out the other side with hell nipping at its heels. Valhalla's sun filled the viewport like a beacon of safe harbor. The wormhole vanished in a searing holocaust, taking the striker with it.

Someone let out a cheer. Others followed, each according to his or her custom, and Cynara let them have their celebration. She grinned at Ronan in the broad, unladylike fashion her mother had so often deplored. He returned the smile—not much of one, to be sure, but a smile nevertheless.

"Thank you," she said. "You gave us the advantage we needed."

"You are . . . welcome," he said. "That is the correct response?"

"It is."

To her private amusement, Janek had holstered his sidearm, though he didn't appear ready to claim undying friendship with their guest. As the clamor died, faces more curious than hostile turned to Ronan. Lizbet Montague stared at him with wide, almost worshipful eyes. Taye Adumbe, for all his scholarly detachment, looked ready to burst with questions.

There were too many yet unanswered. The *Pegasus* could hold its position while Charis and her crew completed full repairs. Plenty of time to resume where Cynara and Ronan had left off.

She met Ronan's eyes and knew he was remembering their last exchange. She had the perfect opportunity to start over on more formal footing.

"I'll be escorting Ronan back to his cabin," she said to Taye. "You have the bridge. Send Kord to me as soon as he's able to dock."

Her second-in-command straightened from his station, eyes glittering behind his visor. "There is another problem, Captain," he said. "It appears that we have once again lost the shuttle."

Chapter 5

Cynara's stomach clenched and the deck rotated under her feet. She reached within for her own strength and Tyr's, aware of the eyes always watching for weakness or instability. Toussaint, Janek—how many others? Kord, Adumbe, Lizbet, and Zheng were the only ones she knew she could trust absolutely.

Yet she sought out the man she knew least—Ronan, whose impassive face showed a deeper understanding than any of the crew who called Kord friend.

She tore her gaze from his. "Was he caught in the wormhole?" she asked Taye calmly.

Adumbe was silent for a time as his visor flickered with symbols only he could see. "No," he said. "It appears that the force of the wormhole's collapse ejected the *Pontos* from our field at high velocity."

"Can you find him?"

"Affirmative. His comlink is nonfunctional, but I've traced the shuttle's transponder signal to the fourth planet in this system, known as Bifrost."

"Then he may have been able to land."

"It is more likely that he lost control of the *Pontos*. I'm sorry, Captain."

She shook her head. "Tell me about this planet."

"Bifrost was once the site of a small mining colony, in spite of its marginal suitability for human habitation. It was abandoned years ago when the shaauri blockade prevented the colonists from receiving critical provisions. Scans indicate that Bifrost is currently in its long winter, average diurnal temperature of minus fifty degrees centigrade."

"Then we need to move quickly." She returned to her chair and tapped her fingers over the console. A holomap of the star system formed in the space above it. "Scholar-Commander, tell Cargomaster Basterra to have the Thalassa outfitted with environmental suits and ready for departure in fifteen minutes." Her muscles felt like springs, compelling her from her seat to pace the deck. "Montague, I need a pilot."

"*Yes,* Captain."

"Captain-*fila*," Toussaint protested. "A man should accompany you."

"Your advice is noted, Toussaint. Lizbet, come with me. Taye, have Zheng meet us in the shuttle bay." She sprinted for the door. Someone stepped into her path.

"I will accompany you," Ronan said.

For a few vital moments she had actually forgotten him. She stood toe to toe with Ronan and felt again the leashed energy of his carriage, the arousal he provoked with his simple presence. Her voice went mute.

"I am trained in the warrior's way," he said, holding her gaze. "I can protect you."

"Out of the question," Janek snapped. "Captain, you should remain on the *Pegasus*. There are others you can send."

She could have embraced Janek for his fortuitous interruption. "Are you volunteering?" she asked. "If not—" She shrugged him off and glanced at Ronan. "Your assistance has been appreciated, but you will be confined to quarters until this situation is resolved."

"Your *ve'laik'in*'s situation exists because of my presence on your ship."

She shook her head. "I am sorry, Ronan. Toussaint, escort *Ser* Ronan to his cabin and set a guard." She shouldered past him, Lizbet at her heels.

"What is he like, Captain?" Lizbet asked when they were safely in the lift. The young Dharman's eyes held a familiar gleam of hero-worship, but for once it was not aimed at Cynara. "He seems dangerous."

"He is." She folded her hands behind her back as if the topic were only of the most casual interest. "We don't know enough about him, and until we do, he must be treated as a potential enemy."

"Yet he aided us against the shaauri," Lizbet said softly, daring contradiction. "There is a kind of . . . stillness about him. I wish that I—" She flushed and stared at the deck. "I understand, Captain."

Curse Dharma for the harsh lessons it taught girls like Lizbet from the time they were old enough to walk. "Your insights are valuable," Cynara said gently. "Never doubt it. And now I need your skills to get Kord home."

Lizbet flushed again, this time with excitement. All she needed were a few chances to prove herself, to learn that she was the equal of any man. God grant she found her calling in an easier way than Cynara had done.

God grant that Lizbet wouldn't live in loneliness, futilely seeking a man disposed to call her his equal.

Ronan's face came to Cynara in all its stubborn tenacity. He had paid his debt to the *Pegasus*. He owed her nothing. Yet she felt that something bound him to her as she was bound to Tyr and to Kord, each in a different way, each loyal unto death.

God grant she was mistaken.

The surface at Ronan's back was wrong, and that wrongness brought him awake in an instant.

He was not in his cabin, where Toussaint had left him sealed and guarded. He stood in the doorway of a cockpit just large enough for two seats and a bank of lighted consoles, screens, and monitors tucked beneath a transparent canopy looking out on a field of stars.

A ship. A ship in space. For an instant he thought he was still on the darter, and that everything else had been a dream.

But Cynara was at the center of his imperfect memory. He had been on the *Pegasus*. He had come to the bridge with no recollection of how he had done so, breaking his word to the captain. He had made some reparation by helping the *Pegasus* escape the shaauri, but it had not been enough.

Because of him, Cynara had lost one of her crewmen. She had been prepared to depart for an uninhabited world to save the warrior Kord. Ronan had seen her driven by an inner fire that almost blinded him, and in her body he had read her fear for her *ve'laik'in.*

But it was Ronan's own fear that had bound him to speak. The fact that Cynara had rebuffed him in his cabin made no difference. He had long since stepped over the rightful boundaries of his position here, as he had done among shaauri every day of his life.

But Cynara had denied his request to accompany her in the rescue attempt. He had not fought Toussaint and Janek when they took him to his cabin. His one thought was that Cynara was about to go into danger, accompanied only by a healer and a female *an'laik'in,* a fragile technician with no skill to protect her First.

And here he was, in the cockpit of a vessel bound for some unknown destination.

The shuttle. He was on the shuttle *Thalassa.* He crossed to the console and scanned the configuration of the controls. They were locked on autopilot, but he could assume command with no difficulty.

"Poseidon!"

He spun to face the voice. The young female Lizbet Montague crouched in the doorway, clinging to its frame as if hard vacuum waited on the other side.

"*An* Montague," he said, raising his hands. "I mean no harm."

"How did you get here?" she whispered. "The captain said—" The skin of her throat quivered. "You escaped from detention."

He tried to smile. "I am not armed. Bring the captain, *sh'eivalin-an.* I will remain here."

Montague scuttled backward, more shock than fear in her posture. Bootheels rang on the deck beyond the door.

Cynara stepped through with her sidearm at the ready, brows arched high.

"I should be surprised," she said, "but for some strange reason I'm not. Put your hands on top of your head, *Ser* Ronan."

He obeyed while Montague reappeared at Cynara's flank and Healer Zheng loomed behind them, her bulk filling the doorway. Cynara strode up to Ronan and patted his shipsuit with one hand. All the insignificant hairs on his body stood erect.

"I am not armed," he repeated.

She stepped back. "I doubt that would make much difference in your case. How the hell did you get on my shuttle?"

"I do not know."

"You just 'appeared' here, the same way you did on the bridge?" Her expression hardened. "How did you escape the guard? What did you do to him?"

His ears twitched in negation before he remembered to shake his head. "I do not remember. The last I knew I was in my cabin."

It was evident from her stance that she did not believe him. "Every one of my crew had better be in good health when we return." She gestured him away from the pilot's seat. "Lizbet, hail the *Pegasus*."

The young female slid into the seat with a swift glance at Ronan. Adumbe's voice answered the hail.

"Taye, has there been any kind of disturbance on the *Pegasus* that you failed to mention?"

"Disturbance, Captain?"

"We have a stowaway on the *Thalassa*. He seems to have escaped a locked cabin and eluded his guard. Perhaps you have an explanation?"

Silence, and the hum of distant voices. "Captain, I have no explanation. Toussaint has just located Bhruic, who appears to have been sleeping on the cabin bunk. He has no recollection of how he came to be there, or how the prisoner escaped."

"I see. Get Bhruic to the infirmary and have Ardith check him out thoroughly. I want a full report."

"Acknowledged, Captain. Will you be returning?"

"Negative. Carry on."

Montague broke the connection. If Cynara had been

shaauri, Ronan would have prepared for imminent attack. He had begun to learn better.

"I'd turn back for the *Pegasus* and toss you in the brig if we hadn't come so far," she said. "But your good fortune is temporary, my friend. When we get to Dharma . . ."

"I came to help you retrieve your *ve'laik'in*," he said. "What you do with me afterward is of no concern."

She paused, pushing a loose strand of russet hair from her forehead. "What do you make of him, Zheng? I suspect that he combines the worst of human and shaauri."

Ronan turned up the corners of his mouth, making another attempt at human levity. "So shaauri and Kinsmen have told me."

"I am inclined to believe him, Captain," the healer said. "He seems to feel he owes you some personal allegiance."

"Scylla's teeth." Cynara moved very close and stared into Ronan's eyes. "Is that what you want to do—swear allegiance? You broke your word to me on the ship, when you came to the bridge and again when you escaped—"

"I am not your enemy, *Aho'Va*."

She measured him so thoroughly that he felt her gaze as a touch up and down his body, arousing him as before. "Perhaps not," she said, "but please don't make any more promises. You maintain this claim that you don't remember how you got here?"

"Yes."

"When we get back to the ship, Zheng, do another full brain scan on our guest. If he's telling the truth, there must be some reason for these blackouts. Zheng, Montague, carry on. I'll take Ronan into the galley." She glanced at her wrist. "One hour to planetfall. Inform me when you're ready to begin final descent."

"Yes, Captain."

Cynara holstered the sidearm and waved Ronan through the door. He preceded her into the galley, furnished with two small tables and three times as many seats.

"Sit," she ordered. "We didn't get the chance to finish our previous conversation, and that was a mistake. I've made the possibly hazardous assumption that you really are human."

Ronan laid his hands on the table. "I am."

"Outwardly, yes. But I think, no matter how much you reject it, you are still part shaauri."

"I had to become like them in order to survive."

"I understand." She kept her hands out of sight under the table, as if she was afraid to let him see them. "But I find it very hard to believe that they taught you how to pilot their ships."

It was a question he had expected, and yet he still had no answer, no explanation to make her trust him. "I was not shut out from all learning—the Kalevi House that took me in accepted me under their protection. It was other Houses on Aitu that wished me gone."

"Gone?"

"Dead."

"They would have killed you, even as a child?"

"It was necessary for me to learn to defend myself and discover how not to provoke attack. When I was very young, Ain'Kalevi protected me. But when I reached the age of Selection, they could not."

"Because you should have been entering adulthood, and they forbade you what you needed to achieve it."

"They feared the tales I might carry to humans, if I were allowed to run free as *be'laik'in*."

"Then why didn't they kill you? Who brought you to Aitu, and where did you come from? Why did the shaauri take you in?"

As he had done so many times in the past, he tried to remember the days of his childhood before he had first come to be among the shaauri. One morning he had awakened in a shaauri dwelling on a shaauri world, understanding almost nothing of what went on around him, or of these great beings who were to be his guardians. Even when he learned to speak the tongue as fluently as any human could, the Kalevii had refused to tell him what he had lost.

So he had learned to stop asking. He had learned, very quickly, how to watch and listen. He had discovered that three Houses of Line Kalevi lived on Aitu, along with several Houses of allied Lines.

At first most shaauri of Ain'Kalevi had treated him with casual indifference, even indulgence, as they did their own young. But when he had ventured away from the settlement, he had learned how much shaauri hated humans.

"You haven't answered my question, Ronan."

"I do not know the answer. It is not the shaauri way to murder children."

"Defending the people who did *that* to you?"

He followed her fierce stare to the back of his hand. Discipline alone kept him from withdrawing it, and he remembered with shame how he had made a display of himself to win her sympathy and trust.

"Shaauri believe," he said slowly, "that all humans are uncivilized barbarians. Humans never return from Walkabout, and so remain unselected and without place or purpose all their lives. Shaauri regard this as a form of insanity, and humans as purveyors of madness. They breed much faster then shaauri, since all may mate where and when they choose. There is much fear . . . that the shaauri way will be infected and devoured by the human."

Cynara sighed and closed her eyes. "Then they are wrong, Ronan. Not all humans are alike. On Scholar-Commander Adumbe's world, learning for its own sake is the great achievement, and all rank comes from academic testing throughout life. Zheng's world, Anvil, is high-gravity, and her people have adapted by altering their bodies both genetically and technologically to cope with the environment. On Sirocco, women hold all property and men gladly cede leadership to them."

"And your world?"

Her pulse increased by increments, and he smelled the faint tang of perspiration. "On Dharma, men rule and women are permitted few liberties. A female goes from her father's house to her husband's and her life is separate from that of males."

With a flash of insight he realized that she was ashamed, and that it had taken her much courage to speak of this to him—to admit a weakness among humans and among her own people.

"This difference in gender does not exist among shaauri," he said. "Most Paths share equally." He leaned closer to her over the table. "Human females do not lead, yet you are First of this ship."

She gave a soft laugh. "That, my friend, is a long and complicated tale. There are many who would like to see me fall from this position."

Toussaint and Janek. Both men had challenged her authority, subtly or openly. "They use my presence to work against you."

"They need very little encouragement. But rest assured— they wouldn't be on this ship if I thought they would undermine our—" She caught herself, brows drawn. "If humans were selected like shaauri—" An almost imperceptible tint of warm color crept up under the clear skin of her face.

"Aho'Va," he said with respect, "you are va'laik'in, of Will. You are First among these of your . . ." He could not say House or Line, for such things did not exist among humans. "You are First of your crew. The one you call Adumbe, he is Second, and should be va'laik'in as well. But you called him scholar. That is kivi, Reason."

"Can shaauri select for more than one Path?"

"I knew only one such shaaurin. He was of riama, Spirit, and vekki, Blood—a warrior and philosopher. He believed that all Paths are One."

"As humans do . . . or should." Cynara leaned forward as he had, so close that their foreheads almost touched. "Perhaps we are not so different."

Ronan breathed in her breath and felt his heart drum within the walls of his chest. "So he taught. So he believed."

"I would like nothing better than to believe in you," she said, with an intimacy reserved for closest kin or mates. Ignorant, he was now certain. Ignorant of what she signaled with scent, voice, and gesture.

"How do I win this belief?" he asked.

"You said that once you had the gift of telepathy, like Kinsmen. Some on Dharma—the ruling families—carry this same trait."

"You are a telepath."

"Yes. Does that disturb you?"

"Do not humans fear those who listen to the thoughts of others?"

"On some worlds, yes. Kinsmen were often held in suspicion even before so many defected to the shaauri."

"You are not Kinsman."

"No. But the first Kinsman—a woman—came from
Dharma."

"Then you can enter my mind, and see if I speak truth."

The deep blue of her eyes swallowed up the black pupil.
She was afraid—not of him, but of something far less tangible. Not merely afraid, but terrified. She did not wish to use
this ability she claimed.

"Yes," she said, "if you'll let me. It is . . . not an easy
thing, to have a stranger come into your deepest self. I
wouldn't ask it, except—"

"You would not be First if you did not make sure of your
enemies."

Her gaze came back to his. "Your mind was tampered
with. Only Kinsmen would have the ability to suppress natural telepathic abilities—Kinsmen or equally strong
telepaths." She hesitated. "Concordat Kinsmen construct
mental shields for agents who may be vulnerable to telepathic intrusion from enemy operatives. I have one myself,
and so does Janek."

"I do not think I have such a shield."

"But you may suffer more from any new intrusions, even
if you don't remember what was done to you."

"You give me the choice, unlike those others."

"Yes."

"Then I accept."

Cynara shivered and leaned back in her seat. "I promise
that I will not go any deeper than absolutely necessary to
confirm your intentions." She brought her hands up onto the
desk and clasped them. "My mind is not as powerful as that
of many Kinsmen, or even some of my kin on Dharma. It will
be necessary to touch you."

All the discipline in the universe could not have kept him
from exulting in that moment. Only the expression on her
face, pinched and grim, held him still.

She was afraid, as he was. He feared that this female he
desired would discover his shame and inadequacy. That she

would realize that her rejection of him had been not only correct, but necessary.

"I accept," he repeated, burying his fear and elation. "What must I do?"

Cynara had fought her own inner battle, and her eyes were clear once more. "Open your mind. Think of it as . . . as space itself, boundless, expanding to infinity. I'll touch your hands. I don't know what you'll feel, but if it becomes painful—"

"Continue until it is finished, *Aho'Va.*"

"I asked you to call me Cynara."

His soul danced. "Cynara. Does it have a meaning?"

"It is a name from an ancient human language—taken from a flower called a thistle."

"And is this flower very beautiful?"

"How would I know what you consider beautiful?"

"Perhaps you will learn."

She looked aside. "We have little time before planetfall. If you're ready—"

He nodded human-wise, and she reached across the table to lay her hands upon his. Heat raced up the nerves of his arms. Cynara's fingers trembled. She almost withdrew them, but all at once her grip became firm and sure.

"Open your mind," she said. "I won't harm you."

Behind his closed eyelids lay the black of space reaching to eternity, and he was only a flicker of light unseen by any but the one who touched him. He felt her enter, illuminating the darkness.

Searing beams plunged like knives, and with them came memory of the other time, when men had held him down and torn at his thoughts until they were stripped bones scattered by scavengers. He embraced the pain and let himself fall.

Chapter 6

Pain. *Such terrible, unendurable pain.*

It came upon Cynara like a killing storm, beating wave upon wave. At first all she caught were blurred images like stones under ice. She was afraid, and fear made her too much at one with her subject.

Too close. His mind was as scarred as his body, bearing the brands of manipulation by telepaths of great skill and no scruples. She withdrew halfway, slipping free gently so as not to further damage his mind in her passing. Only then was she able to see what Ronan remembered.

The images passed swiftly, disordered and jarring as in a nightmare. Visions of felinoid shaauri standing over him, twice giants to the boy he had been, with their pointed teeth and jutting, tattooed claws. Hands reaching. Growls and squeaks and words he could not understand. Terror.

Then a moment of gentleness, unexpected. A soft humming trill, and a face less fearsome very close to his. But the tenderness did not last. For then he was older, his sense of self that of an adolescent. Shaauri were there again, not as tall, their fur unstriped red. Youngsters. They crowded on Ronan like a pod of orcas. Their voices were high with mockery.

Ne'lin, they cried. *Hu-man.*

They came one at a time, but they did not leave him until he lay on the ground, his blood spotting the tree needles that carpeted the ground in the wood. His muscles ached with countless bruises. He rose to his feet, weeping, and found his way home.

It happened again when he ventured too far from the Kalevi settlement. This time he fought. They beat him down. He grew older. Nothing changed.

Another shaauri face. But this one was unlike all the others. The fur, pale sienna with age, was deeply barred with faded stripes. Peace lay in the slanted eyes. The shaaurin held out his hand, and the boy took it.

The pain didn't stop, but something altered. Those who came to beat him hesitated. Some retreated, and others showed the marks of wounds. The boy's terror had slipped behind a barrier they could not penetrate even when they hurt him.

It was victory, of a sort. Cynara searched for emotions of joy, pleasure, even contentment. The last she found in rare memories, those that usually included the old shaaurin. But never true happiness. Never the comfort of belonging, even when other humans came and he lay with females of his own kind.

Cynara found herself caught on those memories as if they were traps deliberately set. The images were focused yet languorous, no longer nightmare but ecstatic dream. Ronan's dream.

It was his first time. For years he had seen shaauri adolescents leave for Walkabout, one by one, free to mate as they chose until the time of Selection. Only he had been forbidden such release. At the age of sixteen, as humans reckoned it, his thoughts had been filled with need and confused yearning.

Then they had sent for the Kinswoman. She had shown him such wonders . . . Cynara tried to remain apart from the memory, but Ronan's emotions were too powerful. Gratitude, elation, release, the fragile sensation of having come home at last.

When it was over, he reached for his lover, his mate, believing with all his heart that she would stay. After what they had shared, how could she do otherwise?

But the face turned toward him was cold, and in it he read the indifference of a tedious duty completed. With that look she wounded him, not in flesh that would heal but in his very soul.

That had been the first of the annual visits. Each time a new Kinswoman arrived to relieve a young man's hungers. No companionship. No love, except when memory touched the old shaaurin, and sometimes other faces that did not turn from him in scorn and loathing.

Cynara tried to conceal her pity, the sorrow for Ronan that he might sense if she projected too strongly. As if aroused by her efforts, Ronan claimed her again—not with old memories, but as he was now, fully aware of her as she was of him.

Emotions washed over her, barely contained. She felt Ronan's desire—attraction, yearning, physical hunger, everything that he had experienced with those other women, but a thousand times more potent.

In his mind he had stripped her naked, and they lay in that forest he remembered from childhood, bodies entangled. Her legs were wrapped around his hips, and he was moving inside her with deep, rhythmic thrusts. She was no longer a captain or a D'Accorso or even a woman of Dharma, but some unrecognizable creature heedless and half mad with lust . . .

Cynara snapped the link far too swiftly, breaking the protocols meant to protect both telepath and subject. It was like lopping off one of her arms. She slumped over the table, breathing hard, Ronan's scarred hands filling her vision.

She pushed up on her elbows. Ronan's gaze passed through her, unseeing.

"Are you all right?"

He blinked and focused. "Is it finished?"

Poseidon. Had it been illusion, her sense that he had been conscious of her presence within his mind? Her entire body felt like a live current, thrumming with Ronan's desire and the memory of his phantom lovemaking.

"Yes." Her throat was too dry for speech. She got up and filled a glass of water from the dispenser, leaning heavily on the counter. After a moment she poured another glass and set it before Ronan.

He touched the glass with his fingertip. "Was it difficult?"

Difficult. She hadn't attempted anything like this since Tyr's death had tripled the acuity of her insignificant talents. She'd always feared that such concentrated use of them would summon Tyr from his restless sleep, compel him to reclaim the life she'd unwillingly stolen.

For she knew he still lived within her. She drew upon his confidence and absolute belief in his own competence and strength. She had no right to prevent him from reclaiming what should be his, yet she avoided any risk that might upset the precarious balance.

Tyr the hero. Tyr the beloved of all Dharma. Tyr the bold, brilliant captain, her childhood idol.

I gave everything to you, Tyr whispered. *Do not deny me, Cynara. Let me live . . .*

"Cynara?"

She winced at the concern in Ronan's voice. "No," she said. "It wasn't difficult."

"Did you discover what you needed?"

Cynara gathered all the images she had collected and realized how little she had seen of his life. Yet it was enough. No man could suffer so and be anything but a fugitive, desperate to rejoin his own kind and find acceptance.

Ronan desired her because she was the first human female to treat him with dignity and friendship, and because his needs had been so inadequately met. It was not her job to heal his wounds with her body or her soul.

Why, then, could she not rid her mind of his erotic dreaming? She forced herself to meet his eyes. The lust she expected was banked, but she could never be unaware of it again.

"Yes," she said. "I believe you are here to rejoin humanity, and to help us."

He closed his eyes. "My thanks."

For what? For having pushed her way into his mind like a rapist, stealing what he held most private?

"Did you ever . . . sense my presence?"

The answer was plain when he opened his eyes. "For a moment," he admitted.

"It may be—" *Poseidon,* how could she find the nerve to raise his hopes? If he'd been a child when they crippled his telepathic abilities, he wouldn't miss them. He might be far better off without them.

She gulped down the rest of the water and set down the glass. "It may be possible to restore something of your telepathy. With the right experts, of course. If . . . if you want to try."

He did not answer but rose, leaving his glass untouched, and paced across the galley to the bulkhead, never quite turning his back to her.

"What is it like, to walk in another mind?"

How could she answer? She'd touched so few, and only two deep enough to brand her: Tyr, and now Ronan.

"It's theoretically different for everyone. There are many kinds of gifts. You'll be able to talk to other telepaths on Dharma. I'll arrange it."

"You don't wish to go back."

"To Dharma? My family is there—"

"But not your heart."

He could have drawn such a conclusion from the clues she'd given him, but the observation was too acute for comfort. "Are you sure you aren't still a telepath?" she asked lightly.

"I recognize your loneliness."

"I don't have time to be lonely."

He faced her, hands folded at his back. "Is Kord your mate?"

Cynara's boots sealed to the deck, nearly tripping her. "Kord is my weapons specialist, and my friend. You remember our discussion of human friendship."

"You risk your life to save his, though you are his First."

"You're willing to risk your life for us—or is that only because you've grown up believing you have no worth to lose?"

She stopped, appalled at her own cruelty. What shocked her far more was the faint, self-mocking smile on Ronan's

face. He had learned to wield human expressions with remarkable skill in a very short time.

"I will risk my life for Cynara D'Accorso," he said, taking a step toward her. "As you would risk much to save this
ship. Your *Pegasus* is not like other human vessels. Why was
it in shaauri space, outrunning a striker as if it were a
ba'laik'in's plaything?"

His sudden change of topic left her mute. If she had not
just probed his mind, she would have suspected his motives
in asking. Janek would do more than suspect.

"Your curiosity is natural," she said, "but it isn't a subject
I'm prepared to discuss."

A shadow darkened his eyes. "You do not trust me as a
friend. Do you need to enter my mind again?"

"It is not a matter of trust or friendship. You are still a
stranger—"

"I do not wish to be." He stood only a meter away, close
enough for the heat of his body to penetrate her shipsuit. He
lifted his hand, palm up. "Cynara—"

"Captain D'Accorso," Lizbet's voice announced over the
intercom. "We are approaching Bifrost."

"Acknowledged." Cynara strode briskly for the door.
Now was the time to decide—to trust or not to trust, to accept
or reject Ronan as he had been rejected so many times before.

"It's time to suit up," she said. "Are you coming?"

He smiled, teeth and all.

Snow blew onto Ronan's faceplate and was swept away
again by the ferocious, icy winds of Bifrost. He had seen
this storm's like before, high in the mountains of Semakka.
But then he had been alone with Sihvaaro, a student in the
care of his elder. Here his companion was one he must protect
with his life.

Cynara tapped her suit's comlink, her face barely visible
through the visor. "I'm picking up the signal from the *Pontos,* south-southeast. Lizbet reports that the terrain between
here and the approximate landing site is broken and treacherous, and the storm is getting worse."

She glanced behind in the direction of the *Thalassa,* al-

ready lost in the blizzard. Lizbet Montague and Healer Zheng
were secure inside; Zheng would ordinarily have accompanied them, but she had declared that she was nearly immobile
under such conditions and would be far more hindrance than
assistance. It was up to Ronan and Cynara to find Kord and
return him to the shuttle.

An Montague had set the *Thalassa* down at the only suit-
able location near Kord's landing site, a half-buried apron
built by the long-departed colonists. Crumbled walls of
buildings framed two sides, blocking the worst of the wind.

Ronan had observed the desolation with a strange discomfort, remembering what Adumbe had said about the fate
befalling colonies cut off from vital supplies. Ronan had no
part in the shaauri blockade; he had been as much at shaauri
mercy as the humans who required trade to survive.

But shaauri would not have been so mad as to settle a
world with such an extreme elliptical orbit. Bifrost had long,
scorching summers and equally endless winters, and it was in
the second season they now found themselves.

Human madness. But Cynara was not mad. Janek must
have thought her so when she permitted Ronan to accompany
her in search of Kord. She had put her life into his hands because she had sifted his thoughts and memories.

He did not know what she had seen. Only at the end had
he felt her and recognized what it must be like to share minds
as Kinsmen did, whole and complete. He had caught a
glimpse of the woman Cynara permitted few to see.

Loneliness. The weight of responsibility for something
beyond her crew, the unspoken fear of failure, the doubt of
her very self.

And desire. Craving touch and rejecting it. Turning him
away for reasons he could not begin to grasp.

She had hurt him with her abrupt withdrawal, raked open
invisible scars he had forgotten. And then she had offered the
return of the abilities he had lost, abilities like those of the
Kinsmen who despised him. Kinsmen who joined, mind to
mind, with their mates.

To be bound so to Cynara, one with her, belonging . . .

Cynara shivered, though her environmental suit held the

cold at bay. Ronan pressed against her. "What concerns you?" he asked through the intercom.

"Imagining what it must have been like to live here," she said, and dismissed the thought with a shrug. "Let's move out."

She took the lead, following the *Pontos*'s transponder signal as she picked her way over obstacles meters deep in snow. She was strong, sure and efficient in her movements, but even the helmet's visual enhancers could not make the going easy. Ronan knew she would be shamed if he preceded her. Her pride was that of a First even when she made light of her rank, and among humans a First always led, even into danger.

Ronan stayed at her heels, straining to separate distinct elements out of the chaos of sound. It was all lost in the whining of the wind. Yet his senses remained alert, warning him that something was wrong.

"You are certain that no humans have remained here?" he asked.

"In this?" Her voice came back to him over the intercom leached of its natural music, but not of its irony.

Ronan searched the barren landscape. "Cynara—"

A hulking shape stepped in front of her, grotesquely furred in a motley pattern of gray and white. Ronan plunged through the snow to knock Cynara aside. He crouched above her and snatched at his hip for the sidearm she had given him.

Not soon enough. The shape raised one upper limb, and Ronan made out a hand with several thick fingers, aiming a rifle at the center of his faceplate.

The fur was not part of this being, but merely a covering. The face was so shrouded as to be invisible.

"What is it?" Cynara whispered.

Briefly Ronan remembered that personal contact was necessary for her telepathic senses to function properly. "I can't smell him," he said. "He must be human. I will disarm him."

"No." She pushed onto her knees. The rifle swung toward her. Ronan moved to intercept it. The muzzle touched his suit just below the helmet seal. At such close range, the beam could penetrate and kill.

"Do what I do," Cynara said. She put her hands above her

head. Against his better judgment, Ronan did the same. The man in furs snatched their sidearms and shoved the weapons among the layers of his covering. He gestured east with his rifle, commanding them to move ahead of him. Ronan kept himself between Cynara and their captor, guiding her along the path the man had already made.

The mouth of a cave opened up before them, rimmed with a jagged fringe of icicles. The fur-clad man pushed them through a door in a wall constructed of broken machinery and paneling.

Inside, the cave was a surprisingly orderly collection of materials undoubtedly scavenged from the colony's remains. Furs were heaped over a cot and broken chairs. A small fire burned at the rear of the cavern, dancing in the draft from some unseen flue.

The man urged them toward the back and made clear that they were to sit or kneel. Only when they had complied did he lower his weapon and begin to unwind the wrappings around his head.

His face was human, clad with its own matted facial fur, and aged with tribulation. The eyes were nearly lost in wrinkles and the rime of frost on lashes and brows. He tugged off his gloves one at a time, never letting go of the rifle.

"Take off your helmets," he commanded.

Cynara obeyed, her hands steady on the seals. Ronan did the same. It took him a moment to adjust to the bitter cold, and he knew that Cynara must be in great discomfort. He edged closer to her.

The man's eyes widened, showing faded brown. "Been so long," he croaked. "So long."

"Who are you?" Cynara asked. "Why have you brought us here?"

He pulled up one of the chairs and sat down, leaning the rifle against his knee. "How did you get to Bifrost?"

"I am Cynara D'Accorso, captain of the Alliance ship *Pegasus*. This is my . . . crewman, Ronan. We came looking for a fellow crewmember forced to land on this world."

"The ship," the man said. He scratched under the collar of his fur coat and breathed out a cloud of mist. "I saw it. Thought it crashed. Was going to look for stuff I could use."

"We have no quarrel with you, *Ser*—"

"Gunter. Sam Gunter." He closed his eyes. "So long."

"Ser Gunter, our shipmate may be injured and in need of immediate assistance. We mean you no harm. Once we have retrieved him, we will leave."

"Leave?" Gunter laughed hoarsely, and Ronan heard an edge of madness in it. This one was truly *ne'lin* as humans understood the concept. Ronan prepared to fight at a moment's notice, adjusting his balance to compensate for the weight of the suit.

"Yes," Gunter said slowly. "Take your friends with you. But I need something first."

Ronan gathered his muscles. Cynara held very still. "What do you want?" she asked.

"That." He jerked his chin toward Ronan. "That suit. It should fit me. You give me that suit, and you can go."

"That will not be possible," Cynara said. "But when we're done, we'll be happy to take you with us to the Nine Worlds."

"You leave. I stay, with the suit."

"You're welcome to any supplies we have on the *Pegasus*—"

He jumped up and grabbed the rifle. "No bargaining. Suit now, you go. No suit—" He took aim at Cynara. "You die, I take both suits. Your choice."

"Ronan can't survive this cold—"

Ronan stood, his hands away from his body. "I will give you the suit."

"Ronan—" Cynara began, scooting around on her knees.

"Hold it," Gunter snapped. "Move, I shoot."

Ronan met her gaze, and she read the stubborn determination in his eyes. He removed his pack, his belt and harness, letting them fall to his feet. Then he unfastened the e-suit, working from the neck down. Cynara could almost feel the cold seep through the double-thick shipsuit he wore beneath. The boots came last, with their element-proof linings and heavy soles. He kicked the e-suit aside.

"Now let us go," he said. Cynara couldn't detect so much as a shiver, though the temperature must have been well below minus ten degrees. He seemed as composed and unaffected as if he stood in the ship's galley with a warm mug of kaffé in his hand.

"Damn," Gunter swore. "You a soldier, man? Too young for the Second War." He moved cautiously toward Ronan and hooked his foot around the suit. "All right. You go now."

Ronan knelt to pick up Cynara's helmet and offered it to her. "You're crazy," she whispered.

"It must be done." He placed the helmet over Cynara's head and fastened it, working efficiently though his fingers must be numb. He grasped her arm and tugged her toward the cave entrance.

It was impossible to reason with him. She considered rushing Gunter and taking his weapon, but Ronan's grip was so hard that she would have to fight him off first. She could hardly see him through the clouds of condensed breath wreathing his unprotected face.

He had asked to disarm Gunter at the beginning, and she had refused. *You still don't trust Ronan. If he dies—*

She cursed Ronan and herself, wondering who was the greater fool.

Gunter didn't follow them outside the cave. Ronan released Cynara when they were a hundred meters away. She found her bearings and pointed back toward the *Thalassa*, hoping they could make it quickly enough.

Ronan shook his head and gestured the way they had been heading before Gunter's assault.

She flipped on the speaker. "I order you back to the *Thalassa*."

He smiled with what she could only assume was wry humor and plunged his bare hands in a snowbank. He raised his ice-covered hands. There was no shivering, no unsteadiness in his fingers. He grasped her wrist and placed her gloved hand flat on his chest.

His heart beat at a normal rhythm, and his breaths were measured and regular. It was impossible, but it was happening. He lifted her hand, folded it into a fist, and rested his lips on her padded knuckles.

Where had he learned such a gallant human gesture? "You're insane . . . you know that, don't you?" She snatched her hand free and shrugged out of her pack, riffling the outer pocket for the thermal blankets meant for Kord. But Ronan had already set off, marching unerringly toward the *Pontos*'s landing site.

Short of a pitched battle, stopping him was out of the question. "Lizbet, did you copy all that?"

It was Zheng who answered. "Affirmative. You have a madman out there with you—two, if you count Ronan. Get back here immediately."

"Negative. Ronan's already out of sight. I'll get us back as quickly as possible. You two remain with the shuttle, is that clear?"

A long, rebellious pause. "Affirmative, Captain."

Cynara cut the 'com and peered through the storm in the direction Ronan had gone. He covered ground at an amazing pace, and she had to scramble to keep up. He disappeared over a rise just as she reached its base.

By the time she had climbed to the top, she was ready to knock Ronan over the head with the nearest convenient rock and drag him back to the *Thalassa* by his hair. The view from the hill instantly halted such unproductive speculation.

On level ground twenty meters ahead, its nose driven deep into the snow, lay the *Pontos*. The hull had blackened and buckled in several places, and the aft section of the shuttle was nearly severed. Cynara picked up her pace and ran after Ronan as fast as the bulky suit would allow.

Once at the ship, she brushed away a thick coating of snow from the cockpit canopy. With her chisel she hammered at the layers of ice. Kord was a dim, unmoving shape within.

She set her scanner against the hull. It blinked green; Kord had survived. Emergency life support had remained operational, but it was near the end of its capacity.

Ronan had already found the hatch release and entered the shuttle. Cynara dumped her pack, unfastened the folded litter, and snapped it open.

Kord's head was first to emerge from the hatch, followed by his body draped over Ronan's shoulder. Ronan laid him out on the litter and crouched in the snow.

"He is breathing," Ronan said, his voice snatched away by the wind.

Cynara clasped Ronan's hand and grinned. She tried to

toss one of the blankets over his shoulders, but he caught it in midair and tucked it around Kord.

Alike as two limpets on a rock, she thought in disgust. Kord had several cuts on his forehead and gashes in his suit, but no visible serious injuries. Most worrisome was his apparent unconsciousness. Cynara pushed up Kord's sleeve and set the medscan against bare skin. The readout indicated broken ribs, a contusion to the forehead, a fractured wrist and tibia, and numerous small lacerations and bruises.

"Zheng," she said into her comlink, "did you get the data?"

"Affirmative. Is he conscious?"

"He seems to be sleeping."

"Get him awake as quickly as you can."

Ronan touched Cynara's arm. Kord's eyes had opened. He seemed to focus on her for a moment, and then his gaze wandered to Ronan. His left arm twitched.

"It's all right, my friend," she murmured. Ronan helped her strap Kord into the litter, and she activated the transparent bubble that would protect him from the elements. Together she and Ronan lifted the litter and retraced their steps.

Kord's weight was far less a burden than Cynara's concern for Ronan. Whatever allowed him to function under these conditions couldn't last indefinitely. He was still only human . . .

The litter jiggled. Cynara half turned, expecting the worst, but Ronan was still on his feet and staring past her shoulder.

She followed his gaze to the man with the rifle pointed directly at her heart.

Chapter 7

Gunter tore the protective folds of cloth away from his mouth and spat in the snow. "The suit," he said. "It stinks of shaauri."

Cynara could only speculate how he'd detected the connection between Ronan and shaauri, but Gunter's obvious disgust explained why he wasn't wearing their "gift."

If she dropped Kord, she might be able to get his rifle, but her only chance was to act before he expected it.

"Don't even think about it, missy," Gunter snarled. "You made a bad deal. Suit's no good. You pay up." He moved to the litter and stared down at Kord. "You want him alive, you pay."

Cynara set down her end of the litter. "Return the suit, and we'll get you another."

"No good." The space between Cynara's shoulders itched, and she could almost feel Ronan weighing his chances. She had no doubt that he'd act just as recklessly as Kord would in the same situation.

"What do you want now?" she demanded.

Much to her surprise, Gunter backed away, rifle cradled in his arms. "You come to my cave, alone," he said to Cynara. "Anyone else comes, I shoot him."

It almost seemed inevitable, though the prospect turned her stomach. "I'm a very poor bargain compared to a suit and supplies."

"That's the deal. You come alone. If you try to pass, I shoot all of you." He backed away over the next small hill, where he undoubtedly planned to wait until she accepted his kind offer or tested his resolve to murder them.

She tugged on the litter, urging Ronan toward a more sheltered place under a rocky overhang. Somehow he managed to place himself with his back facing outward to the storm, making a shelter of his body for Cynara.

"You cannot go to him," he said simply.

"Right," Kord grunted, his voice muffled through the bubble.

"How are you?" Cynara asked, crouching beside the litter.

"I'm alive." He peered up at Ronan. "Don't . . . let her."

"I will not." Ronan met her eyes. "This Gunter is *ne'lin* and without females. He wishes to mate with you by force. This is not acceptable among humans."

A blush was highly incongruous at the moment. "Damn what's acceptable among humans. I think he means what he says. He'll shoot us if we try to pass."

"We do not know if his weapon functions."

"I'm not going to take that chance."

"Then let me fight him."

"In your condition?"

"While I distract him, you take Kord to the shuttle."

"And what if you're hurt?"

He made an awkward imitation of a shrug. "If I were your *ve'laik'in,* it would be my duty."

"If I do as he demands," she said, "no one will be hurt."

"Unless he lies, and decides to keep you."

"Listen," Kord whispered. "Little Mother . . ."

Ronan's hand disappeared into the pocket of his shipsuit and emerged holding a pistol. "I found this in the *Pontos,* and thus I am no longer unarmed. You will . . . *pretend* to obey him. When you go with him, I will come after and take him."

Cynara eyed the gun. "This is mutiny."

"My regret," Ronan said. "Let us go." Tucking the pistol under one arm, he opened the litter and helped Kord sit up.

Cynara had no choice but to assist him. The litter was only a hindrance now, no matter how things went.

Between them they supported Kord over the small hill, where Cynara could make out Gunter's bulk twenty meters off to the side, in the direction of the cave. He could not yet see them.

Ronan took Kord's weight against his side. "Can you wait alone?" he asked the Siroccan, easing him to the ground.

"Yes." The two men exchanged glances that excluded Cynara utterly. "Good water."

"Good ice would be more appropriate," Ronan countered.

A joke from Ronan at a time like this? "Ronan—"

"You go now, Cynara," he said. "Deceive Gunter until I come. I *will* come."

She had never heard a more convincing statement in her life. He would come, and he'd find a way to beat Gunter even if he had to put his life on the line to do it. For her sake. For the sake of her "honor." And that had been lost long ago.

She pushed snarled hair out of her face and glared for all she was worth. "If you die on me, Ronan—" Her throat closed up, and she forgot all the eloquent and vulgar Dharman threats she had been about to hurl at him.

"If you die," she said hoarsely, "you'll never get more of this." She removed her helmet, seized his shoulders in her gloved hands, and kissed him hard, heating his icy lips with the warmth of her breath.

A beat of shock, and then Ronan grasped her upper arms and returned the kiss with interest—no expert wooing, nor the urgent passion of a boy who regarded sex as a kind of miracle.

This was deeply, overwhelmingly personal.

She broke free and pushed him away. "Go!"

He went without a backward glance, vanishing into the blowing snow. With hands that shook more now than they had under the threat of Gunter's rifle, Cynara put on her helmet and tapped Kord's shoulder. She had a feeling he'd have a few things to say to her when they returned to the *Pegasus*.

Leaving her pack with Kord, she set off toward Gunter's cave. He intercepted her at a hundred paces and signaled her to walk ahead. Even through the suit's filters she could smell him—rancid sweat, filthy furs, and the undefinable odor of masculine lust. She had a single, chilling moment of doubt that Ronan could do what he promised.

Within a few meters of the cave her footsteps slowed of their own accord. She stumbled and stopped, expecting to feel Gunter's rifle in her back. But it was not fear that had made her falter. Something stirred in her mind, a sensation she hardly recognized.

She spun on her heel just in time to see Gunter lift his rifle and fire at the figure hurtling toward him.

Ronan touched the ground so lightly that he hardly left a print, dodging the beam by a hair. He sprang again and knocked Gunter's weapon aside with a swipe of his hand. The rifle plunged into a snowbank. Gunter dived for it.

As silent as he was quick, Ronan leaped in front of Gunter and slammed his knee into the hermit's face. Blood spattered the snow. Gunter yelled and rolled onto his back, clutching his broken nose.

Ronan crouched over him, fingers arched and head low. Cynara pushed her way to his side. One look at his face told her that he was ready to kill without hesitation. All Gunter had to do was move.

Gunter did, clawing at Cynara's leg. Ronan fell on him. His arm drew back, fist clenched.

She grabbed Ronan by the elbow and hung on with all her strength. He turned his head slowly, focusing on her; his eyes were narrowed to slits, dark gray in a pale, rigid face. Merciless. The expression of a trained assassin.

If ever she had needed her telepathy, it was now. She forced her fear aside.

No, she projected, closing her eyes. *No, Ronan.*

He flinched and blinked rapidly. His muscles flexed and relaxed in her grip. He lowered his hand.

He had *heard* her. The killer's ardor went out of his eyes. The connection was still there between them: She sensed a vague surprise in him, as if he didn't know where he was or how he had come to be there.

Cynara uncoiled a rope from her pack and held it up, waiting for Ronan to understand. He continued to stare at her in bewilderment, even after Gunter lunged up and sank a knife hilt-deep into his side.

Ronan fell, not as a man falls, but like one of the great trees in Jyri forest, slowly and without grace. His cheek struck a surface both firm and giving that shaped itself to the contours of his face. Melted snow wet his tongue. Somewhere there was pain, but it did not reach him. It had fled to the same place the cold had gone when he prepared his body for its ordeal.

Sharp pellets of sound came to him amid the drone of the wind. Motion flashed in the corner of his vision. Someone touched him with the gentleness of the *li'laik'i* nurturers of Ain'Kalevi, taking him back to his childhood.

Ronan! He heard the voice, but not with his ears. It rang in his head. He tried to turn toward it, but his limbs would not obey. Blackness grew behind his eyelids.

Fight it, Ronan! I'll get you back to the shuttle. Just hold on.

Strange how the sounds seemed unfamiliar, in a language he did not recognize. Yet he understood. He would try to obey, because the one who demanded his obedience held his life as surely as his mind.

"It is when you face the most difficult challenge that you must call upon all Paths," Sihvaaro said. Ronan tried to summon the chant. The words dissolved before he could grasp them, like the snow melting in his mouth.

"There is a time to battle for what must change, and a time to accept what will be."

Acceptance. Relief. All at once he knew that it was better to end here, because what waited on the other side was too terrible, like the death he had seen in his enemy's eyes. On the other side stood a stranger who would steal his soul.

Accept.

No. Curse you, no! Warmth like distant memory caressed his face. Heat scalded his mouth, life-giving fire. He knew the lips that touched his.

Cynara. She was with him, holding him, breathing her will into him with her body as her mind laid siege to his. But another Ronan fought against this woman and her promise of healing as if she brought not life but eternal damnation.

The battle was lost before it truly began. Cynara swept past the ramparts, carrying all resistance before her.

Cold. Pain. Ronan opened his eyes. He smelled his own blood, heard harsh breathing nearby—Gunter, who had tried to kill him.

Something slapped his bared arm. Cynara crouched over him with her lips almost brushing his forehead.

"A coagulant patch," she said. "It'll help stop the bleeding until we reach the shuttle. Gunter won't be any more trouble. I'm taking you back now. Zheng and Lizbet are on their way—they'll carry Kord. Do you understand?"

He understood her perfectly, remembered all that had happened with crystal clarity.

Remembered *everything*.

He knew why he had wanted to die, and why he must not. Laughter hissed between his teeth, jarring the deep wound in his side.

"Don't try to talk. I'll get you back. Just hold on."

She braced her legs and lifted him, and he did what he could to support his own weight. Pain could be ignored, and biting chill. But not what he had remembered. Not the knowledge of why he was here. Knowledge that brought not certainty and confidence but turmoil.

Cynara had embraced his mind, and he would never be the same again.

T*he infirmary was full to overflowing. Three inmates* occupied the permanent beds, and Zheng bustled about like a mechanical babushka, clucking happily over her patients.

Charis had put the hours to good use in repairing the *Pegasus,* and the ship was nearly ready to traverse the final wormhole to the Nine Worlds territory. After leaving Ronan, Kord, and Gunter in Zheng's capable hands, Cynara had seen to her own duties and consulted with Adumbe about the incident on Bifrost and the loss of the *Pontos.*

She wasn't permitted to go about her work unimpeded. From the moment the *Thalassa* docked, Janek had been snapping at her heels, demanding immediate access to Ronan for questioning. She couldn't fault his motives. Someone would have to find out how Ronan had escaped his cabin, overcome the guard, and boarded the *Thalassa,* all without any apparent memory of doing so.

Janek wasn't going to let her handle it alone, but she fended him off and seized a free moment to watch Zheng's charges through the observation window. Kord lay in an accelerated healing field, bones already knitting while his body was pumped full of medications to speed his recovery. Gunter had suffered no serious injuries in spite of his clash with Ronan, and was being held under sedation until he could be assessed for mental as well as physical health. Stripped of his furs, he looked like a harmless old Dharman banker.

But he had nearly killed Ronan, who was recovering much faster than Zheng's best prognosis had indicated. He was awake and exchanging comments with the doctor.

Cynara keyed into the room and worked up a grin for Kord. His body was immobile in the AHF, but he was able to turn his head to look at her. She braced herself for a scold.

"Captain," he said, "what water-sucking demon possessed you?"

"I might ask you the same."

"I did what had to be done."

"So did I." She pulled a chair close to his bed and sighed. "Let's get this out of the way. No, a captain should never go on a hazardous mission. Yes, I took a big risk. Yes, I could have been killed. No, I never considered not going. No, there's no point in arguing with a headstrong seacow like Cynara D'Accorso."

"I would never call you a seacow, Little Mother. It was my disobedient act that placed you in danger. I'm not worth your life."

"You're beginning to sound like Ronan."

He strained to sit up and the field pushed him down again. "Ronan," he echoed. "Why did you bring him with you?"

"It's fortunate that I did."

"He could have turned on you—" His eyes narrowed. "Unless you obtained some new evidence of his trustworthiness."

"Not evidence, my friend. You would call it intuition."

He muttered a string of Siroccan words that she suspected were far from polite. "Is that why you kissed him?"

"You must have been delirious from your injuries."

"My vision was unaffected." He craned his neck toward Ronan's bed. "Have you chosen him?"

The question did not shock her. She had known it was coming, and that Kord would never simply let it pass. Sirocco was a world in which women made nearly all the political decisions and chose their mates, the very reverse of Dharman culture. The crucial difference lay in the fact that men were not regarded as lesser beings, but merely different in nature.

Kord loved her. He had loved her since he'd first come to Dharma as her uncle's protégé, his native brilliance outshining all but a handful of Uncle Jesper's most promising pupils. But he had never presumed to consider her anything but a high-ranking leader, as on his own world.

When she'd become captain, he had sworn himself to her in the way of his people. Nothing could alter that. He was like the most protective elder brother imaginable, held in check only by his innate respect for women. And his love.

"I haven't *chosen* anyone," she said. "But I do trust him. He saved both our lives and nearly lost his own."

Kord digested her statement, leaving her alone with her memories. She'd been frankly terrified when Gunter stabbed Ronan, and that had given her the speed and strength to overcome the older man. After that, her entire focus had been on saving Ronan's life no matter what she had to do to assure it. Fear of her own mind had been as nothing in comparison. She had reached out blindly, hoping to find something in him that would fight beyond hope for survival. She had succeeded beyond her wildest expectations.

When she'd entered Ronan's thoughts on the *Thalassa,* they had come close to an overwhelming intimacy she'd believed impossible to duplicate. But the crisis on Bifrost had engendered a connection that virtually reproduced what she had shared with Tyr just before his death—so profound a blending that to maintain it would have burned her out like the lightning-struck hull of a fishing boat.

She'd held the key to unlocking all of Ronan's secrets, and she had cast it away to preserve herself.

After she'd taken Ronan to the shuttle, he'd collapsed.

Zheng worked quickly to save him and Kord with the limited medical supplies aboard the *Thalassa*. Cynara had spent most of the return trip trying to make sense of what had happened.

"You will take him to your bed," Kord said matter-of-factly. "Be cautious yet, Little Mother."

Cynara bolted from her chair. "You presume too much. This is my ship, and I will not endanger it."

"It is yourself you endanger." His mouth twisted up in a half smile. "But I am only male and lacking in the deeper wisdoms. Disregard me as you choose."

She didn't intend to disregard him, but someone else demanded her attention, someone whose claim on her couldn't be ignored.

Common sense told her that she shouldn't be so acutely aware of Ronan when he lay in a bed meters away. They were not touching. She did not feel his mind, or even the residue of his thoughts or emotion. Yet she sensed his stare raking her body, and that second, desperate kiss seared her mouth anew.

She'd kissed him on Bifrost because it was the surest way of reaching the part of him best able to fight for life. Did he even remember, or was he anticipating a third kiss in the privacy of her quarters?

Deliberately she turned to face him. The intensity of his gaze pulled her across the room, and she fought it every step of the way.

"Captain," Ronan said. "You are well?"

"Shouldn't I be?" She examined him critically. "Zheng says you're lucky to be alive."

"I will heal." He said it with a verbal shrug, dismissing his pain. "*Ve* Kord?"

"He is also healing," Zheng said, stepping up beside Cynara. "You both came very close to death, and it didn't help that you exposed your body to subfreezing temperatures."

Zheng had the full report and knew very well why Ronan had acted as he did. "You continued to function and even fight in conditions that would immobilize or kill an average human," she said. "I'd like to find out how you managed it."

"There are disciplines among shaauri," Ronan said, "that grant the mind mastery over the body's limitations."

"Is that how you learned to fight as you do?" Cynara asked. "One of these shaauri disciplines?"

"There was an old shaaurin who taught me his way."

Cynara hid her surprise. He hadn't spoken so frankly of his past before Bifrost, but she remembered the image of the elderly shaaurin, so vivid in Ronan's mind. A shaauri mentor had taught Ronan to fight with deadly skill. What had his captors thought of that? Why had they allowed it?

"Was it this old shaaurin who taught you to lure an armed guard into your cabin, disable him, and leave him with no memory of what happened—not to mention getting past everyone else to board the shuttle?"

Ronan's brow furrowed in bewilderment. "I do not remember doing this," he admitted. "I thought only of reaching you, *Aho'Va*. The rest is a dream."

"Are you certain telepathy wasn't involved?"

No one could feign such genuine confusion. "Even if such abilities remained available to me, would they not require great mental strength? Would you not have discovered this within my mind?"

He was right, of course. Concealing skills of that magnitude would be extremely difficult—especially after Bifrost.

"I'll need to do more research on these blackouts," Zheng said. "They could indicate some trauma or condition the regular scans haven't identified." She examined his diagnostic screen. "Don't keep him too long, Captain. He needs his beauty sleep."

"No amount of rest will change my appearance," Ronan said. "Will the young male, the one I disabled—"

"Bhruic."

"—accept my regrets for this indignity?"

"You didn't hurt him. He doesn't seem to remember much more than you do." *Though he very well may once Janek is through questioning him.*

"Nevertheless, I regret my actions. What of Gunter?"

He spoke the hermit's name as if he would gladly finish what he'd begun before Gunter stabbed him. Cynara couldn't blame him; she'd like a few rounds with Gunter herself. But she hadn't forgotten the ruthless efficiency with which Ronan had been prepared to end the hermit's life.

A child, beaten again and again, learning at last to defend himself . . .

"I've pulled up his records," Zheng said. "He's listed as a veteran of the Second Shaauri War. Apparently all his living relatives were lost on a colony ship bound for Bifrost, where his family was to join him. Shaauri attacked the ship and presumably killed all aboard. The colony was abandoned, and Gunter refused to leave with the others."

Cynara exchanged glances with the doctor. Such tragedies had been far from uncommon since the blockade. For years most trade between the two human territories had ceased. Only the *Pegasus* had changed the odds back in human favor . . . if its secret was preserved from their enemies.

"*This suit stinks of shaauri,*" Gunter had said. Cynara didn't want to know how he'd made that connection. Perhaps madness had heightened his senses. He had lost his family and become stranded on an abandoned world. Who could blame such a man for his hate?

"Gunter has cause to despise shaauri," Ronan said, "as I do."

Ronan didn't despise all shaauri. He had respected, perhaps even loved, his mentor. Yet it was an apology of sorts, or at least an attempt at understanding.

"Whatever his reasons," Cynara said, "he's mentally unstable and will remain confined until planetfall."

Ronan looked sharply at her. "The *Pegasus* nears its destination?"

"A matter of days."

"Days that you will spend resting," Zheng put in, "either here or in your cabin."

Ronan seemed not to hear. "We are bound for your world, *Aho'Va?*"

How strange his formality sounded after Bifrost. "We have stops at several planets, and finish at Dharma."

"And then?"

And then, indeed. Once she might have promised him the freedom to choose his own destiny, but Janek would make that impossible. He wasn't going to let Ronan wander about

Allied territory without a thorough debriefing. His authority on Dharma was limited, but he still had considerable influence with the Offworld Trade Council.

Cynara had her own kind of influence. She'd left Bifrost convinced that Ronan's telepathic abilities could be on the brink of recovery, perhaps triggered by her mental touch. Specialists on Dharma could be of great benefit to him. And if Ronan volunteered to share his knowledge of shaauri with the Alliance, it would certainly prove his loyalties.

"We can't make any decisions now," she said, hating the need for deception. "You'll have plenty of time to consider all the possibilities on Dharma."

"The captain is correct."

Janek strode into the ward, grim-faced as always. "Ronan VelKalevi will have ample opportunity to contemplate his future as the guest of the Trade Council." He challenged Cynara with a long stare. "Since you seem determined to bar me from questioning him myself, I'll leave the task to the experts."

Cynara stepped into his path. "Ronan has assured me that he doesn't remember what happened between the time he was confined to his cabin and awakened on the *Thalassa*. I believe him."

"His memory lapses are remarkably convenient."

"He also saved Kord's life. I thought that Persephone's laws assured that a person is considered innocent until proven guilty."

"If I were convinced he was a shaauri spy, he'd be in the brig, Captain, regardless of your opinions."

"If he were a shaauri spy, *Ser* Janek, he could have chosen a much safer method of gaining our trust than by risking his life and almost losing it for the sake of a stranger. I'm sure the doctor will be happy to tell you how close he came to death."

"Yet Bhruic has no explanation for what happened to him."

"No one was hurt. Whatever Ronan did—"

"He presents far too much of a mystery," Janek interrupted, "and has too many convenient and unusual skills for a former prisoner. He may be equally adept in the matter of clouding human minds."

"As in telepathic compulsion? Even most Kinsmen can't do it, *Ser* Janek. You and I are presumably protected from such incursions—at least any your Concordat Kinsmen could anticipate. If Ronan possesses residual telepathic abilities, they couldn't be powerful enough to approach such an extraordinary act."

"Forgive me, Captain, but I doubt your objectivity where our guest is concerned. Telepath you may be, but you are not trained to conduct the kind of interrogation necessary to clear VelKalevi of suspicion."

Cynara narrowed her eyes. "You don't speak like a mere observer, *Ser* Janek. Why don't you share with us the source of your expertise in these complex and confidential matters?"

"I'm sure everything will become clear on Dharma," Janek said. He stepped to the side for a clear view of Ronan, who returned his stare. "You're being watched, VelKalevi. Cooperate, and you may find your stay on Dharma relatively pleasant compared to captivity among the stripes."

Ronan smiled. "Perhaps I will, *Va* Janek."

"Until we reach Dharma and contact the Council, you will not obstruct ship's operations," Cynara told Janek. "We'll proceed on the assumption that Ronan is a friend and ally."

Janek clicked his heels and bowed. "As you wish, Captain D'Accorso. Until Dharma."

He left the ward as abruptly as he'd come. Zheng grunted in annoyance. "Bastard, upsetting my patients—"

Cynara patted her shoulder. "For a tech-bureaucrat from the bowels of the Persephonean Space Authority, *Ser* Janek is a little too used to getting his own way. I don't intend to see Ronan subjected to the tender mercies of the Council without adequate representation. I'll be sending a message to my Uncle Jesper as soon as we clear the wormhole."

"Isn't he the most liberal-minded burgher-lord on Dharma?"

"And one of the most powerful. If he's convinced that Ronan is safe, Janek won't have an oar to row with." She turned to Ronan. "You'll have to trust me."

"I do, *Aho'Va*," he said, his eyes bright with something perilously like adoration. *"Ta'i'lai, ta'i'ma."*

Cynara found an excuse to escape soon afterward, evading Kord's knowing gaze. Only when she was on the lift to the bridge did she consult the Voishaaur-Standard database and translate the meaning of Ronan's last phrase.

By my Path and my soul.

It was her own soul most in danger now.

Chapter 8

The mess was crowded with crew, every member except those few required to manage the ship in its last leg of the journey home.

Ronan stood beside Cynara at the captain's table, facing a mob that regarded him with curiosity largely shorn of suspicion. Kord sat in the chair to Ronan's right, relieved of the necessity of standing on his mending leg. The woman Charis sat two seats down from Cynara. Lizbet Montague, Cargomaster Basterra, Toussaint, and two other unnamed males had their seats in this place of honor.

Cynara held up her hand, silencing the murmur of voices. "Ladies and gentlemen," she said, "the *Pegasus* is fully repaired, we're less than a day's travel from Nemesis, and I can think of no better time to introduce the newest addition to our crew." She smiled broadly and laid her hand on Ronan's shoulder. "I take great pleasure in presenting Ronan, the man who saved the *Pegasus* and the lives of myself and *Ser* Kord d'Rhian O'Deira."

The applause was loud and sustained. Ronan listened to it with distant curiosity, comparing the gesture of acclaim to the far more subdued whistling of shaauri commendation.

So easy it was to win human trust. He might have died on

Bifrost, but the unwitting act of self-sacrifice had been well worth the risk.

He was alive and exactly where he needed to be.

Something tapped his leg. He glanced down at Kord, who wielded his crutch very much like a weapon.

"They want you to talk," he said. "Half the crew is Dharman; they always expect speeches, at least from males."

Ronan glanced at Cynara. She nodded encouragement, clearly pleased at the reception and at Kord's change of attitude. Even the young warrior, who should have known better, had abandoned his sensible caution.

Ronan lifted a hand. The crowd fell silent.

"I am not eloquent in the language to which I was born," he said. "I do not know the way of making speeches. I can only say that it is a great honor to repay my debt to this ship and its crew, which preserved me from my enemies, and to serve its captain."

More applause. "Is it enough, *Aho'Va*?" he asked Cynara. She nodded and tapped his shoulder to indicate that he should sit. The others sat as well. Serving crew entered the mess with trays and food, the smells overwhelming in their alien savor.

Conversation broke out immediately, no polite silence maintained during the meal. Ronan concealed his distaste. The food laid out before him was identical to that of the others—fish, a root vegetable, and risen bread. Shaauri, too, were omnivores, but they served meat and vegetable dishes separately. He had not yet become accustomed to the odd feel of human utensils in his hands.

"This is the first time you've sat down to eat with the crew," Cynara said, breaking off a piece of bread. "Does it feel strange? Are shaauri customs similar?"

"They are not so different, *Aho'Va*. But I seldom took meals with the shaauri."

"I see." She smothered her bread with a white substance and took a bite, eyes narrowing in pleasure. "This is the one part of the ship where all are equal, regardless of rank or social position." She glanced about the table. "Some of my officers you've met. Let me introduce the rest. Charis Antoniou, chief engineer."

The tall woman two seats away from Cynara nodded, chewing vigorously on her vegetables. She was well curved and padded in her shipsuit, her pale hair like a cap cut close to her skull. Only her hands were delicate, nails precisely trimmed at the ends of long, agile fingers.

"*Ser* Ronan," she said, swallowing. "Pleasure. Take it you've never been to Persephone."

"Your home, *An* Charis?"

"Aye." She cocked her head. "What's this *'an'*?"

"A prefix indicating profession," Cynara said.

"*Anki*—body," Ronan explained. "*An'laik'in.* You would say . . . those who work with hands, though it is a poor definition."

"Fair enough." She took a sip of her beverage, a sort of weak *arao* that Ronan found extremely bland. "When you lived in shaauri territory, did you ever hear of Lady Kori Galatea Challinor and her consort, Jonas Kane VelArhan?"

Arhan. Ronan grew alert, studying Charis with greater attention. "I have heard the Line name," he said. "He is Kinsman?"

"Was. Lady Kori was second heir to the throne of Persephone. She and Kane tried to stop the Kinsman Rebellion—almost managed it, too. They vanished on a diplomatic mission to the shaauri just before the Second War. The Concordat received reports that they'd been killed by antihuman shaauri, along with their second son."

Ronan's bread grew bitter on his tongue. "The shaauri are killers," he said. "It is their way."

"I wondered if you'd heard of them, raised as you were. The Lady's son might be your age now, if he'd lived."

"I knew no other human children," he said. "I was taken on a raid by *be'laik'i,* wanderers. The Kalevii chose not to kill me."

"Hell of a way to live. Pardon, Captain."

Cynara stared at Ronan. "You've finally remembered how you came to Aitu?"

Ronan realized at once that he had slipped and must be more careful. "Yes, Captain," he said. "Some memories have begun to return."

"Excellent." She leaned back in her seat and addressed the

crew. "We have much to learn from Ronan, and he is eager to learn from all of us."

Ronan caught the gazes of the other officers, including Lizbet. She ducked her head and blushed as a shaaurin might flatten her ears. "I also wish to learn," he said.

Movement from the far side of the mess caught his eye. Janek took his seat in the empty place beside the captain.

"Apologies for my tardiness, Captain D'Accorso," he said. A server brought him a meal, and he picked at it while he cast glances at Ronan. "Have I missed an interesting discussion?"

"Obviously not as interesting as whatever kept you from the captain's table," Kord said. His voice bared his teeth, as the shaauri saying went. "You might have missed your seat if Scholar-Commander Adumbe had been able to attend."

"Because our honored guest is in mine?" Janek said, downing his beverage in one draft. "In that case I'd have to take your place, *Ser* O'Deira. Or do you wish to duel for it?"

Ronan half rose. Kord grabbed his elbow.

"Patience, Brother." Abruptly he stood, drawing the attention of all the crew with his silence.

"I gladly surrender my place," Kord said in a deep, carrying voice, "to my brother Ronan." He held up his hand and drew an exquisite ornamental knife from some hidden pocket in his shipsuit. With its blade he slashed his palm and let the blood drip into the glass of clear water beside his plate. He lifted the glass and offered it to Ronan.

Ritual. Ronan recognized it for what it was, and what it must mean to the young warrior. Kord offered the comradeship of human *ve'laik'i,* a binding made not of birth in House or Line but of choice.

Ronan knew what he did when he lifted the glass and drank the water. He held Kord's gaze, took the knife, and slashed his own palm. Kord tasted his blood, raised both glasses, and tossed them over his shoulder.

"It is done," he said. He cleaned the knife with a cloth and tucked it back inside his shipsuit.

"Bravo," Janek said, clapping. "Deeply moving, indeed."

"My enemies are his, and his mine," Kord said, taking his seat. "Remember that, Persephonean."

"Gentlefolk," Cynara said, "We've had enough drama in the past few days to last until the Opal Tides run black as space. Peace at this table."

"Peace at this table," Cargomaster Basterra muttered.

"Peace," Kord echoed. He leaned toward Ronan and tilted his chin toward Janek. "Watch your back with that one, Brother. He already rides the sword's edge with his insolence to the Little Mother, but she has forbidden me to challenge him. He will try to bring you down."

"Because he fears my intentions toward the Concordat."

"Many Persephoneans hate Kinsmen and their kind, even those who remained with the Concordat. He sees you as Kinsman, whether you are one or not. I believe that he wants this ship for himself, and hopes that by taking you aboard, Cynara endangers her captaincy."

"Does she?"

"She does not answer to Janek, or even the Archon of Persephone. The *Pegasus* belongs to the Alliance."

"And the *Pegasus* is important."

"It is not my place to speak of it. The captain will explain when she judges the time right."

Ronan relaxed in his seat as if the topic held no interest for him. "As you say."

The slight tension went out of Kord's posture. "You desire the captain," he said.

The unexpected question upset Ronan's facade of indifference. He sat up. "I do not understand you."

Kord chuckled. "Come, my friend. You must know she favors you."

"She has done me honor."

"She *favors* you, man. Are you sand-blind?"

Ronan did not misunderstand. On the shuttle, before he had remembered the truth about himself, Cynara had reached into his mind for the first time. That touch had not triggered his memory as had the encounter on Bifrost. Only later, lying in the infirmary, had he realized what she had discovered.

Pieces of his childhood, yes, and faces of those shaauri who had befriended or tormented him. But she had also witnessed his encounters with the Kinswomen who had come at Kalevi behest to serve his needs. She had felt what he felt then, the full measure of his lust and hunger for companionship.

And she had not turned away in disgust. It had been as if *she* lay with him in his bed in Ain'Kalevi, as if *her* body accepted his caresses.

The second mental joining on Bifrost had been brief and deep like a spear-thrust, piercing his carefully constructed defenses and withdrawing just as swiftly. He had been too close to death to fully comprehend it. But it had forged a new bond between them, just as her kiss had awakened his body.

That bond was his advantage and his potential undoing. Cynara did not know how well he recognized her desire for him. She rejected such weakness in herself, but it was so obvious that even her closest *ve'laik'in*—her *friend*—perceived it.

Because of Cynara, Ronan had access to everything he had forgotten—had been made to forget—before he had come aboard the *Pegasus*. He had subdued young Bhruic and made himself invisible to the crew even before he had any understanding of how or why he did so.

Kinsmen had imposed that loss of memory, as they had built the many shields that guarded his mind. It must have served some objective in his mission. Perhaps the false recollections of his past had been designed to convince the humans that he was exactly what he claimed and believed himself to be, the fugitive who hated all shaauri.

Surely his trainers had not expected him to regain his true memory so quickly. They had prepared him for the possibility of sexual liaison as a means of gathering information, but they had not reckoned on one such as Cynara D'Accorso.

He had been sexually drawn to her at first meeting, ignorant of the source of that compulsion. The subliminal drive to accomplish his assignment lay at the heart of all he felt, all he did. In the act of mating, minds were most vulnerable to intrusion.

He had regained memory, but his purpose had not altered. He must guard the changes in himself from everyone, Cynara most of all. As long as she was vulnerable to her desire for him, he would have opportunities to enter her mind as she had his.

"It does not trouble you," he said to Kord, "that the captain favors me?"

"The Little Mother is my sworn lady. Her enemies are mine. One who swears brotherhood to me serves her as I would." His brown eyes held Ronan's. "As you will."

Ronan pretended interest in his piece of fish and glanced down the length of the table. Many of the crew members were finishing their meals and returning to duty, or gathering in small groups to talk. Ronan thought of his own cabin, Cynara's only a few doors down the corridor. His body demanded more rest, but there was a higher priority.

"I'm on the bridge for the next watch," Cynara said. "We'll talk later, Ronan. In the meantime, you have the run of all decks except the bridge."

Ronan stood to face her. "I may move freely, *Aho'Va?*"

"Everywhere but the restricted areas. You'll recognize those by the red and yellow striping on the bulkhead and doors."

He remembered. Such forbidden places were the very ones he must penetrate.

"Perhaps when Kord is off watch, he'll take you on a tour," she said. "Remember Doctor Zheng's instructions, both of you." She nodded farewell and strode toward the mess door.

Kord followed Ronan's gaze. "Don't mistake her ease of manner for weakness," he said. " 'They are most dangerous who keep the blade sheathed.' "

Ronan smiled without humor. "Among shaauri it is said, " 'Who can know the mind of Will?' "

Or the mind of a traitor.

R onan wandered the upper decks for several hours, casually bypassing the forbidden areas as if they held no interest for him. He observed the movements of men and women, noted how few held sidearms or seemed prepared to fight. He counted crew in each sector of the ship from mess to cargo hold. Though he could only guess at crew numbers in the engineering and life support sections, he estimated that three-quarters of the ship's complement had been present in the mess.

Forty crew in all, a reasonable number for a ship of this size. Minimal security. Half of them would be on watch at any given moment.

After his first sweep, Ronan made a second at a more leisurely pace. The humans he encountered were, at worst, guarded, and at best seemed to welcome his presence. Most were curious about him and willing to discuss some element of their occupations, though none was foolish enough to offer essential details. Ronan shared minor anecdotes of shaauri life and left them satisfied that he was more to be pitied than feared.

When he passed the striped doors that led to engineering, he slowed his pace and smiled at the uniformed guards. These men were separate from the crew, in clothing and mien; they were true warriors, like Kord. Ronan took the risk of skimming their surface thoughts.

They knew very little of what lay beyond these doors, of the special engine that enabled the *Pegasus* to outrun shaauri strikers. They did not even have the means to unlock the doors, but they did know who among the crew had such access.

Beyond that Ronan dared not press. He sensed shields within their minds like those Cynara had spoken of possessing, and it was not yet time to test them.

He nodded to the guards and retraced his steps to crew quarters and his own small cabin. At the last minute he altered course for the captain's rooms.

Her door was unlocked. Not a matter of carelessness, not on this ship, but a deliberate gesture of trust. She would hardly keep material pertaining to the *Pegasus*'s secrets in her personal lodgings.

The door slid open at the lightest touch of Ronan's palm. Cynara's scent, and one other he didn't recognize, swept over him.

Though twice as large as his own, her quarters were nearly as spare. Yet the chamber was not entirely without personal decoration. The bunk's coverlet was woven in bright patterns of greens and blues, sea-tones, designed to look like waves. On the bedtable stood a holo, depicting five humans on a sandy beach: an older female, her upper face obscured by a weighted cloth; a mature male in colorful attire; two younger men; and a girl.

The girl was Cynara. Her bright hair escaped the scarf laid haphazardly upon it, and she looked ready to burst into a run. The ankle-length, slit skirt over her close-fitting trousers would not have impeded her for long. Only the adults behind her held her in check.

One of the young men bore a strong resemblance to Cynara: kin, perhaps a genetic brother. The other young man was also similar in appearance, though his hair was gold rather than red.

Ronan found additional objects that he guessed were from other human worlds: a dagger similar to the one Kord kept tucked in his shipsuit; a black, pitted rock; an elaborately coiled shell. Ronan remembered a trick Sihvaaro had taught him the one time they had gone to the sea. He picked up the shell and held its mouth to his ear. The ocean was contained inside it—an ocean within the ocean of space.

Someone spoke. Ronan jumped, unable to locate the intruder until a motion near the deck caught his attention.

The creature was not at all like a shaaurin on four legs, though Ronan had heard it said that humans sometimes regarded shaauri as large bipedal cats. This beast was very small, compact, dark-furred, and flat-skulled. It possessed a long, sleek tail. Its fingers were too short to grasp or manipulate.

Even so, there was enough of a resemblance that Ronan stood very still and let it approach. It was not afraid, though it lifted its head and smelled the air in the manner of any reasonable being.

The cat took another step and abruptly sat on its hindquarters to lick its forepaw. This was, indeed, a sort of Reckoning, a test of Ronan's intentions and an announcement of its own lack of fear.

Ronan crouched closer to its level and displayed his fists palms-up. "Good hunting, *sh'eivalin*," he said.

The beast yawned wide, showing sharp carnivore's teeth. Once shaauri had been strict carnivores and hunters, before they learned the Way of Paths and began to till the soil. Now the most traditional shaauri sought to restore the ancestral features by filing their teeth to sharp points. This creature had no need of such artifice.

"You are Cynara's . . . pet," he said, tasting the human word. Shaauri rarely kept animals in captivity for companionship or amusement. The cat responded by strolling up to his hands and nudging its muzzle against his fingers.

"Ah. You wish to be groomed." Ronan raked his fingers through the animal's fur, taking liberties he had dared with only a few shaauri. The cat rolled over on its back and squirmed its forequarters from side to side.

Ronan examined its belly. There were rows of teats for suckling, but no pouch. It, like humans, must expose its young immediately after birth.

"Are you alone on this ship, Little Sharp-Teeth? Do you miss others of your kind?"

"Cats don't speak," a voice said from the doorway. "At least not in the way we understand it."

He sprang to his feet, prepared for her rightful anger at his intrusion. She cocked her head with a look more puzzled than hostile.

"I've always understood that shaauri were highly territorial," she said. "It seems strange that one raised among them would invade someone else's."

Ronan ducked his head. "You are right, *Aho'Va*. I have trespassed."

"No apology?"

"You have the advantage. You may strike."

She laughed and instantly sobered again. "That's the second time you've said something to that effect. Your shaauri seem to be forever on the edge of violence."

"Only when provoked." He met her gaze. "One who enters OutLine territory uninvited must expect attack."

"As we humans expect attack whenever we try to carry out honest trade." Instead of bidding him leave, she sealed the door and crouched beside her pet. "Have you satisfied your curiosity, or is there something else I can show you?"

Almost as soon as she spoke, her skin flushed pink. It made her seem very young.

"You've already met Archie . . . Archimedes," she said. "He's something of the ship's mascot, though he spends most of his time in my quarters." She smiled at Ronan, close enough to breathe the same air he did. "You've never seen a cat before, I take it."

"Only in a holo. Is it true that humans—that people believe shaauri look like cats?"

"You don't think there's any similarity? Pointed ears, fur, whiskers, claws, sharp teeth—"

"Not as sharp as . . . Archie's." He returned her smile. "And shaauri have no tails. Cats are from your world?"

"We have cats on Dharma, yes, but originally they came from the human homeworld, known as Earth or Terra."

"Will you tell me of this Terra?"

She sighed and scooped Archimedes into her arms, rubbing her face against his shoulder fur. "It's a long story. Centuries ago, humans learned how to build ships that could travel the great distances of space, just as shaauri did. The first ships were very slow. Eventually, they became fast enough to leave the solar system and discover the first wormhole. Then humanity was able to expand to many other planets, some habitable and some less hospitable but valuable in other ways. We formed our first planetary alliances.

"In time, communications broke down among the colonies, and those last settled—the Nine Worlds—were cut off from the original planets of the Concordat. Even Persephone, most prosperous of the colonies, had to struggle for existence. Much of the old technology was lost. We refer to this period as the Long Silence. But Persephone recovered and began to reestablish contact with other local worlds. Her scientists rebuilt much of the old technology and a new fleet of ships to travel between wormholes.

"It was right after this rebirth that humans encountered shaauri, and misunderstandings in culture and language led to the First War. The Shaauriat, as humans named it, formed an immense sphere separating the Concordat from the Nine Worlds, which had fallen into their own dark ages. Though the shaauri did not occupy much of what they considered their territory, they guarded every last system ferociously."

"It is their way," Ronan said.

"So we learned. Fifty years later, Eeva Kane, originally of Dharma, was able to overcome the barriers of communication by entering shaauri minds and interpreting their complex language. Shaauri adopted her into one of their Lines, and she began to gather other telepaths to serve as mediators between aliens and humans."

"The first Kinsmen," Ronan said.

"Indeed. As a result of her work, a new peace was negotiated, and the Concordat was able to reach the Nine Worlds. But we on Dharma had lost so much that it took nearly a century before Concordat scientists, technicians, teachers, and diplomats were accepted and able to encourage a gradual change in Dharma's medieval culture." She smiled wryly. "As you'll see, they hadn't completed their task before the Second War and the blockade cut us off. Only a few Concordat personnel, those who married into Dharman families, remained—including my Uncle Jesper."

"The man you hope will thwart Janek's plans for me."

She laughed in surprise. "I'd almost forgotten you heard that exchange. Yes, my uncle is more than a match for Janek, and he's also on the Trade Council that determines how we use our limited offworld capabilities, as well as the—" She hesitated, and Ronan detected *Pegasus* in her thoughts before she shut them away.

"We've never been sure how the Second War started," she said abruptly, "except that some shaauri were never able to tolerate humans. Many Kinsmen chose defection, which left humanity even more vulnerable." She lifted her hand and let it fall again. "You could be of great value to us, Ronan. You could teach us to understand the shaauri even better than Eeva Kane, so that we can work toward a permanent end to hostilities."

"I can show how to better evade their ships and patrols."

"Perhaps. Does that bother you?"

Ronan held up his hand, displaying the healing slash in his palm. "This is human blood," he said. "The same blood shaauri have spilled again and again."

"They treated you very badly."

He turned his face aside, feeling the unwelcome weight of her sympathy. "It is long in the past."

"Because your shaauri mentor taught you to defend yourself." When he remained silent, she set Archie down and folded her arms across her knees. "He taught you very well, Ronan. He must have cared about you, as you cared for him."

"Sihvaaro was my teacher."

"You don't hate all shaauri."

He looked at her, weighing how much of this question was meant in friendship and how much to discover his truest feelings. "Some were kind. But I was never one of them."

Cynara paced the length of the cabin. "I know what it is to feel . . . different. My life was nothing like yours, but—" She stared at the holo on the bedtable. "You may think all humans hate shaauri, but this war can't last forever. Something will bring it to an end."

"Like this ship."

"Like you."

Archie bumped his nose against Ronan's ankle, demanding attention. Ronan let the feel of fur under his hand soothe away his sudden and inexplicable fear.

"You saw what happened to the Bifrost colony because it couldn't get enough supplies through the shaauri blockade," Cynara said. "It's not the only world that's suffered. Dharma relied heavily on trained personnel and technicians from the Concordat, especially Persephone, to help us rebuild our world after the Long Silence. All the progress we made before the Second War—in medicine, in the exploration and utilization of our own system's resources, in making life better for the people—has virtually come to a halt."

"Yet you have this ship."

"It's little enough. Other worlds have also suffered. Even the Concordat has need of raw materials found only among the Nine Worlds. Lives have been lost because these materials and personnel could not be transported through the Shaauriat."

Now was not the time to ask more about the *Pegasus* and the part it played in circumventing the blockade.

Show human cunning. Keep her trust.

"I am sorry," he said, trying to drive from his mind the images of young humans suffering or elders dying because of his kin.

Remember who you are. It is humans who began this war,

humans who would destroy or enslave every last shaaurin if they could.

"No one blames you, Ronan. You did not choose where you were born."

He rubbed his chin across Archie's supple back. "You grew up on Dharma," he said, guiding her away from unprofitable subjects. "Those in the holo are your kin?"

"Yes. My father, mother, brother, and cousin."

"Your mother wears a facial covering. Does she hide a deformity?"

"It's the custom on Dharma for adult women to wear the veil."

"Does it not restrict vision?"

"I seldom wore one."

"Do your people not regard you as adult?"

The question seemed to startle her, though she recovered quickly. "Oh, yes. I passed that threshold at the appointed time. But certain . . . events prevented me from taking up a 'proper' Dharman woman's role."

Ronan had learned that such a tone of voice was a kind of mockery Cynara often employed, sometimes at her own expense. All the nuances a shaaurin might have expressed in pitch or with tiny gestures of ears or whiskers were contained in mere words. And words were not enough.

Cautiously he opened his mind to receive her surface thoughts, watching for any sign of awareness on her part. "You were different from other females on Dharma."

"Distressingly different, as far as my family was concerned. Women simply do not . . . do the things I've done."

"Such things as ruling a starship?"

"Among others." She sat on the edge of her bed, and Archie jumped up to join her. "I was not the person originally intended for this post."

Humans did not have Selection, he reminded himself. Their Paths were fixed in other ways, sometimes by choice, often by their elders or through the influence of kinship connections.

"Your family did not approve," he said.

"My family had arranged a marriage for me shortly before . . . before the events that led up to my assignment." She stroked Archie's back. "On our world, women of high rank are expected to marry for family advantage and political alliance."

"You were given no choice in your mating?"

"None. But I escaped it nevertheless."

Her emotions grew increasingly chaotic, and Ronan knew she did not wish to speak of her background or how she had come to be captain of the *Pegasus*. Yet a part of her longed to confide some inner pain with one who might understand, one not burdened by a past relationship with her or her world.

Ronan crouched beside the bed and scratched Archie at the base of his long tail. "There is a likeness between us, Cynara."

"As outcasts?"

"As those still searching for the correct Path."

"I've found mine, and I intend to hold to it."

He realized that she spoke not to him, but to some part of herself she needed to convince. An enemy within, like his.

"And if I say I have found mine as well?" he said.

Her hand stopped on Archie's shoulder. "You've hardly left shaauri space. You have entire worlds to discover."

"If all human worlds are like Dharma and treat their females as slaves, I doubt I will wish to."

"They aren't." She shook her head. "You can't learn about humanity in bits and pieces. Once we make planetfall, I'll get you more detailed histories of human colonization."

"It is about you I wish to learn." He touched her clenched fist and worked her fingers open one by one. "Everything, Cynara."

All at once her thoughts swam with images like those she had pried out of his past: naked bodies entwined in this very bed, male and female, *ne'lin* and captain.

Her desire reawakened his own need, never far below the surface. Thought fed on thought, rebounding and redoubling until Ronan could not separate her emotions from those mastering him, her inner battle from the war raging within his skull.

The danger was real. He ignored it and took her shoulders in his hands. She seized the front of his shipsuit. Archimedes jumped off the bed.

Ronan showed her just how much he had already learned.

Chapter 9

For a man who'd had so few opportunities for kissing, Ronan did it very, very well. The pecks she'd given him on Bifrost were nothing, mere throwaway gestures in the midst of crisis. This was entirely different.

Something remarkable was happening, something not defined by his mouth on hers or his strong, scarred body radiating desire. Ronan seemed to blaze from within. She felt his physical lust and an almost frightening sense of triumph—felt even though she made no attempt to touch his mind, even though she had done everything possible to avoid it.

She'd already guessed why he found her attractive. She saw no reason to change her mind. But in the sheer sensuality of this moment, surrendering to her own desire, she didn't care.

Ronan pulled her hair back from her face and kissed her forehead, her brows, her temple, punctuating each caress with tiny flicks of his tongue. She pushed her hand down the collar of his shipsuit. His skin was ridged with scar tissue and warm, so incredibly warm. His heart beat as fast as hers.

Those Kinswomen had viewed Ronan's lovemaking as a duty. She pitied them far more than she pitied him.

The muscles of his back shivered against her palm. He

jerked his hands away and stared at her with cold, stranger's eyes.

"I do not want your pity."

She felt his hurt, the pride he held banked behind his humility, and began to apologize. Then she realized exactly what he had done.

"You read my thoughts," she said.

He was already halfway to the cabin door, one hand pressing his temple. "Yes."

"You *heard* me on Bifrost."

"It was like a voice calling from a great distance."

"Then it's as I suspected . . . you've begun to recover your telepathy." She turned the implications over in her mind. "On Bifrost I was projecting my thoughts, and you were passively receiving. But this time you picked up my surface thoughts even though I didn't intend to send them."

"I am . . . sorry." He met her eyes anxiously. "I do not believe I can control it."

"It's nothing to fear, Ronan. Believe me. I thought something like this might happen—under the right circumstances." The right circumstances, indeed. "You aren't in pain?"

"No." His brows flattened over his eyes. "I am not certain what I feel."

Of course he wasn't. He was untrained, like a baby taking its first step. Yet even a baby could inadvertently toddle into something forbidden. Cynara made a thorough check on the shields Persephonean Kinsmen had embedded when she'd taken the captaincy. They held strong.

"Try again, Ronan. Focus on me, and try to read my thoughts."

He backed up against the door and closed his eyes. "You are thinking . . . of water. Great waves. The ocean on Dharma."

"That's exactly right. What else?"

"Your mother. She is not wearing a veil. She is singing to you . . . I don't know the words."

Cynara relaxed. The childhood melody her mother sang was in the language of Dharma's second largest city-state.

Ronan couldn't interpret it unless he was able to pierce her shield and enter her mind on a much deeper level.

"You ran to your mother because a boy had knocked you down and called you—" Ronan hesitated. "A female who sells her body?"

She had not intended him to see that much, but she wouldn't let him realize it. "The word is 'unveiled'—much like your 'unselected.' A woman who has not taken the veil at fifteen is regarded . . . poorly."

"You defied the rules of your society. You learned from your uncle those things females are not permitted to understand."

"I was what my father called a hellion." She waved distracting memory aside. "I want you to try something new. Say something to me, Ronan, but only with your mind."

He frowned. She felt the fury of his concentration, but nothing came through . . . no more than the emotions she already sensed.

"It's all right, Ronan," she said. "You've done enough today. I think you'd better return to your cabin and rest."

He seemed not to hear her. "Your brother is named Anson. Your cousin . . . Tyr—" He gasped. *"Don't blame yourself, Cyn. It wasn't your doing."*

Tyr's voice, down to the last inflection. Cynara flew at Ronan and grabbed his shoulders.

"Stop it! Do you hear me, Ronan?" She shook him hard, shouting without words. *Get out of my mind!*

He opened his eyes, and for a moment all she saw were black pupils and emptiness. Then he focused, knowledge seeping into his conscious mind and filling his gaze with pity.

"What happened to your cousin, Cynara?" he asked, touching her cheek with his fingertips. "What gift did he give you that brought so much pain?"

Luck. It must be luck, and carelessness on her part, that he'd been able to pry that memory from behind the shield. She backed away and sat down on the bed, shaking. "I'm sorry. I could have hurt you by using such force."

"I was not hurt." He knelt before her. "Your memory of your cousin brings great sorrow. Let me help."

Such compassion from a man raised by aliens, whose

childhood had been a thousand times more difficult than hers. Thank God he didn't fully understand what had happened when Tyr died. "You can't," she said. "It's only a memory." She mastered her trembling and met Ronan's worried gaze. "You must remember one thing, Ronan. Never enter another person's mind uninvited."

"That is the Kinsman's law."

"And ours—those of us born to the gift on Dharma. You'll have every chance to learn."

He recognized the dismissal. He moved toward the door and paused, eyes fixed on the far bulkhead.

"I understand your grief," he said. "I care nothing for your world or its customs. Only for you, Cynara D'Accorso."

The door closed behind him before she could assemble a coherent reply. Once she was alone, she lay back on the bunk and threw her arm over her eyes, fighting the shameful desire to weep.

Shameful to her, or Tyr? Or to both of them, the wild girl grown to womanhood and the man who had been robbed of his life and his true destiny?

A cool nose brushed her cheek. She reached for Archie and pulled him onto her chest, savoring his uncomplicated loyalty.

"I always thought I knew what I wanted," she said into his fur. "I had no conception of life beyond Dharma, only a child's grand illusions. Tyr should have taught me better, but how much have I learned?"

Archimedes purred close to her ear and tapped her cheek with his paw. "On Dharma it was simple, wasn't it? I was a hellion, a rebel. Rebellion itself defined me. Where is my rebellion now, Archie? Who am I fighting?" She laughed. "Don't answer. I know exactly who my greatest enemy is. I'm the captain, a D'Accorso to my Dharman crew, equal or superior to everyone on board. Tell me why I want a stranger as I've never wanted anything in my life? Why do I insist on seeing myself in Ronan, and him in me?"

If Archie had an answer, he kept it entirely to himself.

The Pegasus *had two scheduled stops on its way to* Dharma, first at Scholar-Commander Adumbe's world,

Nemesis, where they delivered a new reactor for the primary dome's life support system, and then at the struggling settlement on Matisse.

Nemesis was a harsh world, and its only city lay under domes requiring constant repair. The atmosphere was a vast cloud of ammonia and other toxic gasses. Outside the dome, the landscape was composed of lifeless volcanic rock. On the whole, the planet reminded Cynara of her own state of mind.

Adumbe disembarked to visit his family while Cargomaster Basterra saw to the offloading of the reactor and supporting equipment. All was as it should be except in one vital and very personal respect.

It was impossible for Cynara to pretend that nothing had happened between her and Ronan. Their minds had opened to each other; she was constantly aware of him, even when he was not physically present.

Thank God he was only beginning to learn how to handle his abilities. As long as she remained alert, she could keep him from inadvertently skimming her thoughts. On Dharma, she hoped that Uncle Jesper would assume responsibility for Ronan and the problems he represented. *Magnus* Jesper Siannas had the power and influence to protect Ronan and see that he got the help he needed.

Then she could go back to routine, free and unencumbered. Or could she?

"The Nemesians couldn't survive if their life support system broke down," she said to Ronan as they stood at the aft viewport watching the *Thalassa* carry its payload into the planet's chaotic atmosphere. "Before the blockade, Concordat engineers were helping them strengthen the domes' systems. Now it's all we can do to keep them patched together."

"Why did humans choose such an inhospitable world to settle?" Ronan asked.

"The colony was founded by a woman who believed that only in isolation could she achieve the intellectual climate she wanted for her followers. On Nemesis there were no distractions from development of the mind. The Nemesians are curious by nature, but also very insular. Few would be willing to leave."

"Yet Adumbe did so."

There was more she could have told him about Adumbe and the contributions Nemesians had made to the *Pegasus* and its mission, but that topic cut too close to secrets she wasn't authorized to share. She was satisfied that she'd made a point: Humans helped each other, even when they faced almost overwhelming odds.

She took Ronan with her on the shuttle to Matisse, a planet well suited to human occupation. But the blockade had prevented the settlers from prospering. They were in desperate need of medical supplies that only the Concordat could provide. On this run, the *Pegasus* brought enough to arrest a particularly nasty illness attacking the colony's children and elderly.

The colonists greeted the landing party with great joy. Ronan moved among the patients like a shadow as Zheng and the colony's medics began to administer the vaccine in the tiny clinic. Once he knelt beside a little girl racked with shivers and laid his hand on her head in tender benediction. Cynara could have sworn she saw tears in his eyes.

Ronan remained very quiet when they boarded the *Pegasus*. Dharma was a quick hop by wormhole from Matisse, but Cynara was not looking forward to journey's end. Ronan's predicament was very much on her mind. Uncle Jesper or no, Janek would be a very unpleasant opponent. And she'd still have to face the Council for debriefing before the *Pegasus* left on its next crossing.

Even before that gauntlet was run, her family would be waiting.

As the *Pegasus* entered the gravity well of Dharma's sun, small mining ships passed on their way to and from the asteroid belt, while others traveled to the cometary halo at the system's outermost borders. These vessels lacked the range to reach other star systems, but their work was essential to Dharma's economy. Dharma itself was metal-poor; the mining operations provided raw materials to be refined and shipped to the Concordat and the Nine Worlds.

The asteroid belt had provided an even greater source of wealth, for there miners had discovered the ancient wreckage of an alien ship—the source of the slingshot drive. The *Pegasus,* with its unique ability to evade shaauri warships, was

Dharma's greatest hope . . . and the Trade Council's deepest secret.

Once in Dharma's system, the *Pegasus* would remain in a geostationary orbit above the planet while the *Thalassa* ferried crew and cargo to and from Dharma's surface.

Cynara, Janek, Kord, Basterra, Lizbet, Ronan, and a half-dozen Dharman crewmen would accompany the first cargo pallets to the planet's sole spaceport. Other crew members who wished to take leave could do so after the first contingent returned to duty.

Adumbe stayed aboard the *Pegasus,* as did Chief Antiniou. She'd requested certain parts for additional repairs to the drive; doubtless the Council would send its few Concordat-trained technicians to verify her work. Cynara almost regretted that she wouldn't be there to see the engineer's scathing reaction to their meddling.

Zheng had chosen to stay with Gunter until he was transported to the hospital in Elsinore. Lizbet Montague would probably have preferred to remain aboard as well, but she was the best qualified shuttle pilot, and Cynara never missed an opportunity to remind Basterra and his cronies that a low-born woman could do something they couldn't.

Always wary of unsupervised Dharman males, Kord accompanied Basterra and his men to the *Thalassa*'s cargo bay, ostensibly to offer assistance with unloading. Janek kept to himself, but Cynara had no doubt that he'd already sent his own messages to the surface.

Once Lizbet had the shuttle undocked and under way, Cynara invited Ronan to observe planetfall on the screen in the passenger compartment.

The scene was always the same, and always different. First one saw the crystal blue of Dharma's interconnecting oceans and seas, obscured here and there by banks of clouds, and then the brown and green of islands. Archipelagos appeared like paint spattered from a brush, all quite beautiful and deceptively peaceful.

As they approached Novaterra, the island that harbored the city of Cynara's birth, the modern buildings and landing fields of Dharma's sole spaceport became visible in the distance. It was no accident that the spaceport lay within the ju-

risdiction of one of the planet's wealthiest and most influential burgher-lords, *Magnus* Casnar D'Accorso of Elsinore.

The shuttle skimmed over the coastal waters, giving the
observers a clear view of oceangoing vessels of every shape
and size. The old seaport was still very much in use, for trade
between islands was still largely a matter of surface transportation, supplemented by Dharma's small airfleet.

The D'Accorso palace stood on a rocky outcrop overlooking Elsinore's chaotic sprawl. Sunlight struck sparks
from the palace's golden roofs and turrets, growing more distinct as the shuttle made its final approach.

"This city is your home?" Ronan asked, standing very
close at her shoulder.

"Yes. Dharma's traditional government consists of city-
states, generally one to each smaller island and several on the
greater. Elsinore is an exception—it's the sole city-state on
Novaterra, the largest island in this hemisphere."

"And the captain's father is its ruler," Janek said behind
her.

Cynara smiled and stifled a yawn. "Thanks for the reminder, *Ser* Janek."

Ronan cast Janek a narrow-eyed glance. "Your immediate
male progenitor is the First of your Line, *Aho'Va*?"

She was glad of his formality. "You might say that, though
most humans reckon political and family relationships differently than shaauri do."

"The captain is too modest," Janek said, gazing at the
screen in apparent fascination. "*Magnus* D'Accorso rules the
equivalent of many of your Lines."

"Dharma has long been an aristocracy," Cynara said. "Our
society is still very rigid in many respects."

"Rather like the shaauri," Janek remarked, "who remain
much as they have always been since their days of savagery.
Isn't that so, Ronan?"

"Humans may change Paths and act independently of
House or Line, in disregard of the confusion that may follow," Ronan said, showing the edges of his teeth. "Is this not
a flaw in your species' evolution?"

"*My* species?"

Cynara moved between them. "Change is never easy."

"It strikes me as very strange, Captain D'Accorso, that *Ser* VelKalevi still defends the shaauri when he claims to hate them."

"You'll have your say before the Council," Cynara said sharply. "Until then, stow it."

Janek's jaw clenched, but he had the sense to bite his tongue. Ronan's gaze never left him until he fled the observation area.

"I am unselected," Ronan said quietly, "and thus unworthy to defend your honor, *Aho'Va*. But if you permit me, I will fight that one by the laws of your world."

Cynara imagined Ronan with a ceremonial sword in hand, facing Janek in a duelist's square. *That* was certainly a savage custom.

"My honor is in no danger," she said. "Whatever Janek does to provoke you, I ask that you do your best to ignore him."

"He is not First, Second, or even Third of this ship, yet he offers challenge in his speech and manner. Will you accept?"

"I'm very tempted, my friend, but with humans it seldom comes to outright violence. Trust me to handle Janek."

Ronan could express the most eloquent doubt with a fractional twitch of his mouth. He looked at the screen. The *Thalassa* hovered above the port's landing field, and Cynara felt vibrations under her feet as landing gear was deployed.

"Secure for landing," Lizbet's voice said over the intercom. Cynara took one of the passenger seats and Ronan the one beside her. An almost imperceptible jolt, and the shuttle touched down on Dharman soil.

PART II

ALLIANCE

Chapter 10

Home. *Cynara could gladly have gone a lifetime with-out seeing it again.*

A messenger from the city was waiting for her on the field, carrying a note sent from Uncle Jesper in response to her urgent request.

> *Captain,*
> *In receipt of your message. Have managed to delay*
> *Council action for a day, but require further discussion.*
> *Bring your guest to the usual place. I'll know when*
> *you've arrived.*

Cynara tipped the messenger and smiled to herself. Jesper had followed through exactly as she'd hoped, and she was sure he knew to the minute when the *Thalassa* had landed at the spaceport.

She tucked the note in her pocket and went to consult briefly with Basterra. The cargomaster's men were already offloading cargo with the help of the spaceport dockhands. As soon as they had finished, they were at liberty to spend the day visiting family and friends before reporting back to the *Pegasus*.

Kord's habit was to follow the Dharman crew, covertly observing the places they went and the people they spoke to. He was always predicting rebellion against a female captain, but Cynara had long since given up trying to convince him that Basterra and the others would obey because they were under the Council's orders to do so. The average Dharman didn't make a very good mutineer.

Lizbet was also free to visit her few relations in Low Town, but she seldom did. She stuck very close to Cynara whenever they stayed on Dharma, and Uncle Jesper always kept spare rooms for former protégés and students.

Cynara hoped he'd have one available for an unexpected guest. She disembarked with Ronan in tow and waited for Lizbet to catch up.

Ronan must have seen a spaceport before, or he wouldn't have been flying a darter. Perhaps his absolute stillness and concentration came from the fact that he hadn't visited a human city since early childhood. Cynara had heard that shaauri cities were hardly cities at all, but sprawling residences surrounded by parkland, inhabited not by many unrelated families and individuals but single kinship groups.

"Your port seems underutilized," Ronan said, glancing at the empty berths and the unoccupied expanse of the field.

"We maintain a small fleet of ships for in-system mining and a few for trade among the Nine Worlds, but most of them are constantly in use. There's been much debate over what remains of the Dharman space program. Some feel it's a waste of resources, like educating girls."

"This is foolish, even for humans."

"I'm glad you agree."

"Where do we go now, *Aho'Va*?"

"To my Uncle Jesper. I'll have to report to the Council, and Janek has certainly made sure they know all about you. He'll see to it that you're summoned for questioning. However, I've received a message that suggests my uncle has managed to delay the debriefing. He's to meet us in the city."

"This is good news," he said.

"So far. While we travel, I advise that you remain quiet and pretend you're a regular member of the crew. Many Dharmans speak Standard—it was fashionable to learn it

years ago, especially among those who aspired to bettering
their positions in society."

Ronan nodded, preoccupied. A few minutes later Lizbet
hurried down the ramp. She wore a veil, as she always did on
Dharma.

Cynara flagged a runabout and the three of them rode it to
the port offices, where she called a cab. Motorized vehicles
were still not commonplace on Elsinore's narrow streets;
they remained very much a mark of privilege and wealth. She
could have summoned a D'Accorso vehicle and driver, but
she was loath to call attention to Ronan until he was safely
under Uncle Jesper's wing.

The cab driver stared at Cynara's unveiled face until he
recognized who she was, and then became considerably more
respectful. He offered Cynara a seat in the front, but she refused and slid into the back seat with Ronan and Lizbet to either side.

No one spoke until they were behind the privacy screen of
the cab. The vehicle's large windows gave all three of them
an excellent view of the scenery, the rolling ocher hills and
sun-warmed vegetation of what had once been called a
"Mediterranean" climate. Through the trees one could see the
ocean, stretching like azure velvet to the horizon.

Whatever Ronan thought of Novaterra remained a mystery until the cab approached Elsinore's outermost gate. At
the foot of the great stone wall huddled the city's poorest
dwellings, cobbled together of every sort of material. Before
Jesper's arrival and his influence on Casnar D'Accorso, the
barrio had been far worse. But change on Dharma was slow.

"These are your *ne'li?*" Ronan asked.

"Not in the sense you mean . . . but yes. Elsinore is a city
of three gates. The people who live outside First Gate are
those who have no steady work or source of income."

"*Ne'li,*" he repeated. "How do they survive?"

"My father and uncle began a charitable foundation some
years ago. Children are encouraged to attend free schools to
learn professions, and are provided with medical care. But
we haven't gone far enough. Much more must be done to
truly civilize this world."

The cab passed through First Gate and into the small but

slightly more prosperous Low Town. Here were all the features of a city in miniature, shops and residences and inns catering to the working poor. Trees were few and far between, and the air smelled of fish and coal. Clothing tended toward the drab with little flashes of color in scarves or caps, and not every woman went veiled.

Lizbet pressed closer to the tinted glass. This was her town, her place of birth; she hated and loved it at the same time. She had worked hard to overcome all traces of a Low Town accent and to develop the talents and intelligence Uncle Jesper had found in her. Cynara knew better than to ask if she wanted to stop.

"This is the dwelling place of your *an'laik'i,*" Ronan said, watching Lizbet intently.

"Human families—Houses—aren't divided by Path," Cynara said. "There are people of most occupations in all sections of the city. The divisions are more . . . economic and cultural. One is born into a part of the city and usually remains there."

"Not unlike Selection, except it occurs at birth."

Neither way pleased Cynara. When she was gone from Dharma, she tended to forget how much poverty and ignorance had yet to be overcome. "No one should be Selected at birth or forced to walk the same Path her entire life."

Ronan made no argument. Another kilometer of winding uphill road brought them to Second Gate and Middleton. The houses were farther apart, some almost large enough to belong in High Town. Gardens held their own trees and flower or vegetable gardens. Attire mimicked the fashions of the elite, but on a much more modest scale. The streets were cleaner, and the sea breeze swept away the odors of Low Town.

"Middleton," Cynara offered. "This is the largest and busiest part of the city. Many from Low Town come here to work."

"For other Houses and Lines," Ronan said.

"It may seem confusing at first, but you'll get used to it." She noted the street signs, watching for one in particular.

"Humans are always fertile and recognize no boundaries

of Path in mating," Ronan said. "Is this why your city is so crowded?"

Lizbet made a choking sound. "Oh, there are boundaries," Cynara said, willing the flush from her skin, "but they aren't always obvious. A subject for some other occasion."

He seemed content enough with that answer and returned to his observation. Cynara found the sign she was looking for and buzzed the driver, who pulled up at the nearest curb adjacent to a busy ale-house.

"We'll get out here," she said. "My uncle asked us to meet him at a pub a few blocks down this lane." She paid the driver and followed Lizbet out of the cab, making sure that Ronan was behind them.

He stood on the cobbled sidewalk, every bit as alert as on previous occasions when he'd been prepared to initiate or fend off an attack. The relatively few midday pedestrians hardly glanced at him as they passed, saving their stares for the unveiled woman. Cynara moved closer to him.

"Are you all right, Ronan?"

"Your uncle lives here?"

"Oh, no. But he thought it best to meet us first on neutral ground where unwelcome observers aren't likely to meddle."

He looked at her in surprise. "You fear for my safety, *Aho'Va?*"

"That's another thing . . . you should know that in Elsinore I am not a First. My family is of high rank, but I am far from the highest of D'Accorsos."

"Then you fear your own enemies," Ronan said with dogged persistence. "Janek?"

The utter grimness of his face did not invite levity. "Not in the sense you mean. I'm not in any physical danger, and neither is Lizbet."

Noises of drunken revelry in a masculine pitch drifted from the ale-house door. Lizbet glanced nervously down the lane. "Captain?"

"Let's go." Cynara took a step toward the street corner just as a man barreled out of the ale-house, followed by several more healthy and inebriated young bucks in brocade sleeves and fine seacow-skin breeches. One of them half car-

ried a very pretty unveiled woman whose hair tumbled loose
as she laughed.

Ronan stopped. "Are these males mating with this female?"

Poseidon. "This is not the time to discuss it, Ronan."

"The woman is unveiled. Is she not adult?"

"She sells her body—her sex—to earn her living. It's best
not to interfere."

Lizbet grabbed Ronan's arm. "C'mon," she said, lapsing
into Low Town dialect.

Cynara had clear prescience of trouble even before she
felt the hostility in Ronan's mind. "A *ne'lin* who trades sex
for food and shelter," he said. "I have heard such things whispered among shaauri, but—"

"What have we here?" One of the men, the least drunk of
the lot, drew himself up before Ronan and grinned. "Want a
drink, stranger?"

Ronan's nose wrinkled in obvious disgust, though he
couldn't understand Dharma's primary language. "I am
Ronan."

"Ronan." The man circled him with exaggerated interest.
"Ronan. Where're you from, *Faber* Ronan?" he asked in
Standard.

Cynara pushed forward. "Your pardon, *Nestus,*" she answered in the same language. "*Ser* Ronan is not from
Dharma and does not understand our ways. If you will permit—"

The man widened his eyes. "Look, gentlemen. Another
whore to entertain us. Maybe our new friend is a pimp." He
punched Ronan's chest. "What say, *Faber*? What's her
price?" He noticed Lizbet. "We'll take both. Maybe we'll let
you watch!"

The other men leered at Lizbet and Cynara. Ronan's nostrils flared. He didn't even wait to ask for definitions of the
gentleman's ugly words. He grabbed the leader's arm,
wrenched it behind his back, and dumped him on the ground
brocade and all.

The male shrieked almost as loud as the receptive female,
flopping on the ground like a snared *hylpup.* The other men

scattered to a safer distance, but Ronan was not deceived by their apparent helplessness. He waited calmly for attack.

It did not come, proving that these men were not *ve'laik'i*. They showed far too much bad judgment to be of Reason, Heart, or Spirit, and were too old to be indulged as children. Even *an'laik'i* did not act so. They behaved like youths on Walkabout, which was not a human custom.

And they had insulted Cynara.

"*Anki-ne'karo,*" he said, turning his back.

He heard the fallen man stir behind him, uttering a stream of human curses. Cynara planted herself between Ronan and his enemies. "I apologize for this misunderstanding, *Nesté,*" she said. "I neglected to introduce myself—Cynara D'Accorso-*fila*, captain of the Allied ship *Pegasus*. I trust that you will forgive my friend's unintentional discourtesy?"

"D'Accorso?" one of the men muttered.

"There is no need to continue this misunderstanding," she said, offering her hand to the man at her feet. "Please accept my apologies in all goodwill, *Nestus.*"

Ronan half turned his head to watch. The man did not take Cynara's hand but scrambled to his feet, waving off the aid of his companions.

"My apologies, D'Accorso-*fila*," he said. "I did not recognize you."

Cynara's bearing spoke of humor, but Ronan felt the anger she suppressed. "I understand. If you require satisfaction, my family will pay the honor-debt."

"No need." The man brushed off his leggings and backed away with one last, burning look at Ronan. "Safetide, *Filia.*"

"Good day." She watched the men stagger down the road as fast as their legs would carry them and released a long sigh.

"*Filia,*" Lizbet whispered. "They mocked you, Captain."

"You and I should be used to that by now." She glanced at Ronan. "All in all, we got out of this easily."

"They offered to buy you—for sex, as they did the other female," Ronan said, showing his teeth. "This could not be permitted."

Cynara laughed. "They would have punished themselves once they realized who I was. No matter how much contempt they have for females, or for me in particular, they can't afford to anger the D'Accorsos." Her smile faded. "I'll require your promise that you won't try that again, Ronan, whatever the provocation to either of us."

"They asked me to sell you," he said. "Why?"

"Because you're male and I'm not wearing a veil. In Middleton, only loose women walk unveiled. It's an advertisement of their wares." She took firm hold of Ronan's arm. He let himself be pulled, thinking over what he had learned during the encounter.

Humans lived in a state of constant ferment. Females sold themselves for sex, and those who did were regarded as *ne'li*. Was this not a kind of Selection in itself? Humans on this world regarded a female's eyes and hair improper to look upon, and any unveiled female was appropriate for mating. Males of unknown Path could insult one of much higher rank, and yet it was she who apologized.

"I do not understand," he said after a few moments. "These males behaved badly, and yet you released them without punishment. Why did you not summon your *ve'laik'i* to deal with them?"

"Because violence isn't the way to change the world," she said. Her grip softened. "By speaking to them as an equal, I compelled them to think about what they'd said and done."

"Scatfish offal," Lizbet muttered. She touched Ronan's arm. "Thank you."

"You are welcome," he said. "Would you have fought these men if they attacked you?"

"Yes." Her voice dropped to a low pitch. "They never let me forget where I come from."

"They are not worthy of you, *An* Montague."

She smiled, and Ronan thought he saw a change in her walk, a longer stride and straighter posture. The three of them continued down the narrow lane, a human-built canyon of walls that pressed in on Ronan as the *Pegasus*'s bulkheads had never done. Shaauri did not have such cities. It would poison them as surely as human influence, destroying the very essence of Aur within them. It had clearly driven Dharman males to madness.

Yet Cynara had not unduly suffered from such debilities.

She had grown in strength in the face of adversity, without the assurance of Path to guide her. She had the loyalty of other humans not-kin. When he completed his mission, would he be able to convince the War-Leader that not all humans were alike?

He realized that he wished to do so—that in spite of the barbarity of many human customs and their endless desire to acquire everything within reach, not all were corrupt. No one could demonstrate this better than Cynara.

If he could take her back . . .

"Here," Cynara said, stopping him.

The place looked little different from the drinking-house they had left. A small sign hung from a pole above the narrow door, depicting a leaping fish spouting water from its forehead.

Cynara led the way into the dim interior. Ronan adjusted his sight and examined the room. Wooden tables and chairs had been arranged haphazardly across the tiled floor, and the smell of alcohol and cooking choked the air. It was unbearably close. Only a few of the tables were occupied.

"Good," Cynara said. "It's quiet today. Follow me."

She wove between the tables to a door at the rear of the room and passed into a short hall. Another door opened to a smaller chamber with only a few tables. Cynara sat at the largest and beckoned to Ronan and Lizbet. Ronan perched on the edge of the chair facing the door.

"Are you thirsty, Ronan?"

"Is plain water available?"

"That is probably safest." She glanced toward the door, and a moment later a man came in. Unlike the males outside the other ale-house, he was immediately respectful of bearing. He began to speak. Cynara interrupted him with a smile. He bowed and continued in Standard.

"D'Accorso-*fila*. Captain. Welcome back."

"Thank you, Wil. *Magnus* Jesper asked us to meet him here. Has he arrived?"

"Not yet, Captain D'Accorso, but he asked me to make you comfortable."

"Thank you. Will you please bring water for my friend, and ale for Montague-*fila* and myself?"

Wil cast a curious glance at Ronan and smiled at Lizbet. "At once, *Magna.*" He hurried away.

"*Magna* is much better than *Filia,*" Lizbet said, wrinkling her nose. "That should be the address for unmarried women of high rank."

"Of any rank. Until Dharma stops identifying women by the men they belong to, the confusion will doubtless continue." She glanced at Ronan. "In that sense, the shaauri have it better than we do."

"Someone always has it better," a new voice remarked. Ronan sprang up from his seat to face yet another male, taller and narrower than the server and considerably older. His thin hair was aged to white, and his clothing was decorated in a manner similar to the drunken men but of much richer material. He carried a stick with a handle carved to resemble a snarling beast.

"I've always liked this place," the man said, taking a deep breath. "Welcome home, Niece. Lizbet." He leaned on his stick. "This must be our fascinating visitor."

"Uncle," Cynara said, rising to embrace him. Their touching was free in the way of humans, but the affection Ronan sensed was that of a *ba'laik'in* for its nurturer. "I'm so glad to see you." She linked her arm through his elbow and turned to Ronan. "Uncle, this is the shaauri prisoner we rescued, Ronan VelKalevi. Ronan, this is my uncle, *Magnus* Jesper Siannas."

"VelKalevi, is it?" the old man said. "How very interesting."

Ronan stood up in the human posture of respect. "Ronan," he corrected. "The other is not of my choosing, *Va* Jesper."

"Ah. Of course." Jesper sat down at the table and leaned his stick against the chair. "Precisely what is '*Va*'?"

"It means 'of Will,'" Cynara explained. "A designation of high rank among shaauri."

"Well, young man, you needn't be formal with me. I've taught far too many youngsters in my time to expect rigid manners."

"A teacher?" Ronan asked.

"Ronan was raised among shaauri, so he tends to categorize people by what he calls 'Path,'" Cynara said. "You

would be of Will, but as a teacher you would also be Reason.
Is that right, Ronan?"

"Yes." He offered a slight smile to the elder. "I know it is
not so simple among humans."

"You're correct in that." Jesper studied Ronan with eyes
as sharp as a warrior's. "You speak excellent Standard for a
man raised among aliens."

"He had human instructors," Cynara said. It was as if she
were defending Ronan, and he grew warm with the memory
of their touching in her cabin.

"He can also pilot a darter. But that's not all of it, Uncle.
As I told you in the message, he's a telepath."

Jesper raised a shaggy white brow. "Like Kinsmen?"

"Like us. His ability was stunted in childhood, but it
seems to be coming back. That's why I asked you to use your
influence on the Council. Janek is convinced that Ronan is an
enemy of the Alliance. He's pushing for an immediate debriefing."

"So I've heard. Janek has connections, but his high-
handed behavior also wins him enemies. That's why I was
able to get the debriefing delayed until tomorrow. I've taken
personal responsibility for you and Ronan."

"Thank you, Uncle. I don't want the Council or anyone
else digging in Ronan's mind until he's fully prepared to face
such an ordeal."

"Quite understandable." He looked at Ronan. "I can offer
you a room at my house, young man, unless you have other
plans."

"Will Cynara be there?"

Jesper's brows rose higher. "Ah. The D'Accorso palace is
not far from my residence. I'll want to hear all the details of
the most recent voyage, so I expect my niece will be visiting
often. You'll be staying with me as well, Lizbet?"

"If you please, *Magnus.*"

"Poseidon's balls. I haven't been *Magnus* to you in
years." He patted Lizbet's hand. "You can show our new
guest around once we're there."

As he finished speaking, the server arrived with a tray of
glasses and, with a bow to Jesper, asked what he wished to

drink. The elder ordered some unfamiliar beverage and turned to Ronan.

"You aren't comfortable here," he said, "in this room, this city."

Was it a reading of his body, or telepathy like Cynara's? "It is not like Aitu," Ronan said, carefully brushing the surface of Jesper's mind.

Jesper seemed unaware. "I suppose it isn't like any shaauri world. But you have an excellent guide in my niece."

Ronan withdrew his probe, fully satisfied that Jesper was a telepath at least as strong as Cynara. She had failed to mention this, though she had said that Jesper was of Persephone, not Dharma. Telepathic abilities were not limited to Kinsmen or Dharmans.

The elder human studied Ronan with a slight frown. "If my niece says that you are to be trusted, I believe her. My own senses confirm her judgment. But it will be a great deal easier to convince the Council if I can tell them you'd be of use to the Alliance in our conflict with the shaauri." He hesitated and glanced at Cynara. "At the very least I can coach our guest in the best way to handle the Council and their questions."

"That was what I'd hoped," Cynara said.

The server arrived with Jesper's drink, and he took his time savoring each sip. "Ah, Remallan Ale. None better on Dharma." He noted Ronan's water. "Very wise of you to abstain, but we old men must be granted our little peccadillos."

"What is your age, *Va* Jesper?"

He laughed, and Ronan saw where Cynara had learned her way of showing amusement. "I am eighty-five, by Dharman reckoning . . . not greatly different from the old Earth calculation. And you?"

"Twenty-nine human years."

"Only a little older than my most precocious niece." Jesper finished his drink and grasped the head of his stick. "My car is waiting in the alley, if you would all accompany me." He rose with Cynara's help and walked purposefully toward the door. Lizbet caught up with him, but Cynara hung back.

"What do you think of him, Ronan?" she asked.

"He is a wise elder," Ronan said. "Very different from the other Dharman males. You are much like him."

"How so?"

"In your assurance as leader, in concern for other humans, in willingness to learn. And in the way you laugh at that which is not obviously amusing."

"Irony," she said. "Absurdity. He did teach me how to look at life." She smiled. "Thank you. I consider that a compliment. Let's go."

She took him to another motorized vehicle parked in the narrow lane around the corner, one much larger than the hired cab. The driver wore a plain jacket and trousers in deep gray with white trim. Cynara sat beside her uncle in the second row of seats, and Ronan took the third with Lizbet.

The car moved as if on water, skimming back to the main street and uphill to the Third Gate. Though it was open as the others had been, Ronan saw the rim of ornate golden embellishments embossed into the polished wood.

This was another world as different from Middleton as the city between the First and Second Gates was different from the *ne'lin* camp. Here the houses were not merely living places, but many-towered habitations with steeply pitched roofs and walls built of colored stone. Elaborately worked metal gates stood around the properties, half concealing gardens thick with growing things and fountains. Men and women in drab clothing worked among the trees and flowers.

The road became much narrower here, winding its way up to the face of a sheer cliff where it made many sharp turns.

"High Town," Cynara said.

The car took them past several even more imposing estates before it turned again between silver posts and into the drive of a surprisingly modest house. Most of the land was given over to a lawn and garden. The driver parked and got out to open the passenger doors.

Ronan felt more at ease in this place, where even a shaaurin might appreciate the open space and the wealth of natural decoration. From the paved walk across the lawn, one could look down upon the city, tiered between its Gates, and out to the ocean and several small islands.

Another servant waited at the dwelling's front door, carved with images of sea creatures. He ushered them into the tiled hallway. Lizbet took her leave and turned down another hall.

"You may wish to rest for a time, Ronan," Jesper said. "And you'll want to visit your parents, Niece."

Cynara's mouth twisted. "They'll be expecting me."

"Because they love you, Spitfire, no matter what you believe."

She didn't answer. "I'll show Ronan to his room."

"Come talk to me in the library when you're done."

"Yes, Uncle." She nodded to Ronan and led him down the high-ceilinged hall where Lizbet had gone, past handsome painted images of water and a number of closed doors to a chamber near the end. It was more spacious than the guest cabin on the *Pegasus,* but the furnishings were spare and utilitarian.

Ronan was pleased. *"Tranquil surroundings make tranquil mind,"* Sihvaaro had often said.

Ronan looked at Cynara, who waited awkwardly in the doorway. Tranquillity? There was no peace in knowing he must guard every thought and deceive these humans who had been kind to an OutLine stranger. No peace until he had completed his task and left Dharma, and this woman, far behind.

"The room once belonged to Kord," Cynara said. "He always preferred a simple living space. If you need anything, touch the buzzer beside the door and my uncle's manservant will attend to it. I'm sure Jesper will invite you to join him at dinner—the evening meal."

"And you?"

"I must see my parents. I'll come for you as soon as we know what the Council intends."

"Do not go."

She was silent a long moment. "I may not be a traditional Dharman woman, but some habits are too deeply ingrained. To ignore my relatives would be unforgivable."

"Yet you do not wish to see them."

He had pushed too hard. Her expression closed, and she stepped through the door. "Please don't leave the grounds. I'll return as soon as I can."

"Cynara." He followed her to the door and held out his hand. "Stay with me."

Chapter 11

Cynara stared at his hand and then at his face. "I can't," she said simply. "Good evening, Ronan."

Once her footsteps had receded down the hall, Ronan retreated to the bed and sat cross-legged on the coverlet, beginning the chant to restore balance. Cynara's rejection meant nothing. She had duties imposed upon her by this world, as his duty belonged to shaauri-*ja*.

Her hesitation had proved one thing. She had understood his invitation and had briefly considered it. Desire remained. He knew he did not entirely understand human courtship ritual; there were signals he was missing, words he must learn to speak. *Must,* for his mission.

And he wanted Cynara for himself, knowing she would take nothing from him but pleasure. Nothing, least of all who he was or why he had come among humans.

He performed the exercises with deliberation, finding it difficult to slow his heartbeat and calm his thoughts. Sihvaaro would have told him that he wanted too much. *To want is to surrender all hope of understanding.*

Ronan stifled his desire. Slowly serenity returned. His mind became a conduit for all possibilities, all Paths, and in the silence of his meditation he felt Cynara's presence like a balm. The sound of her voice told him she was near.

He went to the door and carefully opened it. Cynara and her uncle were out of sight around the corner of the hall, but he could hear every word they spoke.

"You are attracted to him, Niece." Jesper chuckled. "Oh, come now—you're too enlightened to blush at such a discussion between us. You haven't known him long?"

"Not long, Uncle. That's the inexplicable part."

"On Dharma, we've sought to rule human desires as if they were trained seals. It has been my experience that the heart seldom runs in tandem with the mind."

"But if this is only pity—physical attraction . . ."

"If it's mere attraction, it will die of its own accord when the inevitable obstacles arise."

"When you fell in love with Aunt—"

"It was not my first choice to remain on Dharma. But now I know this was my true purpose, to help keep Dharma from slipping into the old ways until full trade is reestablished."

"And Ronan?"

"I like him. He has survived much, hasn't he? He may even prove worthy of you."

"If the Council overreacts to his presence on the *Pegasus*— his mind could be seriously damaged."

"Then we won't let that happen. Trust me, Spitfire. My instincts are seldom wrong. Until we are sure of him, however, he must remain on Dharma. You'll have many opportunities for courtship, and perhaps learn valuable information in the process."

"I won't use my . . . attraction to spy on him."

"I wouldn't suggest such a thing. I hope that your feelings for this man have laid the old fears to rest?"

"Tyr . . ."

"*You* are captain of the *Pegasus*."

Footsteps sounded in the entry hall. Ronan withdrew into his room. After a time he heard a distant door closing and knew the disturbing void of Cynara's absence.

It was strange, that void, almost as if some invisible blade had carved a hollow in his gut—slow leak of blood, vague pain not quite erased by the discipline of the Eightfold Way. Such a wound could become deadly if left untended.

He listened longer for the movements of humans about the house. When they had ceased, he went to the door and looked into the hall. Finding the way clear, he followed his senses to Lizbet's room and scratched on the door.

Lizbet's bare, startled face appeared in the crack. "Ronan!" she said, glancing over his shoulder.

"May I enter, *An* Montague?"

She patted damp brown hair that smelled of recent bathing. "Come in."

Her room was as small as his but vividly decorated in bright hues of red and gold and ocean blue, the bed heaped with cushions and tapestried hangings on the walls. Lizbet settled a sheer woven headcloth over her hair and adjusted the veil so that it covered her eyes. "Will you sit down, An Ronan?"

"I am not *an'laik'in,*" he said gently, taking the offered seat.

"I'm sorry. If I offended—"

"You did not. Ronan is sufficient."

"Yes, of course." She pulled a brightly painted chair opposite his and folded her hands in her lap. "I've been trying to understand, but there is so much I don't know."

"You were chosen as crew for the *Pegasus.* You must know a great deal, *An* Montague."

"Lizbet. In Low Town, we never—" She hesitated, clenched her fists together. "*Magnus* Jesper took me in when I was very young, gave me an education, and prepared me for my duties on the *Pegasus,* as he did with Kord. Except for Captain D'Accorso, I'm the only Dharman woman on board." As if by habit, her hand rose again to adjust the headcloth.

"You wear this veil only on Dharma," Ronan said. "Cynara does not."

"The captain is different from any woman I've ever known." She lowered her gaze. "You saw how it was in Middleton. But Cynara is a D'Accorso. That means a lot in Elsinore."

"Is it also significant that she is a telepath?"

"Many D'Accorsos have the ability, like the other burgher-lord families. But female telepaths aren't allowed to use their abilities. Cynara told me once . . ." She hesitated, biting her lower lip. "The lords are afraid their women will be corrupted by unsuitable thoughts from men, and that they're too weak and irresponsible to control their powers. Girls are punished if they are caught using telepathy. They're supposed to pretend it doesn't exist."

"Is this punishment the reason why Cynara left her House on this world to create her own?"

"There are so many reasons. I used to look up through the haze of Low Town and try to see the stars, imagining places where a woman could be anything she chose, and the people who lived there. Now I don't have to imagine. I think the captain felt the same way." She flushed, as if she had revealed more than she had intended.

Ronan probed lightly, feeling the artless sincerity of her words. He tried to remember when he had last experienced such naive joy about the future. If he ever had.

"Can I help you in some way?" she ventured after a silence humans always felt so obligated to fill. "Would you like me to show you the grounds? There are some lovely views from the garden."

"I have come for guidance, *An* Lizbet. Human ways still confuse me."

"What do you need to know?"

"How human females desire to be approached for mating."

She sprang from her chair, skin very red, and subsided back into it. "Oh. I . . . ."

"Have I offended?"

"No. Not at all. It's just . . . It's strange to be able to talk to a man as an equal, especially—" She placed her palms against her cheeks.

"Are there no males on the *Pegasus* who speak to you as an equal? Others of your Path?"

"The Dharmans ignore me. Kord . . . frightens me. But you don't." Her throat moved. "Do you . . . do you love her?"

"Love." The word so startled Ronan that he was unable to speak.

He knew roughly what it meant. There were equivalents in Voishaaur, one which described the affection between a child and a nurturer, and another used only to express the bond between lifemates. It did not apply to mating-for-pleasure, or even to mating-for-children. The relationships among those of the same Line, or close childhood companions, were described in different ways.

"I do not understand 'love' as humans define it," he said. "When do humans love other humans?"

She frowned. "I never thought about explaining it. We love our mothers and fathers, sisters, brothers, and friends. And if we're lucky, we find one person to love above all others."

"Humans also lifemate?"

"You mean stay together for life? On Dharma, in Middleton and High Town, parents still arrange marriages, and those are usually not based on love. They're made to increase wealth or political power, and for children to bind two families."

"Your culture compels male and female to remain together as lifemates even when there is no true bond?"

"We would consider it . . . immoral otherwise." She radiated apology, shoulders tucked in and head lowered. "A woman who bears a child out of wedlock is outcast."

" 'Wed-lock' is a ritual of binding?"

"Under the eyes of God and Dharman law. Shaauri don't have marriage?"

"There are what you would call 'contracts' between Houses and Lines for the creation of children," he said. "Shaauri mate at will only as *be'laik'in* on Walkabout. It is expected. After Selection, mating-for-pleasure usually occurs between shaauri of the same Path. Only those of Will and Blood produce children except by rare exception."

"Young humans are usually forbidden to . . . mate . . . and anyone can have children," Lizbet said. "But in some ways our cultures aren't so different. There are still many walls built to keep people apart. It's the rules that change."

"Then what rules must I follow with Cynara?"

"I don't know. Cynara was never like other women. And she changed even more, after—after she became captain of the *Pegasus*. Until she met you, I didn't think . . . she was interested in love at all."

"Should I send gifts to her House?"

"Poseidon, no!" She slapped her hand over her mouth and stifled a laugh. *"Magnus* and *Matrona* D'Accorso would die of shock."

It was becoming evident that Lizbet, in spite of her willingness to speak, had no useful advice in the matter of human courtship. But there was another topic of even greater importance.

"You said that Cynara changed when she became captain of the *Pegasus,"* he said, pushing beneath the surface of Lizbet's thoughts. "Is it because the *Pegasus* is not like other ships?"

She blinked. "It's . . . it's not just—" He felt her deliberate effort to evade his question, but under the confusion he found . . . nothing. No shield such as he had discovered in the guards outside the engineering section. No evidence of knowledge that must be protected at all costs.

"I'm sorry," she said, scraping her hands across her face. "I'm very tired. I'm sure that *Magnus* Jesper will be calling us for dinner soon."

Lizbet was no telepath, but she had enough sensitivity to react when her mind was probed by one.

"I, too, feel unwell," Ronan said, rising. "Please tell *Va* Jesper that I will sleep in my quarters, and beg him not to hold the meal for me."

Lizbet only stared at him, trembling.

He listened again for movement in the hall. Finding all quiet, he slipped out of the house and crossed the grounds, moving among the shrubs until he had reached the outer gate.

There were still many things he must learn about this world and its ways, and he could not do so confined to his room.

When Cynara returned, he would be ready.

C ynara was hardly surprised when the tall, ornate gates of Palace D'Accorso swung open before she reached them. One of the garden servants had seen her coming—she did not recognize his face, but he must have known hers as well as every other resident's, baseborn or noble. He bowed and moved quickly out of her way. Another servant dashed ahead to alert those within.

Old Tesar, her father's majordomo for the past twenty years, awaited her inside the pearl-inlaid double doors. He smiled as he bowed, and she was absurdly grateful for such a small and friendly gesture.

There wouldn't be a great many more of those today.

"The *Magnus* is in his library," Tesar said, "and the *Matrona* in the conservatory. Will you wish refreshments first, *Filia*?"

Unlike the drunks in Middleton, Tesar meant no offense by the word. He addressed her as an unmarried adult female—a man's daughter—but he did so with the affection of long familiarity.

"I'll go directly to my father, Tesar," she said, and touched his hand. "It's good to see you again."

"And you, *Filia*." He straightened and led her through the immense entry hall, where the stained-glass skylight painted rainbows on handmade tile, past the portraits of former D'Accorso *Magné*, and into the wood-paneled fastness of her father's realm. Here women, even her mother, entered only by permission.

Cynara had been five when she first penetrated this forbidden domain. Papa had scolded, and then he'd laughed and lifted her up on his knee.

He hadn't laughed with her in a very long time.

The doors to the library were nearly as imposing as those at the entrance, heavily carved with mythic scenes of ocean deities. Tesar knocked, and a moment later he let Cynara into the room.

Magnus Casnar D'Accorso sat in his thickly padded chair, his fingers steepled beneath his chin. Cynara slowed her pace to a more decorous creep. The captain of the *Pegasus* felt like a postulant begging the bishop's favor.

"Daughter," Casnar said in his deep voice. He swung the chair about to face her. "You are well?"

"I am, Father." She touched her knee to the carpet in the ancient convention of respect and brushed his knuckles with her lips. "The *Pegasus* has completed another successful mission."

"I am happy for you." He sighed and waved her to a smaller chair.

"How is Mother?"

He was slow in answering, gazing about at the many shelves of books as if he hadn't spent most of his life in this very room. "She is not as she once was, but you know that, Daughter. She dotes on Elendra, as if . . ."

As if she had no other daughter. It was strange and almost frightening to hear her father hesitate, even to spare her feelings.

"You know that Elendra is to take the veil in a week's time," he said.

She had forgotten. It was not something she liked to dwell on. "I doubt I'll be here in a week, Father. The *Pegasus*—"

"You may explain that to your mother." He touched the buzzer on his desk. "You were visiting Jesper?"

"Yes." No surprise that he knew; he and Jesper had been close since the day the Persephonean married his sister. "Ship-related business."

"Is this alien stranger the business in question?"

That startled her. Jesper would have kept the matter confidential. Casnar had received that intelligence from some other quarter.

D'Accorso spies on the Pegasus. No one beyond the crew, Janek, Jesper, and now the Council knew of Ronan's origins.

"Since you've heard," she said, "you undoubtedly know that I've asked Uncle Jesper to speak to the Council on his behalf. The man is in a delicate position, having just escaped the shaauri who held him prisoner for most of his life. He may be of great service to us."

"Or he may be dangerous. I would hear everything you have learned of him, Daughter."

"If your concern is for me—"

"I fear your foolishness in taking such risks."

"But you would not fear if Tyr did the same thing."

"Tyr thought first of his duty and less of sentiment. His one great error . . ."

Once more he fell silent, tempering his words. Scrupulous

courtesy and strict custom forbade her from entering his thoughts, or him hers, but she could not help but feel what he meant.

Tyr's only great error was in believing I was strong enough to take his skills, his knowledge, his very self, and carry on for him, for Dharma, and for the Alliance.

He believed I could withstand the stigma of his gift. And I have, Father.

Casnar's skin darkened under his meticulously groomed beard. "We will speak no more of this now. You will wish to see your mother." The library door opened, and Tesar entered with a bow.

"Escort *Filia* D'Accorso to the *Matrona*," her father said.

Cynara could have refused the dismissal. Every rebellious instinct she had harbored in childhood rose up again. But now, of all times, Tyr's confidence deserted her. She turned on her heel without farewell and followed Tesar to the conservatory.

Zurine Casnara D'Accorso half reclined on a chaise with a tapestry frame beside her. The stiffness in her posture told Cynara that she was already well aware of her daughter's arrival and had girded herself for battle in the only way she knew. Her eyes were shadows under an embroidered veil much heavier than required for any woman in her own home.

I will not see you, the veil said. *You are a stranger.*

"Mother," Cynara said, bowing her head. She would not seek a benediction her mother would refuse. "It is good to find you well."

"You have seen your father?"

No pleasantries, of course—no affection for the family pariah. "Yes."

"And you have seen Jesper."

"I have. Lizbet Montague is staying with him."

Zurine's lips curled. "That lowborn creature—"

"—can hardly pollute someone already beyond the pale."

Her mother sat up on the chaise. "Do not speak with such pride of our family's shame." She recovered and settled back again, but the bodice of her gown rose and fell with each rapid breath. "Have you come for some reason other than to disturb the peace of this house?"

Cynara was gathering a reply when Elendra sailed into the room. She was fine-boned and petite, like Mother, with Zurine's dark beauty as yet unobscured by the veil.

"Cynara!" she cried, and then drew upon her adolescent dignity. "I am glad to see you. Have you come to witness my veiling?"

It was a reasonable assumption for anyone who did not know Cynara well. But Elendra had taken after Mother. She refused to accept what did not accord with her view of the world.

"The *Pegasus* has just returned," Cynara said gently. "I don't know when we'll be leaving again. I may not be able to stay, Sister. I am sorry."

The lightness left Elendra's bearing. "It is my veiling, Cyn! How can you—" She scrubbed furiously at her eyes, displaying a last hint of childhood spirit. "You don't care about me!"

"Stop that at once, Elendra," Zurine snapped. "You will ruin your complexion."

Cynara met Zurine's hidden gaze. "It would not be advisable for me to stay, El. I wouldn't be welcomed by your guests."

"Because you're not a real woman." Elendra stopped, shocked at her own pronouncement. "I . . . I—"

"Never mind, El. Most of Dharma would agree with you."

Elendra flushed. "Do not call me El ever again. It is Elendra. Elendra D'Accorso-*fila.*"

"Be silent!" Zurine cried.

Elendra lowered her hands and grew very quiet. She, at least, was biddable. A proper female who knew her place, and what the future held in store for her.

"I came to give my respects, Mother," Cynara said. "Now I will leave you."

"You will not." Casnar entered the room without hesitation, for the lord of the house considered even the Women's Hall his own. "Tonight we have guests, Cynara. It would appear most peculiar if you left almost as soon as you arrived— as if we did not support the work you do on the *Pegasus* and the great hope it brings to Dharma and our allies."

"Does that consideration outweigh the shame of my tainted presence?"

Tyr's voice. It must be Tyr, returning to support her and face Father's anger.

Perhaps Casnar recognized it as well. His expression registered disgust and then confusion as he joined Zurine beside the chaise.

"I cannot expect you to remember manners when you're among riffraff and foreigners, but you will watch your tongue in this house. And you will attend us at dinner."

"Veiled, Casnar." Zurine grasped his sleeve, a familiarity permitted only a wife of many years. "She must wear a veil."

"I'm sorry, Mother," Cynara said. "I won't."

"Then you are not welcome at our table."

"Zurine." Casnar shook her off and turned to Cynara. "Tyr would have dined with us tonight."

She knew exactly what he proposed. She would be permitted to sit at the table with his guests—doubtless men of influence whom he had courted with great skill and diplomacy to overlook the stain upon the D'Accorso honor—and reinforce his efforts to consolidate D'Accorso power. Unlike Tyr, she would not be allowed to let her authority and rank speak for itself.

"I will not wear the veil," she said.

Casnar beat at her with his stare. "Perhaps it might interest you to know that *Fico* Nyle Beneviste and his parents will be among our guests."

Never in a thousand tides would Cynara have expected her former betrothed to visit this house again, or for Casnar to use him as an argument against her. Did he think her shame so great that she would feel compelled to don the veil in Nyle's presence?

"You cannot believe he will wish to see me, Father."

"I will be able to show his father that your actions have not in any way weakened House D'Accorso; to the contrary, the *Pegasus* brings great prestige to us and to our allies. Your presence will also remind *Fico* Beneviste that the breaking of your betrothal was essential for the well-being of himself and his family."

Cynara felt as if she'd been slapped. "He has known since

shortly after I left Dharma that marriage was impossible. Why does he need further evidence?"

"They have not seen you since you took up the captaincy. Any lingering doubts or resentment on his family's part will be laid to rest, and our future alliance will be secured once more." He placed his hand on the back of the chaise like an ancient emperor posing for a state portrait. "You owe this debt, Cynara. You will pay it."

Of course he would use any means to further his schemes to expand D'Accorso influence, which could never be taken for granted in Elsinore or anywhere on Dharma. He must simultaneously reinforce his position as one of the *Pegasus*'s supporters, firmly ensconced as a patron of the Council, and at the same time placate his traditional and more backward allies.

"What you suggest," she said, "will hardly be effective if I wear the veil."

He inclined his head slightly. Zurine breathed so hard that her veil lifted away from her face, weights and all.

"I have also invited members of the Council and its supporters. It should be a most interesting gathering."

Interesting, yes—at her expense, caught between those who regarded her as a loathsome freak and those who continued to doubt her ability to captain the *Pegasus*. Her father would stand at the head of the table as the benevolent, reasonable mediator.

"Very well, Father," she said. "I'll stay for dinner, but I will spend the night aboard my ship."

"As you wish." He swept from the room without even glancing at his wife. Zurine, expressionless, rose and hurried Elendra away.

Cynara stood alone in the conservatory, smelling the greenery she had once loved so much. Now it seemed to stink of decay. She strode from the room and found Tesar waiting for her. He conducted her to her childhood quarters. Elendra had been given Cynara's room with its adult sensibilities.

Cynara didn't mind. There was comfort here, and memories of a time when veils and women's duties were far in the future.

Tesar opened the dusty drapes to let in the light. "You will wish refreshments, *Filia,* and an appropriate gown for tonight. I will send a servant to the *Matrona's* couturier with a message to bring her finest selection."

"By all means send for a tailor, Tesar, but don't bother with the gowns. I have my own plans."

The majordomo was experienced enough to regard her with wariness. "Your father—"

"Has asked me to attend as captain of the *Pegasus,* and captain I will be." She smiled to take the sting from her words. "I would very much appreciate a light meal, Tesar."

He nodded dubiously and went to the door. *"Filia—"*

"I know what I'm doing. Thank you, old friend."

And she did know precisely what she was doing. When a tailor arrived—one of the modiste's assistants and not the maestro himself—she described exactly what she wanted and asked if it could be done in a matter of hours. The scandalized assistant, already distracted by her unveiled eyes, took her tip and agreed to do his best.

An hour before the dinner, just as the first guests arrived to gather in the grand hall, the tailor delivered her clothing. She refused all assistance from the maid who came to help her dress. There was nothing elaborate about what she had chosen save for the captain's braid and cravat.

She waited until she heard the bell summoning the guests to dinner, and then she went downstairs to join them in the dining hall.

Tesar took one look at her and seemed to lose his voice. "No need to announce me," she said with a wry smile. "My presence will speak for itself."

As indeed it did. She found an empty seat waiting for her beside Zurine, the only other woman permitted at table tonight save for *Magna* Egona Beneviste, Nyle's mother. Both ladies were superbly gowned and veiled. The gentlemen were as bright as rainbow fish in their brocades and velvets.

Every eye fixed on her as she bowed and took her seat. Zurine stifled a gasp.

"Magné, Matroné," she said, "I apologize for my tardiness. I beg your indulgence."

With a glance at Casnar, she sat. No one spoke. Her gaze

met that of her former betrothed across the table. He half rose as if he intended to desert the gathering, but good manners forbade it. No, only Cynara D'Accorso-*fila* would shatter the rules tonight.

The servants resumed distributing the first course and the light wine that accompanied it, passing over the ladies. Cynara tapped a server's arm and signaled that she wished a glass.

Zurine sat stiffly beside her as if she saw nothing. *Matrona* Beneviste fanned herself discreetly. Her husband was stony-faced.

The other guests, two men of the Trade Council and several other burgher-lords who had encouraged the *Pegasus* Project, were somewhat less perturbed, but even they could hardly approve.

The final guest was Phineas Janek.

She lifted her glass to him. "Good evening, *Ser* Janek."

Everyone stared at her father. He rose ponderously and gazed upon the gathering.

"*Magné* and *Nesté,* I welcome you to the House of D'Accorso. You have honored me with your presence at my table. May the gifts of sea and earth nourish you this night."

The Dharman men murmured the rote response. Casnar let his gaze sweep slowly to Cynara. By not the twitch of an eyebrow did he show dismay at her choice of raiment.

"Tonight I welcome my daughter, Captain Cynara D'Accorso, just returned from space."

Silence. Cynara rose and bowed to the table at large. "Guests of my father, I share this table with joy."

It was a man's response that no Dharman woman would dare venture. If her brother had been here, he would hardly have borne the shame. But he had refused to see her since Tyr's death.

His absent outrage was taken up by another. *Magnus* Egon Beneviste rose to his feet and glared at his host.

"Is this a game, *Magnus*? Do you mock us by presenting this . . . this creature who flaunts her taint before us all?"

"I do not mock," Casnar said. "I merely wish to reiterate my support for the *Pegasus* Project and the ship's crew and captain, who have most ably delivered their cargo once more with no loss of life."

Two of the Council members murmured to each other. Cynara would stand before them in official capacity soon enough, but here they would witness her firm resolve even among her family. It was not a time to speak of business, or she suspected they would have many questions about the guest she had brought to Dharma.

I hope you've done your work well, Uncle. "Without the patronage of the burgher-lords," she said, "there would be no *Pegasus* to stand against shaauri might and help restore the Alliance. *Magné,* I drink to you." She lifted her glass and drank. Three of the men followed suit. Her former betrothed did not, and neither did his father.

Unable to contain himself, young Nyle jumped to his feet. "How can you permit this, *Magnus* D'Accorso?" he cried. "You shame Beneviste honor. You permit this female to wear men's garments and speak freely in honorable company." He flushed almost as red as his doublet. "If it is your desire to provoke—"

"Sit down," his father commanded. "*Magnus* D'Accorso—"

"I will not be silent." Nyle stared at Cynara with bitter contempt. "We were to ally ourselves with this House. I was to bed this . . . this abomination, neither male nor female, tainted with man's thoughts and man's desire—"

Magnus Beneviste turned on his son. No words were spoken, but Nyle went pale and fell back into his seat. Cynara heard the echoes of the furious mental exchange and almost winced for Nyle.

When it was over, Beneviste ignored Cynara as if she didn't exist and faced her father. "I can only presume, *Magnus,* that you have some purpose of your own by permitting this insult to your guests. You had offered your daughter Elendra—"

"Yes, *Magnus,* to make amends for the disappointment you have suffered. I think you will find that Elendra is everything Cynara is not. You have lost nothing by ending the betrothal; indeed, you can have no better proof of my elder daughter's unsuitability as a wife." He smiled. "Is it not so,

Captain? You have no interest in marriage or womanly ways."

Cynara returned his smile, swallowing the humiliation he so casually bestowed.

"Indeed, *Magnus,*" she said, straightening her velvet coat. "My sole purpose lies with the *Pegasus.* If it did not, I would hardly be a worthy captain."

Janek stood. "Forgive the intrusion of an outworlder, *Magné.* As one who has traveled with the captain's crew, I can vouch for Captain D'Accorso's competence and courage. She serves most honorably in Captain Tyr D'Accorso's stead." He sat down again, nodding pleasantly to his neighbor.

Nothing surprised Cynara after the past few exchanges, but Janek's speech was a mystery. She didn't trust any praise from him, and his mention of Tyr could not be an accident. With his very compliments he undermined her legitimacy.

And now, of course, she understood what her father had intended with her presence tonight. To his Council guests, he proved her commitment to the *Pegasus.* At the same time he demonstrated to the Benevistes that they were far better off with Elendra, who had finally come of age—that in fact they had acted with utmost wisdom by agreeing to the unbetrothal and biding in patience for resolution.

Cynara understood, but she could not forgive. She bowed to her father and rose again from her chair.

"Duty compels me to leave this august gathering," she said. *"Magné, Fico, Matroné."* She bowed from the waist and stepped back as a servant hastily moved her chair.

Her father did not try to stop her. He'd accomplished his goal. Cynara strode into the hall and started up the staircase.

You have no interest in marriage or womanly ways, Father had said. Of course she didn't. Except that Ronan hadn't left her thoughts for a moment in all the time she'd been at the palace, and she felt an absurd desire to seek him out and . . . and . . .

"Captain." She turned on the landing at the sound of Janek's voice, reminding herself that it was not her privilege to challenge him to a duel. Persephoneans didn't fight that way.

"*Ser* Janek." She smiled and leaned against the bannister. "I should thank you for your words on my behalf during dinner."

"Why, Captain." He climbed halfway up the stairs and paused, unaffected by his inferior vantage. "I spoke only the truth. I also spoke to members of the Council earlier today." He examined the high polish on the *komor*-wood. "They are most eager to question Ronan and discover what benefits his knowledge may bring to the Alliance."

"Benefits? You've already told them that he's an enemy, haven't you?"

"Unfortunately, *Magnus* Jesper D'Accorso has prevailed with his fellow Councillors to delay the debriefing. I know Ronan is your uncle's guest. This is not a safe situation for Ronan, or Dharma."

"You'd like nothing better than to destroy him."

"We needn't be enemies, Cynara. You know your captaincy is called into question every time you return to Dharma. If you deliver Ronan to the Council freely, I feel sure that they will recognize the contribution you've made."

"And you, of course, will emphasize my suitability to continue as Captain."

"Naturally. That is why I offer advice: If you have any question of sending Ronan for debriefing within the next twelve hours, I would seriously reconsider."

"Ronan has no objection to speaking with the Council if they'll guarantee his continued good health."

"I am, as you have so often pointed out, merely an observer. I am not privy to the Council's decisions."

"Is that really true, Janek?" She descended several steps. "I don't believe it for a minute."

"I would avoid such speculation, Captain. It might not be wise, or healthy."

"Are you threatening me? *I* would strongly advise—"

A man-sized blur appeared behind Janek, and a moment later he was dangling off his feet. Ronan held him casually by his lace collar and slowly lowered him again, one arm locked around Janek's throat.

"You are right not to trust this one," Ronan said, gazing up at Cynara. "Shall I kill him now?"

Chapter 12

The shock on Cynara's face made clear her answer even before she spoke. Ronan released Janek and stepped aside. He scrambled out of Ronan's reach.

"It will be very difficult," Janek said, rubbing at his neck, "to convince the Council that this savage is an ally."

Cynara's eyes lit. "Ah, *now* we speak truth. You'd best leave, *Ser* Janek, before I decide to let Ronan have you."

"As you wish, Captain." He bowed military fashion and strode back toward the dining hall.

"Well," Cynara said. "Your timing is impeccable, Ronan, but your technique needs some refinement." She descended the remaining steps and took his arm. "Does my father or Jesper know you're here?"

"No. I came—" He hesitated and moved closer to her, searching her eyes. He did not need to read her expression to know what she felt; she shouted it at him, all the suppressed anger and humiliation and pain her pride would not permit her to reveal. She had learned to hide her feelings from the world, just as he had.

But all the barriers she raised against intruders were weakening before him. She could not keep him out, but he allowed her to sense in him only those emotions that would draw her closer.

He touched her cheek. "I felt your distress. I came at once."

"You felt—" She became aware of his caress and went very still. "I was guarding my thoughts every minute in this house, but you're obviously linked to my emotions." She sat down on the nearest step. "You're getting stronger, Ronan. It's even more important to take you to a specialist who can work with you."

"So that I, too, can control my thoughts."

"Among other things. Uncle Jesper may not be able to delay our debriefing beyond tomorrow morning."

"And you still fear that I may be concealing something that would alarm your Council."

"No." She stood up, paced away from him, and turned sharply. "There are others like Janek who'll be looking for any excuse to keep you in permanent custody."

"Then we should make preparations."

"Yes. I'll gather my things and return with you to Jesper's. You'd better wait for me outside."

"You do not wish others of your House to see me."

She paused on the steps. "If you read me a little more deeply—which I don't advise—you'd know I'm only trying to protect you."

"And yourself." He listened to the sounds from another part of the house, vast as it was—human voices, mostly male. "It is better when females leave their young to be raised by those suited for it."

"I have no intention of discussing family matters here. Wait outside, Ronan."

She ran up the staircase. Ronan stared at the colored glass several stories overhead, wondering at the waste of space for the purpose of ostentatious ornamentation. This dwelling was far larger than Jesper's, flaunting wealth in the way humans seemed to prefer.

Cynara had grown up to this life of privilege, daughter of the *aho'va* of Line D'Accorso. But she had not been happy. She had no desire to be here among her kin; they made no place for her to fill. She had chosen exile and fought to es-

tablish a new House where she could be First. Now that
House was under threat, by Janek and by this Council.

Ronan's most powerful urge was to protect her from all
enemies. Every time he touched Cynara's mind, even lightly,
he wished to reach further and deeper. Every moment of
sharing jeopardized his resolve to carry out the objective assigned him. Yet what he needed lay in her mind, and he must
risk all to find it.

The male voices came closer, and he went quickly to the
door and slipped into the garden. A few minutes later Cynara
found him. She led him to a path that wound behind the great
house and through a gate in the high wall.

The sun had crossed the horizon by the time they left the
D'Accorso grounds and started for *Va* Jesper's house. The
scents of night were strong in the High City: the cloying per-
fume of some night-blooming flower, fuel from cars skimming along the narrow streets, spices seasoning fish cooked
over an open fire.

Though they had been parted only a few hours, Cynara's
nearness had a curious effect on Ronan. He lost awareness of
the streets they walked and the humans they passed. He did
not forget what he must do tonight, but his reasons for attempting it became more and more confused.

A distraction was necessary. "Your parents," he said.
"They are joined for life, but they are not lifemates."

"It depends on what you mean by 'lifemate.'"

"In shaauri-*ja*, it is a sacred emotional and spiritual bond
between male and female, blessed by the Ancestors. Only a
small percentage of shaauri are so honored. It cannot be
feigned, nor can it be broken. Lifemates are always the
founders of a House or Line; without them there is no prosperity. Alone among shaauri mates, they remain together
until death."

"You make it sound like a kind of Selection."

"In many ways, it is. Your parents' marriage was arranged
by their progenitors?"

"Yes." She began to walk even faster, her gaze fixed on
the ground before her feet.

"This is why they are not contented in their Paths."

"How did you . . ." Her lips thinned. "You'll have to stop

doing that, Ronan. It goes beyond impolite when you intrude on my memories."

"Even if I wish to help?"

They reached the drive that turned into Jesper's dwelling. "Don't tell me that shaauri kin never quarrel. You have the scars to prove it." She came to a sudden halt. "I'm sorry. That was cruel."

"Those I fought were not of Ain'Kalevi," he said. "And I was not shaaurin."

"I know." She touched his arm and continued toward the house, stopping on the cobblestoned walk that led into the garden. "You want to know more about my background. That's fair enough. The more you understand of Dharma and my current situation, the better you'll be able to face the Council."

Her words made a shell of indifference, but beneath them her emotions were in turmoil. She wished to hide herself from him, and at the same time her heart yearned to reveal the burdens she tried to carry alone.

Listen, his instincts whispered, *but do not feel. Speak, but do not judge. Touch, but do not bind. This is the way to court a human female.*

"This garden is pleasant," he said, pausing to touch a silver-edged leaf. "Shaauri, too, keep gardens."

She sat down on a wooden bench flanked by white-flowered vines. "All shaauri, or only those of certain Paths?"

"I knew an *aino'va*—Second of Will—who cultivated his own vegetation," he said. "Is that so strange?"

"It's not strange at all. Uncle Jesper is a wonderful gardener. My parents preferred to have servants manage the grounds."

He sat on the bench beside her. "Your parents hold great power in this city."

"Very great."

"But because you are female, you could not choose your Path."

She gazed into the shadows. "Even in Low Town, where women have more freedom, they seldom choose. Few ever leave their home cities or villages."

"Males may take Walkabout, but not females."

"That's one way of putting it." She smiled and flexed her fingers, catching moonlight on the golden bands of her rings. "If not for my family's authority, and the fact that my father wished to show the Persephoneans that he, at least, had become more progressive . . ." She shrugged. "It was a great blow when the shaauri blockade prevented personnel and materials from moving freely between the Nine Worlds and the Concordat. Because of his marriage to my aunt, Jesper remained on Dharma when most off-planet specialists returned to the Concordat. He and a few others like him were able to continue training technicians, engineers, and doctors on Dharma so the knowledge wouldn't be lost."

"And you also received an education."

"My uncle was happy to do it. My mother was horrified. I thought I was making great strides for Dharman women because I learned alongside the boys and was treated as an equal by my uncle." Her smile vanished. "In the end all my rebellion came to nothing. Because of my family's position, it was even more important to my father that I, his elder daughter, marry advantageously."

"Another arranged marriage."

"He needed all the allies he could find to keep Dharma moving forward so that one day it could join the Concordat as a full member." She sighed. "The man my father selected was the heir of a ruling family on Ikaria, one of our neighboring islands."

Nyle Beneviste. That was the name in her mind, and the image that accompanied it was one humans might call attractive. Ronan snapped a flower from the vine and cupped it in his palm.

"You did not mate with this man," he said.

"No. The month I was to marry, my cousin Tyr returned from his first successful run as captain of the *Pegasus.* We'd always been close, Tyr and I. I worshipped and envied him; all I dreamed of was to escape my betrothal and travel in space. When he went on his second mission, I stowed away on the ship and left Dharma with him and his crew."

"You made your own Walkabout."

"I disrupted the plans of countless people. I was a distraction my cousin didn't need on such an important voyage. Because of me—" She turned her face aside, struggling to hold her grief in check. It swept over Ronan, mingling unexpectedly with his own memories until he could no longer tell one from the other.

Sirens wailing. Explosions. People running, shouting, trying to stem the damage. Fear, and helplessness.

A face, male and light-haired. A smile that rent the heart. "Don't blame yourself, Cyn. It wasn't your doing." Coughing, and bright blood. "Right now we have to save the ship."

Sirens and voices fading. Hands touching, the light dying in his green eyes. But not before the whole world changed.

Ronan snapped the contact. Cynara lunged from the bench, striking blindly into the shrubbery. Just as blind, Ronan pursued her and caught her wrists in his hands.

Vision cleared. Cynara's face was contorted like the mask of a primitive shaauri demon, but there was no evil in it. Only unbearable sorrow and loss.

Ronan pulled her close and folded his arms around her. She stiffened and then went boneless, neither fighting his hold nor responding to it. He did what felt right and natural, stroking her back with the flat of his palm until her trembling stilled. His own heartbeat slowed to match. The top of her head fit just under his chin, and her hair smelled of the white flowers.

He was filled with her—her scent, the blended strength and softness of her body, the complexity of mind and emotion that was Cynara D'Accorso. With a little effort, he could penetrate the outer layers of her thoughts and take what he needed without the cover of seduction.

"You grieve for your cousin," he said. "But his last words to you absolved you of blame. Why do you not believe it?"

"I became captain of the *Pegasus* . . . only because of him. Because of what he gave me."

All at once the tangle of images and memories made sense. Tyr D'Accorso, dying as the result of a shaauri attack, held in his cousin's arms. Two telepaths, one confident and one untried and suppressed, touching minds at the moment of passing. Knowledge bursting into a virgin mind, overwhelming it with everything a man's life could hold.

Memory ended. Cynara stepped away and held up her hand with its glittering golden rings.

"These were Tyr's betrothal gift," she whispered. "I couldn't take them off . . . after he died. I had to remember. Because of him, I inherited the captaincy. Oh, there were protests, and outrage. But there were none as qualified, not even among Jesper's best students." She laughed in self-mockery. "I had finally made progress for Dharman women everywhere."

Any hope Ronan had of piercing Cynara's mental shield was gone. She had thrown up all her defenses with a vengeance, and he could no longer interpret the subtle meaning behind her words. Everything associated with the *Pegasus* was buried and beyond his reach.

He didn't care. He saw her pain, and that was enough. "You doubt your worthiness," he said. "I do not."

"You don't know me, Ronan."

"Our minds have touched. How can I not?"

"Maybe you see what you wish to see. You've been lonely a very long time." She took another step away. "It's getting late. You need sleep, and so do I. First thing in the morning, Jesper and I will prepare you to meet the Council."

Ronan let her go. His opportunity had passed, lost to irresolution and sympathy. He had pitied her—she who rejected pity as he did, and held herself aloof from those who might see emotion as weakness.

Now he understood why she feared any display of vulnerability. It was not merely that she was First with a place to hold against rivals, as he would expect among shaauri, or that she was a woman among humans who regarded females as unfit for high rank.

For her it was personal. She could not forget that the status she possessed, the life she desired above all others, had been bestowed as a gift and not earned in the human way or even properly selected in Walkabout.

There was more to her fears than even those considerations, grave though they were in her mind. And she held those mysteries to herself as fiercely as she guarded the secrets of her unusual ship.

When he learned one, he would learn the other. The plan

he had devised on the *Pegasus* must continue, no matter the penalty to his own peace of mind. That price he paid gladly so long as Cynara did not suffer.

Suffer? If you succeed, you will take from her the very thing she values above all.

He shut such enfeebling thoughts from his mind and followed Cynara into the house. He met Jesper as the old man turned a corner into the entrance hall.

"Well, my friend," he said with generous good humor. "You missed dinner tonight. Quite disappointing. I trust that you enjoyed your tour of our city?"

"You see this in my mind?" Ronan asked bluntly.

He waved his hands. "No, no. I just put myself in your place. If I were a young man with so much yet to discover, I wouldn't waste time puttering around an old man's house. You must have been discreet, or I'd have heard of it by now." He glanced toward the guest wing. "You've been to the D'Accorso palace."

"Yes."

"Fortunate that you didn't run into Cynara's parents. They can be difficult." He paused. "Did she tell you how she became captain of the *Pegasus*?"

"Yes."

"Then you have been granted a rare privilege. I hope you value the gift of her trust." Without waiting for Ronan's answer, he changed the subject. "Cynara wishes to discuss your meeting with the Trade Council in the morning. If you're hungry, I've had my cook set aside a portion in the kitchen." He clapped Ronan's shoulder. "Go to bed, my young friend. I'll make sure you're up in time for breakfast."

Jesper strode down the hall to the second wing of the house, which Ronan had determined held the elder's quarters and the room given to Cynara. Ronan returned to his own chamber, his feet heavy on the polished wood floor.

Va Jesper meant nothing but good for him, like Cynara. These were folk who wished to help and accepted him for what he was, free of suspicion and prejudice.

I must betray you in your own House, Aho'Va. *Forgive me.*

For a time, while Ronan chanted to nourish his resolve,

the house echoed with the light steps of Jesper's *an'laik'i* and the distant clatter of pottery in the kitchen. When all was still, Ronan knew he could wait no longer.

He entered the dark and deserted corridor. A few quick steps to the grand entry hall, and another turn. The family wing was lit by a single glowball held in an outstretched hand. Gentle light bathed Cynara's features and softened every shadow.

She moved almost as quietly as he, wrapped in a thick robe belted at the waist. Ronan could smell damp flesh beneath. She paused when she saw him, lifting the light.

"Ronan?"

He did not answer. Her voice gave his name a thousand meanings, and every one of them shouted wanting. Her mind burned with it, as did his.

She took a step back, globe held high. He followed. At the end of the hall stood an open door. Cynara slipped inside.

There is no other way.

Ronan entered the room, and Cynara closed the door behind him. The dimly lit chamber was twice the size of Ronan's and, like her cabin on the *Pegasus,* arrayed with many curious objects.

"The spoils of my travels," Cynara said. She picked up a small animal carved of black rock and turned it over in her hands. "I try to pick up some memento of every world we visit." She set down the sculpture and sat on the edge of a wide bed laid with a coverlet woven in tones of wood and earth. "This quilt is from Ys, one of the Concordat worlds. The hangings were created by the artisans of Serengeti. I have yet to collect a souvenir from a shaauri world."

Ronan crouched at the foot of the bed. "I have little to offer you."

"No?" She stroked the coverlet over and over with one hand, smoothing nonexistent wrinkles. "Why are you here, Ronan?"

One question concealed many unspoken, but he chose a single answer. "I come for instruction."

"In what?"

"In how to be human."

Her eyes caught the light as she looked at him. "Are you worried about meeting the Council?"

"No. Only one thing concerns me."

She continued to gaze at him, waiting. The scent of her flesh overwhelmed all others in the room. Her thoughts were barely within her control.

He drew closer to the bed, muscles flowing from one position into the next as if he hardly moved at all. "I am concerned only with your judgment, Cynara. I wish to be a worthy human in your eyes."

"You're already that, Ronan. You have nothing to prove to me."

She spoke falsely—not as one courting or being courted, but as a companion . . . a "friend" who bore him some affection and nothing more.

"Do you consider me your equal?" he asked.

"You can't seem to decide if you're a servant or a commander. On the ship—"

"You are captain. *Aho'Va.*"

"You called yourself unworthy then."

"But here it is not the same."

"Because I'm just a woman?"

Anger. Challenge. She tried to dismiss them, but they lay there always, at the heart of her being. " 'Just' is a human term," he said. "There is no 'just' in you, Cynara."

She laughed nervously. "It seems you've learned the human knack of giving compliments. Who taught you? Kord?"

"There is another human word, 'seduction.' Can you explain?"

"It's something I'm sure you could learn very quickly if you tried." She tugged at the ends of her sash. "I'm certainly not the one to ask."

"You have had few . . . lovers."

"Didn't I answer these questions before?"

"You were to be married, and that ended. Your own people turned against you. Kord is not your mate. There have been others?"

She didn't answer, but his mind grasped vague, troubling images of a much younger Cynara, hardly out of childhood,

engaging in another small act of rebellion with a young
Dharman male of her age. Shame accompanied the memory,
but it was not the only one of its kind. She had taken sexual
pleasure several times before she left her homeworld.

He could find no reference to sexual contact after she became captain of the *Pegasus*.

"You have avoided mating," he said, as if he merely
guessed.

"A captain doesn't disrupt the morale of her crew with
personal entanglements." She got up from the bed and
walked across the room. "Discussion of my love life isn't
likely to help you become more human. Maybe you'd better
go back to sleep."

He followed her and stopped within a hand's touch of her
back. "Why did you come to find me, Cynara?"

He heard her internal debate, weighing more deception
against the truth she feared. "Sometimes I'm just not very
good with words."

"Shaauri," he said, "do not use many words when they
wish to mate. The body speaks instead."

Her back stiffened. "And what do you think I'm saying
now?"

"That you are afraid without need." He cupped her shoulders in his hands. A violent tremor shook her body. "I could
not harm you, Cynara. I demand nothing. I know you are
alone among your own kind. Such loneliness may find ease,
if only for an hour."

"As you did with those Kinswomen?"

"It was for the body, which gives strength to the mind, as
the mind strengthens the body."

"Shaauri philosophy?"

He turned her about until his breath mingled with hers.
"Sihvaaro taught me that all beings crave union with something—the universe, perfect knowledge, another of their own
kind. I am not far along the Eightfold Way, Cynara. Since I
came to the *Pegasus,* I have craved only you."

"And you asked me what seduction meant." She brushed
his cheek with the back of her hand. "Just when I think I'm
starting to understand you—"

He caught her hand and pressed it to his mouth. He opened

his mind just enough so that she could see what was in his outermost heart: admiration, respect, and desire so powerful that it made him shake like a *be'laik'in* at his first mating.

This *was* his first. His first with a woman who wanted him, whose own need met his without hesitation or disdain.

"It . . . it makes no sense," Cynara whispered, fitting his hand to her cheek. "When you came aboard the *Pegasus*—even then you weren't a stranger. It's as if I'd known you all my life."

"It is Walkabout," he said. "There is no wrong, no shame. Only discovery."

"I don't know which of us has more to learn. I guess we're about to find out."

And she kissed him. There was no likeness to the previous times. All such comparisons fled his mind. He banked his hunger and gave himself up to this purely human pleasure: lips touching, mouths opening, tongues twining in a dance humans must have known for millennia before they reached the stars.

If he had been shaauri, he would have felt disgust. If he had been shaauri, he would forgo all sexual pleasure rather than embrace a furless, voiceless human.

You are not shaauri. You never will be, no matter what you do to earn the right . . .

He growled and nipped her shoulder. She gasped.

"Is that what you call . . . a love bite?"

He peeled back her robe and licked the sensitized skin beneath. "Does it please you?"

"I don't know yet."

"Remove your covering."

She laughed. "That sounds like a command."

"Do humans not prefer nakedness in mating?"

She clutched the edges of her robe. "What do you prefer?"

In answer he stepped back and stripped off the loose shirt and trousers the house servants had left him for sleeping clothes. He folded the clothing neatly and set it on a nearby chair.

"Is it satisfactory?" he asked, suddenly uncertain. "Does this body please you?"

She closed her eyes. "Mother Sea," she whispered. "It does."

Chapter 13

Cynara had seen Ronan naked aboard the ship, when he was under Dr. Zheng's care in the infirmary. Then he had been a vulnerable patient. There was nothing vulnerable about him now.

His readiness was obvious, and he was certainly not ashamed of it. Why should he be? He'd always been clear about what he wanted, even when he seemed to contradict himself. During his adult life, sex had been virtually his only link to humanity.

For Cynara, sex had become a pleasure unsought and nearly unthinkable. Until now, she had hardly missed it. To crave such contact would mean testing the very nature of her sexuality, discovering once and for all if Tyr had banished all desire or altered it beyond recognition.

But what she felt for Ronan had nothing to do with Tyr. It wasn't just sex. Oh, that was part of it . . . a very large part in more than one sense. She was almost prepared to jump on top of him before he moved a muscle.

She'd known this was coming since the moment Ronan walked onto her bridge, though she'd denied it again and again. Tonight she had gone to Ronan, and he'd met her halfway. There could be no violence in this joining, no matter how urgently they wanted each other. It might be their only chance.

"You are very handsome by human standards," she said, finding her voice. "Did none of those women ever tell you?"

He shook his head. "It would not have mattered."

Because of the scars? Had they looked upon those numerous ridges and stripes on his body and deemed him disgusting?

For the first time Cynara felt no pity for his suffering. He felt none for himself. He was strong, and beautiful.

As she was not.

"I would see you," he said, very quietly. "Will you remove your covering now?"

How very formal and polite. She wanted to laugh, but there was nothing amusing about the knot in her stomach.

Utterly irrational. She knew that when she took off the robe, the body underneath would be exactly as it was before Tyr's dying gift. The various parts would be in all the right places. Nothing would have appeared that shouldn't be there.

She *knew*. Yet, in her mind, the body she wore was wrong. When she dared to look into a mirror, she expected to see her curves vanished, breasts diminished, waist thickened like that of some bizarre androgynous mutation.

"Wait," she said. "Let me turn out the lights."

Ronan grasped the end of her sash. A gentle tug opened the robe from neck to ankle. He rested his hands on her shoulders and pushed the garment down her arms.

Cynara closed her eyes. He was breathing very deeply, speaking not a word. Curse him.

His palm stroked her cheek and slid down to her neck. "Cynara," he whispered. "You are beautiful."

"You may not be the most accurate judge of human beauty."

"You are strong," he said. He began to run his hands over her, illustrating with intimate touches as he spoke. "Your face is symmetrical in its lines, and firm in the jaw. Your teeth are white and even. Your nose is not too small. Your eyes are large and bright." He kissed her closed eyelids. "Your neck is long and graceful, like that of a *la'salo*. Your hair—"

He combed his fingers through it, fanning the strands

about her shoulders. "Your hair is soft and smells of your night flowers."

"Red," she said. "Like shaauri—"

"Like Cynara." His hands sifted her hair and let it fall again. "I am glad that your mouth is not like a shaauri female's."

The kiss was so gentle that she barely felt it. When she reached to take him into her arms, he stopped her with that same firm gentleness.

"I have not finished," he said. He began to massage her tight shoulders with consummate skill. "Your arms are well shaped. Your hands are graceful." He lifted one of her hands and flattened it to his, palm to palm. "So small against mine."

"They're not—" She caught her breath as he drew one of her fingers into his mouth.

"Graceful fingers," he said when he had sampled each one. He stroked his hands up her arms. "Your breasts . . ."

He cradled her beneath, and her breasts felt tight and aching and heavy.

"These, too, are beautiful." His voice grew husky as he ran his thumbs across her nipples. "They give nourishment, but I do not remember what it is like to taste it."

Poseidon. Cynara shivered. "They . . . don't give nourishment unless—"

Words died. Ronan's mouth closed around one of her nipples, and he began to suckle with all the hunger that instinct built into humankind. He used his lips and tongue in amazing ways no amount of experience could have taught him.

He worshipped her, but not as a servant. He celebrated all that was female in her, neither captain nor inferior, but herself whole and complete. He pressed his face between her breasts and she buried her fingers in his hair, swallowing a cry of triumph.

Still he wasn't finished. He kissed a trail from breastbone to belly, rubbing his cheek against the gentle swell. "The shaauri are wrong," he murmured. "There is great delight in this smoothness."

No fur, he meant. Cynara opened her eyes. "Did you . . . you and the shaauri females . . . is it possible—"

His laughter rumbled into her skin, half hiss in the shaauri

way. "Never." He looked up, hands grasping her hips. "Is this
what you feared?"

"No. No." She closed her eyes again, appalled at the direction of her thoughts. "How do shaauri judge beauty?"

"It is not physical perfection that draws one mate to another. Among *va'laik'i* it may be status, or desire for alliance
and strong children. Sometimes it is simply for pleasure."

"Oh, yes. Affection doesn't enter into it."

He cupped her buttocks. "Between lifemates, emotion is
all. There can be no bond without it."

"But we . . . are not lifemates."

What was she saying? She tried to distract herself from
the heat of Ronan's breath at the tops of her thighs. "I
mean—"

"We are human," he said. "I care for you, Cynara."

It was the last thing she'd expected him to say. There was
nothing of the courtier in it, the seducer seeking just the right
words to open a woman's thighs.

No. Ronan meant what he said. She did not know what he
meant by it. Friendship? Affection? Surely not love . . .

"Ronan," she said. Her throat was blocked, and she found
it difficult to speak. "I—"

Ronan had a way with more than words. He rose to his
feet and sealed her lips with his fingers.

"How do you wish to mate, Cynara?" he whispered. "Tell
me what pleases you."

The images that leapt instantly into her mind were quite
astonishing. Certainly those memories she had taken from
Ronan—his encounters with Kinswomen on the shaauri
world—were not nearly so inventive. He and his partners had
been more intent on the result than the process.

But what she pictured did not grow solely out of her own
overstimulated imagination. It was Ronan's thoughts she was
sharing, a veritable catalog of fascinating and challenging
ways to join two bodies. In each image the female was herself.

Ronan couldn't know how strongly he was projecting. He
wasn't that advanced, or that skilled. She must be reaching
out more than halfway, strengthening his thoughts without
any conscious purpose but desire.

"Today I went into your Middle Town," Ronan said, licking her neck. "I observed humans in a place where mating occurs frequently."

Scylla's teeth. He'd gone to the Prostitutes' Quarter. She was afraid to speculate how he'd managed to eavesdrop on the doings there.

"I am not . . . like those women," she said.

He began to draw back, and his absence turned the room cold as an ice floe.

"No," she said, reaching for his hand. "I didn't mean—"

"I will penetrate you in the way you find most comfortable."

She groaned. How could such clinical words have such an unbearably erotic effect? "I thought you said . . . that shaauri don't use words in . . . mating."

"I am sorry." He lifted her hair and kissed the nape of her neck while his other hand was busy elsewhere. She leaned her head against his scarred shoulder. By the black tides of space, he had no need for speech.

"I can't believe," she murmured, "that the men who patronize the Quarter are . . . quite so expert."

He didn't answer. Every part of her was kissed and caressed and stroked by lips and tongue and fingers, and all the while she shared the pictures in his mind.

Unbidden, her mind latched on to one of the images and would not let go. Ronan rumbled deep in his chest. He took her hand and pulled her down to the floor.

"Ronan . . . I think the bed is better."

Without hesitation he lifted her into his arms and carried her to the bed. For a moment he crouched above her, staring with such intensity that she felt flayed bare all the way to the bone.

"The shaauri are wrong," he said, wonder in his voice. Carefully he eased her into position, supporting her waist with one strong arm, and knelt behind her. He steadied her hips with his hands.

Poseidon. There was nothing rational in Cynara's mind, only the excruciating awareness of Ronan pressed to her buttocks, the indescribable feeling as he slid between her thighs.

He entered with a single, unerring thrust, rocking her forward among the pillows.

Pleasure exploded in her mind. Not only hers, but his, joined in a way she had never dreamed to experience. The images he had projected, the sharing of emotions, were as nothing to this. She knew, to the very center of her being, how much Ronan had wanted her. She knew how he had tried to stay away, how every moment in her presence was a kind of agony, desire beyond mere human lust.

It was hunger, to know and be known, to fuse with another of his kind in a way that he had only imagined, that she had only imagined. Each thrust drove him deeper into the core of her very self, body and bodiless. There was no separation. Only rocking, rocking, and a joy so profound that it surpassed every definition of pleasure.

"No," he whispered.

She heard the protest like waves in an undersea cavern, muted and remote. It drew her from ecstasy, to the mundane sensations of the quilt under her palms and Ronan's heat between her thighs.

"Don't," she begged. "Don't stop."

"I must see your face."

He withdrew and turned her about, pulling her into his lap. Suddenly, irrationally, Cynara was afraid. There was no escaping those eyes, no forgetting.

"Cynara," he said, cupping her face in his hands. "Don't fear me."

All she could think, in that moment, was that Ronan had used a contraction like an ordinary human. "I'm not afraid."

He brushed her hair back from her face. "Look at me, Cynara." With infinite tenderness he laid her back, cradling her head among the pillows. He entered her slowly, watching her face.

Humans called this "making love." They used the word "love" so freely, but he knew it for what it was: one more trap to sabotage his resolve.

The struggle to control his simple physical desires required nearly all his attention. There was powerful satisfaction in entering Cynara's body, pleasure beyond any he had known with the other women. But his pleasure was unimportant. She must trust him, give herself to him utterly, or he would never penetrate her mind.

Humans, even telepaths, are mentally most vulnerable in the act of sex, the Kinsmen had told him. *Even the strongest shields may falter at the moment of climax.*

And Cynara's shields were not impregnable. But what he had found beyond the surface of thought and word and physical sensation, what he felt now when her defenses were at their weakest, multiplied his treacherous doubts a thousandfold.

She feared, yes. Not him, nor the act that joined their bodies. No living being could arouse her terror but one: this creature she envisioned when she thought of herself, when she was not captain or leader but a female poisoned by her world's prejudices.

Damaged goods. That was what they said, these Dharman males. She had stowed away aboard the *Pegasus,* unchaperoned among a crew of men. But that was not the ultimate shame. Her own cousin had seduced her—not with his body, but with his mind. She had employed her dormant, forbidden telepathic skills and accepted his thoughts, his male nature into the virginal sanctity of her soul.

It didn't matter that she had saved the *Pegasus.* Nor was she absolved when the Council elevated her to captain, the first Dharman female ever to hold such rank and power.

Freak, they judged. Neither male nor female, with no place except on her ship. In the months before she had learned to protect her mind from the thoughts of others, their contempt and disgust and horror had bombarded her night and day, strengthening her own harsh judgment of herself, multiplying her doubts until all the confidence she had harbored as a child vanished.

If she was captain, she could not be Cynara. If she was a woman—if she ever let them see a moment of female weakness—she would lose everything.

Ne'lin and First, Woman and Captain. A telepath who feared her own abilities because of what they had brought her, and because of what they might set loose.

"Ronan," she whispered. She had closed her eyes again, surrendering all of her body and none of her mind. They moved as one, together and utterly apart. Ronan arched to kiss her breasts without losing rhythm, making her feel, drawing her toward release.

She tossed her head on the pillows, delaying the final Reckoning. Believing that her secrets were safe.

Ronan severed himself from sensation and allowed his body to continue while his mind prepared for the final thrust. It must be timed perfectly. And she must let him in. She must.

Her breath came in short, sharp pants. Her fingers pushed into the quilt. *Finish it,* she cried. Wanting, dreading, demanding.

He moved again. She shuddered, arching against him. He slipped into her mind like a phantom, invisible, enveloped in the blazing brilliance of her release. For an instant all her knowledge lay naked to him. The *Pegasus.* The great discovery. The secret humans held against their enemies.

Her mind closed like an iris to shut him out, reflexive and belated defense, oblivious to what he had done.

"Ronan," she whispered, her hands moving over his chest. "Ronan."

In all the years of his youth, he had never loathed himself as much as he did now. Yet he was safe. If she had sensed even a little of his true purpose, she would not be here with him. His shields held.

But he did not have what he needed—only fragments, pieces of a greater whole. It was not enough.

"I don't know if what we've just done was a very good idea," Cynara murmured.

"Do you regret it, *Aho'Va?*"

"No." *Not even if it creates exactly the complications I can least afford.*

Ronan almost answered before he realized that she had not spoken the second part aloud. He was so deeply attuned to her that reading her outer thoughts had become effortless.

The fact that she was unaware of his violation did not make it less terrible. But he needed to know the source of the technology—neither human nor shaauri—that generated the ship's drive, and how to gain access to the engine room of the *Pegasus* if none of the design information or schematics were available on Dharma itself.

And then, of course, he would have to find a way to escape Dharma.

"You're holding back," Cynara accused, rubbing his shoulders until he found it very difficult to concentrate. "You spent all your effort on me and didn't take any pleasure for yourself."

I took very great pleasure, Cynara. My mate.

"But you—" She sat up suddenly. "What did you just say?"

He realized at once that he had made a mistake, and there was no repairing it save by following Cynara's lead. "Did I speak?"

"You called me your—" She stared at him. "I *heard* you, Ronan. I heard your thoughts. Do you realize what you've done?" She shook her head in bewilderment. "I've been able to project to you, and I've read some of your memories and feelings. This is different. You've transmitted verbal communication in the most explicit way possible. That takes great control. If you've already learned so much . . . *there's no telling what you might do. How deeply can you read me, Ronan?*

Obvious deception would only arouse her suspicions. "I have heard you, Cynara," he said. "I have shared your feelings."

"Is that all? Did you encounter . . . any resistance?"

He put on a mask of bewilderment. "I do not understand."

"I wasn't prepared for this. I should have been."

"I have disturbed you," he said gently. "It was not my intention."

She swung her legs over the bed. "It's my fault, not yours."

"There is no fault in you, Cynara."

"If you believe that, you can't have looked too deeply." She smiled at him, sad and earnest. "I tried to steal a little time for us. I didn't think beyond the fact that we wanted each other. It's my job to consider the consequences of what I do, and in that I've failed."

"Because of what I might discover in your mind?" He frowned. "Is this why you have tried to stay away?"

"There's so much I can't explain. I don't want to shut you

out, Ronan. What we've shared, today and before . . . I won't dismiss it as if it never happened. But there are considerations beyond personal desires." She gathered her robe from the foot of the bed. "We have to remain apart from now on."

He should have made promises then, assuring her that he could never hurt her, that he would sooner die than betray the smallest part of her trust. If he did not do so, her mind, and all it contained, would be closed to him.

"Remain apart," he repeated. "Because I know what you fear most?"

She cinched the robe about her waist, keeping her back to him. "I think we both fear the same things, Ronan. I can no longer be objective where you're concerned. My duty comes first. You have your own future to determine, and I'll soon be gone again."

He moved silently up behind her. "And if I offer my service to you, *Aho'Va?*"

"I can't accept." Her hair fell over her face. "Someday you'll understand."

"Then you, like Janek, believe that I am more shaauri than human."

She turned to him, stark and grim. "If you were shaauri, you wouldn't be here."

"If I were shaauri," he said, grasping her arms, "I would not care once the mating was over."

"Let me go, Ronan."

"You send me away, *Aho'Va,*" he said, "because you are ashamed. Ashamed of this . . . thing you imagine when you see yourself."

Her face lost its color. "And what do you see, Ronan, when you look in the mirror? A man who can never be one of the beings who despised and abused you all your life?"

They stared at each other, shocked into silence. Ronan let her go. She had tried to close her mind to him, but he knew he had the power to force himself in, hold her paralyzed like a *myl'vekk*'s prey and drive past her weak defenses. He could bind her will, just as he had done with the guard on the *Pegasus,* so that she could not act to stop him until he was gone from this world with the knowledge he had come to steal.

It was his one chance. His *duty.*

And when it was finished, he would have earned her hatred—she, who saw him as only one other had done. She who had welcomed him, *ne'lin* though he was, into her body.

Her hatred was an unnecessary complication when there were far less clumsy methods of achieving his end. All they required was patience. His hunger for her remained, but Sihvaaro had taught him well. Let Cynara believe her Reckoning had discouraged him before the battle was joined.

"You are right, *Aho'Va,*" he said. "This body is human. For a time it gave you pleasure. I am grateful for the honor." He tossed his shirt and trousers over his shoulder and strode for the door.

"Ronan."

Her voice was so full of regret that he knew his ploy had worked. It was the human way to accept guilt easily. Guilt was a wedge that would leave her vulnerable to him. Next time he would not hesitate to use every means available to defeat her.

"There is no need for more words," he said. "I understand you."

"No, Ronan," she said. "I don't think you do."

Her grief was past bearing. He left her, seeking the open air beyond Jesper's walls. The garden hung heavy with the scent of white flowers. He stripped three of them from their stems before he achieved tranquillity.

We are not lifemates, she had said. Of course they were not. Humans did not truly lifemate, heart and soul and body joined until death. Even if she were shaauri, he could not win her unless he cast away his purpose, his very reason for being.

The stars seemed unusually bright here in this high place, as they had been on the mountain with Sihvaaro. The Dharmans had not yet polluted their skies with countless motor vehicles and factories.

The technology Ronan brought back from the Alliance would prevent humans from polluting shaauri worlds and culture. This alien drive the Dharmans and their allies had discovered—no human could have invented such a marvel, but they were quick enough to exploit it.

The *Pegasus* was only a prototype. She carried among her crew a Persephonean observer—Janek—because the Concordat was eager to produce an entire fleet of similar hybrid ships. Once the Alliance—the Nine Worlds and the Concordat—had many such ships, they could escape shaauri vessels at will. Nothing could prevent the humans' eventual expanse into shaauri-*ja* or inhibit their rapacious appetite for conquest.

Ronan crouched and ran his fingers over the groomed lawn *Magnus* Jesper kept so tame. Tomorrow the Council that ruled the *Pegasus* and its crew would interrogate him. He must appear cooperative and innocent of all deception, playing upon their hatred for the shaauri with the display of his scars.

Above all, he must sustain his guard against Dharman telepaths of more formidable talent. He had no doubt this Council would employ them, if its own members were not sufficiently skilled themselves.

They, like Cynara, would not be prepared for the enemy they faced.

Ronan scattered white petals at his feet and cleared his mind for a long night of meditation.

Chapter 14

Breakfast at Jesper's table was not nearly as tense as Cynara had expected. Ronan came from his room, greeted Jesper courteously, and took a place at the end with an impartial glance in Cynara's direction.

Lizbet seemed aware of a change, though she kept her thoughts to herself. Jesper made oblivious small talk. Earlier that morning Cynara had given her uncle some idea that Ronan's telepathic skills were stronger than she'd suspected, but she hadn't confided the whole truth. Not even to him.

When the conversation turned at last to the Council meeting, Ronan listened and responded exactly the same to Cynara and her uncle.

Last night did not happen. Ronan had taken her warning to heart. All his restrained anger had vanished, and with it the bond that had begun to grow between them. The incredible bond that had convinced her she dared not trust herself to protect the knowledge she carried in her mind.

Madness, this nagging suspicion that Ronan might betray her and the *Pegasus*. She'd had ample proof on Bifrost that he could be trusted with the lives of her crew. Her heart, the one Dharman men would call weak, insisted that her decision had been right.

But Ronan had learned how to wield his lost gift like a master, and even her Kinsman-built shields weren't meant to hold off prolonged, determined probing by an expert.

Any chance, any chance at all, that she was wrong about Ronan meant the destruction of humanity's single, still-frail hope of victory. Even at the cost of his friendship, she had no right to take that risk.

Friendship. She swallowed the bitter dregs of her kaffé and closed her eyes. Ronan had called her his mate.

"If you're finished," Uncle Jesper said, "we should discuss the debriefing. Cynara, Ronan, if you'll join me in my study?"

Cynara dropped her fork. Ronan had already left the table. She followed him to the study and took the chair farthest away.

"To the best of my knowledge," Jesper said, "this will be a simple interrogation. I have been assured that no telepathic probing will be employed without due notification. However, since you are a telepath yourself, Ronan, I suggest that you focus on keeping your mind open to avoid giving the impression of any subterfuge. You may expect that they'll ask you very detailed questions about your background, your time among the shaauri, your reasons for escaping, etc. They will want to be sure that you harbor no lingering loyalty to your captors. The more you tell them, the more likely they'll be to see you as a potential ally."

"That will be no difficulty," Ronan said.

"I will also be there, and Cynara has been granted permission to remain with you during the debriefing. Her testimony of your actions aboard the *Pegasus* will naturally be a point in your favor, and her faith in you, as a fellow telepath, should speak for itself."

"I am grateful."

"I should also warn you that Janek will be present, but he has little actual power. There are several very reasonable men on the Council who will not judge you based upon your apparent origins. Cynara, have you anything to add?"

"No, Uncle. I'll be there if Ronan needs me."

"But I do caution you, Spitfire, not to communicate with him mentally, since it will only arouse suspicions."

"Of course."

Jesper turned back to Ronan and regaled him with some long-winded but useful advice about the Offworld Trade Council, its history and its members. Cynara listened with only half her attention. Ignoring Ronan was one of the hardest things she'd ever done.

"Cynara, it's time we were off."

Jesper squeezed her shoulder lightly and smiled in such a way that she knew he wasn't as oblivious as he'd seemed at breakfast. He'd always known what went on in his own house.

He was dressed magnificently in a slashed velvet doublet of scarlet and an overrobe of silver, fur-trimmed satin, the traditional costume of Dharman elite that had scarcely changed since the coming of the Concordat. No one in the Council would doubt his loyalties, or his prosperity.

There was nothing traditional about Cynara's uniform. It was the finest she owned, made up of the expensive fabrics the burgher-lords of Elsinore considered appropriate to one of her station, though the color was the conservative dark blue of a standard shipsuit. The braids alone cost a small fortune. She made no other concessions to Dharman sensibilities; the uniform included a sleek-fitting set of trousers that conformed perfectly to her body.

At Jesper's recommendation, Ronan wore a plain shipsuit with no additional decoration. Oddly enough, the choice made him appear at once less threatening and more fascinating, as if the very simplicity of his clothing played up the slightly alien grace of his bearing.

Cynara found herself staring and quickly looked away. Ronan pretended not to notice. He exchanged a few quiet words with Lizbet and answered Jesper's summons with a nod.

"No matter what they ask you, my boy, answer as honestly as you can. Keep your mind open, as we discussed."

Ronan accepted the reminders solemnly and turned for the front door.

"Ronan."

He looked at Cynara as if at a stranger. *"Aho'Va."*

"Good luck."

He nodded. She had never seen his eyes so blank of expression, even when he'd first come aboard the *Pegasus*.

"Good luck indeed," Jesper said, and hurried off to the carport, where his driver stood ready to transport him to the Council chambers. They were located in the small business district of High Town, only a few kilometers' drive from his house. Cynara and Ronan were to follow in a second car.

Cynara was acutely aware of Ronan's proximity when they settled in the passenger seat. She tested the mental void between them as if it were an aching tooth. His mind was sealed shut, but he appeared as relaxed as a hunting cat capable of snapping into killing mode at the tap of a dandy's heel.

God forbid that any of the Council should provoke him beyond his control. She had already come very close.

The ornate building that housed the Trade Council chambers had been constructed to celebrate the discovery of the slingshot drive and the subsequent launch of the *Pegasus*. The average Dharman had no idea that the *Pegasus* was anything more than one of the planet's tiny fleet of trade vessels, albeit an extraordinarily lucky one.

Someday the slingshot drive would become public knowledge—once the Allied fleet was constructed and ready to confront the shaauri on a grand scale. Until then, the secret hid in plain sight, contained in a few minds and locked vaults.

But no one had foreseen the possibility that a Kinsman agent might penetrate the Alliance disguised as a refugee. More than Ronan's future depended upon what the Council decided today. If the Council had any doubts about him, they would not only hold him captive but ground Cynara as well.

Perhaps Ronan would have understood her position more clearly if she'd admitted how much she, too, had to lose. But pride and common sense forbade any such admission.

And so they rode together in silence while Cynara clung to her composure by a cat's whisker. The driver let them out at the high, golden doors of the Council building, but an aide met them at a small side entrance and ushered them into the frescoed hall. As Cynara had expected, the entire building was all but deserted.

A pair of discreetly armed guards accompanied Cynara
and Ronan past murals representing the Nine Worlds and into
the tiny waiting room reserved for the subjects of confidential debriefings. Cynara had come prepared for a wait, and
she was not disappointed. She and Ronan were left to cool
their heels, always in clear view of the uniformed guards.

Ronan looked neither to the right nor left, as smooth as
Tarsian glass. There was nothing more Cynara could tell him.
Either he would pass this test and be set free, or he would
prove her judgment as flawed as her soul.

An hour passed, and then another. The guards began to
look bored. It was only when Ronan turned his head toward
the door that Cynara realized someone was approaching.

The guards stepped out into the hall, and after a few minutes
of hushed conversation Kord strode into the room, his
face set in the unreadable expression that always meant trouble.
He stopped and saluted without a glance at Ronan.

"Captain," he said. "I was told I would find you here. I
have an urgent message regarding the *Pegasus*."

"Urgent" from Kord could never be taken lightly. If he
had come all the way here to find her, the message must be
important indeed. And most definitely not for other ears.

Cynara glanced at the guards. They had no reason to suspect either her or Kord of anything remotely treasonous, but
they'd undoubtedly been ordered to keep a very careful eye
on Ronan.

"Gentlemen," Cynara said, rising to face the guards. "My
weapons officer and I have Fleet business to discuss. If you
will allow us to step outside for a few moments, I'm sure it
can be dispatched efficiently."

The guards, men sophisticated enough to accept her rank
with good grace, exchanged glances. The senior nodded.
"Five minutes, Captain," he said. Ronan made no attempt to
follow when she and Kord left the room.

"Your uncle sent me," Kord said as soon as they were
alone. "He's with the Council now and couldn't approach
you directly, but he managed to get a message to me at the
ship. He said he'd delay them as long as possible. I wasn't
sure I would make it before they called you in."

"What is the message?"

"The Council has taken Janek's advice to have Ronan deep-probed. They've convinced *Magnus* Vidar Larsen to do it."

Cynara absorbed the information with amazement. *Magnus* Larsen was one of the few native Dharman telepaths who had been Kinsman-trained before the Second War. In those days the Kinsmen had actively recruited telepaths throughout the Concordat, and he had been among their most promising students. But though he had been offered a high place among them, he had preferred to remain on his homeworld.

There was no more powerful telepath on Dharma, and few in the Alliance now that most Kinsmen had gone to the shaauri. Larsen was the man to whom Elsinore's aristocrats sent their young men for basic training in mental control.

Damn you, Janek. Damn you to the deepest Anubian hell.

"I don't understand the ways of mindwalkers, Little Mother," Kord said, "but even I know that a man's brain can be destroyed by that kind of examination."

As Jesper knew. The procedure was all but forbidden on Persephone. No one on Elsinore had resorted to it for many years. Even if Ronan cooperated fully, the chances were great that he would suffer permanent damage. If he resisted, even by instinct, he could be stripped to the mental level of a fishflea.

That was why Jesper had undermined the Council and offered this clandestine warning, leaving the rest up to Cynara's judgment.

Her decision. Her choice whether to take the risk that Ronan was everything she assumed, or let him undergo the probe on the chance that he wasn't. Preserve one life, or preserve a secret that might save hundreds of thousands.

One life that had become dearer to her than her own.

The shock of that realization staggered her. Kord caught her arm.

"Cynara?"

"I'm all right. Thank you for getting this to me."

"What will you do?"

No matter what she decided, Kord would accept. But Ronan was his blood-brother. If she refused to save him,

Kord would probably make the attempt, torn in two by conflicting loyalties.

She was captain of the *Pegasus*. There should be no conflict for her. The decision should be as simple as that of choosing between fighting the shaauri or surrendering without a single weapon fired.

Either way a betrayal. Either choice with potential consequences too terrible to imagine.

Head and heart. Man and woman, as Dharman belief would have it—logic the male principle, chaotic emotion the female. She knew exactly what Tyr would do.

She met Kord's gaze. "The *Thalassa*'s waiting?"

"Basterra told me he wouldn't be ready to lift for several more hours."

"If Ronan is what Janek obviously believes, we may be handing the *Pegasus* to the shaauri."

"If he were what Janek believes, I would take his life myself."

Nothing more needed to be said. Kord found concealment behind a potted plant in the hall, and Cynara returned to the waiting room. She gave Ronan a single significant glance.

"Officer," she said, addressing the senior guard, "I have a message for the Council that cannot wait. Can you deliver it for me?"

"Captain, our orders—"

"This information will impact the debriefing. I can't understate its importance."

The guard hesitated and gestured to his partner. "Brion, take the captain's message and return immediately."

Cynara pulled a pad and stylus out of her pocket and dashed off a note with convincing gravity. She folded the paper and presented it to Brion.

"See that this gets to *Magnus* Jesper Siannas without delay."

Brion set off and his senior resumed his post near the door, very much on the alert. Soon afterward there was the sound of something heavy falling in the hall, and then resounding silence.

It was enough to pull the guard's attention away for a few precious seconds. Cynara dived for his gun. Ronan moved at almost the same instant. Cynara kicked the guard's weapon from his hands and flung herself after it, while Ronan leaped like a cat and downed the guard with a chopping motion of his arm.

Cynara rolled to her feet with the gun in hand. The guard was sprawled on the marble floor, apparently unconscious but showing no outward signs of injury.

"Is he all right?" she asked Ronan.

"He will be." Ronan cocked his head at her, a new brightness in his gaze. "Kord has taken the other?"

"If we don't hear an alarm." She shifted her grip on the gun and glanced toward the door. "We have to leave."

"Will you not suffer punishment for this action?"

Trust Ronan to ask the most essential questions. "I'll worry about that later."

Kord appeared in the doorway, breathing hard. "He's out."

"Let's go."

The three of them ran down the hall and took a smaller corridor to the side entrance. Once on the street, Cynara assumed a nonchalant demeanor and pocketed the gun. She led Kord and Ronan to the garage where the Council members often left their vehicles. Several cars were housed there, including Jesper's. Not a driver was in sight.

The key to Jesper's car was still in the ignition. Kord pushed Ronan into the passenger compartment. "I'll see you at the ship," he said. "I have one more task to complete."

"Go," she said, never doubting that Kord would be at the *Thalassa* in time for takeoff. "Be careful." She turned the key in the ignition and the motor hummed to life. "Bless you, Uncle."

No one appeared to stop them as she pulled the car out of the garage and into the street, slipping easily into the light traffic. It was good to feel in control again, even if this vehicle was confined to lowly earth.

"Do you know what happened?" she asked Ronan through the open partition.

"Kord brought a warning."

"From my uncle. The Council was planning to subject you

to a deep-probe. It might have permanently damaged your mind."

"Then I owe you great thanks."

Spoken as sincerely as any diplomat could wish. "Save the thanks. We still may not get off Dharma."

"You will find a way."

"Your confidence inspires me." She clutched the wheel and turned onto Gate Street. Still no pursuit. "I take it that we're on speaking terms again?"

"Are we not speaking now?"

She laughed through her teeth. "We're going to be spending more time together, Ronan, so I hope we've reached an understanding. What I said before still obtains. I won't see you destroyed because of blind suspicion, but neither will I risk the welfare of my people."

He was quiet all the way to Second Gate. "You will take me to the Concordat."

There wasn't really any other choice. None of the other Nine Worlds had native telepaths who could handle Ronan if the worst should come to pass. Persephone's laws wouldn't allow the mental rape of even a convicted criminal, let alone a man who might—Poseidon, *must*—be innocent of any ulterior purpose.

"I'll take you to Persephone," she said.

"Will they accept you if Dharma does not?"

Oh, he knew how much she risked in helping him. "I don't plan to abandon Dharma."

"You will be challenged as First of the *Pegasus*."

"I think what you mean by 'challenge' is not what the Council will have in mind," she said. "I wish it were that simple."

"If Janek challenges you, you would win."

"I'll take that as a compliment."

The sense of camaraderie born on Bifrost had returned. She ached with the warmth of it, ached with the memory of last night and the miraculous, fleeting bond between two minds and hearts.

Losing the *Pegasus* was not the worst thing that could happen.

First Gate still stood open. Likely the alarm had been

raised by now, but it hadn't reached Low Town. Cynara couldn't risk calling the shuttle, for there was a very real chance that the Council might intercept any communication. She accelerated past shacks and stubbled fields onto the highway toward the spaceport. Vehicles here were few and far between, but she and Ronan could still be stopped at the port.

Incredibly, the guard at the sentry post waved her through as soon as he recognized her. She could feel Ronan relaxing, well aware that he had been preparing for a fight.

"This is *Va* Jesper's doing," he remarked as Cynara sped across the field to the service area where the *Thalassa* was berthed. She swerved around a maintenance truck and set a straight course for the shuttle.

Dockhands who had been loading the hold under Cargomaster Basterra's supervision turned to stare as Cynara pulled up fifty meters from the shuttle. Ronan was out of the car before it came to a stop.

"Captain," Basterra called, striding toward her. "We didn't expect you back for two days. I have three pallets left for the *Pegasus*, and—"

"I know, Cargomaster. I need to speak to you. Please come with me."

Basterra glanced at Ronan with a frown. "*Ser* Janek—"

Ronan moved up behind Basterra, who thought better of further argument. The three of them climbed the ramp into the shuttle. Cynara steered Basterra into the passenger compartment and glanced into the cockpit. The pilot for this run was not, unfortunately, Lizbet. Cynara could only hope that Jesper had thought of sending a message to her as well.

"Something has come up, Cargomaster," she said. "Council's orders. I must return to the *Pegasus* immediately. The rest of the cargo can come later."

"If you will show me the orders, Captain—"

"Are you questioning my authority?" She smiled in Basterra's face. "There is at least one informant aboard the *Pegasus,* Basterra. I know you've got your own contacts in the Council, and dubious loyalty to me. Still, I wouldn't advise direct defiance."

Basterra backed down with the usual bluster and bumped

into Ronan, who also smiled. The expression looked uncomfortably alien on his face.

"Ronan, please stay with the Cargomaster while I speak to the pilot." *Don't be too late, Kord.* She caught a final glimpse of Basterra's worried face before Ronan herded him into one of the seats.

Second Pilot Jauregi had more respect than to question her order to prepare the shuttle for imminent departure. "The tower is hailing us, Captain," he said.

"No response." The controller on duty might howl, but they weren't likely to shoot at the shuttle or its crew without explicit Council authority.

Jauregi resumed systems checks while Cynara took a quick survey of the shuttle and retrieved her sidearm from her locker. Some crew were still at large on Dharma, but that couldn't be helped. She'd have enough essential personnel to take the *Pegasus* where it needed to go.

One of the dockhands came up the ramp and stuck his head through the hatch. "Cargomaster?"

"We're preparing for emergency departure," Cynara said before Basterra could speak. "Please seal the hold and move your men away from the perimeter."

The men who loaded cargo, whether onto a starship or a seagoing vessel, were used to taking orders. The dockhand shrugged and went back down. Out the open hatch Cynara saw a car speeding across the field.

Either it was Kord, or someone bent on stopping them. "Strap in, Ronan," she advised. "As for you, Basterra—"

But Ronan was already moving past her into the cockpit. He emerged with an unconscious Jauregi over his shoulder.

"Your *an'laik'in* was disobedient, *Aho'Va,*" he said, dumping Jauregi onto the deck. "He intended to impede our departure. I will take his place."

She threw a hard look at Basterra, little doubting where Jauregi's true loyalty lay. "You can pilot the shuttle?"

"It should not be difficult."

Ronan didn't wait for her decision. He settled in the pilot's seat, his hands flying over the controls.

"Cargo hatch is sealed," he reported. "All systems green."

Down on the field, the dockhands had moved well away

from the shuttle. The approaching car skidded to a stop at the foot of the ramp. The passenger door flew open.

Lizbet jumped out, a pack slung over her back. The car began moving again, and Kord abandoned the vehicle while it rolled in a wide circle away from the *Thalassa.*

"About time," Cynara said as Kord and Lizbet hurtled through the hatch. "Ronan?"

The engine hummed under her feet. "One minute."

"Cargomaster, you may leave the shuttle with your pilot. You will not be seeing the *Pegasus* again."

Basterra eyed her as if he were actually considering attack. Kord heaved Jauregi from the deck and shoved him into Basterra's arms. Siroccan was a language beautifully adapted for elegant cursing.

"Ready, *Aho'va,*" Ronan called. Kord propelled Basterra down the ramp and sprinted back to take his seat.

Cynara ran a final check and strapped in. Bulkheads vibrated. The hatch closed and just as suddenly opened again.

Janek walked into the passenger compartment, turned, and sealed the hatch behind him. He clutched a small black object in one hand. Cynara aimed her gun at his head.

He dropped the object and raised his hands. Lizbet left her seat and picked it up.

"A remote, Captain," she said. "With an override for the hatch lock."

"Well, *Ser* Janek," Cynara said. "So glad you could join us. Ronan, take her up."

Chapter 15

Janek had a few seconds to grab at the bulkhead before the shuttle lifted. He stumbled his way to a seat and strapped in, staring through the open cockpit door.

"Our refugee is certainly a man of many talents," he said. "Do you know what you've done, Captain?"

Cynara relaxed in her seat and smiled. "I'm taking him to Persephone. I'm making sure he gets to the right people who will protect as well as question him."

"You've committed treason, both to your government and mine."

"I understand it was your idea to have Ronan deep-probed, *Ser* Janek."

"You knew it was necessary from the moment he revealed telepathic abilities, particularly after he disabled Bhruic."

"I knew it was necessary, but not your way." She closed her eyes as the shuttle shot skyward. "If you disapprove so heartily, why did you come? You can't expect to change my mind."

"Nor do I intend to abandon my duty as you have done. I'll present my position to Naval Headquarters on Persephone—unless you plan to silence me."

"As much as I'd like to strangle you, Janek, I'm no assassin. You'll have your say, and so will I." She leaned toward him in a confidential attitude. "Did I ever mention that Lord Miklos Challinor was my uncle's good friend years ago, when they both served in the Royal Navy? *Magnus* Jesper encouraged me to go to Miklos if I had certain . . . problems."

"The Archon's brother is much too busy to deal with the likes of—"

"A source of potentially vital intelligence such as Ronan might turn out to be? Or by the same token, a man who could become the downfall of Allied civilization, as you seem to believe? I think Lord Miklos will be most interested."

Janek subsided into his seat with an expression like an overripe gelfruit, but Cynara knew she hadn't heard the last from him. He would bear even more careful watching.

"Lizbet, has Kord briefed you on our situation? You understand that we're making an unauthorized departure?"

"Yes, Captain."

Cynara nodded and glanced at Kord. "As much as I hate to burden you, Kord, I'm assigning *Ser* Janek to your custody until we reach the Concordat."

"Two of my marines are still on Dharma," Janek protested, rising. "There are only two still on board the *Pegasus,* another breach of"—he glanced at Kord—"protocol."

"That is unfortunate, but I'm sure your marines will find no lack of hospitality on Dharma until we return."

"Do you intend to return to face charges, Captain? I can bring them just as easily on Persephone."

Kord moved up beside Janek and took his arm. "Courtesy," he said softly. "I would not wish to have to silence you."

Janek folded his arms across his chest, choosing to preserve his dignity. "What of Ronan, Little Mother?" Kord asked.

What of Ronan indeed. "Our aim is to reach Concordat space as efficiently as possible and deliver him intact to Lord Miklos or his people while preserving the ship's integrity. We'll do whatever is necessary to achieve that end."

Janek jerked his arm from Kord's grip. "I see," he said. "You have 'rescued' Ronan from what you perceive as a threat to his welfare, and yet you clearly do not trust him. What has happened between you, Captain? What has created such a contradictory perspective?" He took a step toward her. "You have learned something, haven't you? You *know* how dangerous he is—"

Kord twisted Janek's arm behind his back. "I warned you," he said. "The captain owes you no explanation."

"But you'll have to explain sooner or later," Janek said, hissing in pain. "If Ronan has penetrated your shields, everything is at risk."

Cynara refused to let him see how close he had come to the truth. "On Persephone," she said, "and no sooner. I suggest that you order your marines to maintain their duties and cooperate, or it may be necessary to throw you in the brig." She turned her back and listened for communications from the comlink, but Ronan either had the volume turned very low or he'd shut it off. Dharma had a few in-system ships it could send after the *Pegasus,* but they would be occupied with the mining operation in the cometary halo and wouldn't be able to reach the wormhole in time.

Ronan handled the shuttle as if he'd been born to it—no surprise given his skill with the shaauri darter. She didn't interrupt him until the shuttle reached rendezvous orbit with the *Pegasus.* Then she joined him in the cockpit and hailed the ship, trusting that Adumbe wouldn't question her orders.

The shuttle bay doors opened without a hitch, and Ronan guided the *Thalassa* smoothly into its berth. Adumbe and several crewmen were waiting when she and the others disembarked.

"Captain," Taye said, one brow raised as he noted the number of passengers, "I did not expect your return so soon."

"I know. I'll have a full explanation for you in the briefing room, once we're under way. Is the *Pegasus* ready to leave orbit?"

"As you ordered, Captain. I—"

"Scholar-Commander Adumbe," Janek said, pushing his way forward, "I advise you that Captain D'Accorso has acted in defiance of the Trade Council and has abducted a guest—"

"Guest?" Kord snorted.

"—before the debriefing ordered by the Council. It is your clear duty to arrest the captain and return Ronan VelKalevi to Dharman authorities, under my jurisdiction."

Adumbe's eyebrows rose still higher. "Indeed. I suspected that something had gone very much awry. Nevertheless, I am sure that Captain D'Accorso had excellent motive for her actions," He turned to Cynara. "*Ser* Janek—"

"I am to watch him until we reach Persephone," Kord said. "Captain's orders."

"In that case—yes, Captain D'Accorso, we are ready to depart at your command."

"Excellent." Cynara suppressed the desire to smile wickedly at Janek. "Lizbet, to the bridge. Ronan, I am confining you to your cabin for the duration of the flight."

Their gazes met. "Yes, Captain," he said.

"The same applies to you, *Ser* Janek," she said. "You will surrender your passcard to *Ser* O'Deira until we reach the Concordat."

"You have no right—"

Kord twisted his arm a little more tightly. Janek went pale. Kord steered his two charges, Ronan cooperative and Janek surly, to the passenger lift. Cynara fell in step with Adumbe and caught the service lift to the bridge.

"All's well?" she asked.

"Yes, Captain." His brown eyes sparkled. "I'll be most interested to hear the story behind this daring escapade."

"Why, Taye—I think you like adventures more than you ever let on." She gripped his shoulder. "I want you to know that I appreciate your loyalty, but if you have any doubts about throwing your lot in with me—"

"No doubts, Captain. And aside from Toussaint and one or two other Dharman crewmen aboard, I believe I speak for everyone."

"With Basterra aground, the Dharmans won't make any trouble. I'll be sure to inform the Council that they had no choice in the matter. As for the two marines left on Dharma, I'll deal with that when the time comes. We'll take the strictest security measures to make up for their absence."

"Janek may file a diplomatic protest on Persephone."

"Let him. Once I speak to Lord Miklos, I doubt he'll have

much to say about it. As for Dharma and the Council—" She shrugged with far more nonchalance than she felt. "I think I'll have enough influence left to recommend you for the captaincy."

"You anticipate being relieved of command."

"They were always looking for an excuse, and now they have it. I trust you to do the job, Taye. If necessary, I'll offer my services to the Persephonean Navy."

"That would be a pity, Captain."

"And perhaps premature. The universe is full of possibilities."

They reached the bridge. Lizbet was back at her post, still in civilian clothing. Bendik Toussaint held the weapons console. He stared at Cynara with obvious hostility.

"If you wish to resign your post, Toussaint," Cynara said, taking the captain's chair, "you may do so without penalty. I will advise the Council that you were an unwilling participant in this action."

Toussaint lowered his gaze. "We will be passing through the Shaauriat, Captain. You will need all weapons personnel."

"Yes. But you will either follow my orders without question, or I will dismiss you to quarters."

"Aye, Captain."

She put him from her thoughts and called the infirmary to exchange a quick greeting with Dr. Zheng, then accepted status reports from all bridge stations. Taye had everything ready, and it remained only to give the command.

She did. The *Pegasus* broke orbit and leaped away from Dharma, grazing the stars with spread wings.

Home. Space was home as Dharma could never be. And if her doubts and fears about Ronan proved as empty as vacuum, the loss of the *Pegasus* would be well worth the sacrifice.

If not . . . Scylla take it, let that ocean be crossed when she came to it.

K*ord closed the door to the cabin and stood just inside,* as grim as Ronan had ever seen him.

"Well, my Brother?" he asked. "What has happened to make Cynara look at you like the bottom of a dry well?"

The metaphor was apt. A man from a desert world might well regard an empty well with longing, resentment, and fear, as a human would look upon lost hopes.

"I'd be sun-blind if I couldn't see what was brewing between you," Kord said, sitting on the edge of Ronan's bunk. "I know—" He glanced at the bulkhead. "I know that you were together at *Magnus* Jesper's."

Together. Did Kord truly know what that meant? "We both had lodgings there."

"And Janek was right, wasn't he? She discovered something about you that alarmed her, even though she was prepared to risk her captaincy to get you away from the Council."

Ronan sat down beside Kord and clasped his hands between his knees. "It is for *Aho'Va* to speak of such things as she wills," he said. "I honor her courage and intelligence."

"Do you? The captain didn't lock you in this cabin without reason." He leaned forward. "Tell me now, Brother. Do you intend harm to her or this ship?"

Did Kord trust that he would tell the truth, that the blood-bond between them was just as serious a matter to Ronan as it was to the Siroccan? How could he assume so much?

Yet he was correct. Ronan owed Kord for the escape from Dharma, but there was more to this bond than gratitude. Ronan could not regard it lightly, not even for the sake of his mission.

"I mean no harm to Cynara," he said, "nor to the crew of the *Pegasus.*"

"I believe you. But my belief is of no importance. Whatever the captain commands, I must do. I swore loyalty to her as my Watergiver—my clan mother."

"She honors you greatly."

"But it is you she has chosen." Kord met his gaze, stark and serious. "There is a new strain between you, Brother. And it is because you are my brother that I warn you again: Do not hurt her. Do not betray her trust. She doubts herself when she can least afford such distractions." He shook his head. "I know little of these powers of the mind, but this thing you share can either bind you or drive you apart. Do not waste this great gift."

He rose suddenly and strode for the door. "Remember what I've said, Brother."

The door sealed behind him—locked, to be opened only by those with explicit permission, or by bearers of the few passcards that bestowed admittance to every part of the ship. Cynara had such a card, and so had Janek before she demanded its surrender. There must be others as well.

Ronan's conversation with Kord had changed nothing; it had only reminded him of the odds he faced. He must find schematics on the *Pegasus*'s engines or, barring that, a way into the engine room without harming the crew of the *Pegasus*.

Seducing Cynara was clearly out of the question, but not because of Kord's warning or even the barriers Cynara had placed between them. The hesitation was in his own heart. He had pushed too hard with her and dared not do so again.

She was his enemy. She always had been, no matter how much he had pretended otherwise. The pain he felt now was apt punishment for losing sight of the truth. Sihvaaro had told him a thousand times that all suffering was transient, meaningless in the face of eternity as one Path apart from the others.

He lay on the bunk, pushing aside the pillows and blankets in favor of the hard, fortifying metal surface. He was still awake when the door opened and Archimedes the cat ran in and leaped onto his chest.

"I'm sorry," Cynara said in the doorway. "Did I wake you?"

"No." He gathered Archie into his arms and held the thrumming animal tucked under his chin. His heart had begun to beat very hard. Stroking the cat gave him some measure of control over his disobedient emotions. "You are well, *Aho'Va*?"

"Quite well. I thought you might appreciate a little company, and Archie seems to like you." She made an odd, dismissive gesture and smiled. "This isn't likely to be a very interesting voyage for you."

"I am interested in the fact that you have saved my life, or at least my mind." He scratched Archie between the ears. "How do humans pay such debts?"

She folded her hands behind her back and leaned against the door. "You don't owe me anything."

He chose not to pursue that course. "Have we entered shaauri space?"

"Not yet, but we're approaching the first border crossing. Unless something goes very wrong, we should be able to evade shaauri patrols and make an uneventful run." She cleared her throat. "When this is over—" She looked at him, skin taut and pale. "If you join us, I hope that we can remain friends."

Friends, that odd and very human word. He set Archie down and stood. Cynara tensed.

"I know you no longer trust me," he said. "I understand. Because of you, my mind has reawakened and I cannot yet master it. I also know what you may have given up for my sake. Whatever the future holds, I will never forget."

"Neither will I. Not as long as I live."

Though she guarded her mind, her feelings washed over him, mingling with his own so violently that he found it necessary to lean back against the bulkhead.

Cynara pounded the door lock with her fist. She was halfway into the corridor before she stopped.

"Swear to me, Ronan," she said in a whisper. "Swear that you will make no attempts to enter my mind."

What she asked was impossible, as desperate and hopeless as a *ne'lin*'s challenge for First. Yet she waited for his answer. Waited, as if she believed she, like Kord, could still trust his word.

"I swear," he said. "I will not try to enter your mind without permission."

She turned her head, and he caught a glimpse of her distress. Then she was gone.

In the silence of the cabin, Ronan began to shake. Archie's rubbing and kneading offered little comfort.

There was no day or night on the *Pegasus.* Ronan felt the ship's vibrations change when it entered and exited a wormhole, or engaged the mysterious alien drive. No alarms sounded, nor indications of shaauri interference or pursuit.

Meals were delivered to Ronan's cabin, and he ate them to maintain his strength. He performed Sihvaaro's *vek'riam* exercises, designed to develop absolute command over muscle and movement, warrior's strikes slowed to a fraction of their usual speed.

And he prepared himself for what must be done. When his fourth meal was delivered, he cautiously touched the crewman's mind, seeking a single piece of information. Unlike Cynara, this man had no shields and went on his way unsuspecting.

Ronan pushed his meal aside untasted. What he planned was within his powers. He had used the technique all unknowing on a *Pegasus* guard before he regained his memory and sense of purpose. He had felt his mental strength building with each passing day. But to walk in another mind at a distance—a mind he had never touched, certainly shielded—and then to compel such a mind to do his will was a dangerous and terrible matter.

The Kinsmen had claimed to despise mental intrusion, yet they used such methods on Ronan. They had sent him here expecting that he would not hesitate to do the same. At the very least, the process weakened the wielder and brought grave discomfort and illness.

Ronan had not lied to Kord when he'd said he would not harm the crew. The one he sought to move to his will would have only vague memories of dreams, unable to explain if others questioned her later. No permanent damage would be done to her mind or her being.

Lying back on the bunk, Ronan recited the Eightfold Way until his mind was calm and his heartbeat slow and steady. For a time he simply breathed. At last he began the seeking, stretching his mind beyond his cabin, into the corridor, past the crewmen and women in their quarters or at their posts, down and down into the heart of the ship.

Seeking. He avoided the guarded mind of the single Persephonean marine who watched the door to engineering and envisioned another face he had seen only once: the close-cropped hair, the tall and sturdy body, the ease of manner he had observed in the mess.

Charis. Charis Antoniou.

She did not answer, for she did not truly hear. Yet he found her, caught a glimpse of her surroundings through eyes not his own. Numerous consoles, screens alight with complex graphics and scrolling numbers, were attended by crew in shipsuits marked with the designation of their post.

In Charis's thoughts was the contentment of one engaged in a true Path: concentration, devotion to her work, and benevolent feelings toward her fellows. She had no telepathic abilities whatsoever, and did not sense Ronan's presence. So much was simple enough.

But almost the moment Ronan touched Charis's mind, he felt the shield. This female who ruled engineering, who knew the ship's secrets as well as the captain herself, must also be protected from the very trespass Ronan attempted.

That was why Cynara had considered it enough to confine Ronan to his cabin during the voyage to Persephone. Her own shield had given way only when she and Ronan had engaged in sex, but she did not realize how much. If Ronan could not reach Charis, the engineer must be safe.

Ronan floated on the edge of Charis's mind, forcing nothing, allowing her to concentrate on her work without venturing to interpret it. Gradually he inserted a thought into the flow of ceaseless mental chatter, so delicately that her shield was not disturbed.

Go see Ronan, the thought suggested. He did not try to produce a reason that might seem implausible to one he did not know, and who did not know him. He let it take gentle hold and work its way deeper until it became fully a part of her consciousness.

Go see Ronan. He felt her mind trip on the notion, move away, and return to it until it became a nagging buzz she could no longer ignore. He saw through her eyes again as she left her console, exchanged a few words with one of her assistants, and walked toward the door.

She did not speak to the guard as she entered the corridor. Ronan clung to the fringes of her consciousness, allowing the compulsion to carry her to him.

Time was measured in heartbeats. Charis's presence grew nearer. He heard footsteps on the deck outside the cabin, and then a scrape on the door. It slid open.

Ronan was already on his feet, light-headed with the effort of influencing Charis's mind and controlling his own. The engineer stood in the entrance, her passcard in one raised hand. Her eyes held the blankness of surprise.

"*An* Charis," he said, bowing his head. "I am pleased to see you again."

Chapter 16

C *haris blinked.* "Ser *Ronan. I*—" *She glanced around* the cabin. "I had to see you. But I seem . . . I seem to have forgotten—"

"Will you sit?" he asked. "I have little to offer, but I have kept this cake from the morning meal. You have not eaten today."

"As a matter of fact, I—" She sat down heavily, legs sprawled, and dropped the passcard onto the bunk. "Captain said the Dharmans tried to do something to your mind and we had to get you away. You all right?"

"Very well, thank you." He unwrapped the cake in its napkin and presented it. "I wished to express my admiration for your extraordinary skill in maintaining such a vessel."

"Thanks." She took a bite of the cake with obvious pleasure. "This isn't bad. They're always nagging me to eat down in engineering, but I forget—" Her brow wrinkled, and she pinched the bridge of her nose. "I had something important to tell you, but damned if it hasn't slipped my mind."

"Perhaps when we reach Persephone," he said, "you can tell me more of your world."

"Be glad to. Goddess knows I'm happy to help anyone who's been through what you have." She finished the cake and dusted her fingers on her shipsuit. "Well, I have to apologize. My memory just isn't what it used to be when I was younger—but it's enough to get this bucket of bolts around, I guess." She stood, and her hand felt for the passcard.

You don't need it, Ronan suggested. *It is necessary only for emergencies. This is not an emergency.*

Charis froze, staring at the bulkhead. Then she shook her head and blinked one of her eyes in a gesture humans used to indicate shared secrets.

"Well," she said, "I hope it works out between you and the captain. I'd better get back to work." Leaving the passcard on the bunk, she strolled out of the cabin. Ronan quickly closed the door and dropped the passcard in his pocket. He did not entirely leave Charis's mind until she had reached engineering, spoken to the marine on duty, and returned to her console. It was, for her, as if nothing had happened.

Sickness overwhelmed him. He fell to his knees on the deck and clutched his stomach, which threatened to spill its meager contents. A pounding darkness crouched behind his eyelids.

He had succeeded. Charis wouldn't notice the absence of the card until she needed it again—unlikely, since retinal scans were usually sufficient for access to every restricted portion of the ship. She would simply assume she'd misplaced it.

But it was Ronan's way in, once he got past the marine at the door. He must act quickly to gather information before the ship arrived at Persephone.

Without a few hours of rest, he would be useless for such an operation. He crawled to his bunk and fell across it, summoning the Way to hold his unruly gut in check. He slept, and when he awoke again, it was to the wail of sirens.

The clock by Ronan's bunk showed that several hours had passed. He remained where he was, fighting the blackness in his skull, and listened. The ship shuddered.

"Repeat, all crew to stations," the intercom spat from the overhead. *"We are under attack by shaauri vessels. Brace for return fire and drive activation."*

Adumbe's voice. The ship shuddered again, hit by enemy fire.

There would be no better opportunity than this. The crew must be aware of the circumstances of Ronan's rescue and the fact that he was confined to quarters. But few crewmen or women would be in the corridors during an attack, and Ronan counted on the probability that the current crisis would prevent any crew he met from pausing to question him.

He was far from certain that his strength would sustain him long enough to complete his job and return to his cabin undetected. Should the shaauri succeed in catching or destroying the *Pegasus,* that would hardly matter.

He got up, tested his balance, and opened the door left unlocked by Charis's passcard. He paused there for several minutes, waiting for his vision to clear. Voices echoed at the far end of the corridor. The siren continued to wail.

The way to engineering was still imprinted in memory from his first boarding of the *Pegasus,* though he had noted it without knowledge of what he would do with the information later. He crouched and ran near the wall to the lift that served crew quarters. No one saw him. The lift was empty.

He took it down two decks and pressed to the bulkhead as the door opened. A technician waited outside. Ronan touched the man's mind, envisioning emptiness, and the crewman stepped into the lift without noticing him. Ronan slipped past him into the corridor.

Immediately he relinquished control and staggered the next few meters, gathering strength. He evaded the next woman he encountered by dodging into an empty storeroom. Most of the corridors on this level were deserted, because the crew who maintained the *Pegasus* were all at their posts.

That meant he would have many minds to cloud once he penetrated engineering. But first he had to pass the guard. The marine stood alert, rifle held across his chest as if he expected imminent attack.

Ronan flattened to the bulkhead just out of the guard's view and probed the man's mind with a touch light as morning mist. The man had been trained to expect mental intrusion, and his shield held firm. Ronan could not compel the marine to perform even the simplest task, but he might create an image the man would believe for a few essential moments.

One chance, and one only. *The corridor is empty,* he projected, wrapping the suggestion in a pleasant, innocuous fog. *No one approaches from any direction. No movement, no threat.*

The marine looked through Ronan as he stalked to the doors. *Silence. Emptiness.* Ronan punched the passcard into the slot. The guard glanced toward him. Ronan went still. The man stared in the opposite direction.

The door opened. Ronan made himself small and stole inside, and the door closed automatically. Space opened up before him, dominated by a massive central structure, ovoid in shape, a dragon's egg piercing the deck on which he stood. Its base rested on the deck below, visible from a railed landing circling the egg. Walkways provided access to the ovoid's surface, its multifaceted metallic skin made of no material Ronan had ever seen.

Extending from the egg to the bulkheads were numerous frosted conduits and thick cables, haphazardly laid across the deck or suspended above it with no apparent thought to order or harmony. The entire assemblage was a kind of grotesque hybrid, very much like the *Pegasus* itself appeared from the outside.

Ronan crept closer to the edge of the landing. Banks upon banks of electronics hugged the bulkhead from the lower deck to the overhead of the second deck. Nearly every centimeter of deckspace was filled with consoles. Crewmen and women hurried among them, consulting monitors filled with scrolling data, complex equations, and multicolored waveform displays—far too many screens for a single technician to remain at any one post. *An* Charis moved from station to station, giving orders or answering questions. Her aspect was both stern and apprehensive.

Ronan kept to the deck and the shadows, relying on simple stealth. The very air hummed with the agitation of beings intent on survival, their minds focused entirely on the preservation of the ship and its precious drive.

Such grim preoccupation made it easier for Ronan to cloud minds, for the crewfolk were already convinced that nothing existed outside of their vital duties. Even so, the strain was great. Any inattention on his part would expose him to discovery, yet he had to reserve some part of his mind for the work at hand.

The datastream displays were in a technical language mostly beyond Ronan's experience, but he understood enough of it to know what he was looking for. At last he found it on a single monitor left unattended for a few crucial minutes.

Ronan scanned the room for a data slide and found one at the adjoining console. Moving slowly to maintain the illusion of invisibility, he inserted the slide into the recess of his console.

Only one step remained. He searched for the download icon on the screen.

And stopped, as if someone had stayed his hand.

"I know little of these powers of the mind, but this thing you share can either bind you or drive you apart. Do not waste this great gift."

Ronan's concentration wavered. One of the crew turned toward him with a frown.

You cannot.

He withdrew into himself, becoming small and insignificant once more. The technician looked away. Sickness gathered in Ronan's throat, and tremors seized his legs. He could no longer feel his fingers. Abruptly the sirens ceased, fading into a whine that deafened Ronan to every sound but that of his own heartbeat.

"Attention all sections," a distant voice announced. "We have cleared shaauri space. Status and damage reports to captain's console in ten minutes."

Other voices, other thoughts crowded Ronan's mind. He was beginning to lose control of them. Now that the crisis was over, someone would seek him in his cabin and find him absent. Cynara would know him for what he was.

He turned blindly toward the section door. It opened without warning and the marine stepped through.

"Chief Antoniou," he called.

The man's suspicion swept over Ronan like suffocating vapor, and he dropped into a crouch. Centimeter by centimeter he crawled along the deck. The guard walked past him. Ronan felt for the door panel and slotted the passcard. It jammed, and he wasted costly seconds prying it loose. With the last of his fading concentration he stumbled out the doors, maintaining the facade of invisibility until he had reached the nearest cross-corridor.

Only his instinct for survival and Sihvaaro's training got him back to his cabin undetected. Sight and sound ran together in a nauseating miasma. His brain was a heavy, useless organ, incapable of the least or simplest exercise. He fell to his knees and reached the cabin's facilities in time to empty his stomach.

Failure.

Not strong enough. All the training, all the preparation was insufficient to make up for his weakness. But the greatest shame lay not in his lack of skill, but in his hesitation.

The very moment he could have succeeded, he had thought of Cynara. And Kord, and Lizbet, and all the others he must betray. He had remembered, too well, that he was born human.

If they came for him now, he would be glad.

He crept to the foot of his bunk and lay on the cold deck as once he had lain on pebbles as a child, learning to bear discomfort and sleep under any conditions. But he did not sleep. A warm, fur-covered body grazed his cheek, and he remembered *Li* Hanno's gentleness when she had cleaned and bound his wounds.

Archie settled at the hollow of Ronan's neck, feet neatly tucked under his body, and purred consolation. Ronan permitted himself to remember a time when he had dreamed of such unconditional acceptance.

"And what do you see, Ronan, when you look in the mirror? A man who can never be one of the beings who despised and abused you all your life?"

Ronan rolled to face the bulkhead and drew his knees up to his chest. Dreamless sleep came at last. He woke again long enough to climb onto the bunk and pull Archie into the crook of his arm. He was functional again when Kord tapped on the door and let himself in.

"You're awake," Kord observed. "The last time I came, you slept like the serpents of Iskar."

Ronan sat up against the bulkhead and ran his hand through his hair. Kord's surface thoughts were empty of suspicion or memory of disturbance other than the shaauri attack, but he was puzzled and concerned. The cabin stank of sickness.

Ronan set Archie aside and stretched his muscles one by one. He had no valid reason for asking about Cynara. "Is all well with the ship? There was no damage from the shaauri?"

"None of importance. It was simple misfortune that we encountered the patrol." He cocked his head. "You were ill."

"It was nothing. I must have eaten incompatible food."

Kord was unsatisfied, but he let it pass. "We're only sixteen hours from the last wormhole to Persephone Station. The captain intends to take you down as soon as we make orbit." He wrinkled his nose. "You'd better change your clothes. Even a fool of a Dharman burgher could smell you ten kilometers away."

"I will not disappoint those to whom I owe so much."

Kord sat on his heels. "If I spoke too harshly before—"

"That would not be possible." Ronan got up and unsealed the neck of his shipsuit. "I will be ready to meet the captain's allies."

"Be wary of them, Ronan. Their world is named for a woman, but its ways are not those of the Mother."

"I will remember." He tossed his soiled shipsuit into the laundry chute and stepped into the shower. When he emerged, Kord was gone.

Ronan cleaned the cabin, dressed in a fresh shipsuit, and fed Archie his evening meal. He dropped Charis's passcard in the disposal, where it would instantly be reduced to its component atoms. Then he sat cross-legged on his bunk and waited for any indication that his activities had been discovered.

No one came for him. No alarm was raised. He had ruined his greatest opportunity to acquire the drive's schematics, but his mind was calm. He understood the nature of his defeat. Cynara and the crew of the *Pegasus* had become important to him. They were not kin, nor even of his kind, yet he perceived his debt to them as if they were born of his House and Line.

But Persephone meant nothing. It was undisputed enemy. Somewhere on the Concordat's central world, among the powerful rulers Cynara claimed to know, he would find what he had failed to obtain on the *Pegasus*.

Adumbe's voice announced the approach to the final wormhole. Ronan brushed feline hair from his shipsuit and waited for Cynara to set him free.

C*ynara had been to Persephone station many times, but* Persephone itself was still a marvel to her eyes. The capital city of its largest continent, seat of the Archon himself, had grown to become the center of the entire Concordat and its constituent worlds.

Utopia, the ancients had called it.

"Eos," she said to Ronan as they looked down upon the city from the spaceport tower. "City of the Dawn, the place where humans first awoke from the Long Silence."

Any man might be silenced by awe at such a sight. Eos was as different from Elsinore as Dharma's largest city was from a Siroccan camp. Here the baroque scrollwork, gilded carvings, and velvet hangings gave way to the clean, simple lines of bleached columns that rose many stories to sculpted pediments, and even the meanest dwellings were in perfect harmony with their neighbors.

No narrow, stinking alleys marred the nobility of its streets, nor did gates exclude those of lesser wealth from the rich and mighty. Elsinore had its ground cabs for the rich, but here the privileged flew skimmers above the earthbound traffic and resided in apartments that seemed fit homes for mythic angels.

At the center stood Eos's Acropolis and the Archon's palace with its hanging gardens and obelisk piercing the sky. Beyond the river were the estates of the nobles, and then the countryside with its farms preserved as a reminder of a former way of life.

"My Uncle Jesper was born in this city," Cynara said. "I'm sometimes amazed that he chose to settle on such a provincial world as Dharma."

Ronan didn't so much as glance in her direction. She had
released him from his cabin during their final approach to the
system, but he had maintained this same stony silence.

She knew the reason. She'd forced him to swear an oath
to keep out of her mind as if there had never been any trust
between them, let alone the intimacy of that night on
Dharma.

A hundred times she had considered various apologies
and dismissed every one. She had done what she must to protect the ship. When—if—Ronan realized what was at stake,
he would understand why she had acted as she did.

When. Let there come such a time, and a chance to tear
down the walls. Let her testimony balance that of *Ser* Phineas
Janek, who was already on his way to present his case to the
High Command at Naval Headquarters.

"You have nothing to fear, Ronan," she said awkwardly,
gripping the guard rail until her knuckles ached. "Dharma's
ways are primitive in comparison to Persephone's. Your
mind won't be at risk here, I promise you."

"Will you be present when they question me?" he asked.

The sound of his voice was a gift, fertile land and fresh
water to a sailor lost on the sea. "I intend to be. I didn't expect Lord Miklos to agree to see us so quickly. Apparently
Uncle Jesper wasn't overestimating his friendship with the
Archon's brother."

"You trust these friends of *Va* Jesper."

"Law is sacred on Persephone, even among its rulers. You
won't be assumed guilty—" She broke off, staring out at the
city.

"Will I see this Archon, who rules so much of human
space?"

"The Archon is a very busy man. Lord Miklos can provide
what we need as long as we convince him that—" What?
That Ronan could become the valuable asset she wanted to
believe he could be, that her virtual theft of the *Pegasus* had
been necessary, that she was still competent to captain the Alliance's most precious treasure . . . that she had not risked
everything for the sake of a single man?

"Captain D'Accorso?"

She turned from the rail as a dark-suited man and woman

approached from the tower kiosk. Ronan shifted into his subtle warrior's stance, moving closer to her. She thought briefly
of the sidearm she'd left aboard the *Pegasus*.

"I am Cynara D'Accorso," she said.

"I am Gajda, and this is Mains, at your service, my lady,"
the man said. "Lord Miklos sent us to escort you to his offices at the palace."

Lord Miklos's people. She had been expecting a personal
escort from the spaceport, though the Lord's secretary had
not provided details on transportation. The captain of the *Pegasus* was not required to wade through the numerous levels
of complex Persephonean bureaucracy. The knowledge she
carried was far too valuable . . . and dangerous.

But it was entirely possible that she and Ronan were
under arrest. These two in their dark suits were hardly common messengers. She suspected they were of Miklos's personal guard, or perhaps even from the Archon's legendary
Royal Intelligence.

And if they were under arrest, then Janek had already
done his work. Adumbe had promised to send immediate
word if the *Pegasus* was boarded by Persephonean authorities, and she had prepared for that as well. There was little
more she could do.

"This is *Ser* Ronan?" Gajda asked.

"I also speak," Ronan said, so dryly that Cynara almost
suspected him of humor. "You are *Va* Miklos's *ve'laik'i*."

"Warriors," Cynara translated. "Are we guests or prisoners, *Ser* Gajda?"

"Guests, Captain. Lord Miklos wishes your visit to be free
of any inconvenience."

Indeed. She tugged the hem of her formal tunic and nodded. "We're ready."

Gajda stared at Ronan with a cool, measuring gaze and
gestured Cynara to precede him. Ronan hung back, but
Mains was careful to keep behind him. Cynara knew they
were armed and wouldn't hesitate to stun Ronan if he made
the slightest hostile move.

She kept half her attention on him and half on the agents
as the four of them took the lift to the tower lobby and
walked out to the skimmer parked in an area cleared of all

other traffic. Mains got in front with the driver, and Gajda sat in the wide rear seat between Ronan and Cynara. Even without benefit of sharing Ronan's thoughts, Cynara felt his tension.

Why should he trust them any more than he had the Dharmans? He might even suspect that Cynara had transported him from one predicament to another even worse.

There is no other way. If he has nothing to hide, he has nothing to fear. Yet she found no solace in the thought, or in the alien blankness of Ronan's face.

The skimmer lifted above the pavement, leaving its common terrestrial brethren far below. Deftly its pilot settled into a course that carried his passengers past the outskirts of Eos and into the city's brilliant center.

Cynara hardly noticed the stunning view. She was grateful when the skimmer landed on a pad on the palace grounds, letting her escape the oppressive confinement.

The first security check waited at the edge of the pad, and it was only one of many. Uniformed personnel very thoroughly scanned Cynara and Ronan, always accompanied by Gajda and Mains. Ronan was cooperative, almost passive, allowing the guards to touch him in a way he must hate. Cynara had no opportunity to offer a word or touch of encouragement, and wasn't sure he would accept either.

The palace interior was spare of decoration and yet handsome, walls subtly textured and punctuated with murals rendered in a deceptively simple style. Men and women, palace staff and clerks and bureaucrats in efficient garments, went about their business without a glance at the visitors. Endless corridors, more security checks, and finally admission to the outer chambers of that portion of the palace assigned to the younger brother of the Archon of Persephone.

Guards stood at every doorway, each one doubtless armed with some compact and highly efficient Persephonean weapon. Pompous though the burgher-lords of Elsinore might be, their security measures were pitiful by comparison. This was true power.

But Cynara was still captain of the *Pegasus*. When it appeared that their escorts would attempt to separate her and Ronan, she stood firm and refused. Ronan did the same.

Gajda and Mains chose not to force the issue, but showed them to a private sitting room painted in muted sea colors that could only have been chosen by someone who believed the ocean was peaceful.

They waited. No word came from Adumbe, though the guards had actually permitted her to keep her comlink. They could jam the signal easily enough if they chose. Ronan was a statue, hardly blinking. Cynara struggled with a dangerous desire to charge Gajda and demand to speak to someone in authority.

Such drastic action proved unnecessary. The door opened, and a woman in a conservative suit spoke briefly to Lord Miklos's people. They waved Cynara and Ronan through and into yet another room, larger than the first but still clearly an antechamber complete with a reception desk and potted plants. Cynara felt a buzz in her skull, and then the agents led them to another door.

Everything changed. On the other side was a room unlike the others, warm in tone and clearly designed for occupation by a person with a desire for comfort rather than conse- quence. Deeply padded chairs invited long talks, and the walls held shelf after shelf of old-style books.

The guards took up positions to either side of the room. Before Cynara could complete her internal debate as to whether or not to avail herself of one of the chairs, a wood- paneled door opened and a man stepped through.

She knew at once that it was Lord Miklos. The Challinor family was said to be extraordinarily attractive as well as gifted and much beloved by the Persephonean people, but she had seen the Archon and his family only at a distance. Those men and women she had dealt with during her brief- ings and layovers on Persephone had been less exalted lords, officials, and naval commanders assigned to the *Pegasus* Project.

None of those previous meetings could have prepared her for Lord Miklos Challinor. He was of middle years but still handsome, dressed in gray tunic and trousers with only a touch of braid to indicate his rank. She sensed immediately what Uncle Jesper had loved in this man, and why he was so confident of his royal connection.

Lord Miklos glanced from her to Ronan with keen interest, but it was Ronan's face that caught him. He stared, and Ronan's muscles tightened in a way Cynara had learned to recognize as portending trouble. If he'd possessed shaauri fur, it would have stood on end.

"Lord Miklos," Cynara said quickly, "I thank you for agreeing to see us. It is a great honor."

Blue eyes met hers with a trace of humor. "Captain D'Accorso," he said, his voice deep and warm. "Ronan VelKalevi. I am Miklos Challinor." He smiled at them both. "Please be seated. What would you care to drink?"

Cynara edged closer to Ronan. "Nothing, my lord."

"I understand." He glanced from Ronan to the guards. "I believe your friend regards me as an enemy."

His bluntness surprised her, but it did not seem out of his character. She couldn't help but like him. "Ronan has been through a great deal," she said. "I don't think he knows who to trust." *Including myself.*

Lord Miklos gestured to his men, who hesitated a moment and then left through the front entrance. No doubt they would be waiting just outside, easily summoned by a hidden buzzer.

"We are quite alone," he said, addressing both Cynara and Ronan. "No one outside this room will hear us. Now, sit."

Cynara took the nearest seat, with a direct look urging Ronan to do the same. He obeyed with obvious reluctance. His muscles were bunched to launch him from the chair at the slightest warning of danger.

"Good," Miklos said. He sat in one of the matching chairs next to the heavy wood desk and crossed his legs. "Now we may speak frankly. When Jesper first went to Dharma thirty-six years ago as part of the Concordat team assisting your government, he wrote to me many times about his experiences there. I remember well that he fell in love with the people—one in particular."

"My late Aunt Donata," Cynara said. "Dharma was deeply fortunate to keep *Magnus* Siannas after the blockade. Without him, I don't know what would have happened to the Nine Worlds."

"Or to any of the human worlds, considering the part your uncle played in—" He stopped, looked at Ronan, and contin-

ued smoothly. "I heard regularly from Jesper until the blockade, and very little since. But I knew he was fond of his
niece, and of course I have had reports of your progress each
time you've completed a run. I am delighted to meet you in
person, Captain D'Accorso."

"Thank you, my lord."

Miklos chuckled. "Jesper was certainly never so respectful. It's amusing to think of him as one of Dharma's elite."
He clasped his hand over his knee. "Call me Miklos, and I
will call you Cynara."

"Thank you, my . . . Miklos."

"That isn't so difficult, is it?" He grew serious. "You said
in your message that you knew that Observer Janek would be
reporting the events of the past few days in a prejudicial
light, and you wished to present another perspective before
any hasty action was taken. Is that correct?"

"It is." She curbed her impatience and waited for him to
finish.

"I have already heard something of *Ser* Janek's story. He
paints quite an ominous picture. However—" He raised his
hand to forestall Cynara's protest. "I fully intend to hear you
out. *Ser* Ronan."

Ronan's attention had never left Miklos, but he had not
expected to be addressed. *"Aho'Kei."*

"First of Clan . . . indeed, I'm afraid not. My brother is
Archon, and I am quite content to be Second."

"You know Voishaaur," Ronan said with wary respect.

"A little. My family was closely involved in negotiations
during both shaauri conflicts." He continued to appear relaxed, as if the subject were not one to arouse powerful emotions. "Ronan is not a shaauri name, is it?"

Once again Ronan was startled, though he hid it quickly.
"It was given to me by Kinsmen."

"Of course." Miklos leaned forward. "Have you ever been
called by another name?"

"No, *Aino'Kei.*"

"Do you remember anything of your earlier childhood?
Your parents?"

"I do not."

"VelKalevi is a Kinsman designation, but you do not

claim Kinsman descent." He steepled his fingers under his chin. "The Kalevi Line is said to be one of those most opposed to peace with humans; in fact, they have a reputation for murderous hatred of humanity. These were the people who raised you."

"Lord Miklos—" Cynara began.

He ignored her. "Is it not true, *Ser* Ronan, that you hate all humans, including yourself?"

Chapter 17

Cynara shot up from her seat. "Lord Miklos," she said, "you said you would hear us out—"

He raised his hand. Ronan's expression was stretched tight, as if the muscles in his temples sought to pull back large, expressive ears he didn't own.

"The Kalevi raised me," he said in a near-whisper. "They hate humans. They fear that humans will destroy the way of life they honor."

"They tortured him," Cynara said. She felt herself shaking and clenched her fists to assert some control over her body. "They beat him and broke his bones when he was still a child. They tried to destroy his natural telepathic ability."

"He *is* a telepath."

She dropped back into her chair, still shaking. "*Ser* Janek must have made that clear."

"Among other things." He made a calming motion with his hands. "What may seem cruelty to you, Captain, is necessity if I am to understand and judge the situation as you requested." He looked at Ronan. "Be at ease, young man. I intend you no harm. You will suffer no beatings here."

"They would have destroyed his mind on Dharma," Cynara said.

"And that is why you brought him to us." He got up and went to a blackwood sideboard, where he poured clear liquid from a crystal decanter into a glass. Instead of drinking it himself, he skirted the desk and brought it to Ronan. "Water," he said. "Unadulterated, I assure you."

To Cynara's shock, Ronan accepted the glass, sniffed it, and drank the contents in one swallow. Miklos resumed his seat.

"*Ser* Janek," he said, "appears to suspect that your relationship with this young man has become dangerous to Alliance security. Having witnessed your defense of him, I can see that you care for him a great deal."

"He's saved my life and the lives of my crew," she said. The words felt thick on her tongue. "I realize that Janek questions my objectivity."

"*Ser* Ronan sought refuge on the *Pegasus,* which you granted contrary to Janek's advice."

"As long as I am captain of the *Pegasus,* Lord Miklos, no one seeking sanctuary will be left to die alone in space."

"Indeed." Miklos had lost his air of good humor, and he spoke as if Ronan wasn't there. "Nevertheless, there was always a possibility that Ronan was a shaauri agent. You chose to accept him at his word, though you knew the risks. Was it your own telepathy that convinced you of his good faith?"

"My telepathy, Lord Miklos, was never very reliable."

"You did receive a shield here on Persephone before you took the captaincy."

"Yes."

"It seemed evident to *Ser* Janek that something had happened during your brief stay on Dharma to arouse your suspicions against Ronan and even to doubt his motives. In spite of this, you took him out from under the Dharman Trade Council's nose."

"Perhaps you should invite *Ser* Janek here, Lord Miklos, since you give such credence to his report."

"Do you deny his suspicions, Captain?"

She could have lied. She knew that some Persephoneans were telepaths, though the gift was far less common than on Dharma. But even through her anger she recognized that this was not a man who deserved, or would tolerate, deception.

"I do not," she said calmly. "There are details of recent events that Janek does not know. Ronan has been gradually recovering the telepathic abilities taken from him when he was a child. I am aware of the risks involved in such a recovery, and my own possible vulnerability. It is for that reason that I brought him here to be questioned, rather than allowing the Dharman Council to destroy him with the assumption of guilt that has not been proven."

"Then you concede that he may not be what he claims."

Ronan half rose from his seat. "It is me you should question, *Aino'Kei*. You may do with me as you wish, but do not doubt the captain's loyalty to you and your people."

"My people," Miklos repeated. "Where does your loyalty lie, Ronan?"

"With Captain D'Accorso."

Miklos turned on Cynara. "Were you intimate with this man, Cynara?"

In a blur of movement, Ronan leaped across the room, stopping centimeters from Lord Miklos's chair. He no longer looked remotely human.

"It is enough," he said, hissing between bared teeth. "Do not question her further."

"Ronan." Cynara got up carefully and held out her hand, fearing far more for him than Miklos. "Please."

"It's all right." Miklos glanced from Ronan's face to his arched fingers. "I see that his allegiance in at least one area is indisputable."

"Lord Miklos—"

The door burst open, and Miklos's guards jumped into the room, vicious little guns fixed on Ronan. He turned to face them without a trace of fear.

"Stand down," Miklos ordered. "I'm in no danger." He smiled at Cynara. "My security insisted that I be fitted with a monitor that alerts my guards when it detects an elevated heartbeat."

"Ronan," Cynara said firmly, "back away slowly, and sit down."

He obeyed, watching Miklos's people with their lowered weapons. Miklos let out a slow breath. "Dismissed," he told the guards.

"My lord—"

"Out."

They went. Miklos laughed, but Cynara recognized it as genuine relief. In spite of his assurances to his people, he'd been very well aware of the real threat to his life.

"Well," he said. "I don't believe I've had that much excitement since I was younger than you are, Captain." He looked at Ronan. "I was once a boy of considerable recklessness myself, but I was compelled to recognize that some situations require patience. I advise patience now, *Ser* Ronan VelKalevi."

"You won't have him arrested?" Cynara demanded.

"I admire his devotion to you, however overzealous. It will be necessary to question Ronan at length, as you expected, but I reiterate my personal assurance that he will not be harmed mentally or physically, and your report will be given full consideration."

"I would like to remain during the questioning, Lord . . . Miklos."

"I'm afraid that won't be possible. You do have a personal interest in this, Captain, as well as the complication of telepathic sensitivity. And your ship requires your presence."

She sat very still. "You won't advise that I be relieved of my command?"

"To the contrary. You may have acted with some lack of restraint, particularly where *Ser* Janek is concerned, but I believe you are a valuable asset to the Alliance." He smiled. "I'm sure Jesper will agree with me. I will send a communiqué with your return voyage recommending that any discipline be light, and that you retain command of the *Pegasus*."

Cynara was profoundly grateful that she was not prone to tears. "Thank you, Lord Miklos."

"I'll also supervise the questioning myself. I trust you will find this satisfactory, *Ser* Ronan?"

Ronan inclined his head. "I hold you in great respect, *Aino'Kei* Miklos Challinor," he said. "I will cooperate."

"I don't think I've ever been given such a sincere compliment." Miklos rose and extended his hand to Cynara. "Rest assured that I will have a detailed report for you on your next return to Persephone, which I presume will be soon. No matter what we discover, your friend will be given fair and humane treatment, and all the circumstances of his life will be considered."

If Ronan was a shaauri agent—God forbid—he meant that judgment would be tempered by compassion for what he had suffered as a child among them. He would be confined but wouldn't face the severe punishment he could be dealt on Dharma, or if *Ser* Janek had the deciding of his fate.

She met Miklos's gaze. "If I believed for an instant that he was truly betraying my crew and the Alliance, I would never have brought him here."

"I know." He clasped her hand. "I look forward to a more thorough and leisurely discussion when you return to Persephone, Captain. Perhaps next time you can bring Jesper with you."

"Perhaps." She squeezed his fingers and released his hand. "I hope that one day I can repay the debt we owe you."

"Perhaps you have already done so. Continue in your mission with the same level of courage and commitment, and you will more than requite any obligation." He turned to Ronan. "Ronan, I'll escort you to your quarters. Any questions you may have will be answered before debriefing begins."

"I understand."

"Then I will wait outside." He nodded to Cynara and strode to the door his men guarded, leaving her and Ronan alone.

"You are satisfied?" Ronan asked softly.

"Satisfied?" She banged the back of the chair with her fist. "I won't be satisfied until you're cleared and . . . life returns to normal."

"What is normal, Cynara?" He moved closer, bathing her in his warmth. "To risk your life evading shaauri whose only purpose is to kill you? To hold yourself apart from others who would give you what your heart desires?"

She smiled. Her chest ached, and she didn't care what vulnerability she revealed to him now. "Even I don't know what that is anymore."

"You will find it." He touched her hand, so small a gesture

and yet so charged with emotion. She wanted him, and he wanted her, and it was impossible.

"How do they say good-bye in Voishaaur, Ronan?"

"There are many ways. *'Sil akai'* means 'With the Ancestors.' It indicates a final parting. *'Kei'lai'* is said to *be'laik'i* when they leave on Walkabout. It means 'Fortunate Path.' Once a youth has selected, she seldom leaves her House or Line permanently. Among kin, shaauri say *'Tan uri-kah.'* 'Until we are whole again.' "

"And which kind of parting is this?"

"I do not know, *Aho'Va.* Because we are human, our Paths can never be certain."

"I think I prefer—" He caught her words with his mouth, kissing her with heartbreaking tenderness. It was as if he truly believed they would never meet again.

With the Ancestors.

She returned his kiss almost angrily, wanting to punish him, make it impossible for him to forget what they had shared. Yet she had been the one to raise the corrosive doubts and build bitter walls.

He had forgiven her.

"No good-byes, then," she said, stepping back. "On Dharma we say 'safetide.' It comes from the days when all Dharmans, great or small, made their livings from the sea. It still holds true in space."

"Care well for yourself, Cynara," he said, stroking her cheek.

"And you." She turned abruptly and strode for the door, clenching her jaw to dam her tears. Miklos politely averted his gaze until she had overcome her weakness. His men had retreated to the far end of the antechamber.

"I knew a woman once," Miklos said, "who would gladly have sacrificed everything she possessed for the man she loved. And he would have done the same. In fact, one might say they both sacrificed everything for love—of each other, of their people, and of peace."

She couldn't bear to examine his implication too closely, yet her trust in Miklos was stronger than ever. "This woman was someone you also cared for," she said.

"She was my sister, Lady Kori Galatea Challinor."

"I'm sorry. I know what it is to lose family."

"I still hope that Kori's work, and her husband's, was not in vain. What has happened today encourages that hope." He set his hand on her shoulder. "If anything in the universe can bridge the gulf between opposing forces, it is love." He smiled as if at his own romantic folly. "My people will escort you back to the ship. Good-bye, Captain."

"Safetide, Lord Miklos." She bowed with deep respect and joined Gajda and Mains. Their dispassionate presence kept her emotions well in check until she boarded the shuttle for the *Pegasus*.

Crew took one look at her face and wisely declined to question her. She gave a sketchy report to Adumbe, asked him to brief her officers, and considered his suggestions about possible cargo to carry back to the Nine Worlds. Then she retired to her quarters and stretched out on the bunk with Archie, her thoughts in such turmoil that she couldn't hold on to any one of them long enough to examine it.

Her door buzzed sometime later, and Kord entered at her invitation. "Adumbe asked me to deliver this to you, Captain," he said formally, though his eyes gave away his concern. "It just arrived from Lord Miklos Challinor."

She jumped from the bunk, snatching the message cube from his hand. She opened it impatiently and read the dispatch.

A second reading and then a third were required before she was certain that she understood correctly. Lord Miklos had almost gone too far, and yet she wasn't offended. How had he come to understand so well? Or was there some other purpose behind his generosity?

"Good news, Little Mother?"

She had almost forgotten that Kord was still in her cabin. "I've been . . . called back to the palace," she said. "I'll probably be gone overnight."

"Should I accompany you?"

"No. It will be perfectly safe. Adumbe can prepare to move out sometime tomorrow with whatever cargo we can acquire and load by then."

"Is everything well with Ronan, and with you?"

She met his gaze. "Lord Miklos has taken personal interest in Ronan's case, and I trust him." She smiled. "I know that look, my friend. I can't let you remain here with him—I need you on the *Pegasus*."

Kord inclined his head, though he wasn't happy. He would consider leaving his brother on Persephone to be nearly as bad as abandoning Ronan to the Dharmans. Cynara knew the difference, but she was no happier than he was.

That made this last night all the more precious.

Lord Miklos's message didn't require a reply. She checked in with Adumbe and the woman he had assigned as temporary cargomaster before taking the shuttle back down to the surface. The sun was setting in glorious gold over the city, catching the pearlescent gleam of its towers.

They said that the streets of Persephone proper were safe enough for a child to walk at midnight. Cynara caught a public cab to the foot of the Acropolis and walked up the steep stairway, ignoring the escalators installed for the less vigorous. At the perimeter walls she presented the pass Miklos had sent with his message and was ushered through without hindrance.

Six more times she passed through security checkpoints until she was within the palace proper. There a guard offered escort to the guest wing that contained the address Miklos had provided. They walked through night-scented grottos, crossed an elegant artificial stream, and entered an annex of guest apartments with patios overlooking the garden. As open as it seemed, Cynara didn't doubt that escape from this place would be near impossible.

The guard left her at a door identical to all the others in the wing, decorated much like the more public portions of the palace she had seen before.

She hesitated, suddenly afraid. Surely Ronan knew to expect her. Miklos would have warned him.

Warned him, indeed. Did Ronan want this? Would he have preferred the simple farewell they had shared in Miklos's office?

The door opened. Ronan stood looking at her as if he had known she was outside—a simple matter for a telepath of his strength. But perhaps it was a subtler sense that brought them together, awkward in the silence, each weighing the emotional cost of this gift they had been given.

Ronan moved out of the doorway, leaving her a clear path into the apartment. Cynara stepped over the threshold. The quarters were clean, comfortable, and entirely colorless. They suited Ronan well. They suited the circumstances perfectly.

The bed stood in a separate room off the living area. Ronan offered his hand. She took it. There was no touching of minds; she couldn't risk it, and he would not press. But the understanding was there.

Tonight was not for words, or prolonged farewells. Tonight was for the ardent language of flesh and desire.

During their night on Dharma, Ronan had taken control. She had let him. But this time she needed more than ever to feel strong, brazen, anything but passive. She pushed Ronan until the back of his knees hit the bed, and then she kissed him.

It was difficult to keep from feeling his thoughts when he responded. Perhaps some of them slipped through her guard, because she was gripped by a sexual hunger surpassing any that had gone before. Ronan pulled her onto his lap, and she straddled him without interrupting the kiss. His erection strained against his shipsuit.

She put her hand on him, squeezing lightly. He groaned into her mouth. She opened the fly and touched his hot, silky flesh.

Ronan had no qualms about showing his pleasure. He bent back his head, breathing fast, as she stroked him up and down with her fingertips. He seized her about the waist, but she wriggled free and slid to her knees before him.

When she took him into her mouth, she knew immediately that none of his Kinswoman lovers had gone beyond the basic necessities in their servicing. His whole body went rigid, and then he released a shuddering breath. The feel of him in her mouth, the anticipation of taking him into her body, inspired her to try things she'd hardly imagined.

But she wanted to touch more of him than this. She paused, ignoring Ronan's wordless protest, to unfasten his shipsuit from neck to belly. She peeled the suit back from his shoulders, half trapping his arms, and rubbed her cheek against the hard swell of his pectorals and the ridged muscle beneath his ribs. She kissed his nipples one by one. He tried to lift his hands, but she forced them back and pressed him flat onto the bed.

Their eyes met. His were slightly glazed, but in them she saw the depth of appreciation and affection he couldn't express in words or even in thoughts. He had no masculine pride to surrender by letting her take the lead.

With his willing cooperation, she finished undressing him and tossed his 'suit to the floor. Even though she had seen him naked more than once, his body still seemed a magnificent work of art, scars and all. She stretched out atop him, kissing his face from brow to chin, letting her hair fall across his face in a sensual caress.

When she began to work her way down, kissing every scar in her path, he resisted for the first time.

If she opened her mind to him, she knew she would feel his shame. This bed wasn't large enough to carry such extra weight. Deliberately she lingered on each healed slash or cut, licking the scars as if she could make them disappear. She forced Ronan to endure until she was satisfied that every point and plane of his body had been thoroughly touched, indulged, and cherished.

Only then did she permit him to pull her up and hold her against him. He nuzzled her temple, crushing her so tightly to his chest that she hoped he remembered his own strength. But then he released her, just enough so that he could peel her dress tunic beneath her breasts, trapping her as she had trapped him.

She straddled his waist, and he eased her down so that her breasts were within reach of his mouth, steadying her above him with one hand. His tongue flicked, teasing, tasting with implacable hunger and unfailing gentleness.

Cynara closed her eyes and tried to remember to breathe. But she didn't want this to be a repeat of the previous time. Her desire had reached the point of pain, and she was in no doubt that Ronan's was equally pressing. Arching up, she shrugged the tunic from her shoulders. Ronan tugged her trousers down around her hips, and she finished the job. Her undergarments were discarded even more swiftly.

Then she resumed her position, her thighs to either side of his, hands braced on his chest. She eased down, taking him into herself, making the exquisite moment last to the very brink of torment. Ronan remained still. Only when she released her breath and began to move did he take up her rhythm.

Cynara hadn't expected this joining to be as profound as the one on Dharma, or as complicated. But the knowledge that her mind was safe, that Ronan would never breach her trust, set her free to take and give pleasure without fear. She rode him hard. He was tireless. No mental communication was required to tell them both when the time had come to let go.

She allowed her bones to melt and folded her body over Ronan's. He licked the perspiration from her neck and rolled to his side, keeping her within the crook of his arm. They lay thus long into the night, unspeaking, warming each other with heated flesh and intertwined limbs.

Cynara fell asleep with her head on Ronan's shoulder. Even in dreams she felt his arms enfolding her, protecting, claiming as if this were only the first of a thousand nights to come.

She woke at dawn, disturbed by the unfamiliar chatter of birds in the trees outside the window.

The apartment seemed bleak and alien in the morning light, and not even the gentle shadows could soften the harsh reality of the clock on the bed table. She rolled over carefully, trying not to disturb the sheets tangled around her legs.

Ronan lay with one hand sprawled across his chest and the other on the pillow above his head. Some said that the true human soul was revealed only in sleep. If that were so, she didn't know how she could bear to leave him.

He seemed asleep; his breathing was slow and steady, the muscles of his face relaxed. But he was not. She knew it, and he must know she was aware of his deception. Yet he kept up the pretense, making it easier on both of them.

No words.

She crawled out of bed and pulled on her suit. It smelled

of Ronan. She held her tunic to her face and breathed him in, imprinting the scent in memory.

Ronan hadn't moved when she left the apartment. Gardeners were already at work among the shrubs and walkways, raking and pruning. Once she entered the more public corridors, she passed palace staff who nodded to her with formal and impersonal recognition. At the innermost security post, the guard called ahead to assure that she could pass through the remainder without stopping.

It seemed strange that she could walk so quickly when her heart felt twice its normal weight. But she had work to do; today the *Pegasus* would return to the Nine Worlds with a cargo of essential goods in its hold. A few days to Dharma, the inevitable confrontation with the Council—eased by Jesper's and Miklos's influence—and another cargo of fissibles back to the Concordat.

Then she would know the truth.

If anything in the universe can bridge the gulf between opposing forces, it is love. She prayed that Miklos was right. If not, then the universe had played a very cruel joke. And it would be a very long time before she laughed again.

Chapter 18

Ronan spent the hours after Cynara's departure settling his mind and sealing his heart from all emotion,
chanting the Eightfold Way and preparing for the worst the
Concordat might cast at him.

Concentration was more difficult than he had ever found
it, even in the early days of his training. Cynara's scent clung
to his body and everything he touched in the soft and over-
large rooms assigned to him. Though not a word had passed
between them during the night, though he hadn't so much as
skimmed her thoughts, she had left an indelible mark that no
discipline could eliminate.

He had taken the gift *Aino'Kei* Miklos had offered, knowing it might be a ploy to make him more vulnerable. In his
heart was the conviction that he might never see Cynara
again. He could not determine the source of that fear, nor
why he felt such despair when he considered the completion
of his assignment.

You will not betray Cynara. That knowledge should have
severed any ties that restrained him. But he had found much
to honor in Lord Miklos, despite his disrespectful questions
to Cynara.

Ronan was not even a true prisoner here, though he knew

escape would be no simple matter. Escape was not an option. In order to acquire the unrestricted freedom he needed to search out vulnerable and knowledgeable minds, he had to pass the tests these humans set him.

But when the guard came, an hour after a server had brought him a breakfast of bread, thinly sliced meat, and fruit, it was not to take him to a place of questioning but to Lord Miklos's room of books.

"Good morning," Miklos said, waving him to a seat. "I hope the morning meal was to your liking."

Ronan listened for mockery in the *aino'kei*'s voice and did not hear it. He answered with neutral courtesy and attempted what he had not dared at their first meeting, a swift and shallow touch of Miklos's mind.

It was, as he had expected, fully shielded. Miklos was no telepath, but he had been prepared to deal with one. He smiled, unaware, and leaned across his desk.

"I won't pretend that you don't have an ordeal ahead of you, Ronan," he said. "But I wanted to reassure you that no one here wishes you ill. I will be present during the questioning. Before then, however, I'd like to show you something of the palace."

Ronan kept his face expressionless as he examined *Aino'Kei* Miklos's motives. He did not behave as if he faced a potential enemy. Nor was he a stupid man. It made no sense for him to invite Ronan within the walls of his House as if they were kin.

Miklos had his *ve'laik'i,* to be sure, and they would be ready for any aggression. But still it made no sense—unless Miklos had a hidden plan of his own to draw out Ronan's knowledge by subtle and devious means.

"I am honored," Ronan said, inclining his head.

"No formality, please," Miklos said. "You see, Ronan, I'm convinced, like the captain, that you will be of great assistance to the Alliance in understanding the shaauri. Understanding is the first step toward peace, and that is what we desire above all."

"Why should humans want peace when shaauri have stopped their trade and killed their kin?"

"You speak of humans as if you weren't one yourself,"

Miklos said, smiling to lighten his words, "but I suppose that's no wonder. You were only a child when the shaauri took you." He pretended interest in one of his books and half pulled it from its shelf. "You were kidnapped, I understand."

"I was taken on a raid, such as shaauri youths often venture during Walkabout."

Miklos sighed and pushed the book back in place. "It seems likely that our database will turn up the names of families who lost a child that year, or who were killed in a shaauri attack. You do wish to find your human kin?"

Were these questions part of Miklos's scheme? Of what use could they be to him? "Yes," Ronan said warily. "It was my purpose in escaping the shaauri."

"Of course." Miklos straightened the tunic of his dark brown suit. "Come. We can talk as I show you the palace."

He led Ronan out the private door behind his desk, and as expected, two of his men fell in behind. Miklos apologized with a chuckle, as if their presence were an offense rather than a necessity.

"Persephone is a peaceful world," he said, "but my grandmother used to say that peace is founded on strength."

"So the shaauri would say as well. 'The House strong in ve'laik'in is sure in Path.'"

"Indeed. My brother-in-law, Jonas Kane VelArhan, came to believe that the differences between our species are not nearly so great as either side would believe. Jonas married my sister after they stopped the first Kinsman coup attempt thirty-odd years ago. We had every reason to believe that their efforts would assure a continuation of the peace we enjoyed after the First War. But it was not to be.

"My sister and the man she chose as husband saved my life that day," Miklos said, turning down a corridor toward the center of the palace. "I told you that even I had been young and reckless once, before responsibility came to rest on my shoulders. There are times when I wish I could go back to those days, dangers and all."

"You were selected for your Path at birth," Ronan said.

"I'm afraid you're right. Ah." He paused at immense double doors flanked by guards in more elaborate costume. "In a few moments, I hope to be able to introduce you to some of my family."

There was a great wrongness here. Ronan stopped when Miklos would have approached the doors. *Ne'lin fool. Take what he offers.*

But he could not. "I do not understand you, *Aino'Kei*," he said. "You take me among your kin, though I may be your enemy."

Miklos held his gaze. "Are you, Ronan? Are you my enemy?"

He is OutLine, OutClan. There is no shame in deceit. "No."

"I haven't telepathic gifts like my sister had, but I have a certain sense, if you will. And I trust your captain's judgment. She thought you were worth saving. So do I."

Ronan looked away quickly, unable to trust his voice.

"Well," Miklos said, "come along, then."

The doors swung open, held by two of the decorated attendants. The wide hall was carpeted, its length punctuated by numerous tables set with sculptures of naked human figures and containers of flowers. The colors were warm, earth tones such as those preferred by shaauri.

Many smaller corridors and antechambers opened up from the hall, but Miklos passed them by. The security men and women here were not so conspicuous, but Ronan recognized and noted their positions. It was information he might require later.

A second set of high doors led to another hall, and then to a glass-walled room, furnished with padded chairs and heavy woven carpets, overlooking a hidden garden. Miklos stopped at the window and invited Ronan to join him.

In the garden several young humans of various ages were at play, tossing a ball back and forth as an adult looked on indulgently. Ronan saw a resemblance among some of the *ba'laik'i,* markings of kinship that were not so readily apparent among shaauri.

"My great-nieces and -nephews, the grandchildren of my elder brother Hector and offspring of my nephew Ambros." He smiled with genuine pride and pleasure. "I have none of my own, so I tend to spoil them. Do shaauri spoil their children?"

Ronan remembered the little treats Hanno had often brought him after a particularly nasty beating, the way her fur had smelled when she held him close with crooning songs passed down among the *li'laik'i* of Ain'Kalevi.

"All children are valued," he said seriously.

"Even you?"

Startled, Ronan stared through the glass. Had Cynara found the means to speak to Miklos of his childhood, the portions she had taken from his mind and those he had confided to her?

Use it. Make him pity you, as she did.

"I was human," he said. "I had to prove my worth."

"That's how you received the scars?"

"Janek reported this to you."

"I have several reliable sources of information, but you need have no fear that any will be used to Cynara's detriment."

"The captain can care for herself."

Miklos merely smiled. "Ah. The one who has the ball now, with the freckles and brown hair? That's my favorite great-niece, Melanthe, Kori's granddaughter and the child of my nephew Ambros. Quite a little spitfire even at the age of ten."

Ronan remembered that *Magnus* Jesper had referred to Cynara by that *bali*-name. "A child of strength and spirit," he said.

"Do you hope for any of your own?"

"I never considered it."

"You're lying." Miklos turned a pleasant face on him as if he had not just delivered a breathtaking insult. "You want children. You want a family, to make up for what you lost in your own childhood."

"I was adequately cared for by the shaauri."

"So well that you escaped and betrayed them."

Ronan made his emotions disappear. "I could never be one of them."

"But now your life has changed. You may find a mate of your own kind. The captain—"

"Do not speak further of her, *Aino'Kei.*"

"Because you see no future between you?" Miklos kept his mild manner, refusing to react to Ronan's deliberate insolence.

Ronan bared his teeth. "No more."

"Very well. I apologize for my inquisitiveness."

Apology from one of high rank could be interpreted as disadvantage. Ronan's confidence returned. In the garden beyond the window, a man walked out among the children and paused to speak to their *li'laik'in.*

Janek. He stood among the children, smiling, as if he belonged there. A moment's study of several of the children convinced Ronan of a resemblance between them and the Persephonean Observer.

Ronan glanced at Miklos to gauge his reaction. The Second's face revealed a moment of chagrin and then resumed its bland, pleasant expression.

"I did not know," Ronan said softly, "that *Ser* Janek was of your House."

"That was why he was chosen to observe aboard the *Pegasus*—he always preferred working behind the scenes. It was highly unlikely he'd be recognized." Miklos sighed. "I see no reason to withhold information from you now that you've seen him in the palace. Phineas Janek is, in fact, my nephew Damon, another of Kori's children."

"A Challinor."

"Yes."

"He works in your intelligence division, to gather information about enemies?"

"And allies, where critical projects are involved." His eyes narrowed. "You have divined a great deal during your journey aboard the *Pegasus,* telepathically or otherwise. You know the ship is not an ordinary one."

"I know."

"We must, of course, ascertain exactly how much you know and what you might do with the information if given complete freedom."

"No matter what you decide, *Aino'Kei,* you cannot release me. I know who Janek is, and I would report it to Captain D'Accorso."

"Who already has suspicions of her own." Miklos looked as though he wished to touch Ronan, and Ronan backed a step away. "Your honesty in this matter goes far in convincing me that you are as trustworthy as Cynara claims."

Ronan shook his head. "I do not understand these human ways."

"Not even humans always understand them." The child Melanthe waved, and Miklos waved back. Janek—Damon—glanced up and seemed to see Miklos and Ronan for the first time. His expression darkened.

"I know that you and my nephew were not the best of friends aboard the *Pegasus*," Miklos said, "and he has made his opinion of you quite clear. He doesn't trust you, Ronan. I must take his opinion into consideration. But his is not the only one."

Damon's mouth moved, but his voice was muffled by the glass. Melanthe ran up to the window and pressed her face against the surface, flattening her nose in a deliberately grotesque mask. She laughed up at Miklos. He made a face in return.

The affection was real. Ronan tried to imagine what it would have been like to grow up with such closeness—not only the kindness any *li'laik'i* might show a child, but the true knowledge of belonging, of acceptance. He smiled at the girl, hesitantly, and she grinned back.

"Come," Miklos said. "There are others I wish you to meet." He stepped away from the window, expecting Ronan to follow. Damon Challinor's eyes met Ronan's in open challenge, and then Ronan turned his back and went after Miklos.

They passed adjoining corridors connecting various office and sitting rooms and came at last to a wing that seemed devoted to practical affairs rather than family comfort. Miklos walked through a pair of ordinary doors into a reception area, where an administrative clerk rose from his desk and quickly bowed acknowledgment.

"I haven't an appointment," Miklos said, "but if *Mes* Carter VelShaan is available, I would like to speak to her."

VelShaan. A Kinsman name. Ronan made swift assessment of his own telepathic defenses.

"I'll check at once, my lord," the clerk said. He spoke into his headset, and a moment later he nodded and addressed Miklos. *"Mes* Carter VelShaan is in her office, Lord Miklos. I'll escort you at once."

"Unnecessary. I know the way." He smiled at the clerk and led Ronan through another set of doors. At once Ronan strongly felt what he had been expecting: the sensation of many powerful telepathic minds in close proximity.

Kinsmen—the men and women who had chosen to stay with the Concordat when the Second War had broken out, splitting off from those who had gone to the shaauri. It was said that the strongest telepaths had allied with the shaauri. Yet Ronan knew that these were not weak or ineffectual minds.

Concordat Kinsmen such as these would have placed the mental shields in Cynara, Charis, Damon, and Miklos. Such minds might break through Ronan's own shields and expose his true purpose.

Unless he proved himself their superior, as his masters had been so certain he would.

"I'm taking you to see the leader of our contingent of Kinsmen based on Persephone," Miklos said. "I am aware that you occasionally dealt with shaauri Kinsmen, but you weren't accepted among them. I think you'll find a better welcome here."

"Is my questioning to begin now?"

"No, indeed. This is informal introduction. Please be at ease." He reached the end of a corridor and paused at an open door. The Kinswoman was already there to meet him, a female of average height, age, and build with thick black hair and golden skin.

"Lord Miklos," she said with a smile and a glance at Ronan. "Please, come in."

They did so, while Miklos's men remained just outside. The Kinswoman's office was large, with a pleasant view overlooking another part of the garden. She greeted Miklos and then offered chairs to both her guests.

Miklos sat. Ronan continued to stand even when VelShaan chose another seat across from them.

"I believe you know why I've come today, *Mes* Carter VelShaan," Miklos said. "This young man is, of course, *Ser*

Ronan VelKalevi, who has just come to us from the *Pegasus* and Dharma. Ronan, may I introduce *Mes* Brit Carter VelShaan."

Ronan met the woman's eyes. If she had lived among shaauri at all—which her age made possible, since Kinsman children generally spent part of their childhood with their adopted Line, and she might have done so before the outbreak of war—she would grasp the fine nuances of his gaze. He did not offer challenge, admit lesser standing, nor acknowledge kinship. This was her territory, and hers was the first move.

"Welcome, *sh'kei'eivalin*," she said in stilted Voishaaur. "Here are you among kin."

The swift acknowledgment amazed and troubled him. She called him "Clan brother," acknowledging him as distant kin, not of Line but Clan, granted the protection of her House. Not all Clan-kin were given such privileges. Clans were large, like nations, and Lines within them might be at conflict.

As his Line must be with hers.

"I am honored, *Aho'Ken*," he answered, with the inflection that acknowledged her courtesy and rank.

She smiled, close-mouthed. "As am I, *sh'eivalin*. We will speak in Standard," she said with a nod at Lord Miklos.

"Very good," Miklos said. "You and your fellow Kinsmen, *Mes* Carter VelShaan, will be invaluable in reintroducing *Ser* VelKalevi to humanity after his long stay among shaauri."

VelShaan studied Ronan more carefully. "I know this will be a difficult time for you, Ronan. We'll do all we can to help."

"After you probe my mind."

She, like Miklos, failed to take offense. "It is necessary, as I'm sure you understand. A human raised since early childhood among a human-hating Line like Kalevi may have . . . suffered far more than physical scars."

"Shaan was allied to humans, like Arhan."

"Still is, we believe, though communications have been sporadic at best. The prohuman Lines have been under constant pressure since the War began. Perhaps you will be able to update our incomplete intelligence on current shaauri politics."

"It is why I am here."

"Of course." She offered refreshments, which Miklos accepted. A moment later she returned with three steaming mugs of liquid that Ronan immediately recognized as *arao*. His mouth watered.

"Ah," Miklos said with approval. "I've developed a taste for this stuff ever since Kori made me try it."

Ronan took his mug and savored the complex aroma of spices, fruit, and nuts. He drank the *arao* with real gratitude, only recalling afterward that it was the human way to drug potential enemies.

"There is so much we have yet to learn from the shaauri—those Lines that don't hate humanity," VelShaan said. "Our goal is, and has always been, lasting peace and understanding. As long as the antihuman factions control shaauri politics, we have little hope of progress. You may provide the key." She finished her drink and set it aside. "I understand that your telepathy was tampered with when you were a child. We'll do everything possible to heal and train you to use your gifts properly. You'll become one of us."

Ronan could find no response. Whatever VelShaan's motives, there was genuine kindness in her, and sympathy that did not extend to offensive pity. She treated him almost as an equal.

Yet when she spoke of peace, could she truly mean it? Was it not simply a lie among other lies to cover rapacious human plans for conquest?

"All your life you've been punished for being human," VelShaan said. "That has ended. You will be yourself, Ronan, and valued for all your qualities, human and shaauri." She turned to Miklos. "Have you scheduled a time for the debriefing, Lord Miklos? I'll want to be sure that my seniors are available and prepared."

"If Ronan is agreeable, I'd thought tomorrow morning. I'd like to spend the rest of the day showing him something of Persephone."

"We'll be ready."

"Excellent." Miklos rose. "Until tomorrow, *Mes* Carter

VelShaan." He nodded and walked toward the door. Ronan hesitated.

"Why?" he asked VelShaan. "Why did you and your people choose to remain among humans?"

"Because we're human, and we saw a chance to serve. Because we saw what hatred and misunderstanding could do to two intelligent species. Because people like us are needed if there is ever to be peace again. *Tan uri-kah,* Ronan."

"Tan uri-kah." He caught up with Miklos and the guards followed at his heels.

"It's nearly time for the noon meal," Miklos said. "Please join me in my quarters—our chefs here are excellent and can cater to your particular preferences on very short notice. Afterwards there is one other person who would like to meet you. I think you'll find it worth your while."

"*C*aptain," Charis's *voice said over the intercom, "I'm* sorry to disturb you, but I need you in engineering immediately."

Cynara woke from her light doze and glanced at the clock. It was the middle of second watch, not yet time for her next shift. She'd slept a little more than an hour.

Since the *Pegasus* had left Persephone at dawn that morning, Cynara had thrown herself into her duties, making up for the fallow time on Persephone and Adumbe's long watch. She'd relieved him on the bridge and taken the ship out of orbit, setting course for the wormhole that would propel them to the edge of Concordat space and into shaauri territory.

Most of the crew, sensing her mood, hadn't troubled her with questions. Adumbe was glad enough to get away to his own quarters, and Cynara adjusted the watch schedule to permit a longer break for those who had stood at their posts for an extended period.

Working kept her thoughts away from Ronan and their last night together. She was almost convinced that Ronan would be all right, that Miklos's advocacy would counteract Janek's hostility, and that she would be able to return to Persephone as captain of the *Pegasus.*

Almost.

She would gladly have continued on the bridge all day

and through the following night, but Adumbe returned after the eight-hour watch and admonished her to take a brief rest. Miya Zheng seconded the suggestion.

She hadn't known why they insisted until she saw her face in the mirror. Her eyes were dark hollows surrounded by pale, drawn skin, haunted and hectic at the same time. She looked as though the blow of a child would knock her over. She felt almost as bad.

Once she slept, she had plunged into nightmares that grew mercifully dim when she received Charis's call. She threw her legs over the side of the bunk and punched the 'com. "I'll be right down, Chief."

She hadn't changed her shipsuit since boarding the *Pegasus,* so she undressed quickly, put on a clean one, and took the lift down to engineering. The marine on duty admitted her through the heavy doors. Charis was waiting inside.

"Thank you for coming, Captain," she said, rocking nervously on the balls of her feet. "I have a report . . . one I wish I didn't have to make. I'm sorry I couldn't tell you earlier, but I had to be sure my suspicions were correct."

Charis had never seemed so grim. "What is it, Chief?"

The engineer held up her hand. On her palm rested a standard data slide. "I found this in one of my consoles a few hours before we left Persephone. I didn't think much of it at first, but I never leave slides out when I'm not using them. I asked the other crew, and none of them had done it either. Still nothing so terrible, but then . . ." She ducked her head. "I checked the log, and found that someone had viewed several pages of the schematics file. Then I started to remember."

Cynara shivered. "Remember what?"

"That I'd felt strange the day of the shaauri attack—a little off, somehow, like I was on meds, but I wasn't. I asked if anyone else had noticed. They said I'd gone out suddenly for some reason, while we were tuning the drive, and didn't say why. Crew also mentioned having experienced similar sensations after I returned—feelings of disorientation, as if their eyes weren't quite seeing straight.

"That was when I couldn't find my passcard. I usually keep it in my pocket, so I thought I'd left it in another 'suit.

No go. It just disappeared. And I started remembering conversations I knew I didn't have with any of my crew.

"Well, I knew something wasn't right, so I ordered a thorough sweep of all stations in engineering. We came up with a few drops of perspiration on my console and asked Doc Zheng to take a look. She checked the mitochondrial DNA. It wasn't mine or any of the crews.' "

Cynara knew what Charis was about to say. "Whose, Chief?"

"I'm sorry, Captain. Doc says it's Ronan's."

Chapter 19

The meal in Miklos's quarters was elaborate by ship-board standards, but Ronan hardly tasted the food his host's servers delivered on silver platters from a private lift serving the distant kitchen. He ate just enough to avoid giving offense while Miklos lingered over his meat and wine with every evidence of pleasure.

After he was finished, he took Ronan on a tour of the prosperous and busy neighborhood at the foot of the Acropolis, where merchants of every kind kept shops catering to the aristocracy of Eos. Subtle as they were, Miklos's guards doubled in number as soon as their master left the palace grounds, ranging just out of sight so as not to alarm the citizenry.

Miklos was clearly proud of his people and his city. He spoke of the freedoms the Concordat's citizens enjoyed, the high standard of living, good health, and ambition of Persephoneans. The heart of Eos was beautiful by human standards, with the symmetrical, unbroken lines of the architecture, the bright stone and orderly progression of buildings. The blocks of greenery Miklos called "parks" were as flawless and contained as everything else.

Even so there was life—couples walking hand in hand in

the open way of humans, children racing about the parks, passers-by offering respectful and affectionate greetings to Miklos when they recognized him. Eos was not ruled by tyrants, and signs of human violence were absent.

Yet Miklos brought his warriors with him wherever he traveled, and these *ve'laik'i* were not merely for *sh'ei*—honor—but protected their lord from dishonorable assault.

"You see why we wish to retain what we have fought to build since the Reunion and founding of the Concordat," Miklos said as they began the walk back to the Acropolis. "Humanity crawled out from the dark and rebuilt all we had lost. Now we're on the verge of new discoveries, new possibilities beyond the regions we know. That's why the blockade must end. Without the possibility of growth and freedom, humans wither and die."

His passionate speech left no room for argument. It sickened Ronan, for it illustrated the very nature that Kalevi, Rauthi, Aarys, and their allies feared in the enemy. Humans recognized no limits; they saw only new opportunities to swallow up whatever they discovered, to expand without restraint and impose their own inverted order on the universe.

"Ronan?"

He came back to himself and found Miklos regarding him quizzically. *"Aino'Kei."*

"I hope you've found our tour of some interest, but it's nearly the hour I promised to take you to meet another member of my family."

The angle of the sun told Ronan that the day already approached its end, and he had achieved nothing of worth. But he had obviously won Miklos's trust, and there might be opportunities tonight, before the questioning, to explore further. One of Miklos's servants could have a weakness in his mental shield. One vulnerable mind, in a human free to move about the palace, was all he required.

"May I know the name of this one I am to attend?" he asked with a show of courteous interest.

Miklos smiled. "You'll discover that very soon." He picked up his pace, choosing the steep stairway rather than the private lift. He, Ronan, and the guards entered by a back entrance to the palace. A series of concealed doorways and narrow corridors led to a more familiar section of the complex, and into a wide hall Ronan had not seen before.

The grandness of it reminded Ronan of the Council building on Dharma, and he knew it was a place of ceremony. The servants and guards wore livery and were openly armed.

A new alertness gripped Ronan, anticipation out of proportion to the circumstances. He half expected a trap of human devising. Miklos strolled along the hall at his ease, and his *ve'laik'i* maintained their positions well behind.

The doors at the end of the hall were greater than all the others Ronan had seen, pale stone embossed with scenes of naked human figures, stylized planets, and sleek starships. They swung open as Miklos approached. The chamber beyond was broad, walls lined with hundreds of chairs, and at its end was a dais and a massive throne carved much like the doors.

This must be the public receiving room of Persephone's ruler, the Archon. But the throne was empty. Miklos strode halfway down the room and then turned to a small, unobtrusive door set in the wall. Two uniformed attendants within moved quickly to admit the visitors.

A tall, thin man rose from a chair beside a simple stone hearth and held out his hands. "Miklos," he said. "I am glad you could come."

Miklos bowed his head briefly. "My Lord Archon, I present to you Ronan VelKalevi, brought to us by Captain Cynara D'Accorso of the *Pegasus*."

The Archon. The Archon himself, a pleasant gentleman in his sixth decade who might have been a common *an'laik'in* save for the intelligence in his eyes and the grace of his bearing—an unremarkable human with white hair and a long face drawn with care and old sorrow. All Ronan's nerves sharpened to needle points, stabbing his body in a thousand places at once.

The Archon. The man you were sent to find.

Hector Challinor turned to Ronan and stared, directly and without apology, like a First to one of lowest rank. "I believe you are right, Miklos," he murmured. "It is quite remarkable."

Ronan hardly heard him. He shielded himself from the

stare and struggled to make sense of the bizarre thoughts and images in his mind. They did not come from the Archon, or Miklos, or any of the men who watched their masters from the room's perimeter. All the minds here were shielded from interference by anyone of telepathic ability, and none were telepaths themselves.

But something, someone was driving him to a kind of madness he could not control, robbing him of will, demanding instant obedience.

"Welcome to Persephone, young man," the Archon said. "I am very glad you have come to us."

Ronan tried to speak. The Archon smiled in understanding. "My brother has told me what you have endured," he said gently. "I hardly expect eloquence under the circumstances. My name is Hector Challinor, and I hope . . ."

His voice faded to a murmur behind the clamor in Ronan's head. It was said that at the moment of Selection, a shaauri youth felt perfect unity with all matter, total comprehension of her place in the order of things.

What Ronan experienced was far more terrible. He had felt so once before, when he had recalled his purpose in requesting sanctuary from the humans, when he knew what he was meant to achieve for the sake of his people.

Only the message had changed.

Kill the Archon. It was as simple, as unspeakable, as that. *Kill the Archon, and destroy the unity of the humans.*

Vision blurred. Muscles locked. This was the true reason he had been sent to human space. The quest for new human technology had been only the cover, a secondary objective if he did not reach the Archon. But his masters had done everything within their power to send him here, to this moment, to this fatal decision that was no decision at all.

The room. The tiny room where they had kept him during the training, as they called it, honing his mind to hold layer upon layer of deception. The darkness and solitude, no voices save those of his trainers; the men and women, Kinsmen, who had reminded him again and again of his chance to win an honorable place among shaauri with courage and sacrifice. Kinsmen, who had invented and imposed a false past of hatred for the aliens, hatred that would propel him on the right course until the time came to remember.

But he had not been meant to remember until he reached the Archon. It was Cynara, and his union with her mind, that had disrupted the Kinsmen's careful work. Now his memory was complete.

Kill the Archon.

He could do it easily, moving faster than any human eye could follow, snapping the Archon's neck and then turning on Miklos as well before his guards recognized the danger.

No.

Kinsman faces watched him, filled with cruel purpose. *For your people, Ronan. For your House and your Line.*

I will not.

His body shuddered like a *ba'laik'in*'s rag doll. Something touched him, and it was as if scalding metal had been laid against his skin. Then other hands grasped, held him still, confined him in a cage of flesh. Janek's eyes—Damon's—stared into his.

"You," he whispered. "Take him to a holding cell and set two teams to watch him until I order otherwise. Go!"

"Damon!" Miklos said sharply. "He—"

"This is my charge, Uncle," he said. "He was mine from the moment he boarded the *Pegasus*." He bowed stiffly to the Archon. "My lord. Forgive this intrusion."

The Archon could hardly be seen behind a wall of *ve'laik'i*, bristling with drawn weapons. Ronan was incapable of fighting. His limbs had lost their strength, severed from the mastery of his brain. The guards half dragged him from the room and out another door, into narrow, featureless corridors and a lift that carried them down beneath the palace into the rock itself.

They threw him into a cell and activated the transparent containment field. Ronan collapsed against the far wall, between the narrow bunk and the facilities, and closed his eyes.

He had betrayed them all: shaauri, their Kinsman allies, his House and Line—the crew of the *Pegasus,* Kord and Lizbet and Miya Zheng, *Magnus* Jesper, Lord Miklos with his ready smile and welcome. Not one had he served with honor.

And Cynara. Even she had not guessed the possible extent of his betrayal. She had believed in him.

Cynara. Strange that he almost felt as if she were with him, though she would be aboard the *Pegasus* and far across space on her way to Dharma. Her faith had been for nothing, yet still he sensed her like a pinpoint of light in the back of his brain, never quite extinguished.

He tried to sleep for a while, and wakened again when a new presence touched the edge of his consciousness. The Kinswoman Brit Carter VelShaan entered the corridor, passed through the wall of guards, and stood before the containment field with her hands clasped behind her back.

"Ronan VelKalevi," she said with a slight nod. "I've heard why you are here."

He looked beyond her to the *ve'laik'i*, and she smiled. "I have permission to be here and speak to you in any manner I wish."

Ronan approached the field, careful not to touch it. "What is there to say?"

"As much as you're willing to share." She glanced about the cold, gray cell. "I regret that it has come to this."

"Why did Damon Challinor send me here?"

"He believes you intended to kill the Archon."

It was not Damon's suspicion that surprised Ronan, but the fact that he had guessed a truth hidden from Ronan himself.

"Did you, Ronan?"

"You have the means to find out, *sh'eivalin.*"

"Means I prefer not to use except in direst extremity—no matter what the shaauri Kinsmen do." She sighed. "I don't believe that you meant to kill the Archon. But I am not confident of your loyalties. Lord Damon's word is influential on Persephone."

"Is he a telepath?"

"We didn't believe so, but we have apparently overlooked certain talents he chose not to share with us."

"If he believes shaauri sent me here to kill the Archon, it will not matter what I say."

"I disagree. Perhaps your reasons for leaving the Shaauriat were complex, and perhaps you didn't have complete control over your fate."

"I determine my own fate."

"Do you?"

Suddenly his fragile discipline wavered, and the images that had come to him in the Archon's presence returned in all their horror. Kinsman faces, Kinsman voices, demanding and promising, minds pushing into his with commands hidden within commands like the pieces of a *ba'laik'in*'s nesting puzzle.

VelShaan caught her breath. "VelRauthi," she whispered.

Ronan retreated to the back of his cell and turned his body toward the wall. Her violation was as nothing to what he had endured on Aitu, but for a time he had thought her better than the Kinsmen who had selected him for murder.

"I'm sorry, Ronan," she said, and silently walked away.

He hissed shaauri laughter and dropped his head to his knees.

Cynara walked up to the first palace checkpoint as if she were on official business, flashing her pass with the easy confidence of one who expected immediate admittance.

The woman on duty examined her and the card and called a superior, who duly sent another guard to conduct Cynara past two more checkpoints and to a third, where he put in another call. Fifteen minutes later, a uniformed attendant led her to a public antechamber in an outer wing and asked her to wait.

She waited, reviewing the events that had led her to return to Persephone with such haste. After Charis's stunning revelation of Ronan's trespass into engineering, Cynara had ordered the *Pegasus* back to Persephone. She had struggled with her anger and despair and overcome them, keeping her deepest fears to herself.

There had been no question of what must be done. Whatever his purpose—even if he had taken nothing, as the evidence suggested—Ronan had deceived her and the crew, and she had to face him down and demand the truth.

Curious that she had considered the personal first—confronting *him,* not immediately reporting his actions to Lord Miklos or, God forbid, Janek.

God forbid she would have to admit Janek was right all along. Once she'd seen Ronan and looked into his eyes, she would know. Then no more secrets, no more protecting the man Miklos had dared to suggest she loved.

At this moment she hated Ronan more than she had loved anything in her life.

She sprang to her feet and paced the length of the antechamber twenty times before another clerk led her into a small office, where she presented her full credentials and repeated the urgent need to speak to Lord Miklos Challinor on a matter of Concordat security. More calls, more waiting, and finally an official-looking and dignified personage appeared to conduct her into the heart of the palace.

But it was not Lord Miklos who met her. It was Janek—dressed with elegant simplicity in tunic and trousers, less arrogant and more confident than she could ever remember seeing him aboard the *Pegasus.* The office he occupied might have belonged to a prince.

"Captain D'Accorso," he said formally. "I am surprised to see you returned so quickly. I understand there is an urgent matter you wish to discuss."

"It was because of this urgent matter that I came back," she said. "I would like to speak with Lord Miklos."

"I'm afraid that isn't possible at the moment." He picked up a stylus and tapped it on the desk. "You may tell me, and I will inform Lord Miklos when he is available."

Cynara clenched her teeth and held on to her patience. "In that case, I must speak to Ronan."

He smiled briefly, freezing her blood. "That is also not possible. You see, Ronan is in custody for the attempted murder of the Archon."

"What?"

If he took satisfaction in her stunned disbelief, he had enough courtesy to hide it. "It's quite true, Captain." He dropped the stylus. "Is the *Pegasus* in orbit?"

She swallowed. "I sent the ship back to Dharma without me."

"Then your news must be urgent indeed. What is it?"

She'd been wrong before in thinking she hated Ronan more than anything or anyone else. "I think I'll wait for Lord Miklos, Janek," she said, "even if I have to sleep in your office."

"I trust you don't hope to win Ronan's freedom," Janek remarked. "Now that he has proven himself a traitor and assassin—"

"It hasn't been proven to me," she said, contradicting her own furious doubts. "Or, I presume, to a court of law."

"We shall see. Oh, and to spare you any future embarrassment, I should inform you that my name is not Phineas Janek."

Her heart was too heavy for surprise. "I didn't really expect Janek to have an office like this," she said. "Who are you?"

"Damon Challinor." He tucked his hands behind his back. "Head of Security for the *Pegasus* Project."

Challinor. Cynara found that her capacity for shock had not quite reached its limit. "Damon Challinor," she repeated. "I should have realized. You're a member of the royal family."

"Nephew of the Archon," he said casually. "But I consider that less important than my rank in Royal Intelligence. I assure you that I take my duties most seriously."

"As do I." Miklos Challinor walked into the room and stopped halfway between Cynara and Damon. He nodded to Cynara. "I heard you'd already returned. Have I missed your report?"

"Not at all, Lord Miklos," Cynara said with a hard glance at Damon. "I've just been informed that Ronan has been arrested. May I know the evidence against him?"

Miklos sat in one of the guest chairs and stretched his legs. "As yet we have only one witness."

"He was seen trying to kill the Archon?"

"No," Damon admitted, jerking up his chin. "Not in the usual way."

"Then why did you—"

Miklos held up his hand. "Patience, children. First, Captain, I'd like to know why you've come back to us so quickly."

"I prefer to speak to you alone, Lord Miklos—"

"Does this matter in any way involve Ronan or the *Pegasus*?"

She hesitated, deliberately looking away from Damon. "It does."

"Then my nephew is entitled to hear it."

Nothing could be worse, in light of what Damon had told her of Ronan's arrest. "While we were en route to Dharma," she said slowly, "my chief engineer reported that there had been some unauthorized access to the engine room computers, specifically the schematic files for the slingshot drive."

"Ronan," Damon said.

"As best we can determine, he acquired a passcard, managed to get past the marine at the door, and evaded the notice of the crew. There is no evidence that he actually stole any information."

"I knew it," Damon said, his voice oddly devoid of triumph. "I *saw* it."

"And you didn't report it until now?" Miklos demanded.

"I wasn't sure until now."

Miklos rose and tapped the intercom. "Send *Mes* Carter VelShaan to Lord Damon's office at once."

"I don't understand," Cynara said. "Lord Miklos—"

"The Archon wished to see Ronan," Miklos said. "I took him to the Archon's private sitting room and introduced them. Shortly after that, my nephew entered the room and claimed that Ronan was about to kill my brother."

"I had reason," Damon said. "I saw what he was about to do."

"You *saw*?" Cynara repeated.

"That's why I've asked *Mes* Carter VelShaan to join us," Miklos said. "There is as yet some confusion as to what exactly my nephew did see, and how."

"Captain D'Accorso's report will be vindicated by other evidence once Ronan is questioned," Damon said. "He will face just retribution as a traitor to his own kind."

Miklos drew up straight and glared at his nephew. "Don't be so hasty to condemn him," he said. "He is, after all, your brother."

Chapter 20

Under other circumstances, Cynara might have been delighted to see Damon so startled. She took no pleasure from it now, for she shared his shock.

"My brother?" Damon echoed, and began to laugh. Miklos's expression didn't change. Damon's laughter dwindled and stopped.

"Your brother," Miklos repeated grimly. "Evidently that was one small fact you failed to 'see' because of your own prejudices. I began to suspect almost as soon as Captain D'Accorso brought him to meet me. I had never met anyone who so closely resembled both my sister Kori and her husband, Jonas Kane VelArhan." He glanced with sympathy at Cynara. "I had tests run this morning, after Ronan left his room. They confirmed my suspicion."

No one spoke. Damon sat down heavily. Cynara locked her knees and remained on her feet.

A Challinor. Ronan was a Challinor, like Damon. She also had the hysterical urge to laugh.

"Of course," Damon whispered. "Now it makes even more sense. He didn't die with my parents—the shaauri took him. They knew we would want to trust him as our long-lost relative. The perfect weapon." He slammed his fist on the desk. "When he first came aboard the *Pegasus,* he claimed to remember nothing of his past. I knew something was wrong with his assertion. It was all a deception, a trick."

Cynara felt ill, half afraid that the room's walls would close in and crush her. The door opened, and a black-haired woman entered the office. She stopped, nodded to Damon and Miklos, and turned toward Cynara.

"Lord Miklos," she said. "Lord Damon."

"*Mes* Brit Carter VelShaan, I present to you Captain Cynara D'Accorso of the *Pegasus.* Captain D'Accorso, *Mes* Carter VelShaan."

The Kinswoman offered her hand, and Cynara took it without reciting the usual empty words of greeting. Carter VelShaan seemed to understand.

"You wished to see me, Lord Miklos," she said.

"You spoke to Ronan?" he asked.

"I did."

"Were you able to glean anything at all from his thoughts?"

"Yes." She hesitated, and Miklos offered her a seat. One by one each of them took the nearest chair, though the tension was palpable.

"He has very powerful shields, as we already realized," she said, "and it would be impossible, short of a true deep-probe, to discern everything he may be hiding. He is, without doubt, loyal to his adopted shaauri kin. But I was able to detect some vivid images which I am sure he did not intend to share."

Damon looked ready to interrupt, but Miklos silenced him. "And what were these images, *Mes* Carter VelShaan?"

"Faces," she said. "Faces all around him, voices giving commands—Kinsmen, in fact, in the process of doing something to his mind. They were definitely not our people. I suspect that his mind was manipulated, and the effect was devastating for Ronan."

"Scylla's teeth," Cynara swore.

"Manipulated," Miklos said. "As in given hidden compulsions? Fraudulent memories?"

"It's very possible. The Kinsmen who went over to the shaauri included many who were not so eager to follow the rules we set for ourselves long ago. They might force their wills on a vulnerable mind."

"Ronan said at the beginning that his telepathy had been suppressed," Cynara said.

"Perhaps it was. Unraveling what really occurred may take a great deal of time and patience."

"Time we don't have," Damon said. "You said he was loyal to the shaauri. Even if his mind was manipulated, there is no evidence that he didn't agree to it."

"None thus far. But I sensed that he resisted the compulsion to kill the Archon, and his feelings about the Kinsmen are unequivocally negative. However he came to be a shaauri agent, I'm certain he didn't expect to suffer what was done to him. He's no hardened assassin."

"Just how strong is Ronan's mind?" Miklos asked.

"I can say with certainty that its power is considerable. This means that whoever tampered with him had to be a very strong telepath as well, and ruthless enough to cut through Ronan's natural defenses. He doesn't grasp the range of his own abilities."

"This could be yet another ploy—" Damon began.

"Unlikely. Emotion is not so easily feigned as thought. Ronan is far too disturbed to have anticipated recent events. Even a disciplined mind cannot control everything."

"He *was* sent by our enemies to act against the Concordat and humanity."

"But his willing, conscious participation in those actions remains to be determined."

"It will be."

"Only if I and my people consent to do a deep-probe, Lord Damon, and that is by no means assured."

"Does he know who he really is?" Miklos asked.

"No. His captors must have known, but they kept it from him." She looked directly at Cynara. "I would swear on my name that Ronan has been suffering from artificially imposed amnesia and is not wholly responsible for his actions. He is lost, Lord Miklos."

"He's dangerous," Damon said. "Too dangerous to leave alone."

"Perhaps he is not the primary danger," VelShaan said. "I

told you that I'd seen certain faces among those who manipulated Ronan's mind. One of them was very clear, and I recognized it instantly. Artur Constano VelRauthi."

The name sounded familiar to Cynara, and she could see the others knew it as well. Damon paced across the room, and Miklos ran his hand through his white hair.

"Constano," Miklos said. "We'd heard he was dead—"

"We also heard that about my parents and brother," Damon said. Unexpectedly, he turned to Cynara. "Constano was the leader behind the first Kinsman conspiracy, which my parents helped to put down. He and his coconspirators were taken prisoner, but some later escaped, and that proved a devastating event for the Concordat. We've believed for some time that he had a large part in the troubles that led to the defection of two-thirds of our Kinsmen to the shaauri, and the subsequent conflict, war, and blockade. But we had been told he was killed in a skirmish near the border some years ago."

"Constano was hungry for power," Carter VelShaan said grimly. "He wasn't satisfied with the privileges given Kinsmen by the Concordat and the shaauri. He believed that Kinsmen should rule human space, and he was confident that he and his followers, with antihuman shaauri assistance, had the means to bring it about. If anyone in the universe had reason to want the Archon dead, it would be Constano and his kind."

"Why Constano?" Damon asked. "Why not the shaauri? You speak as if they are working independently, when they're close allies."

"As close, perhaps, as humans and aliens can be," she said. "But there are many shaauri who will never fully accept any human. We still don't know why Ronan survived and was raised by Kalevi—his original story of being taken on a raid doesn't match the facts."

"This could have been planned from the beginning," Damon said. "Kinsmen and shaauri could have ambushed my parents' ship to prevent them from brokering a lasting peace. They kidnapped Ronan knowing exactly who he was."

"Shaauri might have held him for ransom—such things are done among them—but they didn't. They kept him alive well into adulthood, and accepted him after a fashion." She pursed her lips. "It's also my understanding that they leave any actual espionage to Kinsmen. I think it likely that Constano has never abandoned his plans for ruling human space. The shaauri might have been convinced to give Ronan over to Kinsmen for training as an agent."

"Shaauri don't have telepaths of their own," Miklos said.

"Precisely. Once it was discovered that Ronan had his parents' gifts, the shaauri would not have been sure what to do with him. If Constano had schemes within schemes, they would be hard pressed to learn of it."

"Are you suggesting Constano used Ronan to further his personal ambitions?" Damon asked.

"It's certainly possible. Given what I know of Constano, even probable. And Ronan may have had very little to say about any of it."

"Why wouldn't the shaauri want the Archon dead?" Cynara asked.

"Because shaauri would not think in terms of killing one leader and disabling an entire system or alliance. Their society rarely has a single powerful leader over many Lines or Clans, except in time of war—their *A'Aho-Kei'hon-vekki,* the War-Leader. Even Constano must realize that the Archon's death would not destroy the Concordat, but it might disrupt its function long enough for a carefully orchestrated assault to have a greater effect."

"All of which changes nothing about the danger Ronan poses," Damon said.

"Which you somehow sensed without any overt telepathic skills," Miklos said. "You have always denied inheriting any ability from your parents."

Damon laughed with a touch of bitterness. "I was the only son who didn't carry on the gift. But when Ronan came aboard the *Pegasus,* I began to catch glimpses of events before they occurred. At first I thought these visions arose from my legitimate concern for the Project. But when we returned to Persephone and I saw him—I *saw* him kill the Archon . . ."

"Precognition," Carter VelShaan said. "It's not common even among Kinsmen. Your gift may actually have been awakened by your brother's proximity. You see the future possibilities—what *might* happen, not necessarily what will."

Damon clenched his fists. "Could I risk believing I was wrong?"

"No," Miklos said. "You did what you felt necessary. But now it's time to decide what to do about Ronan."

"The only way to learn the truth is to probe him. Even you must concede as much, Uncle."

"Why do you hate him so much, Lord Damon?" Cynara asked. "He's your brother, and he's suffered more than you can imagine. What has he done to you?"

Damon paled. "*Mes* Carter VelShaan," he said, ignoring Cynara, "if you refuse to carry out the probe as requested, I'll find someone who will." Without another word, he strode from the office.

Miklos let out a long breath. "I must apologize for my nephew," he said. "You asked a legitimate question, Captain D'Accorso. Damon does appear to hold an irrational grudge against Ronan that goes beyond any danger he may present. I'm afraid it stems from the circumstances of his parents' deaths—or presumed deaths. They chose to take Ronan—he was Achilles, then—with them into shaauri space, leaving his brothers on Persephone."

"Ambros and Damon," VelShaan said.

"Indeed. Damon is only a year younger than Ronan, but he recognized that he was being left behind. He knew that Achilles was the only son gifted with telepathic abilities."

"He resented Ronan," Cynara said.

"Ronan was considered quite a prodigy, and his parents wanted him exposed to shaauri culture at an early age. But Damon didn't understand. When the reports came in of Kori's and Jonas's probable deaths—"

"Misplaced guilt?" VelShaan surmised.

"I'm no specialist, but I believe that Damon, in his childish mind, thought he could have stopped the tragedy if he'd gone in Achilles' place."

"A five-year-old boy?" Cynara shook her head. "Can he still believe it after so many years?"

"Ronan's experiences are proof of the mind's complexity and contradictions," VelShaan said. "Damon may have decided that Ronan's apparent treason is evidence, however unlikely, that he bore some responsibility for the loss of their parents."

"He has no right," Cynara snapped.

"It's hardly just," Miklos said, "but if we refrain from judging Ronan, how can we do less for Damon?"

"Ronan didn't know what he was intended to do until the moment came to do it," Cynara said.

"That is my theory," VelShaan said. "He was given a mental 'false front,' so to speak, to make his original story appear authentic to any casual telepathic reading. He was quite literally 'programmed' to remember just as much as was required for a given purpose, triggered by specific circumstances or events."

Cynara averted her face so that the others couldn't see her profound relief. Ronan *hadn't* been a deliberate traitor from the beginning. Depending on these "triggers" VelShaan postulated, he could have remembered his objective any time after his rescue—when she'd first entered his mind, later on Bifrost, when they made love.

At least some of his amnesia must be real. Risking his life to save her and Kord couldn't be beneficial to his mission, even to win their trust. His "programming" was flawed.

He deceived me, but he swore not to enter my mind uninvited. If he'd broken that promise on the Pegasus, *he wouldn't have needed to use Charis and steal the drive schematics. Is that the act of a cold-blooded killer?*

"Whatever Damon believes," she said, "Ronan can't be condemned in the absence of all the facts. He didn't kill the Archon. I shared Ronan's thoughts and memories more than once while we traveled on the *Pegasus*. I can't be sure how much was real, but some of it had to be."

Miklos stared at her. "You neglected to mention this before, Captain."

"I take full responsibility for my mistakes, Lord Miklos. But I can assure you that if I had sensed in Ronan the intention to harm the Archon or anyone else, I would have informed you immediately. Until we discovered the infiltration of engineering, I had no reason to suspect him of anything but an understandable disorientation."

"Damon was sure that something had happened on

Dharma to bring you closer to Ronan, and at the same time arouse your suspicions."

"I'll gladly tell you—or *Mes* Carter VelShaan—all I experienced, if it will help Ronan and the Concordat."

"And if it harms Ronan?" Miklos asked.

Cynara didn't answer, and Miklos sighed. "If you consent to open your mind to *Mes* Carter VelShaan, I'll leave this interrogation to her."

The Kinswoman nodded. "There is much we might learn if Ronan and Cynara shared any kind of link, even if Ronan carried spurious information. Telepathic communication is extremely complex. That's why it has been so useful in interpreting the language of the shaauri, and negotiating diplomatic and cultural hazards inherent in interspecies communication."

"And it becomes even more effective in the presence of profound emotion," Miklos added. He turned to Cynara. "You do love him, don't you?"

Cynara choked. "Lord Miklos, I assure you that my personal feelings—"

"We generally prefer to give the benefit of the doubt to those we love, and defend them in the face of the most daunting odds," he said. "Ronan is my nephew. You can rest assured that I will speak to Damon about his prejudices, but he has ultimate authority in any matter pertaining to the Project. If I could find a good reason to spare Ronan . . ."

"I had no idea that love was involved in this," Carter VelShaan said. "If we could turn Ronan to our side, and be sure of him, the advantage could be enormous. He could learn what became of Lady Kori and Jonas, what Constano intended if the Archon was assassinated, and how much the shaauri Kinsmen are behind the blockade and continued hostilities."

Even love had become just another calculation. "You're suggesting that he become a counteragent for the Concordat," Cynara said.

"His mind was tampered with before," the Kinswoman said. "It could be done again, *if* he were willing. He could even be implanted with false information for the Kinsmen who programmed him."

"The Kinsmen probably expected him to die carrying out their schemes. Assuming they take him back, they'd be very likely to kill him."

VelShaan looked at Miklos. "Am I wrong in presuming that he is already under a possible sentence of death, at the very least severe mental damage?"

"I'm afraid, given the circumstances—" Miklos paused, frowning. "It seems a long shot, but if Ronan truly wished to atone for his actions—if he cares for you, Cynara, as I believe he does—he might even turn the tide in this cold war."

"You can't ask it of him," Cynara said. "Even if he agreed, you could never be sure . . ." Her mind went blank, and then filled with impossible, absurd notions she was almost afraid to speak aloud. "Unless someone goes with him. Someone who knows him as well as anyone can."

Miklos looked up at her. "Are you volunteering, Cynara?"

"What are the alternatives? I'll do whatever is necessary to spare Ronan death or permanent brain damage. He'll have a far better chance among the shaauri."

"Though I honor your courage," Miklos said, "I can't permit you to give yourself to our enemies. They would most certainly kill you, and you're still a valuable asset to the Alliance."

"Maybe it isn't necessary for me to cross the border. *Mes* Carter VelShaan—"

"Brit."

"Brit," she said slowly, "bear with me. I have a very unconventional idea that just might work."

R onan woke from a dream of Cynara in his arms, whispering secrets he could not quite understand. The moment he opened his eyes, he knew that it had not all been a dream.

Cynara was here, on Persephone, in the palace. He did not know how long ago she had come, but she was on her way to him now.

There was only one logical reason why she would have returned to Persephone so quickly. He was on his feet, as close to the field as he dared, when she entered the corridor and spoke to the guards.

"Ronan," she said.

He expected accusation, anger, the bitterness of betrayal. It could not have been much worse if *An* Charis had accompanied her to confront him with his deceit and manipulation of her mind. But Cynara was alone, and the way she looked at him made his legs as weak as an unweaned *ba'laik'in.*

"Cynara," he said. "I am sorry."

"I believe you are," she said. "Chief Charis doesn't seem to have been harmed." She hesitated. "You made her deliver her passcard to you, and clouded the minds of the marine and the other crew. That must have taken a great deal of skill. But when you faced your final decision, you didn't take what you'd come for."

Her words were like blows, reminding him of every failure and betrayal, great and small. "You returned to report what I had done."

"Yes. But matters aren't nearly so black and white as they may seem." She braced her legs apart and clasped her hands behind her back, all First and commander. "Did you come here to kill the Archon?"

"I did not," he said, "but the compulsion was within me. They put it there."

"The shaauri Kinsmen."

He nodded once, letting his eyes speak for him. "I did not know their full purpose. I still do not—"

"You don't know what else they had in mind for you," she finished softly. "It must be terrible, Ronan."

"You speak so to me after what I did on the *Pegasus*?"

"I can't punish you any more than you punish yourself." She lifted her head, and he felt in her a new confidence that made his own helplessness all the more contemptible. "I know some of what you've done has been within your control, and some has not. But I don't hate you, Ronan. Believe that."

And then, without warning, she opened her mind to him. He saw that she did believe him; he felt that incredible generosity of spirit and courage that allowed her to forgive and yet find regret for what he might have suffered. If there was any fear, it was so well hidden that he could not discover it.

She challenged him to take what he could of her thoughts

and what lay beneath. He refused the temptation. But in his refusal, he let her feel what should have remained locked in his own heart. She shut him out as firmly as she had done at the end of their night on Dharma.

"I'm here alone," she said. "The *Pegasus* is en route to Dharma, as before. I won't leave you until this has been resolved."

"If I am judged a murderer, I will be punished," he said. He reached toward the field, irrationally wishing to touch her even if that touch brought him pain. "Do not stay, Cynara."

She shook her head fiercely. "You won't be executed. I can't explain it all now, but—"

Her words were interrupted by the sudden attention of Ronan's guards and the entrance of Lord Miklos. He came to stand beside Cynara, his gaze hard and uncompromising.

"Ronan," he said. "I've spoken to Lord Damon, and I have convinced him to let you go."

"He believes . . . you also believe that I was sent to kill the Archon."

"It doesn't matter what I believe." He gazed at the floor between his feet. "Even among humans, kinship means something more than social advantage and accident of birth. You are the son of my sister, Lady Kori Galatea Challinor, and her husband, Jonas Kane VelArhan of the Kinsmen. For that reason, and for that alone, you will be permitted to leave Persephone and return to your adopted people."

PART III

SHAAURI-*ja*

Chapter 21

*C*hallinor.

Ronan heard the words, and there was a part of him that understood instantly, even accepted as if in some way he had always known.

But the part that was shaauri revolted. He sat down on the cool floor of the cell, placing his hands flat at his sides to support his unsteady weight.

All his life he had wondered about his human parents. He had been told that they were human colonists on a backwater world, left alive but childless when he was taken in a *be'laik'i* raid. Even when he had doubted the story—even when he had fled shaauri-*ja* convinced his escape was real—he had never seriously believed he would see them again.

Lady Kori Galatea Challinor. Jonas Kane VelArhan.

"You are Damon's brother," Cynara said. She came nearer to the field and knelt, one hand lifted. "Lord Miklos is your uncle. Your mother and father were lost in shaauri space on a diplomatic mission twenty-three years ago, and presumed dead along with one of their three sons, Achilles. You, Ronan."

Ronan was not his real name. He had known that, too. But Achilles meant less than nothing.

Damon was his brother. Phineas Janek, the man who hated him, was as close to him as any human could be by birth.

"The Archon feels some sense of obligation to his sister," Miklos said coldly, "as do I. We recognize that it was not your choice to be raised among our enemies, and that your will has not always been your own. Nevertheless, you'll be allowed to leave only with the understanding that any attempt to return to human space will meet a lethal reception." He looked away, as if he couldn't bear to see this pathetic creature that was his kin. "We can't risk the danger you present to all humanity. Go back to the shaauri, and remain there."

Sickness bent Ronan to the floor. He wrapped his arms around his stomach and let his forehead rest against the hard gray surface.

"Ronan," Cynara whispered.

"I understand, *Aino'Kei,*" he said. "But if you let me go, I will promise nothing. I cannot."

"Captain D'Accorso has agreed to escort you to the edge of the Shaauriat, and I have made my yacht available for this purpose. Its lifepod's engine has the range to get you through the wormhole and into the hands of the shaauri—if that is where you wish to go."

Ronan almost laughed. There was nowhere else to go, even if his loyalty did not pull him back to Aitu. But he had nothing to give them—only word of new drive technology that must be retrieved by an agent far more capable and ruthless than he. It was quite possible that his failure merited punishment with the execution his human kin spared him.

But he would not go willingly to the Kinsmen.

"Do not return, Ronan," Miklos said, his voice breaking, "or we'll be forced to kill you."

Ronan struggled to his feet. "I will go," he said. "But let another of your warriors take me from human space."

"No, Ronan," Cynara said, rising. "That decision is final."

"There is a risk," he said, forgetting Miklos and everything he had learned. "I will not let you take it."

"What are you afraid of, Ronan?" she countered. "That you'll become deranged and ravish my mind? You've been my responsibility from the beginning, and I intend to see this through."

There was no yielding in her eyes. He knew it would not be possible to escape and leave her behind.

"Lord Miklos," he said, "I ask that you convey my regrets to the Archon."

But Miklos had already gone. Cynara stood with Ronan a little longer, and then she, too, left the detention area.

Without the Eightfold Way, Ronan could not have passed through the next few hours with his composure intact. He recited the chants over and over again until his mind could accept Miklos's revelation, emotionless and serene.

They had known, of course, those Kinsmen who had trained and prepared him. They had relied on his kinship with the Archon to permit him access, and perhaps even to win his freedom should he fail. More likely they had expected him to die in the attempt.

At least there would have been some honor in death. He would have earned his place among shaauri, even in failure. What purpose could he serve now?

Guards brought him a meal, and then a second. Hours later they took him from the cell and escorted him through the corridors and to the edge of the palace grounds. It was night; the Acropolis was quiet, though the lights of traffic flashed in the city below.

Cynara was waiting for him. Together they entered a palace skimmer and rode to the spaceport, where Lord Miklos's yacht was ready for departure. One of the Challinor pilots was on hand to instruct Cynara in the peculiarities of the ship's helm; the guards took Ronan to the passenger lounge and installed him in one of the plush seats.

At last the guards and pilot disembarked. The ship hummed under Cynara's hand and lifted, unchallenged, in that peculiar darkness that always comes just before dawn.

The yacht cleared the atmosphere and settled into its course. Cynara emerged from the cockpit, her hair loose about her shoulders. She sat down in one of the swivel chairs opposite him.

"Are you all right?" she asked.

"You should not have come, Cynara."

"Haven't you figured out that this—these things that have happened to us—are not entirely within our control?"

"It is a most disturbing philosophy."

"Shaauri don't control Selection, do they? It just happens. And lifemating—it strikes me as almost a kind of destiny."

Her question took him unaware. "Humans believe such things?"

She dropped her head so that her red hair veiled her face, but her shoulders moved in silent laughter. "Never mind. What's done is done. You're on your way home." Suddenly she looked up again. "Unless you'd rather go somewhere else."

Miklos had asked that question on Persephone, and the answer was the same now as then. "I must return to my people on Aitu."

"Did they know why you left?"

"The *Arva'Kir*—our leaders—and a few of the high-ranked *va'laik'i* knew, for they approved my original purpose to gather intelligence."

"They gave you to the Kinsmen."

"I wished to serve. But my status as an agent would not have been widely circulated. Ain'Kalevi was informed that I had finally gone on Walkabout."

"From which you might not return. But you're coming back empty-handed, Ronan. You'll be punished."

"I have allies. I will be given the chance to speak."

"You'll still have nothing to give them." Her anger beat against him like the heat of a midsummer bonfire. "I can take you . . . anywhere, Ronan. Anywhere other than the Shaauriat."

"To Dharma, where they already believe you to be a traitor? The Challinors would learn of it, no matter where you left me. I will not permit you to betray your loyalties for my sake."

"And what if your shaauri brothers cast you out, Ronan? What then?"

It was a possibility he had considered, more terrifying than any other. To become *ne'lin* in truth, a ghost, unseen, unable to win his way from the twilight of a half-life . . .

"It will not matter, as long as I know you are well."

"That isn't good enough." Abruptly her mood shifted, and she compelled him to meet her gaze. "When you were in the cell on Persephone, Brit Carter VelShaan saw images in your mind—images of the Kinsmen who trained you. She also said that shaauri would not have sent you to kill the Archon."

"They do not hire assassins. It would be dishonor and cowardice."

"And they wouldn't think that killing a single human leader would paralyze the Concordat, no matter how important the Archon is. But humans—your Kinsmen—might have other, more subtle reasons for wanting the Archon dead. That's why I believe these Kinsmen are as much your enemies, the shaauri's, as they are humanity's. It was Kinsmen who programmed you to assassinate the Archon. They're operating clandestinely for their own purposes."

"Programmed." It seemed a most appropriate definition. "I have reached the same conclusion," Ronan said.

"We know you weren't aware of everything the shaauri Kinsmen intended for you. They corrupted your memory, even your emotions. That was one reason Miklos let you go." She paused, becoming suddenly fascinated by the pattern of the carpet. "When did you begin to remember, Ronan?"

He could not misunderstand her. "On Bifrost, when you forced me to remain alive. Our sharing . . . released my memory."

"That was also when you began to regain your supposedly lost telepathic abilities."

"They were lost to me, for a time. I was meant to employ them, but not until it was absolutely required."

"The Kinsmen didn't expect you to recover your memory so soon."

"I am sure they did not, but they did not anticipate your . . . interference in their work. After Bifrost, I remembered only that I was to gather information about the new technology that permitted human ships—the *Pegasus*—to pass through shaauri-*ja* unscathed."

"That wasn't your ultimate goal."

"It was a secondary objective, in the event that I failed in my first."

"To assassinate the Archon."

"I believe that I would have been driven to use any means necessary to reach Persephone."

"And I took you there." She looked away. "You did an excellent job of deceiving me. I didn't become wary until that night at Uncle Jesper's . . ." Her words slowed and stopped.

He wanted very badly to touch her, hold her, but he dared not. "I intended to retrieve the intelligence just as I was instructed, but it brought me no pleasure to deceive you."

"I've wondered how many of the things you said were genuine."

"Not all was deception."

"But your first loyalty is to the shaauri."

"I knew much less of humanity than I do now. I believed what I did would protect shaauri-*ja* from Concordat invasion. Matters are not so clear as they once were."

"That is a vast understatement." She looked as though she wished to attack the bulkhead with her fists and teeth. Gradually her anger gave way to poorly feigned indifference.

"We'll reach the wormhole any minute," she said. "I'll need to take the yacht through manually. Stay webbed in."

She disappeared into the cockpit. It was only then that Ronan considered the one question Cynara had failed to ask: why he had not taken the *Pegasus* intelligence directly from her mind when they had joined on Dharma.

He would have found it very difficult to answer.

Ronan lay back until the alarm sounded and he felt the ship enter the wormhole. After a moment of disorientation, he knew the yacht had reached the other side.

"Two more legs," Cynara said at the door, "and we'll reach the border. You have six hours to make up your mind, Ronan."

"I do not require it." He unwebbed and rose to face her. "I cannot go to any human colony. I would live on an uninhabited planet if humans could survive there, but I do not wish to spend the rest of my life alone. Shaauri go mad when they are alone, Cynara. I think humans do the same."

"Like Sam Gunter on Bifrost," she said. "Yes, humans do the same." She stood before him, hands on hips. "Have you considered that the Kinsmen aren't just going to leave you alone? You know too much. They'll find you on Aitu, Ronan."

"I expect it."

"And you have a plan to deal with them?"

"My plan is to find proof that they are enemies of shaauri, and expose them."

"You think you can accomplish this on your own."

"At least it will be my choice. No one will steal that from me again."

Cynara returned to the cockpit and spent the hours en route to the next wormhole cursing herself for believing, if only for a moment, that Ronan would allow her to save him.

He didn't know she'd planned to accompany him to the Shaauriat from the moment they'd left Persephone. Lord Miklos had hoped she wouldn't, but he was no fool. He and Carter VelShaan had taken the necessary precautions in case she chose to do so.

It was clear to Cynara that Ronan would rather die than continue to live among his adopted people as an outcast, and there were certainly those in the Shaauriat who would oblige his wishes. Only one thing might compel him to fight for himself, and that was her presence at his side. She must either convince him to take her with him, or take the decision out of his hands.

Cynara tried to rest in the pilot's seat until the next alarm sounded. She took the yacht through the wormhole, laid in the course for the final leg, and then went looking for Ronan.

He had gone aft to examine the lifepod that was to carry him through the final wormhole into the Shaauriat. The pod had been designed for two passengers, with room for a third if necessity dictated. In effect, it was almost a miniature starship with the capacity to travel a certain distance under its own power.

Ronan was stretched out on one of the reclining seats, familiarizing himself with the overhead control panel. Cynara poked her head inside the hatch and wormed into the second seat.

"I have to talk to you," she said.

"Are we approaching the border?"

"Soon." There was so little extra room for movement that she brushed his arm or side with every shift of position. Each touch increased her sense of urgency. "Ronan, look at me."

He turned his head. His gaze was direct, unafraid, and filled with sorrow. *"Aho'Va."*

"Stop it. Don't treat me like some kind of distant superior you wouldn't dare to touch."

"You are still angry. Would it not be better if we parted in friendship?"

"Friendship, Poseidon's balls." She grasped his arm and pulled him about to face her. "I have no intention of letting you go back to the shaauri alone."

"You must. I cannot allow—"

"You stiff-rumped, landlocked . . . Haven't you realized by now that I love you?"

He went very still. "This is not wise, Cynara."

"No. It's not wise at all." She waited for his answer, knowing she hadn't the slightest idea how he would respond. Yet she was strangely at peace with herself. Nothing he said could hurt her, for she saw her path clearly, more clearly than at any other time in her ineffectually rebellious life.

"It is not possible," he said, pushing her hand away. "You would be regarded as an enemy among my people, and by the Kinsmen most of all."

"I'm not as defenseless as you think."

"I am the Challinors' enemy, Cynara. I will not betray my House and Line."

"I'm not asking you to choose. I'm only demanding the right to protect the life I saved at considerable cost on the day you left the shaauri."

"Protect." He laughed with an edge of cruelty. "Protect me from *your* enemies?"

She seized the hair at the nape of his neck. "You owe me. You deceived me and my crew, and by Scylla's teeth I'm not letting you do it again." Dragging his head down to hers, she kissed him, biting into his lower lip.

There was no question of stopping. Ronan ground his mouth against hers with equal savagery, and in moments they were wrestling out of their shipsuits in the pod's cramped quarters, flailing arms and legs and frantic caresses.

Cynara sat astride him, thighs pressed to his hips. She plunged down, swallowed him up, and began to ride him without mercy. But he did not allow her to finish. With that remarkable strength that could still surprise her, he braced his feet on the deck and stood, carrying her with him. He held her impaled and neatly laid her back on the adjoining seat, fully reclining it without interrupting the flow of his motion.

She wrapped her legs around his waist and let him set the new rhythm. When he slowed to kiss her, she drew him back. They had to stay together, be together every moment, in every way.

"Cynara," he whispered, half groan. She locked her hands behind his neck and pulled his head into the crook of her shoulder. His breath scalded her neck. He pierced her through, all the way to her soul.

Their minds touched, but nothing so crude as thoughts passed between them. It was all emotion.

Love.

Love swept every lesser passion before it, burned the simpleminded schemes of mere humans to cosmic ash. The yacht's frame dissolved around them. Two beings freed of mortal constraint spread wings and soared on the tides of space, gathering warmth and nourishment from a thousand suns.

They danced, as ancient legend said angels did in heaven. They passed through the artificial constructs humans and shaauri called borders and scorned the petty conflicts far below. Ronan flung himself into a star and emerged again whole, every scar erased from his body, glowing like some glorious creature constructed of light and dreams. Then, laughing, he plunged through Cynara's incorporeal body and wrapped her in the vastness of his embrace.

No one, nothing stood in their way. They were gods, complete in understanding, invulnerable to the fetters that bound ordinary creatures. They were one.

The universe exploded, casting forth its countless multitudes of stars. Cynara returned to her own body, shivering with astonishment. The transcendent emotions she had grasped so briefly had faded. She knew mortal intelligence was not meant to live that way, that the human mind could not compass such perfection and survive.

But she felt no regret, no fear. Her body was sated, and her mind was at rest. A part of her had remained separate, inviolate even during the height of passion, and that part smoothly assumed control once more. She looked on the universe with calm, dispassionate reason.

Love. Was that truly what she'd felt in Ronan, or had it been an illusion? Could she trust emotions dredged up in the midst of sublime physical union? She'd admitted her feelings, but Ronan couldn't freely return them while he harbored such conflicting loyalties.

Whatever they'd shared during their lovemaking, she was quite sure that Ronan hadn't glimpsed her immediate plans. And when he discovered them, he wouldn't be able to prevent them.

The proximity alarm sounded with sharp finality. Ronan stirred but didn't open his eyes.

Cynara rose to dress, carefully guarding her thoughts. She touched the panel on her wristcom to silence the alarm.

"You'd better dress and web in," she said.

He groaned softly but obeyed, and she stepped outside the pod to set the yacht's autopilot. When she returned to the pod, Ronan stood beside his seat, bent under the low overhead, and gazed at her solemnly as if he expected a wrenching farewell.

Don't slip now, she told herself. "Sit. We still have a little time left."

With a slight frown Ronan perched on the edge of his seat. Cynara lay back in the second seat as if to make herself comfortable and tapped her wristcom.

The hatch sealed with a click, and then the pod shuddered and broke free of its clamps.

Ronan half rose. "What have you done?"

"I instructed the yacht to eject the lifepod on my command. Too late to stop it now." The pod's engine came to life, and she pulled the webbing over her hips and chest. "One minute until we enter the wormhole. I suggest you web in."

He spat some alien curse and did so. His emotions could easily overwhelm her if she let them. But she wouldn't, because she felt strong and sure of her purpose. She concentrated on the overhead displays. "Ten seconds," she said. "Five."

The pod shuddered and entered the wormhole. Ronan stared straight up, jaw set. In seconds they were on the other side, where a shaauri reception committee was waiting.

The alien vessel was of the striker class like the one that had pursued Ronan. The pod's small screen gave very few details of design or decoration, but Ronan had already unwebbed and was studying it intently.

"Can you read the designation?" she asked.

His anger remained at low ebb, where it couldn't interfere with the far more pressing business at hand. "I am not sure," he said. "Let us hope they know of my mission."

"You seem to have expected them to be here."

"There are regular patrols at most shaauri wormholes, but junctions to Concordat territory are most closely watched. It is possible this ship is expecting my return."

"I always meant to ask if the shaauri vessel that chased you to the *Pegasus* was part of the plan."

"Few shaauri knew of it," he said. "Pray to your gods that these do, or that they are Kalevi allies."

"Not Kalevi themselves?"

"My Line does not have its own ships, or any interest in worlds beyond their own. But Clan Moikko, to which Line Kalevi belongs, does possess them. If this ship is Moikko, its First will not have us killed immediately."

"That's a relief. What now?"

"We wait." He moved close, his arm touching hers. "Do not speak to the shaauri. I will say what is necessary, and do whatever I must to protect you."

"I knew what I was doing when I came. I'm prepared to take the consequences."

"I am not." He almost smiled, though it was not a pretty expression. "Do not stare at any of the shaauri; keep your gaze averted. We are inferiors until our place is established. Do not show your teeth, or smile, or offer your hand. Remain quiet."

"I plan to." *And I'm not prepared to have you risk everything for my sake.*

That is my decision. You are in my territory now.

She heard him clearly, more than ever before. There was a new ease in such communication, one that did not require physical contact, and she found that she could keep that mental channel open without exposing all her thoughts and feelings. Even so strong an emotion as love couldn't fog her mind when survival itself depended on absolute awareness and control.

The image on the screen changed as the striker came about. Its grapples struck the pod with a muted thump, and the cable began to reel them in like a well-hooked fish.

For Ronan it must have seemed a repeat of his "rescue" by the *Pegasus,* but this docking might not end nearly so well. A single shaaurin might be waiting, or a thousand.

Stay close. Ronan opened the hatch and stepped out ahead of her, hands at his sides, palms out and fingers curled tightly to conceal his nails. Evidently a clenched fist was not a sign of hostility among shaauri. Cynara bit hard on her lower lip to stifle an untimely laugh.

Do not show fear. Cynara ground her teeth and nearly bumped into Ronan when he stopped. His head was slightly turned to one side, neither bowed nor lifted, as he met the armed shaauri who confronted him.

Warriors. No one could mistake the size of these shaauri, or their aggressiveness. Cynara struggled to keep her head low and still assimilate the incredible vision so few humans had ever been privileged to witness.

The warriors—*ve'laik'i,* Ronan called them—stood well over six feet tall, and their spare and functional clothing did nothing to conceal the muscles flexing under deep red, black-barred fur. Cynara remembered that shaauri rank was determined visually by the number of stripes on the body fur; these warriors had a large number collected on the upper torso and arms.

Ronan had always been incredibly graceful in his movements. Now she understood what he attempted to mimic, for the shaauri did not so much walk as flow over the deck. Their limbs were formed differently than humans', yet there was no hint of awkwardness in the aliens' physiques. Feet were bare, and the hands, bearing sinister weapons, were armed with curved, sharpened, and tattooed nails.

Their faces were indeed catlike, as much as an ancient Terran monkey's was like a human's; the shaauri's whiskers grew like parentheses on either side of the face and formed two bristle-like clumps on the jaw. Ears, set slightly to the side of the head, were large and pointed and extremely mobile, never quite still.

But it was the creatures' eyes that were most extraordinary, large and tilted and red-gold, with vertical oval pupils. Those eyes were staring at Ronan in open challenge, waiting for a single false move.

One of the shaauri spoke. Its voice—Cynara couldn't tell if it was male or female—was utterly unexpected. There was nothing feline about it. Recordings could never do it justice, for human hearing was not meant to absorb its incredible complexity. Cynara sensed pitches too high or low for her to detect, rumbles she felt in her chest, hissing sibilants and minuscule alterations in tone that must have held great meaning for other shaauri.

Ronan listened intently. How he understood with his human senses was beyond her, unless he—like "true" Kinsmen—relied on telepathy and had done so in the past without realizing it. After the shaaurin finished speaking, Ronan waited several minutes in silence and then began his reply.

Human voices were no more designed to make those sounds than human hearing was to perceive them, yet Ronan came so close that Cynara couldn't tell the difference. His throat and tongue and chest manipulated tones up and down the scale and well beyond it. She concentrated, seeking explanation in his mind.

The shaaurin warrior had challenged, and Ronan answered simply, with Line, House, and name. "Ronan" had never sounded so peculiar. There were honorifics, including the prefix "Ve," which Ronan had applied to Kord on the *Pegasus,* and much that she interpreted as additional courtesies due those who were, at least for the time being, in a position of greater rank and power.

The one thing Ronan did not do was back down. He kept his gaze averted, but never lowered; his stance was straight, unapologetic, and his body and hands moved almost imperceptibly to accent his words. Cynara guessed that his small and immobile ears were his greatest disadvantage. It must have been difficult to grow up among shaauri lacking those marvelous appendages.

It must have been difficult not to be afraid of these beings every minute of every day. But Ronan was not afraid—not for himself. His only fear was for her. Even that he did not let the warriors see.

When he had finished, there was another silence, not so long, and one of the warriors turned to the three shaauri standing behind. More whistling, growling, and hissing, and then one of the three stepped forward.

The difference in its fur was immediately apparent. Where the dark bars on the warriors' shoulders were heavy and numerous, those on this individual turned its upper body nearly black from neck to waist. It also wore minimal clothing, consisting primarily of a long robe open at the sides and lightly held in place with a sash. It, like the others, wore little personal ornamentation, as if the striking fur were enough.

Ronan stood still, if possible even more alert than he had been facing the warriors. The new shaaurin moved up between the *ve'laik'i* and made a gesture with one graceful, long-nailed hand. Ronan answered an unspoken question. Cynara heard some semblance of her own name, honorifics attached.

The robed shaaurin answered, Ronan responded at some length, and the shaaurin made a single perfunctory sound that could only be a command. Ronan hesitated and then slowly moved aside.

She is Third of this ship, Ronan spoke in Cynara's mind. *Let her see you. Do not be afraid.*

He had, she thought with some irony, decided to be funny at the worst possible moment. Cautiously she moved forward, standing shoulder to shoulder with Ronan and hoping the shaaurin would interpret her stance as one of perfect unity with him.

Silence. Cynara's own breathing seemed deafening. Ronan was with her, all around her, though he didn't so much as twitch a finger. She felt the shaaurin's stare, undeniably rude by human or shaauri standards.

Then she lost her temper, and stared back.

One of the warriors moved. The robed shaaurin barked another order, and both *ve'laik'i* lunged toward Ronan with the butts of their weapons raised to strike.

Chapter 22

N*o!* Had there been other telepaths aboard, every one of them would have heard Ronan's warning. The *ve'laik'i* saw it clearly enough; instinct stopped them in their attack, and Ronan seized on that hesitation.

"No," he repeated firmly, staring past the warriors into the *arvi'va*'s eyes. "You will not take her, Tala Aarys. This female carries intelligence vital to shaauri security, and it is information only I can access. She is my hostage, and I will deliver her to my Line, alive and well."

The Aarys ship's Third was so stunned by his assumption of equality that she halted her warriors and simply stared back. Had Cynara asked him what he did, he could not have explained; so much of shaauri nature was incomprehensible to humans, especially that behavior not defined by words.

At this moment he held the advantage, and he must continue to do so. Boldness was his only hope. Tala Aarys was young, clearly inexperienced and new-come to her rank; the First and Second of the Aarys striker watched from behind a rank of *ve'laik'i,* waiting to see what she would do. It was as much her test as his.

If the young shaaurin chose to continue with her attack,

her superiors might or might not stop her. He had to make
sure that they did.

"I have told you my name and purpose, *Va* Tala," he said.
"You are of Moikko. You know why I was sent into human
space. If you take my hostage, you will challenge Line
Kalevi, and I will fight. Is this wisdom, when all shaauri suffer by such conflict in time of war?"

"*Human,*" Tala Aarys spat, anger in the set of her ears.
"You are not shaaurin."

"I am Ronan VelKalevi, sent forth by the War-Leader and
the First of Ain'Kalevi."

"And by Kinsmen."

The hatred in her words was manifest. Before the Second
War, Aarys had allied itself with Kinsmen rebelling against
the Concordat. The human rebels had turned against their
shaauri allies to save themselves. Now it was well known
that Aarys, like Kalevi, hated all humans. That was another
advantage Ronan must exploit.

"I am not Kinsman," he said. "Because of my birth, I was
deemed best suited by *A'Aho-Kei'hon-vekki* to seek word of
new human technology that threatens shaauri-*ja*. Now I have
returned, and I ask in the name of *Kei* Moikko that you deliver me to Ain'Kalevi."

"Humans lie," Tala Aarys said.

"But Ronan VelKalevi is no ordinary human." The ship's
First stepped from behind her guardian *ve'laik'i* and flicked
her ears to signal that Tala Aarys should retreat. The youngster did so with barely concealed resentment.

"I have heard of you," the First addressed Ronan, ne-
glecting even the most neutral honorific but considerably
more courteous than her Third had been. "Aarys was asked
to watch for your return, but we were also given word to
transport you to the Kinsman holding on Luhta." Her teeth
flashed. "It is to Ain'Kalevi, and not to these Kinsmen, that
you wish to be delivered?"

A trap lay within the simple question. Ronan did not mistake the First's easy manner for friendliness. Whatever the
orders she had received from the *A'Aho-Kei'hon-vekki* regarding Ronan's disposition, his immediate fate rested with
her alone.

"I am not Kinsman," he repeated, meeting her gaze. "I was raised in Ain'Kalevi."

"You have no Path except among other humans."

"Better *ne'lin* than First of Kinsmen."

She absorbed this in silence, the eloquent shaauri silence Ronan had missed among humans with their constant noise and chatter. Cynara released a long, slow breath. He knew her fear as his own, but he could not risk a moment's inattention to address it. Every blink or shiver held significance to shaauri and could betray him.

"We have heard the words of *A'Aho-Kei'hon-vekki*," the First said at last. "We have heard your words." She glanced at each of her subordinates in turn. "It is my judgment that this human will be taken to Ain'Kalevi, who may collect this intelligence and deal with Ronan VelKalevi's hostage—and Kinsmen—as they choose."

Ears twitched and whiskers vibrated in argument. When the First faced him again, Ronan knew the others had agreed with her decision.

"Ronan VelKalevi, you will go with this female to secure quarters."

Ronan bowed to the precise degree necessary, offering honor and thanks but yielding nothing of his neutrality. It was good that the Aarysi didn't know what to make of him; they would proceed with caution because his place in shaauri society was not in accord with any they knew. *Ne'lin* he appeared, but no *ne'lin* was granted such responsibility and adoption into a shaauri House.

So he remained an enigma. He had trusted that very confusion, along with unprecedented boldness, to protect him and Cynara. His assumption had proved accurate . . . for the time being.

The First and her subordinate *va'laik'i* left the bay escorted by six warriors, and four other *ve'laik'i* fell in around Ronan and Cynara. They took the humans at a brisk pace up a companionway to another deck and what Ronan presumed to be one of the ship's holding cells. What the cabin lacked in comforts it made up for in privacy, and Ronan was grateful when the door was shut and locked behind them.

Cynara slumped against the bulkhead and slid down to the

deck. "Poseidon," she whispered. "I wasn't sure we'd survive that encounter."

"Nor was I." Ronan brushed her hair with his fingertips and sat against the opposite bulkhead, focused on bringing his heartbeat to a reasonable pace. His palms were sweaty, and his hair stuck to the nape of his neck. The shaauri would have smelled his perspiration, but they had chosen to overlook it. Perhaps they had not been sure exactly what he felt.

"You did very well, Cynara," he said, willing her to feel the depth of his pride in her. "They did not sense your fear."

She smiled, one corner of her mouth turned down. "I was terrified."

"Is that not the essence of courage—to act in spite of fear?"

The wry humor left her face. "Courage wouldn't have been enough. You were magnificent, Ronan."

Her admiration was quite real, and harrowing. Now that he could allow himself to consider the things she had revealed on the yacht, he was close to being overwhelmed.

Her withdrawal from him, that first night on Dharma, had been devastating. He had only begun to test his abilities against Cynara's. But the time had come when he was grateful that she did not share his thoughts, or he hers.

On Persephone, they had joined in his apartment without so much as a single mental touch. It had not been so in the lifepod. Something remarkable had occurred. A new passage had opened up between them, and if she had not been guarding her mind, he would know her every thought, her every emotion as if it were his own.

She must be just as aware of the difference as he was, yet during their joining she had managed to conceal the small matter of her intent to remain on the lifepod while her mind gave up far more vital information.

There seemed to be no pattern or sense in this change. Cynara was not prepared to embrace it, and neither was he. Their minds walked an uneasy border, neither daring to take a step over the line lest it provoke a most terrible Reckoning.

Still she believed she loved him. That was impossible to doubt. And he did not understand.

"Why did you come?" he asked.

She glanced at the overhead. *Do shaauri keep surveillance on prisoners?*

"Our status is not yet determined," he said aloud. "And shaauri—" *Do not spy.* But that was not the entire truth, for both the War-Leader and the Kalevi had agreed to send him to the Concordat for just such a purpose.

He was human, and so could not suffer dishonor.

"No one will hear us," he said. "Answer, Cynara."

"I told you." She hugged herself. "Do I have to say it again?"

He recognized how difficult the admission of love had been for her—as difficult as it would be for him. Hers was indeed the greater courage.

"That was not your only reason," he said, more gently.

"Just what do you think my other reasons are?"

"I do not know," he said. *You are concealing something important,* he thought, and quickly silenced it. "You have heard me speak into your mind, as I have heard you," he said.

"Very clearly."

"Did you understand what happened when I spoke to the shaauri?"

"Only a little. I . . . haven't got the knack for interpreting alien thoughts." She hugged her knees up to her chest. "Tell me, Ronan. I need to know everything if I'm to help."

"I will try," he said. In simple, terse sentences he translated the conversations between him and Tala Aarys, conveying some sense of the emotions that had accompanied the shaaurin's words. "Aarys, among other starfaring Lines, was instructed to watch for me, but their original orders were to deliver me to the Kinsmen."

"Then the Kinsmen did expect you to return from the assignment."

"Or perhaps by some unknown means they heard that I had failed."

"You mean via shaauri Kinsmen agents on Persephone? Security is almost impenetrable in Eos."

"Lord Miklos must be aware of such a possibility." A strange thought darted through his mind like a *vil*-nymph, too swift to catch. "Aarys would not be pleased to carry out any order remotely beneficial to humans, Kinsmen above all.

Therefore, I bespoke the common Clan Aarys and Kalevi share—Moikko—and requested that they transport us directly to Ain'Kalevi on Aitu. I claimed you as my hostage."

"I assumed as much. This Tala Aarys intended to take me away from you?"

"She attempted it. You must understand that it is shaauri habit to constantly test for weakness in any meeting between kin of certain Paths, strangers, or enemies. Had I been of obvious Path, her reaction would have been much more predictable. Because I acted as an equal, one of Will or Blood from an allied Line meeting another of similar Path, she did not know how to treat me. She assumed my inferiority as a human and tested my resolve. I had to counter her assumption."

"You stood face to face with huge aliens armed to the teeth and never flinched."

"Among shaauri, sheer . . . what you would call 'bravado' . . . can go far to counteract other disadvantages, if one is prepared to risk one's life. I had the disadvantages of no Path, no Linekin beside me, my human form, and the fact that I stood in Aarys territory. I had to behave as if none of that troubled me."

"It worked." She smiled crookedly. "What did they decide to do with us?"

"Shaauri are not like human military, nor are they bound to obey even a War-Leader's dictates without question. Each Line is to some extent autonomous, and first loyalty is always to House and Line. Had the ship's First determined I was a threat, she might have killed us both."

"Did they know what you'd done on Persephone?"

Memory of the near-assassination thickened his words. "They showed no sign of such knowledge. I told them only that I had acquired information I must deliver to my Line."

"What information?"

He could tell her now. It would be best for her to know the truth and be prepared.

"On Dharma," he began slowly, "you began to fear that I might take vital intelligence about the *Pegasus* from your mind. I swore to you afterward that I would not, but—"

"But I have no knowledge worth stealing," she said. "Lord Miklos and *Mes* Carter VelShaan saw to that."

He suffered a moment of shock. "They knew you would come with me?"

"They didn't know, but I wasn't willing to make any promises. I submitted to a process by which VelShaan . . . wiped my memory of all technical knowledge that could be used against the Concordat." She smiled, as if the procedure were as simple as a tooth cleaning. "I know it must seem as if I don't trust you, but Lord Miklos wouldn't let me go without the guarantee—"

"That I would not take such information from you," Ronan finished. Cynara had sacrificed much in order to accompany him into danger. She believed she had eliminated any obstruction to such an action, any risk of betraying her own people.

Something had gone very wrong.

"We found no evidence that you took anything when you broke into engineering using Charis's passcard," Cynara said, catching his gaze. "Did you?"

"I did not."

"Then what you know must be very general. It can't be enough to satisfy your Kalevi."

The *vil*-nymph thought intruded again, buzzing between his ears. He had broken the promise given to her on the *Pegasus*. He had unwittingly uncovered important information in her mind during their mating in the lifepod, though it was not what he'd expected. In many ways it was even more valuable—and dangerous.

How could she claim such information had been erased? If she had not felt him take it from her and denied possessing it, VelShaan's procedure, undoubtedly similar to the one he had undergone on Aitu, had failed in some vital respect.

Just as the shaauri Kinsmen's programming had failed.

He pressed his temples, drawn into a nauseating spiral of speculation. If he were to question Cynara further on the procedure, he would only arouse her suspicions and destroy the trust he must keep if he were to save her life.

How he had learned to hate these games of deception.

Cynara was sketching invisible runes on the deck with her

finger, tension evident in her posture. "When you spoke to the shaauri," she said, "did you mention the people who trained you?"

He gladly pursued her change of subject. "Aarys is aware that Kinsmen were involved in my mission."

"And they hate the Kinsmen. Did you know any of the men and women who worked with you on Aitu?"

"I did not know their names. Their shields were very strong. They trained me with the War-Leader's approval, and Kalevi agreed."

"One of those Kinsmen was Artur Constano VelRauthi. Do you know the name?"

Ronan searched his memory. "It is not unknown to me. Rauthi is not at present a powerful Line."

"But Constano VelRauthi was important to both shaauri and humans thirty-two years ago, when he led the Kinsman rebellion prior to the Second War."

"I do remember. He became Aarys's enemy."

"Constano had some human-hating shaauri convinced that the Kinsman rebellion would lead to the eventual expulsion of *all* humans from shaauri space. But he betrayed his shaauri allies when he saw an advantage in doing so. Your parents were instrumental in stopping the rebellion and capturing Constano VelRauthi. He was returned to the Concordat, but he managed to escape and was presumed dead . . . until his face turned up in your mind."

"If he was known to be living among shaauri Kinsmen, Aarys would hunt him down."

"Then they must not know he's alive and working incognito. Why would your War-Leader and your Line permit a treacherous bastard like Constano to conduct intelligence operations?"

Ronan bared his teeth in a smile. "They would not. This is information Aarys would wish to obtain."

"The desire for vengeance is something humans and shaauri have in common." She returned his smile and moved closer, brushing his temple with the softness of her hair.

He put his arm around her, sinking into the forbidden warmth of contentment, the rightness of her firm and supple body close to his.

"You want to know," she murmured, "if these Kinsmen have their own agenda, and why they sent you to kill the Archon."

"And you desire the same thing."

"Among others." She nuzzled his neck. "It benefits your people and mine. Peace is what we all want."

"You do not know how much many shaauri hate humans."

"I think I do." She glanced at his hand flat on the deck, and he became aware of the netting of old scars. He clenched his fist.

"Line Kalevi . . . and my own House, Ain'Kalevi . . . tolerated Kinsman presence on Aitu only because of me."

She took his hand and deliberately opened each one of his fingers until his palm lay flat against hers. "Would they be able to distinguish one human from another easily?"

"Unless the circumstances were extraordinary, they would not pay attention to individual markings and features." Her hand, so small in his, seemed infinitely precious. "All humans appear alike to them."

"Then they might not recognize any given Kinsman. The Constano I've heard of wouldn't be foolish enough to risk his life carelessly. He may harbor the same ambitions he did during the rebellion, and he has a faction of shaauri-allied Kinsmen on his side. He might have been involved in your programming without shaauri knowledge, hiding among the Kinsmen who are accepted by the shaauri government."

"The only government ruling all shaauri Clans is that assembled by the *A'Aho-Kei'hon-vekki*."

"But *he* knew about your mission. He should also be very interested to learn that Constano is active among the supposed shaauri Kinsmen."

"Indeed." He got to his feet and looked down at Cynara: the luxurious fall of red hair, the supple body, the clever mind behind a face humans called beautiful. If that mind contained motives she refused to admit, he dared not look for them. Not yet.

"Shaauri are coming," he said. "I will give them word of this Constano—just enough to rouse their interest and to suggest that I may be of benefit to Aarys as well as Kalevi."

"And once we get to your world . . . the Kinsmen may already be waiting."

"Let us hope that we reach Aitu before them."

"That's a very good plan." She tilted her head back and smiled, stopping the breath behind his teeth. "I have faith in you, Ronan. In your intelligence, your strength, and your courage."

He turned his face from her. "Let us hope it is enough."

The spaceport on Aitu was hardly more than a field cleared of brush and a cluster of small stone and wooden buildings, just sufficient to permit the landing of a midsized ship. If Ronan hadn't told Cynara that the Kalevi disliked space travel, the conditions here would have suggested that precise state of affairs.

It was also obvious that the Kinsmen hadn't arrived yet. Ronan visibly relaxed, though "relaxed" was very much a relative term. Cynara had to fight the desire to give and receive comfort, here on this alien world where two humans stood against thousands of shaauri. But Ronan was holding back, hardening himself for the inevitable confrontation. The best support she could give him was her vigilance.

As Ronan and Cynara left the Aarys ship, surrounded by hair-trigger *ve'laik'i* with constantly twitching ears, Ronan quickly summarized what they would encounter in the Aitu settlements.

Aitu was a fairly recent colonization effort by several Lines belonging to the Moikko Clan. Three Houses of Kalevi, and three each of their allied Lines Darja, Keisho, and Soraan, occupied the coastal and inland areas of one of Aitu's continents, comprising a population of less than ten thousand individuals. Shaauri, Ronan emphasized, did not like to be crowded. Clans, and sometimes individual Lines, searched constantly for habitable worlds on which new colonies could be established.

The one characteristic common to most of Moikko's Lines was that they were rabidly antihuman and committed to what they regarded as the ancient shaauri way of life. Aitu was a world little changed since its first colonists had arrived. They maintained sufficient technology to assure survival of the majority, and regarded any greater dependence as weakness.

Militant, human-hating separatists, Cynara thought as the shuttle's hatch opened to Aitu's biting air. *These are the people who raised Ronan. The people he has to convince.*

Convince them that he carried information of sufficient value to make his and her own continued existence worthwhile. And that perhaps the shaauri Kinsman allies were not such loyal allies after all.

Cynara had felt the excitement in the Aarys warriors ever since she and Ronan had been released from their cell. The name "Constano VelRauthi" had worked its magic, and Ronan had at least one Line very interested in any conspiracies he might expose.

An armed *ve'laik'in* grunted to Ronan, who took Cynara's arm and started down the ramp. The young female Tala Aarys followed. She addressed Ronan at length, and after a pause he answered. With a disdainful flick of her side whiskers, the shaaurin marched back up the ramp.

"I assured her," Ronan said, "that I will see that the *Aho'Ah'Aarys*—the First of First House of Aarys—is informed if I learn anything of Constano VelRauthi."

"They aren't staying to meet your family?"

Family. The word felt wrong to her, but she used it for Ronan's sake. He needed complete support and no hint of doubt.

"Shaauri of different Lines do not intrude upon one another without good reason," he said. "By such custom is conflict avoided."

There would be conflict enough in store for both of them. Cynara looked toward the few one-story buildings that comprised the spaceport facilities. "No welcoming party?"

"Only one shaaurin watches the spaceport. It requires time for Aarys's message to reach Ain'Kalevi."

"Because they don't keep advanced communication systems." Even with Ronan's description, she wasn't sure what to expect of the Kalevi settlement. Woods crowded close around the cleared area of the spaceport, and she could see the white tops of mountains to the north and east. The sky was blue, heavily overcast in the west, with a brisk wind threatening to blow the storm directly toward them. The look of the place reminded Cynara of the northern islands of Cabiria on Dharma, lands where summers were brief and winters often snowbound.

According to Ronan, Kalevi House compounds were widely spaced, sprawling communities divided by natural borders. Their people grew cold-hardy crops, kept domestic animals, and hunted as their ancestors had done.

Given Ronan's experiences in childhood, the colonists were as primitive in their behavior as they were in their chosen way of life.

She shivered. Ronan moved closer to her, sharing his natural warmth.

"It is cold for you here," he said.

"No worse than the Cabirian taiga during Solstice. Don't worry about me."

"Remember what I told you—"

"Keep quiet, avert my gaze, and don't speak unless spoken to." She grimaced. "It's not in my character to be quite so . . . retiring."

"I know." He brushed her hair away from her face. "At least your hair is red."

She was about to ask if he intended that as a joke when he looked sharply toward the edge of the clearing opposite the buildings. A lone shaaurin emerged from the trees. He—it—was very tall, and its fur was faded with age, but it carried itself like a warrior.

Ronan had stopped breathing. She grabbed his cold hand. His mind was in the grip of emotions so intense she could not help but feel them.

"Who?" she asked.

He tugged on her hand, pulling her toward the shaaurin. The thump of his pulse leaped from his palm to hers. Only as they neared the shaaurin, so close that she could see his broad, bewhiskered face, did she realize who the alien must be.

"Sihvaaro," Ronan whispered.

Cynara released his hand. He strode the last few steps and dropped to his knees, overcome.

The old shaaurin gazed down on him with as benevolent

an expression as a nonhuman face could hold. "Ronan," he said, the name recognizable to Cynara's untrained ears.

Ronan bent his face skyward, exposing the length of his throat, and Sihvaaro took his head between long-nailed hands. It was a welcome, and a benediction. Like a child meeting a much-beloved uncle, Ronan jumped to his feet and embraced the old shaaurin. Then he turned toward Cynara. His face shone with a joy and serenity that took her breath away.

"Sihvaaro," he said, followed by a string of sounds that included her full name. His eyes were warm with pride.

"Cynara D'Accorso," he said, "my teacher and friend, Sihvaaro Kio'laii."

Sihvaaro inclined his head. "It is an honor," he said in fluid Standard, "to greet Cynara D'Accorso, lifemate of Ronan VelKalevi."

Chapter 23

Cynara barely remembered not to stare. "Pardon me?" she stammered.

Ronan flushed. He spoke rapidly to Sihvaaro and joined Cynara.

"He does not understand," he said quietly, not meeting her gaze. "Sometimes he . . . senses things, and can be mistaken."

"Are you saying he's a telepath?"

"There are no shaauri telepaths. Sihvaaro has a . . . gift."

Cynara decided that circumspection was better than awkward questions. "Did you expect him to be here?"

"I hoped." He smiled with an almost childlike pleasure. "It will be easier with Sihvaaro's aid."

She studied the alien more carefully. Ronan had never said anything but good about his teacher, yet their relationship remained a mystery to her. Sihvaaro had taught Ronan how to defend himself, and how to bear his difficult life. He had given Ronan something like love. That was enough for Cynara.

"Honored teacher," she said, hoping the salutation was adequately respectful. "I value your welcome."

Sihvaaro's ears flicked forward and back. "I welcome

you," he said, "but I do not speak for Ain'Kalevi. They will be here soon, and perhaps others." He turned to Ronan. "Your mission?"

Ronan's eyes widened in real surprise, and the sides of his mouth stretched in a grimace.

"You knew?"

"These Kinsmen thought their work most secret, and prevented you from telling me," Sihvaaro said with hissing shaauri laughter, "but they underestimated us both, did they not? You are here alive, with your full memory, a mate, and perhaps the means to catch certain humans in their own trap."

"I should have expected you to unearth their plans. How much do you know?"

"Not enough. But perhaps you have what I lack."

"We must speak further of this."

Sihvaaro laid his hand on Ronan's shoulder, dwarfing him. "You wonder why I vanished at the time you needed me."

"No, Sihvaaro."

"I will tell you. It was necessary for me to play ignorant so that I could learn as much as possible. When I discovered the full nature of their plans for you, and that they intended to take your memories, I considered who best to approach with this information. I spoke to *Aho'Ain'Kalevi,* but she, as you remember, had always been circumspect. I was prepared to take you from the Kinsmen myself.

"But these humans are most clever. They convinced the First that I wished to deliver you to one of the former prohuman Lines, where you could serve no useful purpose or might even work against Kalevi. Soon after you departed, *Va Pohomi* was challenged and deposed by Lenko. He now rules as First."

Though she missed the subtleties of Sihvaaro's tale, Cynara couldn't mistake the gravity with which he spoke the final sentence, or Ronan's reaction to it. "I assume this is bad news," she said.

"Pohomi was a shaaurin of reason, though cautious in her decisions," Sihvaaro said. "She accepted Ronan's presence and supported his wish to aid shaauri-*ja,* though she could not know the Kinsmen's hidden purpose. Lenko not only despises humans, but has great hatred for Ronan."

Cynara met Ronan's gaze. "Personal hatred?"

"Lenko is of Arv'Kalevi, Third House. Their settlement lies some kilometers away, near the mountains." Ronan hesitated. "Arv'Kalevi is the most intransigent in hatred of humans. Before he left for Walkabout, Lenko was one of those who took pleasure in hunting me when I ventured away from Ain'Kalevi-*ja*. Sometimes he and his fellow *ba'laik'i* caught me alone."

The shaauri "children" who had beaten and scarred him. "And no one defended you or tried to stop them until Sihvaaro?"

"Many hated me even here in Second House holding. It was necessary to prove my worthiness to survive."

Cynara could not contain her loathing, even for Sihvaaro's benefit. "I'd very much like to get my hands on this Lenko and his friends."

"Do not consider such a move," Sihvaaro said. "You would be killed. It is necessary to act with prudence."

"Sihvaaro is correct," Ronan said, touching her hand. "Lenko is my enemy, but others are not."

She curbed her anger. "I'll do my best to follow your instructions, but don't expect miracles."

"I do not." He displayed the edges of his teeth. "But if Lenko offers to harm you, I will have to kill him."

Then I'd better make damned sure I don't provoke Lenko and get you killed. "At least the Kinsmen aren't here yet."

"It is surely a matter of days before they arrive," Sihvaaro said. "They have longer ears than many shaauri." He turned back to Ronan and resumed his story. "When Lenko became First, it was necessary for me to depart from Aitu. I did not know where you had gone and had no way to warn you of the change."

"Yet you anticipated my return and risked Lenko's anger to meet me on Aitu."

Sihvaaro's fingers flicked in a rippling gesture that might have been a shrug. "I am old. You are my student and my chosen kin."

"You are accepted at Kalevi-*ja* once more?"

"I believe that others of Kalevi have also begun to suspect these Kinsmen of some illicit purpose," Sihvaaro said, "though even the *va'laik'i* will not approach Lenko without sure proof. As long as the First thinks only of his hatred for humans, he will not be reasonable."

"Then we should not remain here," Ronan said, "but go directly to *A'Aho-Kei'hon'vekki* on Aur."

"This would be logical if we had a ship for such a voyage. It may be that one will come. Until then, we must be prepared to act swiftly and with cunning." He tilted an ear at Cynara. "Yes, even with human deception."

Cynara smiled. "It's comforting to know that we humans can teach shaauri something useful."

"I have taken my old dwelling on the east border of Ain'Kalevi-*ja*," Sihvaaro said to Ronan. "Lenko and his allies have not troubled me there. Others watch, however."

"The Kinsmen will want to silence Ronan," Cynara said, "and that's assuming this Lenko doesn't get him first. I admit my ignorance of shaauri politics . . . but will any Kalevi listen to Ronan if Lenko is against him?"

"Even a First is not all-powerful," Ronan said. "The Second and Third also have great influence, and any of them are subject to challenge. Others will listen. But even if they believe, Kalevi is not enough."

"What exactly do you plan to tell the ones who will listen?"

"First I will approach Lenko and determine his knowledge and intentions. He will not simply kill me without warning. I will tell him that you are my hostage and under my protection."

"And if they try to take me, like the Aarys youngster did?"

He answered with his eyes, suddenly cold and utterly determined.

"Sihvaa—" She looked for the big shaauri and discovered him vanished, as silent as a mouse in the tall grass of the clearing. Not even a ripple marked his passage. "He's gone!"

"To watch for those who come. He will warn us." Ronan brushed the tips of his fingers along the back of her hand. "You are not afraid."

It was a statement, not a question. Cynara was warmed by

his confidence, and unaccountably aroused by his caress. "I should be, if I had a gram of sense—enough for both of us. Sihvaaro seems a good man. He obviously cares for you."

"He likes you, Cynara. Shaauri do not express such things as humans do, at least not in words."

"Sihvaaro seems to have many talents."

"He is unlike any shaauri I have known."

"But he isn't Kalevi?"

"He is of all Lines, and none. In his House of origin, he was selected *ve'laik'in,* of Blood. But he learned a different way and won rare exemption to follow a second path—that of *riama,* Spirit. Sihvaaro believes that Selection is not a biological necessity, and can be set aside. That is why he is called Sihvaaro *kio'laii—* of all Paths."

"All Paths. Surely that's a challenge to shaauri social order."

"He belonged to a group of—you would call them 'warrior-monks'—who were honored a hundred years ago on many shaauri worlds. They traveled from House to House and world to world, teaching their ancient fighting techniques and the philosophy of the Eightfold Way. Nearly all of them have vanished. Sihvaaro found a place on Aitu because he won the respect of Kalevi and the other Lines here, surpassing their skills in tracking, hunting, and combat. Still he is considered strange, almost *ne'lin,* and can never rest easy."

"He recognized someone like him when he began to teach you."

"I do not know why he chose me. Someday I will explain—" He broke off as a harsh, rising whistle sounded from a stand of conifers a hundred meters distant. "They come." He cocked his head. "Darja."

He gave the word an explosive sound. "Enemy?" Cynara asked.

He opened his mind. In the fraction of an instant she saw through a child's eyes and recognized shaauri who, like Lenko, had beaten Ronan whenever he wandered away from the Kalevi compound.

"How many enemies do you have on this planet?"

"Do not worry," he said, pushing her behind him. "I am not so easily defeated as I was in childhood."

"If you think I'm going to let you fight alone—"

He faced her and grasped her shoulders. "You are brave, Cynara, and skilled in defense. But you must leave this to me."

"Not if you're going down."

"I will not."

Shaauri loped out from the cover of the woods, five individuals who looked very much like Sihvaaro and the Aarysi. Each of them bore at least one visible firearm. As they drew closer, Cynara saw that all of them bore the stripe pattern of ve'laik'i warriors. Bullies.

Instinctively she reached for her sidearm, which of course she had left on the lifepod. There was only one thing to do: Trust Ronan . . . and show absolutely no fear.

"Will they shoot us?" she asked.

"No. They will fight as I do." He shifted his weight and flexed his muscles. "Bodies only."

"Ronan—"

"Do not interfere unless there is treachery." To her surprise, he reached out with his mind and bestowed the gift of his pride in her, his warmth, his affection . . . what she almost dared call love. It fortified her like full body armor and a whole array of crack marines. She set her legs apart and watched the Darjai come with a wicked smile.

One ran ahead of the others and stopped, ears cocked forward and shoulder fur standing on end. "Ne'lin!" it called, and spat a phrase that couldn't possibly be anything but insult and challenge.

Ronan answered, hardly lifting his voice above a whisper. The challenger clicked its teeth and charged.

Ronan had five seconds to brace himself before the ve'laik'in was on him. He took the full weight of the alien, turned his hip, and sent the shaaurin flying over his shoulder. It happened so quickly that Cynara missed the individual elements of his counterstrike.

A second Darja moved forward and issued another, longer challenge, rasping like chisel on stone. This time Ronan met the attack by dodging to the side at the last possible moment, making his body small as if he'd folded in on himself. The shaauri's filed nails struck him a glancing blow. It recovered its balance and sprang up only to be felled by a brutal chop from Ronan's right foot.

Cynara had already turned to watch for the first shaauri's recovery. It struggled to its feet, and she prepared to fight it off by any means she had. But it did not attack. It backed away, ears flattened, glaring hatred.

The second shaauri did the same, clutching its belly as it joined its companion.

"These will not attack again," Ronan said between breaths. His shipsuit was torn where the second attacker had scored him, and three parallel red lines marked his skin. He seemed not to notice. "They will come one at a time, by custom, and retire only when shoulders touch the earth."

"That's comforting. Only three to go."

"They send their lesser *ve'laik'i* first." He flexed his arms and performed a gliding, graceful exercise that turned his muscles liquid. "Stand apart."

Their conversation had muted the third warrior's challenge. Its charge shifted abruptly to the right, directly toward Cynara. Ronan sidestepped to meet the warrior. The shaaurin slammed into him full on, and both fell. Blue shipsuit and barred red fur mingled in striking limbs and heaving bodies.

Do not interfere, Ronan shouted into her mind. She clenched her fists to the point of pain and forced herself to wait. Briefly the shaaurin gained the upper hand, straddling Ronan with nails like razors poised to strike. Cynara snatched up a fallen tree branch. In the same instant Ronan flipped his enemy over, knelt on the shaaurin's back, and forced its head to the ground.

But the *ve'laik'in* didn't quit as Ronan had promised. It heaved its bulk with ferocious strength, kicking Ronan up and away. Ronan rolled as he fell, recovering quickly, but the Darja warrior crouched and launched itself at Cynara.

In a second, it was on her. In another, Ronan had the warrior by the neck. He snapped his opponent's head to the side and threw the shaaurin to the ground.

The *ve'laik'in* lay absolutely still. Ronan staggered back, holding his hands out to his sides. His shipsuit was torn in a dozen new places, his lower lip was split, and two of the fingers on his left hand were bent at awkward angles.

Cynara grabbed him before he fell. "Dead?"

"Yes. I did not intend—" He broke off and pushed Cynara away as the other warriors dropped to their knees beside their fallen companion. One of them lifted its face to the sky and roared. The others swung their heads to stare at Ronan and Cynara.

"They didn't follow your rules," Cynara said. "They'll try to kill us now, won't they?"

"Perhaps not." Cynara followed Ronan's gaze to the tall grass moving with as many as twenty shaauri, Sihvaaro among them.

"Kalevi?" she asked.

He nodded and touched his injured lip. "Watch."

The Darjai had also noticed the approaching Kalevii, and began to make sounds so high-pitched that they hurt Cynara's ears. At once they gathered up their comrade and bounded away.

"They know they cannot prevail . . . now," Ronan said, hearing her thoughts.

"I thought Darja and Kalevi are of the same Clan."

"They are. That does not mean they are always close allies. The Darjai avoid a beating or worse by retreat."

"Would they have let you go if you retreated?"

"I am not shaauri."

Cynara was in the mood to tear out several fistfuls of red shaauri fur. Instead, she carefully took Ronan's arm to examine his broken fingers. "How badly are you hurt?"

"Kalevi healers will cure me." He urged her to readiness with his mind and stood very straight. "*Aino'Ain'Kalevi* Samit, the Second of my House."

"Male or female?" she whispered.

"Female. As a majority of *ve'laik'i* are male, so most *va'laik'i* are female."

"That's useful to know." Cynara shut her mouth as the leader stopped several meters from Ronan, Sihvaaro a little apart from her attendants. Unlike the Darja warriors, Samit carried herself with neutral dignity, wearing robes not unlike those of the Aarys leaders but in mingled tones of red that nearly matched her fur. She clutched a tall, carved staff in one hand, and a silver pendant hung from her neck.

To either side and behind her ranged Kalevi warriors, distinguishable from the Darjai only by the color and cut of their spare surcoats. Cynara suspected there were shaauri of other Paths present, but their respective decorations and markings were obscured by those in front.

Ronan did not speak human language again for many minutes. He ignored Cynara entirely, his head slightly tilted and averted as he addressed the Second. Sounds, sometimes distinct as words, flowed and volleyed between them. Ronan's voice was always soft, respectful, never submissive.

At long last there was a pause while Samit considered what Ronan had said, and Cynara tried to make an educated estimate of his success. The fact that the Kalevi warriors hadn't moved forward seemed a very good sign. The long silence did not. Ronan's back was a firm, unyielding wall blocking Cynara's view.

If ever she had needed patience, it was now. She met Sihvaaro's slanted eyes over the heads of Kalevi warriors. He nodded almost imperceptibly. Five minutes passed, and then ten. Her legs were going numb.

It is the shaauri way, Ronan said.

Curse the shaauri—

"*Akai'po,*" the Second said clearly.

Tension flowed out of Ronan like a flooding river. "*He'i, ri hi'ir kala, Aino'Va.*" He reached behind to touch Cynara's waist. *We go to Ain'Kalevi-*ja.

Are we safe?

Samit has accepted my return. She will advise Lenko to listen to my words. You are acknowledged my captive, unless I am challenged.

Next time I'd prefer fighting for myself.

You may yet do so. He silenced her with a warning thought and fell in among the Kalevi warriors. Cynara went along with feigned meekness. Somehow Sihvaaro insinuated himself next to her, and she was reminded that at least one shaaurin could be trusted.

The party of humans and shaauri entered the woods, made up of conifers very much like those she had known on the northern islands of Dharma. There was little undergrowth, and only the occasional rustle of branches indicated other life high above. The path through the forest was unobtrusive, though clearly often used, and Cynara wondered if the shaauri here built roads.

The air grew noticeably colder when they left the woods for a meadow just awakening with new spring greenery. Clouds obscured the sun. Far below lay a cultivated field tended by several shaauri workers, all laboring with what appeared to be hand tools. There were no fences or obvious boundary markers save for distant woods and the silver thread of a stream.

From the hill Cynara could see other fields stretching out to the south and east. In the center of it all was a compound of low, sprawling wood and stone buildings of a color and design to blend in with the landscape. Structures of various sizes were separated by what must be irregularly shaped gardens, large and small, lacking the symmetrical order she expected in human design.

Ronan moved close enough to touch her shoulder with his. "Ain'Kalevi's primary settlement," he said in a low voice. "There are two others, just beyond that wood and to the west."

Cynara knew from his tone and the sense of his mind that this was the place where he had grown up. Such a landscape would have seemed paradise for an adventurous child, if he had been among his own kind. For Ronan it had been hell. He should have hated the idea of going back, but he walked with a light step and raised head.

Nevertheless she reached for his hand and squeezed it briefly. He looked down at her with that profound warmth and ran his thumb along the hollow of her palm.

The path widened into a dirt and gravel road. Curious shaauri field hands paused to stare. Cynara noted that most of these shaauri had little in the way of black stripes, their fur more solidly red than that of the Kalevi escort.

Ronan searched every face, though he did not raise his hand. Some of the shaauri workers seemed to acknowledge him; others turned their backs in clear rejection. Cynara despised them for it.

A half-kilometer across the fields took them to the first of the settlement's outbuildings, some kind of barn or byre for storage or the housing of animals. Many such buildings were scattered along the perimeter, and after another kilometer the party reached the garden bordering the central village.

Now Cynara could make out the heavy wooden walls, pitched roofs, and downswept eaves of the individual, single-story buildings. Some of the doors and walls were carved with geometric or spiral designs. The gardens were still dormant from winter, but obviously well tended. Shaauri workers moved among the buildings with calm purpose, differing only in the cut of garment and striping of fur. Like the field hands, many of these turned away from Ronan, and several made gestures of obvious hostility.

Cynara soon became lost in the twistings and turnings of the paths and gardens. Samit finally brought the group to a halt before a plain one-story structure. Two Kalevi guards herded Ronan and Cynara into the building and shut the door.

The interior was somewhat warmer than the outside air, though not quite comfortable by the criteria of furless humans. There were no partitions in the single room, only a series of beds with wooden box frames, toilet facilities at one end, and a simple table and chairs in the center. The windows were shuttered against the elements.

"Well," Cynara said, "we've survived so far." She steered Ronan to the nearest bed. "You did say you have friends here, didn't you? Most of the Kalevi seem to hold you in considerable dislike."

"Did I not tell you that Kalevi—"

"Hate humans. And you were lucky enough to be stuck with them."

"Do not be so hasty in judgment," he chided, wincing as he eased onto the bed. "There is much you have not seen."

"I hope I get the chance." With gentle fingers she tilted back his head and examined his lip. "These wounds need tending, and your broken fingers have to be set. Where is this healer of yours?"

"The Second will send him." He met her eyes. "Once again you did well, Cynara."

"As I remember it, you did everything and I watched." She pulled the torn edges of his shipsuit away from a particularly nasty cut. "I don't know why you haven't bled more than this."

"I stopped the bleeding."

She rocked away from him. "That was useful."

"Yes."

"You also stopped the pain, I suppose, as Sihvaaro taught you."

He cocked his head at her. "It hurts, but I can bear it."

Oh, yes. "You need to lie down until the healer arrives." She pushed him gently back on the cot. "This is where you lived as a child?"

"No. Wrongdoers are kept here, though there are seldom many at a time."

"Shaauri wrongdoers. I'd like to see more of those."

"I doubt it."

"Humor, Ronan?"

"We have, as you said, survived. I will have my time to address the *va'laik'i,* and Sihvaaro will also be permitted to speak."

Cynara was sorely tempted to demand a complete accounting of everything he had said and what he planned to tell them, but he truly did need rest. "Are they going to keep us in here until then?"

"I hope to be permitted to return to my own lodging."

"Off on the edge of the settlement, like Sihvaaro's?"

"Not as far." He laced his fingers through hers. "It was what I preferred."

She sighed and adjusted the roll of cloth that served as a pillow. "Will you try to find out what happened to your parents?"

"If I can."

Cynara suspected that he felt much more strongly about the subject than he let on. If he could learn the fate of Lady Kori Challinor and her Kinsman mate, it would be of great comfort to Lord Miklos. And such a discovery might convince Ronan, once and for all, to change his loyalties.

A faint scratching came from outside the door, and two shaauri entered the room: Sihvaaro and another with a medium concentration of stripes and a benign manner. He carried a pouch slung across his chest. Ronan propped himself up on his elbows.

"The healer," Ronan murmured, and offered a shaauri greeting. The healer replied briefly and approached Ronan's bed. Cynara retreated to the next bunk and watched curiously as the shaaurin examined Ronan's wounds.

"*Va* D'Accorso," Sihvaaro said, coming to stand beside her. "You are well?"

She decided against sarcasm. "Yes, Sih—how should I address you?"

"Sihvaaro is sufficient."

"You speak my language extremely well."

"It is a simple tongue, and I have had much time for study. Do not be concerned; few other shaauri understand it." He dropped into a crouch with easy grace. "I know that you are a female of some importance among humans, but Ronan has told me that you are to be considered his hostage for your protection. This was not *sivuj'avar,* kidnap-for-mating. How is it that you have accompanied him here?"

She well remembered how he'd immediately assumed she was Ronan's lifemate, and felt heat rise under her skin. "I didn't want him to be alone among shaauri, or Kinsmen."

"You hoped to protect him?"

There was no mockery in his question. "I didn't realize you would be here, and I wanted him to have at least one ally."

His ears flattened and rose again. "It is more than that, *Va* D'Accorso. You serve human interests and wish him to remember the species of his birth. You are also bound to him, even if you fear to acknowledge this."

"I was among those who rescued him from shaauri pursuit."

"And you know that he was sent with his memory impaired, to work against humans."

Cynara met his gaze. "I must ask whom you serve, Sihvaaro—Ronan, or your own people?"

He hissed laughter, earning a startled glance from the healer. "Humans believe that shaauri loyalties are simple, but it is not always so. Ronan's welfare is of great importance to me. So are my people, and yours."

"Mine?"

"All Paths are one. I will listen with great interest to the tale of your meeting with my apprentice, when circumstances permit." His whiskers quivered. "You prevented him from serving Kinsman interests. Your will is strong. The others must not realize your importance."

"Will you protect Ronan from those who would harm him?"

"I will do all I can." He turned his attention to the healer, who was applying a sticky substance to Ronan's wounds and wrapping them in pale cloth. The fingers of Ronan's left hand were already splinted and bound, but he hadn't made a single sound while they were set.

"You taught Ronan very well," Cynara said. "Thank you."

Sihvaaro inclined his head. After a few moments the healer completed his work and spoke to Ronan at length as he packed his supplies in the woven pouch.

"Rest is indicated," Sihvaaro translated for Cynara, "but it must wait. Ronan, the *Arva'Kir* is prepared to hear you now."

Ronan nodded and pushed himself up, only the slight tension in his face marking discomfort. Cynara hurried to help, but Sihvaaro barred her way.

"He must not show weakness, now above all times," he said. "I will stand with him." He anticipated her protest before she spoke. "You may not come, *Va* D'Accorso. Your presence would remind them he is human."

She pushed past him. Ronan held up his good hand and smiled, benevolent and very far away.

"They will not kill me," he said. "Wait. Food will be brought to you. Eat to maintain your strength, and do not worry."

"That you can't prevent, my friend." She took his face between her hands. "Keep yourself safe. Whatever you have to do—stay alive and come back." She leaned forward and kissed him, ignoring Sihvaaro and all the alarms going off in her head. "Come back to me."

Chapter 24

Cynara was pacing back and forth just inside the door when Ronan returned. His wounds burned in spite of every discipline he had employed during the interrogation; his eyes were blurry from lack of sleep, and his broken fingers throbbed with each beat of his heart.

Yet when he saw Cynara, he forgot everything but the brightness of her eyes.

"Ronan!" She ran toward him and stopped, afraid to touch him lest he shatter. "You look ready to collapse. Lie down."

He let her support him to the nearest bed and half fell onto the pad. She sat beside him, settling his weight against her shoulder.

"Thank God you're safe. It's been hours since you left—do you realize it's already dark?" Anxiously she smoothed his hair and peered into his eyes. "Did Lenko threaten you? Did they listen to our suspicions about the Kinsmen?"

"They listened." He sighed and closed his eyes. "Lenko did not wish to, but Samit and the *Arvi'Va* pressured him to do so. I explained that the Kinsmen had altered the assignment for which I was originally intended—not simply to gather information about new human technology, but to kill the First of the Concordat by dishonorable stealth."

"They believed you."

"They did not deny the possibility." He flexed the un-damaged fingers of his right hand. "I also told them that I would not deal with Kinsmen, but must report to the War-Leader and his advisors directly. *Arva'Kir* agreed to consider this."

"And if the Kinsmen demand your surrender?"

"They can demand very little on Kalevi soil." He opened his eyes and looked upon her face, the lines of tension be-tween her brows and about her mouth that spoke of hidden fear—not for herself, but for him. "You are still in my charge, and I have been given the freedom of the settlement."

"Scylla's teeth—"

"Listen to me, Cynara. I promised them that I had infor-mation that would benefit Kalevi and all shaauri-*ja*—not only of possible Kinsman treachery, but of the human tech-nology that permits Concordat ships to evade shaauri pa-trols."

"We've discussed this before. You can't know anything that will help them—only that the *Pegasus* exists."

Once more he was sure that she truly believed her mind contained nothing of worth he could trade to the shaauri for her life. Yet there was a new unease in her surface thoughts, a fear that his knowledge could indeed harm the Concordat.

"What did you offer them?" she demanded.

He sank back on the bed and stretched his legs. "Only a promise, in exchange for your safety."

"No, Ronan," she groaned. "Not for me."

"As an enemy human, you are not afforded even the min-imal protection of one adopted by Kalevi. If they believe you have information I do not, they will give you to the Kinsmen to obtain the contents of your mind. The Kinsmen would de-stroy you without hesitation, no matter what shields you pos-sess. Only by claiming I fully share your knowledge was I able to prevent this."

She scrambled off the bed and paced wildly across the room. "And when they find out you know nothing of real value?"

He closed his mind so that she would not feel the doubt and self-contempt eating at his gut. "We will face that as it comes. It is enough to know that we have the freedom to move as we will, and much may still be done." He held out his hands, and she took them. "I do have allies—friends—who will help us. I will show you—"

"Not now. You need sleep."

He could not deny it. He permitted himself the luxury of accepting Cynara's generous little acts of solace, obeying her command to lie down and let his body heal.

Though the bunks were meant for only one shaauri apiece, they were just wide enough for two humans. Cynara lay down beside him, careful not to disturb his injured hand or touch his wounds. She pulled up the blankets and tucked her body against his side.

For a time he lay awake, savoring the uncomplicated joy of her nearness. But his limbs grew heavy, and he drifted into a half sleep filled with images of accusing human fingers pointed at him, faces contorted with rage, shaauri ears flattened and teeth bared to drive him from shaauri-*ja* forever.

"*Ronan.* Ronan, wake up."

He opened his eyes to darkness. Cynara's face, loving and beloved, replaced the cruel masks of his dreams.

"You had a nightmare," she said, smoothing the damp hair from his forehead. "Sometimes it helps to talk."

Talk, as if they lay together in a soft bed on a human world, mate and mate, with no concern other than unpleasant dreams. Ronan breathed out the lingering terror and shook his head. "They were only dreams."

"Then you should go back to sleep. I'll be here."

But he knew sleep would elude him. Just as the dreams were absurd and irrational, so was the desire Cynara awakened in his bruised and battered body. At least one part had been completely unaffected by the fights.

He cupped her face in his hands and kissed her tentatively, giving her the choice. Her answer could not be misinterpreted. When he began to roll her beneath him, she locked her muscles and stopped him.

"Your injuries," she protested, wincing in sympathy. "You need—"

"I will be very careful," he said, kissing the soft skin under her jaw. "I need you, Cynara."

She released her breath and relaxed her muscles. "Yes."

For a time Ronan only held her, and they exchanged gentle caresses, resisting the urgency that had driven them on Miklos's yacht. Their fate was no more certain than it had been then, but Ronan knew, as Cynara did, that they would remain together until it was over.

Together they felt their way to a new tenderness, a healing of more than physical wounds or harrowing visions. They shed their shipsuits. The blankets hoarded their warmth and captured Cynara's scent, distilling it to an intoxicating, seductive vapor.

Ronan tasted her skin, lingering at every slight variation of her body's essence. She accepted his leisurely exploration without protest, responding with gasps and moans. She opened her mind, and he felt what she felt: not merely physical pleasure, but the very love she had professed at the cost of pride and security.

He tried to show her that her gift was not in vain. The fullness of his heart guided his hands and his mouth, caressing her breasts and her belly and the soft, fragrant place below. She signaled her readiness with nectar that flowed over his tongue, crying out when he licked her clean.

She grasped the hair at the nape of his neck and pulled him back to her mouth. "I want you, Ronan," she whispered. "Now."

He had never found a surer welcome. Her body enfolded him like an ocean of peace where time had no meaning. He moved, and she moved with him. He murmured words she could not understand, and she gave him the universe in the unsparing gaze of her blue eyes.

They were not gods, nor angels. Their shared humanity was the greatest gift that Cynara's love had bestowed, and he could never repay her.

Completion came as softly as the loving. Cynara shuddered and sighed beneath him, her hands massaging the throbbing muscles of his back and shoulders. He remained inside her as long as he could, chest to chest and thigh to thigh. At last her eyes closed and her head sank into the pillow. He kissed her brow and tucked the blankets under her chin. Even in sleep her grip on him could not be broken.

He cradled her in the hollow of his curved body and tried to sleep. There were no nightmares.

Dawn came with the smell of an unseasonably late snowfall. Ronan worked his way free of Cynara's arms and went to the shuttered window. The sky hung heavy with clouds; there would be concern among the *an'laik'i* field workers.

He glanced back at Cynara and denied the temptation to return to her side. There was no more he could give her now. His body ached, but his wounds were already healing; they must both be fit to meet the new day's challenge. He sat in the center of the room and practiced the Eightfold Way three times before Cynara awoke.

She sat up and pushed the blankets away, seeking him in the dim light provided by the single open shutter. Her skin appeared flushed, as if in memory of their joining. "How long have I been asleep?"

"Do not be concerned," he said. "Nothing has happened."

She combed her fingers through her hair, ordering it as best she could, and draped one of the blankets about her shoulders. "I meant to keep watch while you slept. I'm sorry."

"No need. Shaauri would not enter without warning."

"But humans would. And Kinsmen are human."

"When they come to Aitu, everyone will know."

She swung her legs over the bunk, shook out her shipsuit, and put it on. "How are you feeling?"

"Better." He smiled, watching her small, graceful motions as if they were steps in a captivating dance. "You helped. I can still fight."

She hesitated and then came to sit beside him. "You believe it'll come to that?"

"The settling of disputes can be very simple, especially among Lines such as Kalevi. It is an ancient way that any shaaurin may seek if other methods prove inadequate."

"Fighting each other?"

"Among certain Paths, yes. Among others, like those of Spirit, the competition may take a different form. Once the challenge is given and accepted, the outcome is final."

"Those Darja warriors weren't following the rules."

"There are always those who behave with dishonor."

"Then it's the strong who ultimately conquer."

"Not always the strongest. Sometimes it is the bravest and most determined. There are old tales of weak shaauri who defeated great warriors because of their use of what you would call psychology."

"If it was a matter of courage, you'd win. But we're sentient beings, Ronan, not wild animals."

Her scorn for the shaauri cut worse than Darja nails. "You understand so little of shaauri ways. Poverty as you know it does not exist here. Each has his or her place and function, and will never starve or be cast out except as punishment for the most severe crimes. And crime itself is rare."

"Because people's lives are preordained by Selection. And your *ne'li* . . . aren't they outcasts without recourse? You condemn them because they don't fit neatly into your social structure."

"Even *ne'li* are provided for by most Houses."

"But they live on the outside, always apart."

"Is it so unlike the way females are treated on Dharma, or those of different body shape or color or doctrine on other human worlds?"

She shook her head. "Humans make the same mistakes, Ronan. But you idealize the shaauri far too much."

"And you judge them too harshly." He got to his feet and offered his hand to her. "Come. There are things I would have you see."

She took his hand. "Won't some shaaurin or other challenge you if you go out again?"

"Not yet. And you are under my protection."

Her dubious expression spoke almost as clearly as shaauri body-speech. "Will they think it a weakness if I keep this blanket?"

"We will go first to the weavers' lodge and get you an outer garment."

She tossed the blanket on the nearest bed and accompanied him to the door, casting an uneasy glance at the leaden sky. Ronan kept her close to him as he followed the labyrinthine paths between buildings to Anki-*ja* and the workshops of *an'laik'i* crafters.

Ronan was very much aware of the shaauri they passed.

Many reacted with hostility, as Cynara had observed, but others were warily cordial in ways she would not be likely to recognize. They had reason to be guarded, especially those of the more docile Paths who avoided conflict.

Yet Ronan had no doubt that if he required it, assistance would be forthcoming. Soon he would visit his old companions and renew the *ba'laik'i* bonds he, unique among Kalevi, maintained in adulthood.

He and Cynara soon reached the weavers' lodge, situated among those of other *an'laik'i* crafters. He asked Cynara to remain in the anteroom while he went to the First of Weavers with his request.

As he hoped, the crafters were curious to see this new human. The First was not personally known to Ronan, but he was amiable and quite willing to provide covering for Kalevi's furless guest.

"They don't hate us?" Cynara asked when he returned to fetch her.

"They are not warriors or leaders who make policy or fight battles. They take satisfaction in their own work, and most have never left this world."

"Not even on Walkabout?"

"There are shaauri who remain very near their House or Line Holdings, and such almost always select as Body. *An'laik'i,* by nature, are not aggressive. But they do hear of all that passes in the settlement. I am the only other alien they have ever observed."

The weavers crowded as close to Cynara as courtesy permitted, faces averted, silent only in voice. She allowed them to look their fill. The First offered a neutral greeting and came forward with a heavy vest made for a youth near Cynara's size.

She took the folded garment carefully, smiling with her lips closed. "How am I to pay for this?"

"Since you are my responsibility and I am still of this House, you owe nothing."

"I see," she murmured, though he knew she did not. "How do you say 'thank you' in Voishaaur?"

"*Ina-sh'ei vai kana*—it means, roughly, 'My honor to you.' "

She repeated the word with a comprehensible accent, and the *Aho'An*'s ears twitched in amazement. He answered eagerly and mimicked her smile.

"He asks that you come again if the vest proves inadequate to cover your body," Ronan translated. "He is very sorry that you have no fur of your own."

"At the moment, so am I."

Ronan thanked the weavers and helped Cynara into the vest. It was vastly oversized, but it was warm and would cut the worst of the chill.

"You didn't ask for one yourself," she chided. "I presume your usual immunity to pain, hunger, the elements, and other human hazards is still operating at full capacity."

"I am accustomed to the cold," he said humbly.

"Someday I expect you to teach me these tricks of yours. Where now?"

"To *Riama-ja* . . . Place of Spirit."

He led her through a new-budding garden to the compound of the *ri'laik'i*. Cynara paused to admire the intricate, interlocked designs carved into the walls and doors of the lodges. "These buildings are different from the weavers'," she commented.

"They reflect the disciplines of those of Spirit—philosophers, artists, those who seek the intangible."

"You've never mentioned shaauri religion. Are there priests as well?"

"There are shaauri who study the wisdom of the Ancestors and interpret for all the House. They are of great importance to Kalevi, because my Line is committed to tradition in all things." He entered the door of the first lodge and walked without hesitation to the inner door. The shaauri within did not look up from their work. Two sat at huge desks, poring over fragile books brought from Aur itself. Others simply gazed at some inner vision.

In the next lodge, shaauri artisans carved ceremonial staffs and painted pictorial records of Ain'Kalevi history on handmade scrolls. They hardly noticed the humans' presence.

"Selection gives much easier jobs to some shaauri than others," Cynara said when they had left the second lodge. "I'd far rather be one of these than a laborer in the field."

"Yet each is suited to his or her task, without the need to seek elsewhere for contentment. Humans search always for such a place. You were not satisfied to remain a breeding female on Dharma; your Selection at birth was flawed."

"So it was." She met his gaze gravely. "But at least I still have a choice."

"Sihvaaro teaches that all Paths are one."

"They allow him to speak of such revolutionary concepts freely?"

"Few listen, or believe."

"Do you, Ronan?"

"I would follow Sihvaaro's example and be content."

She shook her head. "I think you still have your own Path to make."

Her words said far more than what their simplest meaning implied. She still feared his loyalties and where they might lead him.

She feared for his soul.

"I have one thing more to show you," he said.

Cynara ran a few paces to catch up to Ronan, dividing her attention between him, the environment of an unfamiliar culture, and the winding path behind them. Every corner or garden thicket provided possible cover for ambush; she had none of Ronan's confidence that shaauri would disdain a covert attack, and a very healthy respect for the damage razor-sharp nails could do to human flesh.

She was also disturbed that Ronan found it necessary to convince her of shaauri worth. *You have nothing to prove to me,* she wanted to tell him.

But she would be lying. These aliens were not worthy of Ronan's loyalty; nothing he'd shown her had changed her opinion. She felt only pity for the low-ranked shaauri stuck with menial labor and no hope of advancement through hard work or simple determination.

Like women on Dharma, she reminded herself. *This is hardly the time to debate philosophy when both of you are in very real danger.*

But if she was to turn Ronan completely to the human side, she had to be able to counter his arguments, even when they came from his heart and not his head. Their mutual affection and regard was not enough. She had to understand him and his adopted way of life better than she ever had before.

Ronan stopped, and she realized they'd reached the next compound. *"Linei-ja,"* he said. "Place of Heart."

Unlike the others, this compound was made up of many smaller dwellings, with broad gravel yards in between. The arrangement reminded Cynara of nothing so much as a schoolyard. Even as she thought it, a group of very young shaauri trotted out into the yard and began to play with a ball, tossing it from hand to hand and butting it with their heads. The hissing of shaauri laughter was like water rushing over stone.

"Ba'laik'i," Ronan said. "The children of Ain'Kalevi."

Children, like children everywhere. Their bodies were small and still learning to move with shaauri grace; fur was tones and tints of solid red, no sign of barring. The youngsters were so absorbed in their play that it was several moments before one of them noticed the humans.

Immediately they fell silent, as if the message had been passed from one to the next on a single breath. Eyes grew very wide and ears waved madly. All at once one of the children bounded forward, stopped, and then hurled itself at Ronan.

Cynara hadn't a hope of putting herself in the shaaurin's path. It crashed into Ronan and sent them both tumbling to the ground. Cynara lunged to pull the little hellion away, but Ronan had already flipped the child onto its back.

"Silta," he hissed, followed by a string of vowels and consonants, squeaks, and rumbles. Then he did something utterly unexpected and entirely human: He tickled the youngster until it rolled up into a tight ball and yowled for mercy.

The attack had not been an attack at all. Cynara swallowed her amazement as the other children drew closer.

Ronan hauled the youngster up by the collar of its loose vest and grinned at Cynara. "Silta is the child—son—of Annukki, who bore him during her Walkabout and now lives as *ki'laik'in.* She was among the *ba'laik'i* I knew when I was a child."

Cynara crouched to the youngster's level. Red-gold eyes stared into hers. "Please tell him I'm glad to meet him."

Ronan translated, and Silta's ears flattened in a look of astonishment. He asked a long and obviously complex question.

"He asks," Ronan said with a very straight face, "if I have brought you back from Walkabout as my mate."

"This seems to be the general assumption," she said with feigned amusement. "What will you tell him?"

"If I were *va'laik'in* or *ve'laik'in,* I could tell him that you are pregnant with my offspring, and I kidnapped you so that our child would be of Kalevi and not your Line." His eyes sparkled with unexpected mischief. "Shaauri children are not so protected about the necessities of mating as humans seem to be."

She touched her stomach, hot with the image of Ronan's child inside her. It could have happened, even last night. She had never thought to bear children.

"Isn't it enough that I'm your hostage?" she said.

"Not to Silta. He knows there is something more."

She couldn't mistake the way he watched her, as if he waited for a definitive response. What did he expect her to say that she hadn't already? What more could she give?

"He wouldn't understand if you told him we were friends," she said.

The light died in Ronan's eyes. "Perhaps I can explain another time." He turned to the boy and gave him a gentle push toward the other youngsters. Cynara felt as though she'd struck Ronan down, and she didn't know what to do about it.

He'd never said he loved her, far less suggested a permanent mating. And if he had . . . if he did . . . was that what she had been hoping for, like any proper, desperate Dharman female?

What she'd offered Ronan demanded no repayment, no promises. He must know that. He'd already agreed without saying a word.

"The children seem very happy," she said as Silta rejoined the game.

"They have all they want or need."

"Silta's parents don't take care of him."

"His father is of another Line and has no claim on the boy, though his genetic signature has been carefully recorded in the annals of Ain'Kalevi. His mother has her own work."

"Humans would regard that as—"

"Wrong. But humans raise their offspring even if they are ill-suited to the work, and the child suffers. No shaauri child is without love or proper care. Those adults drawn to nurturing, *li'laik'i,* can never be driven to unhappiness or cruelty toward their charges. Their patience is endless."

"What about your own children? You aren't of any one Path. Would you care for them yourself?"

His face lost its color. "I will have no offspring."

"What makes you so sure of that, Ronan?"

He looked ready to respond and then swallowed his words. Tension, feral and erotic, laced the air between them.

"It's the old claim of unworthiness," Cynara said, snapping the angry silence. "You don't think you have the right to pass on your many defects to another generation." *And that's why you hold back, Ronan. That's why you wait in stoic patience until you've proven yourself to me and the world.*

Unworthy. Never the true equal of Cynara D'Accorso.

"We will speak no more of this," he said, turning away.

Cynara hung back to watch the shaauri children. They squabbled and tussled and tested as children will, but without the bloodthirsty intensity she had seen in boys on Dharma. They seemed to understand each other's limits instinctively, and not push beyond them.

"What happens when a *ba'laik'in* needs to be punished?" she asked.

Ronan's shoulders relaxed, and he smiled at her as if in apology. "Very little behavior is punished. It is the time of *rhoka-toi'sun,* irresponsibility. Much is tolerated of *ba'laik'i* before Walkabout, when they become *be'laik'i* and are free to go where they will until Selection finds them."

"It's a shame they didn't treat you with such tolerance."

"Come," Ronan said, taking her hand. They walked up a low ramp to the door of the nearest building. The moment they stepped inside, warmth embraced them.

"*Linei-ja* is built over natural hot springs," Ronan said, "to provide the young with extra comfort." He crossed the antechamber, very like those in the other buildings with its padded benches for visitors, and into a room bright with light from numerous windows and painted in rich earth tones.

Three shaauri children sat on floor cushions, two playing with what appeared to be a wooden, three-dimensional puzzle, the third reading aloud as an adult watched over its shoulder. The second adult in the room sat cross-legged at a low desk and looked up at the sound of footsteps.

Ronan stopped. "*Li* Hanno," he said. The name was an endearment, thick with emotion and memory.

The shaaurin stood up. It—*she,* Cynara decided, certain without knowing why—laid her ears to the side and made an odd, keening sound.

"She who raised me," Ronan murmured to Cynara. Hanno circled the desk and passed the wide-eyed students and second *li'laik'in.* They met in the center of the room; there was no hesitation, no formality in their embrace.

"Ronan," Hanno said, still keening in a way that would have alarmed Cynara if not for her obvious delight. She was Ronan's height, small for a shaaurin, and her fur was a bright mahogany but lightly marked with black. If any shaauri face could be called gentle, hers met the description.

Human and shaaurin fell into rapid conversation. Ronan had not looked so relaxed since he had come to Aitu. Hanno expressed herself with great vivacity, her hands and whiskers and ears in constant motion. She touched Ronan again and again, like an anxious relative making sure that a loved one had returned whole from a long journey. Her feelings were plain even to human eyes.

She loved Ronan, and he loved her. This was his mother as no human had ever been.

"Hanno," he said, a world of affection in his voice, "*ilku se Va* Cynara D'Accorso."

The shaaurin turned immediately to Cynara. Her entire being smiled. She spoke softly and inclined her head, ears lowered.

"Hanno greets you," Ronan said. "She apologizes that she does not speak the human tongue and asks your forbearance. I have told her that you understand."

"Please convey all that is necessary," Cynara said, "and

tell her how pleased I am to meet the one who cared for you as a child."

Ronan translated, and Hanno virtually beamed. She hurried back to the other shaauri, spoke to them in low tones, and vanished through a door at the rear of the room.

"Hanno brings tea and refreshments," Ronan said, smiling faintly. "She always feared that I did not get enough to eat."

Cynara felt a rush of gratitude. "She is quite . . . radiant. I can see that she would be very good with children, of any species."

"I am glad you think so." He took both her hands in his. "It is important to me that you understand."

That was why he had brought her here last of all, to prove that shaauri could love, that he had known true caring in his time among them.

The gap between species had never been narrower than it was here, in a nursery that might have been transplanted from any human world. She had begun to like Sihvaaro; she liked Hanno already, knowing that she had loved Ronan unconditionally when others had hurt and abused him.

Did two individuals atone for the sins of all the rest? And if they did . . . if she began to believe that the shaauri deserved equal consideration in the long war with humanity . . . how could she hope to persuade Ronan that only the human cause was just?

She dodged Ronan's gaze and watched the other *li'laik'in,* who was speaking in a soft voice to the children. "What is she saying?"

"She tells the story of the First Selection. Would you hear it?"

"Please."

"In ancient days," Ronan began in the measured tones of ritual, "when all shaauri lived upon Aur, there was no Selection. Though every other creature had learned its place and purpose, shaauri rebelled and refused to seek harmony with the land.

"In ancient days, before shaauri journeyed to the stars, Clans fought among one another in the manner of savages, without order or purpose.

"In ancient days, all fur was of a single pattern, so that one shaaurin might not be known from another.

"Because there was no Selection, a shaaurin might follow any Path regardless of need or ability, and there was much sorrow and unhappiness.

"Because there was no *be'rokh-kaari'la,* the young did not know when to become adults.

"Because there was no *an'lai,* the land was not cultivated, and Clan fought with Clan over hunting rights to feed the people.

"Because there was no *li'lai,* children were left orphaned with none to care for them.

"Because there was no *ri'lai,* shaauri lacked the beauty and the depth of spirit that raises us above the beasts.

"Because there was no *ki'lai,* reason was abandoned for unreason, and shaauri could not learn better ways.

"Because there was no *ve'lai,* all shaauri fought each other regardless of age or strength, and thousands died in the chaos of battle.

"Because there was no *va'lai,* all shaauri were ruled by their own wills and heeded no other, caring little for the harm they wrought in their selfishness.

"So it was the elders of those ancient days who saw that shaauri must change or die, and they gathered in council to call upon the First Ancestors. 'What must we do,' they asked, 'to bring peace to our people?'

"The First Ancestors took pity upon the ancient ones and said, 'You must send the young of each Clan into the wilderness and bid them find a new Path. This alone will bring peace to Aur.'

"So it was that the elders gathered the young as they were bid, but the *ba'laik'i* of those ancient days were stubborn and did not wish to follow the word of the First Ancestors. Then came upon them a great desire, sent by the First Ancestors, to leave their Clans and seek that which they did not know.

"Many seasons the elders waited. When the young returned, they had changed. Each bore the blessing of the First Ancestors in marks upon her fur. Each sought a new place in her Clan, according to her desires and talents: *an'laik'i* to work the fields and weave the cloth and build the houses;

li'laik'i to nurture the young; *ri'laik'i* to carve and paint and bestow the beauty of spirit; *ki'laik'i* to teach and discover new ways; *ve'laik'i* to fight in honorable battle so that others might not die; *va'laik'i* to lead.

"But there were those who returned with no Path and threatened the new way with their envy and discontent. All who looked upon these Pathless ones were troubled in spirit, and the Elders feared once more for shaauri-*ja.*

"Then the First Ancestors said to them: 'Let any who fails in Selection walk as a wraith, *ne'lin,* unseen and unheard.'

"So it was that the way of Paths became the way of the people of Aur. So it was that the First Selection brought order and peace to shaauri-*ja.* So it was, and so it will be."

Ronan let his voice die to a whisper. Cynara shivered. *Let any who fails in Selection walk as a wraith, unseen and unheard.*

Alien. Utterly, inexorably alien.

"I've seen enough," she said. "I'd like to go back to our quarters now."

"Hanno—"

"Please offer my apologies and regrets."

He searched her eyes. "You are not ill?"

"No."

His jaw tightened, and he strode across the room to the rear door. He returned with Hanno behind him, and the two spoke and embraced once more. He passed Cynara without a glance and left the building at a fast walk.

Ronan's anger was rare enough that Cynara was keenly aware of it with both body and mind. She couldn't explain her behavior until they were alone. But Ronan didn't take the path she had expected, back to the shaauri jail; he turned north and made for the perimeter of the settlement, where buildings thinned out and the first fields began. A small hut or cabin stood by a grove of conifers, and she knew this must be his home.

The door was unlocked, like all doors in the settlement. Ronan entered and opened the shutter of a small window. The light was just enough for Cynara to make out a single room, more austere than the brig on the *Pegasus.* A narrow cot, a plain wooden chair that he might have made himself, a table stacked with earthenware pots, shelves of folded cloth, and supplies in simple containers. The packed earth floor was bare, and so were the stone and plank walls.

Cynara looked for a source of heat and discovered a small hearth built into the corner, which Ronan brought to life with logs and kindling retrieved from a stack outside. Once the fire was burning, he left the hut with one of the pots and returned with water. He poured half of it into a pitcher, and suspended the pot from a bar running the width of the fireplace to heat the rest.

He worked with such efficiency that Cynara knew he had followed this same routine a thousand times, caring for himself with no expectation of assistance or company. Yet the surroundings suited him, quiet and spare as they were. He wanted no luxury. He was, in some strange way, happy here.

"I would not see Hanno hurt for any reason," he said, after the silence had stretched for many uncomfortable minutes. "She believes you disapprove of her."

"*Poseidon,* no. Nothing of the kind." Cynara sat on the lone chair and gathered her thoughts. "I liked her, very much."

He crouched on his heels before her. "Something is wrong between us," he said. "It is not about shaauri. If I have displeased you in some way—"

"Stop. It isn't what you've done, but what you still may do." She held his gaze. "I ask you again not to share any information you may have about the *Pegasus,* or human vulnerabilities, with the shaauri government. Especially not for my sake."

His brow creased in surprise. "Is this still your fear? Miklos would not have let me go if he thought I could harm the human cause."

His words made sense, and yet Cynara couldn't escape the conviction that going to the shaauri War-Leader was the worst possible action Ronan could take. She clenched her fists on her knees. "What will you say to them?"

He turned to stare into the fire. "I will tell you, Cynara, if you allow me to look deep into your mind."

"For what purpose?"

"To prove that you trust me." He tossed a twig into the fire. Sap popped and crackled. "That we trust each other."

Cynara's chest tightened. "Is this what it's come to, Ronan?"

His eyes held infinite sorrow, a hopelessness that sucked into its depths all the tender intimacy they had shared in the night. "Can you swear never to use what you have seen here against my people?"

"Your people are mine, Ronan. You are human."

"There is only one way to be certain. Let me in, Cynara."

Chapter 25

It was an ultimatum beyond all others they had faced. Either she trusted him, or she did not.

"Very well," she said, cold in the pit of her stomach. "Do what you must." She closed her eyes, unwilling to see his face. He was quiet for a time, and then she felt the first tentative probing of her surface thoughts. He slipped between them, seeking deeper levels.

His touch caused no discomfort. It was a beloved reunion, an embrace rather than an invasion. They had been too long apart, too little sharing this most profound of all bonds.

Ronan stroked her mind with sensual delicacy, driving her body to shivers nearly erotic in their intensity. She opened to him gladly. Deeper he plunged, and there came a moment when she saw into her own mind as a reflection in the shining brilliance of his.

Then she remembered. She understood fully what Ronan must have felt when he discovered his mind had been manipulated, memory overlain with memories false and true and somewhere in between.

Tyr was laughing.

In horror she cast Ronan out. He pulled away, rocking

back on his heels. Cynara folded her arms around her stomach, sick in body and spirit.

So strange and bitter that Tyr filled her thoughts when so much more was at stake. She understood the reason they— VelShaan and Miklos—had planted the fraudulent intelligence in her mind. She not only had agreed to the ruse, but had suggested it. Ronan had taken the bait exactly as planned.

But VelShaan had taken additional action that Cynara had neither proposed nor expected. Since the time she had left Persephone, Cynara had lost all recollection of the turning point in her life: Tyr's death. The horror struck her anew as if it were happening all over again.

The horror, and the sure knowledge that she was no longer Cynara D'Accorso, but an unnatural synthesis of two souls, two beings contained in a single body.

For a handful of days she had actually believed she was whole and complete unto herself, bound and beholden to no one. She was free. But Tyr had never gone away.

She laughed, earning a bewildered glance from Ronan. She was hardly less bewildered. She'd hated the idea of deceiving Ronan, but she hadn't been afraid of what might lie ahead—capture and probing by Kinsmen, possible death at the hands of shaauri. No. She'd given herself up to VelShaan's expert ministrations terrified that the telepath's influence of her mind and memory would release Tyr from his prison. Cynara D'Accorso would finally lose herself.

The decision had been taken out of her hands. VelShaan had buried Tyr, but not deeply enough. Like a supernatural creature out of ancient myth, he rose again from the dead.

Poor Cynara. Tyr wouldn't pity himself the way she did. Her petty fears simply didn't matter anymore.

"Ronan," she whispered. "I'm sorry."

He blinked, his forehead creased in pain. "What?"

"You were right," she said. "My mind did hold information about the *Pegasus.* You were meant to find it . . . when we joined just before crossing the border."

Comprehension flooded his eyes. "Planted . . . for me."

"False information intended for the Kinsmen who used you." She leaned forward, trying to make him understand. "It was my doing, Ronan. Lord Miklos, *Mes* Carter VelShaan, and I discussed the idea just after I returned to Persephone and learned of the incident with the Archon. VelShaan removed from my mind any technical knowledge specifically related to the slingshot drive. It was done to make sure that the Kinsmen couldn't steal it if we fell into their hands. But she also erased my memory of the secondary plan—to provide any Kinsman interrogators with planted intelligence they'd have every reason to believe was genuine."

"As I must believe."

"The only way to make the plan work was if you were also convinced, and—"

"You anticipated that I would attempt to steal this information because of what I did on the *Pegasus*."

He turned his anger inward, and that hurt far worse than bearing it herself. "I know you didn't take anything then, or before when we were together on Dharma. But I had to make sure you did this time. Since telepathic bonds are most acute during sex—"

"You initiated mating so that I would penetrate your shields, discover this information, and accept it as truth."

"I didn't remember what I was supposed to do, any more than you remembered that you were supposed to assassinate the Archon. The difference is that I . . . truly wanted what we shared, Ronan."

He seemed not to hear. "Did you believe I would go to the Kinsmen?"

"We knew that you'd go directly to Aitu if given a choice, that your first loyalty was still to Kalevi. But we also assumed that once you'd entered shaauri territory, Kinsmen would eventually find a way to question you. If you reached your shaauri before them, you might find allies who would give you some protection and compel the Kinsmen to compromise." She almost smiled at the irony. "And I'd be with you."

"In the past, you did not accept that I had friends among Kalevii."

"But you always believed in them. I've finally begun to understand why. Sihvaaro won't give you up without a fight. If Constano and his crew behave as we predicted, they'll insist on questioning you but won't find it so easy to make you disappear."

"There is no predicting what Lenko will do."

"We couldn't know that your personal enemy would be running this place."

Ronan bent his head, deep in concentration. "You were not meant to remember this plan within a plan."

"I underestimated . . . the effect deep mental sharing between us would have on my memory."

"Yet you tried many times since our arrival to discourage me from giving information of humans to Lenko, even to preserve your life."

"When you mentioned going to the War-Leader with your suspicions about the Kinsmen, I was afraid. You didn't have real proof of their disloyalty, and I truly didn't believe you had anything else to offer." She wrung her hands in her lap, struggling to reach him. "We want the same thing, Ronan— to expose these Kinsmen if they're acting for themselves against shaauri interests."

"By making us both Concordat tools."

"It was the only way to get the assassination charges dropped and secure your release from Persephone. I didn't trust Damon. I knew you must despise what the Kinsmen had done to you. Lord Miklos wanted to let you go, but he needed a reason. And you needed the freedom to face your own demons without Challinor threats hanging over your head."

Ronan laughed softly. "Then Lord Miklos's last words to me were untrue."

"Not completely. He's still unsure of you and the part you were intended to play. But he was willing to try this, for your sake and for the Concordat."

"And I would serve a real purpose against the Kinsmen, as I wish to do."

"You'd offer them a temptation they couldn't resist—the supposed location of the original alien excavation that gave us the slingshot drive. And if they failed to share this intelligence with the shaauri—if they acted alone in raiding the world in question—they'd fall right into the trap Lord Miklos has prepared for them and expose themselves as traitors."

Ronan finally met her gaze. "There are many 'ifs' in this

plan. What if I gave the information to Kalevi before the Kinsmen arrived, or if the Kinsmen proved to be loyal allies? It would be my people springing this trap."

"That was a possibility Lord Miklos was prepared to face. He still regards shaauri as the adversary. For him, the end result would be much the same."

"Destruction of the enemy."

"That's why I came with you. I didn't remember the plan, but I sensed that my presence would be important." She flushed and looked away. *And what I said before, about love . . .*

If Ronan heard the thought, he gave no sign. "By accompanying me to Aitu, you have given me the opportunity to discover the truth."

And thereby undermined the scheme completely. She tried to laugh. "It obviously wasn't a very good idea."

"Would you have urged me to cooperate with the Kinsmen?"

"I don't know. Until now, intuition was all I had to go on."

"You also proposed destinations other than Aitu when we approached the border. Did this intuition suggest that we should escape before your plan could be implemented?"

Escape. That was exactly what she'd wanted, knowing in her gut that the forgotten scheme might end in disaster.

"Lord Miklos never insisted that you return to Aitu," she said, "but we knew you wouldn't go anywhere else."

"In spite of your hope to divert me." He reached up to touch her knee, and the heat in his eyes flowed through skin and cloth, turning her spine to rubber. "Now that I know of the deception, it will not be so simple to deceive the Kinsmen."

"No. But I still have faith in you. I would never have done this if I didn't." She covered his hand with her own. "You'll have to keep bluffing Lenko."

He let his hand fall and got to his feet. "He expects to win honor for Kalevi, and himself, by sharing my knowledge with the *A'Aho-Kei'hon-vekki*. I cannot allow my House and Line to be shamed and made vulnerable by promising intelligence they cannot deliver."

She rose to face him. "You can't tell Lenko you have nothing. He'll kill you."

"You are in danger from both shaauri and the Kinsmen. I must salvage what I can."

Cynara took several steps toward him and stopped, checked by his rigid posture and her own shame. "We can still make use of this, Ronan. There must be a way, if you'll only—"

A figure appeared in the doorway, its shadow falling across the threshold. Ronan looked up, as startled as she.

"Sihvaaro," he said.

"Ronan," he said in Standard. "I have come to warn you. Arv'Darja has arrived in force to demand possession of the female Cynara D'Accorso, in restitution for the death of their *ve'laik'in* at your hands." He met Cynara's gaze over Ronan's shoulder. "By shaauri custom, the kin of a shaaurin wrongly killed by one of another House or Line may demand payment for the life, in goods or in kind."

"Ronan was defending himself," Cynara protested.

"Darja considers your presence here an abomination, and not worth a single shaauri hair. Therefore, any death associated with you or your defense is regarded as *nemii,* 'unlawful.'"

Ronan's entire body had become a crackling coil of energy. "Cynara is not a thing to be taken in blood-settlement."

"*Va'laik'i* may debate this point," Sihvaaro said, "and stand firm against Arv'Darja. But I fear they will not. Of what value is Cynara D'Accorso? Better to surrender her and spare the risk of battle."

"I will fight."

"No, Ronan," Cynara said, gripping his shoulder.

"Darja would be pleased to see you die, Ronan," Sihvaaro said. "Then the life of Cynara D'Accorso will still be forfeit."

"I will speak to *Aho'Ain'Kalevi* at once."

"He will not see you, but it may be that Samit will listen. They already gather at the *Da'amera-ja,* Place of Challenge."

Ronan shook off Cynara's hold and pulled Sihvaaro aside. They spoke in hushed Voishaaur, Ronan agitated and Sihvaaro unshakably calm. At last they seemed to reach a conclusion, and Ronan turned back to Cynara. He kissed her, grinding his mouth into hers with a warrior's passion.

"*Sil akai,*" he said harshly, and strode for the door. *With the Ancestors.*

Cynara charged after him, running full into Sihvaaro. "Stop him," she demanded. "Don't let him do this."

"You love him."

The question barely penetrated the roaring in her ears. "Yes—in the human or shaauri way, take your pick." She glared up at the big shaaurin. "He gave me the final farewell. He thinks he's going to die."

"Arv'Darja will send its most skilled and powerful *ve'laik'in* against him. It is their right."

"Will they let me fight for my own life?"

"Challenge permits no weapons. You would die."

"But Ronan would be safe."

Sihvaaro's eyes seemed to reach inside her head. "He was angry with you. Why?"

There was no point in prevarication. "He discovered that my mind carried planted Concordat intelligence designed to mislead the Kinsmen who sent him to kill the Archon. Ronan previously believed this information to be genuine, and had used the promise of it to bargain with your First for my life. I'd hoped the Kinsmen would take this intelligence, act on it independently, and reveal themselves as traitors to shaauri."

"So you deceived my student."

"In the interest of peace, yes. But that changes nothing." She tried to push past Sihvaaro, which was very much like attempting to move a boulder. "Let me go. I've got to try—"

His powerful hands stopped her. "This information may still damage the Kinsmen if they do not know others possess it."

"That's what it was designed to do."

"Then you may yet have an opportunity to give it to them." He released her. "Follow the rightmost path to its end, and you will find *Da'amera-ja.* I will come when I can." Nimbly as a young foal, Sihvaaro bounded away. Cynara set off at a run, shooting past shaauri in ones and twos headed in the same direction.

She expected to have to fight her way to the Place of Challenge if she encountered any *ve'laik'i,* but it seemed they had all gone ahead of her. The path ended in a cluster of impressive buildings that she assumed must be the Kalevi administrative center. A large assembly of shaauri, all adult but of many fur patterns, formed a silent circle about the space that resembled a primitive arena. A banner of black and gold had been planted at one end, and a blue banner at the other, clearly marking two camps. Darja, and Kalevi.

Ronan stood with the Kalevi, speaking to a shaaurin that Cynara recognized as Samit, the House Second. Even from a distance she could see that the conversation was an argument; Ronan's hands swept in broad gestures, as if he were shouting, though his voice wasn't raised.

He was arguing for Cynara's life, urging Kalevi not to give her up. Asking them to permit him to fight for her. Cynara picked up her pace and dashed across the open space of the arena.

A hundred shaauri faces swung toward her, accompanied by ominous sounds of anger. Ronan didn't turn until she was at his shoulder.

"Be silent," he whispered, and resumed his speech with the shaaurin. Cynara stepped past him.

"Aino'Ain'Kalevi," she said, "I have brought this conflict upon your House. I ask permission to make it right."

The shaaurin's ears swiveled in amazement. She spoke sharply to Ronan, who hesitated so long that the Second repeated her demand. Ronan shook his head in human denial and answered.

"Did you tell her?" Cynara asked. "I want the chance to fight."

He swept back his arm, pushing her behind him. The words he addressed to the shaaurin had a desperate sound of finality to them, half plea and half threat. Cynara braced herself for attack.

None came. After a long pause, the Second turned to another dark-striped shaaurin. They consulted in almost inaudible tones. Finally the Second spoke to Ronan again, and her words were those of grave ceremony.

Ronan bowed deeply and took three steps back, coming to stand at Cynara's shoulder.

"What have you done?" she demanded.

"You have impressed *Va* Samit with your boldness," he said. "You will not be given to Darja without challenge."

"Will they let me fight?"

"No. Even shaauri have the concept of what humans call 'fair play.'"

"You can't do this, Ronan."

"Your confidence inspires me, *Aho'Va.*" The twinkle of amusement in his eyes died almost instantly. "It could have been much worse if Lenko had made the decision, but he sent Samit to deal with us."

She grabbed the front of Ronan's shipsuit, heedless of their audience. "How could it be worse? They'll send their strongest against you. No matter how good you are, your chances . . ." She pulled his head down to hers. "I won't let you die for me."

"But you must." He caressed her cheek with the back of his hand, so tenderly. "I have declared you my lifemate, and under shaauri law this gives me uncontested right to fight in your place for any cause, and preserve your life with my own no matter what the offense. To do otherwise would dishonor me forever."

Lifemate. Mother Sea. "Do you think I care about honor— yours, mine, or anyone else's?"

"It is all I have, pathless as I am."

Ronan saw the fury in her eyes, desperation so strong that it filled his whole mind and threatened to undermine the preparations he had made for the coming fight. She would give her life for him. She would throw away her command, loyalty to her people, her bright future for his sake.

His greatest desire was to reach out to her, share the way they had done in joining, know once more the deepest essence of her soul. But he was afraid. He felt nothing when he regarded the Darjai and knew what they would send to meet him. He did not fear death. This woman, with her fierce courage, terrified him. The thought of losing her terrified him.

He must survive, and win.

He took her face between his hands and kissed her lips. "Forgive me," he said. Then he released her and sought his kin who watched on the sidelines, shaauri who had been his companions in childhood.

Though they followed different Paths, his old friends defied convention and stood together now: Annukki, returned from Walkabout as *ki'laik'in;* Mairva, now a Kalevi warrior; Riko, who had come back *va'laik'in* and helped administer the settlement. There were others as well, those who had accepted him as a boy, and Hanno stood behind them, her ears pressed low with anxiety.

Va Riko made the sign of affectionate greeting. "We are pleased to see you returned safely from *be'rokh-kaari'la,*" he said, "and that you have found a lifemate. But the circumstances are indeed unfortunate."

Ronan bit back a laugh. "Indeed," he said, bowing. "I am grateful for your presence."

"We would have come to see you at an earlier time," *Ve* Mairva said, "but you were confined, and then Arv'Darja came." She glanced at each of her companions in turn. "Your appearance has not changed since *be'rokh-kaari'la.* What Path have you followed?"

Ronan didn't have the courage to admit the truth. "It sometimes requires . . . many Walkabouts for humans to find the correct Path."

"This is regrettable. You are strong, but not *ve'laik'in.* It is foolishness to fight the Arv'Darja champion. I will do so in your place."

"You know that will not be permitted. But I do request your assistance in one small matter."

"It is yours."

"My lifemate would put herself at risk and intrude upon the challenge. I would have you hold her, with respect, until the battle is finished."

Mairva's whiskers rippled. "She, too, has courage, your lifemate." She blinked solemnly. "I will keep her safe until the battle is finished."

"If you lose the fight," *Va* Riko said, "your mate will be forfeit to Darja. Is there a thing you would have me do to prevent this?"

"I, too, offer assistance," *Ri* Annukki interposed. Hanno whispered agreement.

Their proposal was extraordinary. Shaauri did not interfere with lawful challenge given and accepted. Shaauri did not band together across Paths . . . unless they held in common childhood affection for one who had no Path and thus remained an adolescent who must be protected.

Cynara had wondered if shaauri could love.

Ronan bowed. "*Sh'eivali,* I honor you greatly," he said, his voice heavy with emotion. "I ask that you do what you can to preserve my lifemate from harm and find a way to return her to her own people in the Concordat. Sihvaaro will aid you."

"We hear," Riko said.

"We hear," the others echoed.

There was no further speech, no expressions of good luck such as humans used, no cries of encouragement. Ronan met each gaze in turn, conveying respect and affection. Hanno was last. To her he sent all the love in his heart, and smiled.

He turned away before they could see the tears in his eyes, that shameful badge of his inescapable humanity. He moved with slow, measured steps to the center of *Da'amera-ja* and sat cross-legged on the gravel to begin his preparations. Cynara pushed at the fringe of his consciousness, protest and anger and outrage. He cast her out. One distraction could see him dead, and Cynara in Darja hands. He must be all warrior now, single-minded for battle like any *ve'laik'in.*

He must cease to be human.

Minutes passed in silence. Even the enemy respected this time; it could last for hours if he wished. But he did not. He repeated the chants of the Eightfold Way until only that endless, perfect circle existed.

He opened his eyes and rose to his feet. Arv'Darja had sent its champion, a deceptively small *ve'laik'in* whose stance and confidence told Ronan that he was among the House's best fighters. He wore no covering but his own fur, as required by tradition.

No one would object if the pitiful human retained his garments over naked skin. Ronan stripped off his shipsuit and tossed it to the edge of the arena. He bowed to his opponent and then turned to acknowledge the leaders of his House.

Samit no longer stood to the fore. Lenko had taken the place of honor to preside over the combat, and his eyes glowed with satisfaction.

Ronan bowed again, cold as winter's kill. He knew that Cynara stood in the custody of his friends, safe and restrained. More than that knowledge he did not seek. He waited calmly for Lenko to bid the challenge begin.

Someone shouted. The voice rang so clear that all ears flattened in shock, and every face turned toward it.

Sihvaaro stepped into the arena and set himself before Lenko, hands folded at his waist. He bowed.

Ronan's detachment faltered. He could hear only fragments of the conversation between Sihvaaro and Lenko, but what he understood was enough. He abandoned his position and ran to stop his teacher.

Sihvaaro bowed to Lenko once more and turned to face Ronan. His eyes were eloquent, full of pride and sorrow and a calm that could not be touched.

"It is done," he said softly. "*Aho'Ain'Kalevi* Lenko has given me leave to fight in your place, *ina-ma.*"

"*No.*" Ronan charged past Sihvaaro, but the shaauri stepped neatly into his path and hurled him to the ground. Ronan was on his feet instantly. Sihvaaro held him with a grip like a *koinno*'s jaws.

"You cannot," Ronan begged, the air gone poisonous in his chest. "There is no precedent—"

"Nevertheless, Lenko has agreed. You must obey."

"If he agreed, it is because he believes you will be defeated," Ronan said desperately. "He wants to be rid of you as well. Arv'Darja will still win the right to take my lifemate, and you will die for nothing."

Sihvaaro's eyes lit. "So that was not only a deception. I am pleased." He touched Ronan's chin. "There is little time left. Hear me, *ina-ma.* When the challenge was given by Arv'Darja, I tried to convince Lenko to expose our mutual Kinsmen enemies by helping to lay a trap for them, as you wished."

"Cynara—"

"Lenko refused, as I expected. He only wishes to be rid of all humans, at the expense of the welfare of shaauri-*ja*. But he is far too conservative to take direct action against your lifemate, and I have planted enough doubts in his mind that he would never share suspicions about your Concordat intelligence with the Kinsmen. He is happy enough to let Darja rid him of all his problems."

The muscles in Ronan's temples tightened to the point of pain. "He may succeed in his desire."

"Do I look so old and weak to you, *ina-ma?*" Sihvaaro hissed a chuckle heavy with irony. "I also believe Lenko hides some plan of his own, and that may yet be turned to your advantage. His cunning is limited, and he is by no means an able leader. Eventually he will fall. Be prepared and hold your mind clear." He gazed over Ronan's head at the waiting Arv'Darja warrior. "I must prepare. Do not disobey this last request."

He turned his back, and Ronan felt the complete severance of all contact between them, more irrevocable than a thousand light-years of space. Sihvaaro would not be moved.

If Ronan had been raised as a human, he might have prayed. Shaauri were stoic by human standards, not given to weeping and wailing over what they could not change. And he could not change this.

Without thought he reached for Cynara, a child seeking comfort from one trusted and loved above all others. He stopped himself before he found her mind. She alone would understand. She would willingly take the burden of his sorrow, but he would return nothing but affliction and grief.

He sank to his knees where he was, at the edge of the *Da'amera-ja,* ignoring Lenko, Samit, and the others behind him. The Eightfold Way brought no consolation. He watched, dry-eyed, as Sihvaaro stripped off his robes and faced the Arv'Darja warrior.

The rituals that followed were meaningless noise. Lenko spoke, and then the *Aino'Arv'Darja* who had brought the challenge. Sihvaaro and his opponent bowed.

Then the fight began. The Darja warrior attacked. Sihvaaro moved in a blur to counter the strike, and flung the *ve'laik'in* aside.

So each strike and counterstrike, attack and defense followed in blinding succession, the opponents so evenly matched in skill that it seemed the fight must continue past nightfall. No one but Ronan saw Sihvaaro begin to falter; no one knew or loved him so well. He seemed invincible, and ageless.

He was not. A small misstep, and Sihvaaro came away with deep scratches on his thigh. Another tiny miscalculation, and one graying ear was half torn from his head.

Ronan bit down on his lip until he tasted blood. He felt every blow. He wished the human gods would strike him down in Sihvaaro's place.

They had no mercy for one such as him. Sihvaaro fell at last, tumbling onto his back, and rose too slowly. The Arv'-Darja warrior did not hesitate. He struck a killing blow and leaped away.

Sihvaaro lay unmoving. The *ve'laik'in* uttered the cry of victory, and his fellow Darja warriors took it up.

Ronan did not wait for final word. He sprang up from his place and threw himself between Sihvaaro and the victor, cradling the old shaaurin's head in his arms.

"Sihvaaro," he whispered. "Sihvaaro!"

Eyes focused. The third eyelid was already drawn half closed like a veil, signaling the nearness of death.

"*Ina-ma,*" Sihvaaro sighed. "It is not . . . what I would have wished. But do not give up hope." He chuckled. "Hope is very human. I . . ." He coughed, and blood stained his whiskers. "I have learned of your true past. You must go to Arhan, those who adopted your father. They will . . . defend you."

"Sihvaaro."

"Hear me." *Hear my last secret, which I kept even from you.*

Sihvaaro. You speak . . .

I, too, know the way of mindwalking. There are others like me, in hiding. I summoned Arhan as soon as I sensed your approach to Aitu. Ancestors bid them come quickly. He visualized a series of numbers and letters, code to be used if Ronan had to reach the Arhan ship. *Go with them, my son.*

Ronan bent his head to Sihvaaro's. The old shaaurin

licked the corner of his mouth. "Tears are another human custom I envy." His breath rattled. "All Paths are One. The circle will be complete."

He sighed, and then his body loosened in Ronan's gentle hold.

Ronan flung back his head and bellowed, the mourning cry harsh and terrible in a human throat. He sang in petition to Ancestors not his own. No shaaurin moved to stop him.

In his grief he reached for one mind, one heart. She did not hear him. He clambered to his feet.

"Come," he said to the Darja warrior, baring his teeth. "Come, you and your brothers, and take me."

Chapter 26

*C*ynara heard Ronan's cry, first with her ears and then
with her mind. His grief pounded her down, turning her
bones to jelly, overwhelming any hope she had of rational
thought.

The fight was over. Sihvaaro had lost. Ronan had lost. The
maelstrom of his emotion held nothing of hope or even the
determination to survive. He meant to die defending her,
avenging his teacher.

And she could not reach him. He was cut off from her
more surely than at any time since she had known him, even
before he had recovered his memories and his telepathic
skills. His absence gaped like an open wound.

She was alone—captive, paralyzed, outmatched. Inadequate. Fatally weak. Unable to devise a single worthy plan to
get them out of this mess. A shaauri warrior held her in an
iron grip, and a hundred more surrounded her.

But she wanted Ronan to live. Suddenly she loved life itself more fiercely than her family, her command, her freedom. No sacrifice would be too great if it was within her
power to make.

What would you give, Cynara? a voice demanded.

Her lips moved to answer before she realized that the words came from within.

Not alone. Of course. Ronan had banished her, but she had another ally.

Tyr. Tyr, whose nerve and assurance she had admired all her life. Tyr, who never panicked or hesitated. Tyr, who always found a way.

She turned inward, ignoring the *ve'laik'in*'s grip, the howls of shaauri threat, the terror that blocked the breath in her throat.

I know you're with me, Tyr, she began. *Ever since I was a child, I wanted to be you. You gave me yourself, but I was always afraid to let you share this body. Afraid your strength would overwhelm me, prove I was nothing.*

Now I set you free. I call on you to purge me of all weakness, all fear. Give me your courage, your confidence, your cool reason. Make me strong, and I'll never restrain you again.

She waited in her private silence, light-headed with terror and a wild surge of hope. Her stomach heaved. A presence stirred in its place of exile, rising up in triumph.

Tyr had answered, like an ancient god of war presented with an offering of flesh. New strength flowed into Cynara's chest and shoulders and legs. Her muscles seemed to expand, the flow of her blood increase. The remnants of fear vanished.

This was what it was to be truly superior, to be secure in one's place in the scheme of things. Emotion and doubt no longer clouded her thoughts. Remarkable how very clear matters seemed, how obvious her priorities now that her sentimental frailties had been left behind.

This was what Tyr had tried to give her, what she'd so mistakenly refused out of womanly fear. She smiled Tyr's smile and weighed the situation with cool detachment.

She hadn't resisted Ronan's warrior friend Mairva when the female had taken her into custody just before the fight; better a shaauri well-disposed toward humans than one of Lenko's cronies. Then Sihvaaro had offered to fight in Ronan's place. Even without the most rudimentary understanding of shaauri language, she had recognized Ronan's protest, his grief, his ultimate surrender.

But the old shaauri was no match for his opponent. He'd died, and Darja had won. Driven to madness in his anguish, Ronan faced a hundred hostile shaauri in defiance of tradition and the leaders of his House. If the Darja warriors didn't see to his death, Lenko would.

Ronan's torment no longer influenced her, nor did she owe any loyalty to his friends. She turned her head slightly to observe her captor's face. Mairva's grip on her shoulders had loosened; she, like all the other shaauri, seemed mesmerized by what had occurred in the arena. Perhaps she wished to rush to Ronan's defense, but shaauri custom restrained her.

The *ve'laik'in* would naturally assume that her human captive was incapable of resistance in the face of impossible odds. If shaauri were in any way susceptible to telepathic suggestion, such an assumption might be strengthened at just the right moment.

Cynara estimated the precise angle of the bone-hilted blade held in a sheath at Mairva's waist, and calculated the most economical move to take it. She called upon her combat training and all Tyr's personal tricks. When she struck, she struck true. The knife's carved hilt bit into her palm. She writhed free of the startled *ve'laik'in*'s hold and launched herself toward the First of House Ain'Kalevi.

Astonishment was her ally. The shaauri moved belatedly, and most didn't move at all. Cynara reached Lenko an arm's length ahead of the nearest Kalevi warrior and thrust the knife's point straight up under the First's bewhiskered chin.

Lenko froze. So did Samit, and the third heavily striped shaaurin beside her. The approaching warriors stopped.

She could just feel Ronan, very far away.

"Listen to me," she said, her face inches from Lenko's half-open mouth. "And don't move."

Lenko stuttered a protest. Cynara grinned. "If you don't understand, you'd better find someone to translate."

The First squeaked, and Ronan's friend Annukki appeared. She glanced at Cynara without expression and answered her leader.

"I know a little of human tongue," she said. "Speak."

"Good. Tell Lenko that I expect him to release me and

Ronan. I don't care what he has to do or say to convince
Darja, but that's the only way he's staying alive."

Annukki translated. The remaining shaauri, Kalevi and
Darja alike, held absolute silence. They were utterly confounded by this unprecedented and unlawful attack on a
leader by a weakling human.

Lenko was frankly terrified. He began to speak. Several
ve'laik'i moved. A human voice shouted warning.

All at once the Darja shaauri moved in a mass toward the
Kalevi, rumbling sounds that could only be threats. Cynara
turned her head just enough to observe Ronan blocking their
way as though he could stop them single-handedly.

"Do it now," she hissed at Lenko. The First cried out
again, flinching from the bite of the blade. Kalevi *ve'laik'i*
turned as one to face the Darjai. Two hundred armed shaauri
stood opposite each other, only a few body lengths and a lone
human keeping them apart.

The surprises were far from over. Samit stepped forward
and addressed Cynara gravely.

Annukki's ears flattened in what Cynara had begun to
recognize as extreme dismay. "*Aino'Va* Samit says," she
translated, "you have right to fight *Va* Lenko for leadership
of Ain'Kalevi." She hesitated, her ears still firmly lowered.
"*Va* Samit did not have to tell you this thing, Human. It gives
great power." Samit spoke again, and Annukki's ears pricked.
"*Va* Samit says that if you grant her right, she will fight *Va*
Lenko in your place. But you must give up right to lead
Ain'Kalevi."

Cynara laughed. Lenko whimpered. "One small rebellion
opens the floodgates," Cynara said. "*Ki* Annukki, tell *Aino'Va*
Samit that I accept." She fell back and tossed the knife toward
Samit, who caught it deftly in midair.

Samit spoke to Lenko, who cringed as if he had lost whatever skill and courage had won him his position. It was clear
that he wasn't going to put up much of a fight to retain it.

"Come," Annukki said. "*Va* Samit will soon take leadership from Lenko, and must deal with Darja. She will let you
and Ronan depart, but she must go now."

Cynara searched for Ronan behind the wall of Kalevi warriors. Mairva pushed through with her human friend in tow.

Ronan's expression was blank, and Cynara knew that she should be terrified of what she saw in his eyes. She felt nothing. Hanno ran up to Ronan and stood trembling, expressing with ears and eyes what Cynara couldn't.

"*Ve* Mairva says that there is time to go to Ronan-*ja* to collect supplies," Annukki said, "then you must go to forest. Ronan is in madness. Will you help him?"

"Yes." She took Ronan's arm. It was rigid and at the same time lifeless, and she felt no response from his mind. "Take me back to Ronan's hut."

Mairva turned and led Cynara through a gathering of dazed shaauri and onto a path leading away from the arena. Ronan allowed himself to be steered along; his utter lack of mental presence convinced Cynara that he was in a state of emotional shock. He'd have to snap out of it once they were clear of the settlement.

At Ronan's hut, Mairva efficiently gathered up provisions—dried fruits and meat, a rolled length of canvas-like material, hunting implements—and arranged them in a large pack made of tanned hide. The *ve'laik'in* tossed Cynara a heavy shirt and trousers woven of animal wool much like her vest. Cynara helped Ronan dress and settled the pack over her shoulders.

Annukki appeared at the door, ears cocked behind to catch any sounds of pursuit. Another black-barred shaaurin joined her.

"Human," Annukki said, "This one is *Va* Riko, also Ronan's . . . friend." She spoke the word gingerly, testing its strangeness. "He it was who made *Va* Samit think of challenge. *Va* Riko bids me tell that a ship comes to the port. There you must go."

"A ship?" She glanced at Ronan, who remained unresponsive. "What ship?"

"We do not know. But you must leave Ain'Kalevi-*ja*. *Aino'Va* Samit let you go, but she cannot guarantee safety from Darja."

None of the possibilities looked promising. Trying to survive in the wilderness was not Cynara's idea of a tenable long-term solution. If the newly arrived ship were any kind of shaauri vessel, it wouldn't be likely to provide sanctuary to a pair of humans—especially when Ronan was incapable of communication.

But if it were the Kinsmen's ship . . . she might have bargaining power.

"Show me the right direction," she said. "I'll take Ronan there."

"*Ve* Mairva and I will accompany you," Annukki said. "Come."

Cynara followed the two shaauri to the edge of the settlement. Distant noise hinted at ongoing conflict in the arena, but no one had yet come looking for the errant humans.

Ronan fell into a steady pace beside her, gazing straight ahead. She concentrated on the path that led up the hill and into the forest. A few small, white flakes of snow powdered her shoulders and the shaauri's fur. She had a sudden, vivid memory of Bifrost, and Ronan virtually naked in the howling fury of a perpetual storm.

He was responsible for that storm and the turmoil that followed. He'd been nothing but trouble since the day he'd come aboard the *Pegasus*. If she had it to do over again . . .

She shook such irrelevant speculation from her mind like the snow from her hair. Sometime later Mairva signaled a halt, and they paused at the edge of a familiar clearing.

On the other side lay the spaceport buildings, the landing field, and the ship. Cynara recognized it as some kind of shaauri vessel, but its markings were indecipherable to her eyes.

"I must find out who they are," she said to Annukki. "Can you identify the ship if we go closer?"

The shaaurin indicated agreement, and all of them, including Ronan, crouched in the tall grass. They worked their way forward, Mairva in the lead, until they had a clearer view of the ship and the several figures moving on the ground beside it.

Human figures.

"Kinsmen," Annukki hissed.

Cynara settled onto her haunches, drawing Ronan down beside her. "You see how it is," she said coolly, as if he might answer. "Your friends have made it clear that we won't be welcome in the settlement, and Darja will keep coming after us. Even if you were in your right senses, I don't know how long we could live off the land with little hope of rescue." She laughed. "We did want the Kinsmen to take the false intelligence. Now we have our chance."

Ronan blinked, and the first flicker of life came into his eyes. "Yes," he croaked. "Let them take us."

Mairva moved closer and spoke to Ronan in a low voice. He reached out, palm up, and she laid her huge hand over his. After a moment he exchanged the same gesture with Annukki.

"Kei'lai," the shaaurin said. She looked at Cynara. "Ancestors watch and guide." With only the faintest rustle of dried grasses, she and Mairva vanished.

"They go back," Ronan said, staring at the Kinsman ship. "They have done all they can."

"Can you do what needs to be done?"

"Yes."

"There's a good chance they'll realize the intelligence is a trap."

"They will not discover it from me. But you have lost the barriers the Persephoneans put into your mind."

"I'm prepared to take that risk. We'll tell the Kinsmen at least part of the truth—you were caught on Persephone trying to assassinate the Archon, and they let you go because they discovered that you were a Challinor."

"And what will we tell them is the reason that you are with me?"

"You believed I had knowledge that might be of use to the shaauri, so you abducted me. Convince yourself, and you'll convince them." She smiled coldly. "Unfortunately, an old rival took over your House, and your enemies here are trying to kill both of us. You don't even have to pretend that you like the Kinsmen, as long as they believe that going to them was our only chance of survival."

"You have it very well planned, *Aho'Va.*"

"I plan for both of us to survive. Let's go."

They stood up, chest and head above the grass. One of the distant figures turned toward them.

A silent alarm was given. At the edge of the tall grass, where it had been mown short to accommodate landing ships, three armed Kinsmen came to claim them.

The two men and single woman wore uniforms of dark red with black bars on back and shoulders designed to mimic the striping of shaauri fur. They stopped well short of Cynara and Ronan, weapons raised.

Cynara felt the assault of several minds on her own, sifting her surface thoughts. If Ronan suffered the same scrutiny, his face didn't show it.

The Kinswoman raised her brows. "We were expecting you," she said to Ronan. Her gaze sought Cynara's. "You must be the Concordat agent Lenko told us about. Artur will be very happy to see you both."

The ship lifted from Aitu as soon as the Kinsmen and their prisoners were aboard. Its interior was very much like the one Ronan had seen before they had stripped his mind of memory. Perhaps it was even the same vessel. It was modeled after a shaauri striker but on a smaller scale, adapted for human use and heavily armed. Artur Constano VelRauthi was clearly prepared for attack and defense.

But by whom? Did he already fear what the shaauri might discover?

Ronan glanced at Cynara again, clearing the last confusion from his thoughts. He had been mad for a time after Sihvaaro's death, and thus had forfeited the chance to protect her until the Arhan ship arrived. Sihvaaro had been wise to summon them, but they would come too late.

He had lost more than Sihvaaro in the past few hours, but he had no one to blame save himself. He had withdrawn too far, disgracefully abandoned Cynara in her time of greatest need.

And she had changed. She had taken command in spite of her limited knowledge and many disadvantages, never hesitating to do what must be done. She was true *aho'va,* as he had known from the beginning. That was not what convinced him that she had inexplicably altered.

She looked as she always had, except for the utter coldness of her eyes. But her voice had undergone an unmistakable transformation, along with everything she did and said—sometimes in only a subtle nuance, at others so blatantly that it was as if another soul spoke through her mouth.

That other soul was unreachable. She had closed her mind from him as well as the Kinsmen. He had begun to believe that she was invulnerable to any probe to which they might subject her.

She was lost to him. All that remained was to keep her alive until she had the opportunity to escape.

He shut such thoughts behind a barrier thick as the ship's hull and let the Kinsmen push them through the main corridors, past stations manned by Kinsman technicians and into a narrower corridor of many doors. One of these led to the inevitable holding cell, cold and sparsely furnished.

Ronan had learned to expect dry humor from Cynara under such circumstances. He waited for her to speak, but she simply sat down against the bulkhead and ignored him.

Sihvaaro, my father, you are my only Ancestor. Guide me now.

He sat opposite Cynara and stared at her until she looked up. Her eyes were glazed with ice like Lake Ashti in the Month of Brittle Branches. What agonies had she suffered for his sake?

"Cynara," he said. "Tell me what has happened."

She looked through him. "I want to stay alive."

Ronan had not believed himself capable of breaking under rightful chastisement, or even her justified contempt. But it came to him then how much he had come to rely upon Cynara's warmth, her unfailing concern for others, the affection he had taken far too much for granted.

"You have changed," he whispered.

"Because I fought for both of us?" She smiled. "What did I do that you found so disturbing? Escape your warrior friend? Threaten Lenko and start a coup among the Kalevii? Or take you out of there when you were as helpless as an infant?"

She mocked him, and yet she spoke as if those very feats must excite his amazement. The Cynara he knew was courageous and determined, and none of her recent actions were beyond her abilities.

"You fought bravely and well," he said. "You saved my life and confounded Lenko. You have won the respect of many who would have killed you."

"Their respect means nothing," she said. "You're allowing yourself to be vulnerable, Ronan. They might be listening even now." She turned her face aside. "Sihvaaro's dead, and you can't bring him back."

Her words clawed at his heart. "He died for me. For us."

"And you feel guilt. You should have died in his place. Poor Ronan." Her profile was carved of granite. "If I hadn't acted as I did, Lenko would have handed us both to Darja."

Ronan drew his knees up to his chest and closed his eyes. *You believed she was my true lifemate, Sihvaaro. I never believed she would accept me. But at least she will not grieve. She will be free.*

"You are right," he said quietly. "I am not strong. I would have failed."

"Your self-pity becomes tiresome. All I expect is that you do what is necessary."

To survive. But mere survival had never been enough for this woman, not at any cost. "Who are you?" he asked. "Whose voice speaks to me now?"

She didn't answer, but her fingers trembled when she pushed at her hair.

He opened his consciousness, listening for Kinsmen. The nearest minds seemed otherwise occupied; either they were overconfident of ultimate success, or they paradoxically held to the convention that forbade them from entering an unsuspecting mind.

It did not matter, as long as they stayed away. "I ask nothing of you but your name."

Her eyes squeezed shut. "Stop."

"Who are you?"

"No." Her hands tightened into fists, and she gasped as if invisible forces buffeted her body. "Tyr was always stronger." She hunched her back away from him. "You didn't know. You didn't see."

He caught at the very edge of an idea so fantastic that he could not quite accept it. "Your cousin," he said. "He is here now."

Cynara looked into his eyes with such bleak resignation that he knew he was right. "Stay out," she said. "Leave me alone." The emotion, and the voice, were Cynara's. But then she vanished, and the cold calculation of a stranger returned.

Tyr. It could be no one else. As Ronan had become a different person when the Kinsmen had taken away his positive memories of the shaauri, so she had somehow taken on the characteristics of the cousin who had helped shape her destiny.

Had she called upon this hidden part of herself when she found the situation on Aitu too difficult to bear? Had memories of Tyr arisen to take possession of her being, beyond her control?

Ronan feared for her, but he could not allow that fear to rule him. Cynara's mental state might become a wedge for Kinsmen to pry into her past and her unique knowledge.

He must not fail her as he had failed Sihvaaro. Deliberately he relived the final battle, the moment of his teacher's death, heard again the words that brought so little comfort: "Do not give up hope."

Hope was a human emotion. Ronan could make his body function under conditions that would kill most humans, numb his senses to extreme heat and cold and hunger, ignore pain, speed the healing of wounds. He could not stop his grief.

"You must go to Arhan, those who adopted your father."

Sihvaaro had learned the truth of Ronan's parentage. But only upon his death had he revealed the secret he had concealed even from his beloved student: his own telepathic abilities.

There are others like me, Sihvaaro had said. The rest of his knowledge, like his devotion and serene courage, had died with him.

But the Kinsmen must also know what had become of Ronan's parents. Constano had been the enemy of Arhan, and Arhan was Jonas Kane's adopted Line. If the Arhani still bore any loyalty toward Kane and Kori Challinor, hope remained.

All Ronan had to do was reach this vessel's com station and send a message to the Arhan ship Sihvaaro had summoned.

He laughed. Cynara regarded him impassively across the cabin. The door opened.

"Come," the armed Kinsman said, jerking his rifle. "Constano wants to see you."

Cynara got to her feet and walked past Ronan without a glance. The Kinsman, joined by a second guard, herded them back down the corridor to a larger cabin that could only belong to the First of the ship.

A man rose from his chair behind a broad desk. Ronan knew him immediately.

Artur Constano VelRauthi—the man whose face and name he had for so long forgotten, traitor to the Concordat, the Kinsman who was behind the assassination plot, Sihvaaro's death, and Cynara's present danger.

The guards set Ronan and Cynara before the desk and took up stations to either side of the cabin. VelRauthi smiled behind his dark beard with all the ease of a man certain in his power.

"I see that you remember me, Ronan," he said, "though I'd hardly expected to meet again. Ronan Kane VelKalevi— what irony in that name." He chuckled. "Or do you prefer Lord Achilles Challinor?"

"I did not carry out your bidding," Ronan said. "The Archon still lives."

"So I understand." VelRauthi moved an object on his desk to a new position as if it were of great importance. "Bravo. Your mind is far stronger than even we suspected when we sent you. But it seems you still cannot control your thoughts or your emotions. I feel your hate." He glanced at Cynara, who had neither moved nor spoken. "And I feel something more . . . Is it possible that a human raised by shaauri can love?"

"You are not interested in my emotions," Ronan said, holding VelRauthi's gaze. "You came to Aitu when you learned I had returned, though I was not meant to survive your mission."

"And we discovered that you had a very interesting companion," VelRauthi added. "Sit, Cynara D'Accorso, captain of the Alliance ship *Pegasus*."

Cynara remained standing. "What do you want?"

"Admirable directness, Captain," he said. "Perhaps you will tell me why you were watching us at the landing field?"

"We had no choice," Ronan said. "After the Challinors discovered my purpose and sent me from Concordat space—"

"Curious that they let you go."

"—I returned with Cynara D'Accorso to share what I had learned with my House. But circumstances on Aitu have changed since I left. It was necessary to escape by any means possible."

"Indeed—Lenko is an old enemy, isn't he? Of course you had no intention of contacting us until you were driven to it."

"I regained my full memory and recognized what you had done to me. I am no assassin."

"Nor, apparently, are you ever to be anything but an outcast among shaauri." He clucked with mock sympathy. "Lenko was most eager to be rid of all human presence—he was not so amenable to our mutual goals as the previous First of Ain'Kalevi and had no interest in what we had done with you. He allowed you to think that you might buy safety with the knowledge you promised, while all the time he was waiting for us to take you away."

"What will you do with us now?" Cynara demanded.

"I sense a certain chagrin, Captain. Though Ronan would have us believe he took you hostage, it is clear that you accompanied him out of sheer devotion, having supposedly saved his life from the shaauri striker. It must make a fascinating tale."

Cynara laughed. "Look a little deeper, Constano, and you may find that my feelings are not as tender as you suppose."

VelRauthi narrowed his eyes. "Ah, yes. A change of heart that *seems* to be genuine." He glanced at Ronan. "Yet you are still determined to protect her. How very touching."

"All I want is to be returned to the Concordat," Cynara said. "To my own kind."

"I do sympathize with your feelings, Captain. When you came with Ronan, you did not expect him to probe your mind and take vital intelligence that might harm the Concordat. Alas, betrayal all around. But since he has already retrieved this intelligence and you have little to lose by sharing it, you and I may be able to reach an agreement regarding your future."

"Perhaps," she said coolly. "Why did you want the Archon dead?"

"If I told you the reason, dear Captain, I might never be able to let you leave."

"You're human, and so am I. Your war is not with the Nine Worlds or my people; it's with the Concordat, who have never treated us as equals."

"And you imply that our interests may coincide more than I might assume? You intrigue me, Captain." He glanced at Ronan. "And I see she shocks you. You expected her to remain loyal to her own kind, as you have to the shaauri, who have rejected you." He bowed to Cynara. "Naturally I can't take you at your word, Captain. I know you're a telepath of limited ability and privy to certain Concordat secrets. Secrets within secrets, perhaps?"

"By now the Concordat must realize that I left with Ronan," she said. "They didn't authorize it. They'll be prepared for the possibility that an enemy might penetrate my defenses. I know very well I can't hold out against Kinsmen."

"Sensible. Still, your sincerity remains in question . . . for the time being." He turned to Ronan again. "We were always aware even you might fail, but you may still serve some purpose."

Ronan knotted his fists. "What became of my parents? Who sent me to Aitu and Ain'Kalevi?"

"Ah, your parents. Such a tragedy. They came to shaauri space hoping to avert a Second War, but were intercepted by shaauri . . . less enthusiastic about a lasting peace with humans."

"And by Kinsmen."

"Perhaps. In any case, I understand that Jonas Kane Vel-Arhan and his Challinor mate escaped the ship in a lifepod before it was destroyed, just as you did. They were never found. You, however, were rescued."

"And sent not to my father's shaauri kin, but to those who hated humans."

"There was always some debate as to whether or not you should be allowed to survive. Aitu was a test. You were relieved of your memories of your true parents and the time before your arrival on that world, and given to Ain'Kalevi. When you not only survived but made a place for yourself in House Kalevi—and displayed signs of your parents' skills—it became clear that you might be an asset after all."

"You hated my parents."

"They had caused me some inconvenience in the past. But you were to atone for their sins. A few conferences with the

War-Leader and Ain'Kalevi—who didn't hate Kinsmen nearly so much as the Concordat—and you were given to us."

Ronan was sucked into a memory of the small room, the human faces, the burning in his mind as they stripped it bare and filled it again with their schemes and thoughts of death.

"The pain was a small price to pay for what you might have accomplished," VelRauthi said.

"For you, not for shaauri-*ja*."

"You seem convinced that there is a difference. Shaauri need the benefit of human cunning and human strategies if they are to win this war."

"The *A'Aho-Kei'hon-vekki* knew about the assassination attempt?"

VelRauthi pursed his lips. "He approved our plans to use you as an agent ideally suited to evading Concordat defenses against our people. The details he left in our hands."

"Will you tell him I have failed?"

"The information you and the captain carry should be more than sufficient to satisfy the War-Leader."

"I will give him my knowledge directly. Release Captain D'Accorso and deliver me to Aur."

"No, no." VelRauthi's eyes glinted with humor, barely concealing his hostility. "You are only a tool, Ronan, and a flawed one. You're of no more importance to *A'Aho-Kei'hon-vekki* than a gnat on the tip of his whisker. You live on sufferance now, just as on Aitu."

Ronan swallowed his anger like rancid meat. "Do with me what you wish, but release Captain D'Accorso. I possess all the knowledge in her mind."

"We shall see." VelRauthi leaned against the desk, his eyes sharp behind their amusement. "You and the captain have been lovers?"

"Yes," Cynara said. "That's the only reason he has my knowledge. I did care for him, before . . ." She let the contempt in her voice complete the sentence.

"I see that you have lost your taste for alien lovers. A little too exotic . . . Lifemate?" He smiled at Ronan. "So that was your strategy to save her from the human-haters. Unfortunately, I feel the lady's distaste for the prospect. Such a high honor wasted."

Ronan shut out the Kinsman's mockery. It didn't matter if Cynara truly believed what she said, or if Tyr spoke for her. As long as she remained alive and safe.

Silence. Silence your thoughts.

"You seem distracted, VelKalevi," Constano said with feigned concern. "It is sad to lose the regard of a loved one, but it will make it easier for you in the long term. You see, I won't be able to let the captain go until I am quite certain that her information is of use to us. One of you will provide the initial intelligence, and the other will confirm it under deep-probe. Unfortunately, that confirmation may result in severe and permanent damage to the subjected mind.

"You'll have to choose which of you is to remain sane."

Chapter 27

R onan took a step forward, and the guards snapped to attention. "Captain D'Accorso will give you what you demand," he said. "I will not resist your deep-probe."

"Very noble," Constano said. "Have you any objections, Captain D'Accorso? Cooperate and keep your sanity, and your life if not your freedom. I give you my word. You'll be rid of the man who led you to this, along with the unwelcome burden of his pathetic devotion."

Cynara continued to stare straight ahead, an exquisite statue gracing VelRauthi's quarters. "I need time to consider."

"Of course." He moved back around his desk and sat, steepling his fingers in an attitude of profound gravity. "You and Ronan may return to your cabin to . . . discuss your options."

The guards closed in about Ronan and Cynara, and for a moment Ronan's impulse to attack VelRauthi was so powerful that the Kinsman shot up from his seat and shouted in warning. A rifle butt struck Ronan in the belly. He doubled over, sucking in air, and came up to meet Cynara's stony gaze.

"Enjoy your final moments together," VelRauthi said, and laughed.

The Kinsman guards marched Ronan and Cynara back to the cell, where they were provided with rations and water. Cynara retreated to her side of the cabin.

"You must let him have what he wants," Ronan said, sinking into a crouch. "VelRauthi will not spare me, whatever you decide."

He might as well have been talking to the bulkhead. Cynara didn't move.

Before the meeting with VelRauthi, Ronan had feared to touch Cynara's mind lest he prematurely reveal his intentions. Now there was no choice. VelRauthi was convinced that Cynara would break with very little encouragement, and that she might even prove useful beyond the intelligence she contributed. But Ronan had no doubt that he would deep-probe Cynara in spite of his promise.

What she needed was a way to preserve her sanity when VelRauthi attempted the probe. Ronan had a very limited window of opportunity in which to give her that ability.

Cynara had said or implied many times that all her strength came from her cousin. What had happened on the day Tyr died? Her memories made his act a noble sacrifice, essential to her position as captain of the *Pegasus*.

There must be something more.

"Cynara," he said gently, "you must trust me." Without waiting for a reply, he sat cross-legged on the deck and began the practice of the Eightfold Way. One by one he renewed his mental barriers, constructing a scaffolding of surface thoughts and fears to distract any Kinsman observers. The barricade would hold for only a short time, but its labyrinthine structure would conceal what he attempted to create behind it.

He released his grip on his fabrication and sank deep beneath its meaningless chatter, retaining just enough physical awareness to reach for Cynara. Her hand was ice-cold, fingers unresisting.

Cynara. Hear me.

It seemed that he walked in a fog, lost as she was lost in

the caverns of her mind. The bright presence of her being was muted and cold.

Cynara. You have nothing to fear. Come to me.

No response. But within the mist shone a faint luminescence, ghost-lights to guide the weary traveler home. Ronan made his way toward them, memories sucking at his legs with every step.

Memories.

They danced before him like the veils worn by Dharman women, floating within his grasp and then snatched away by invisible fingers. He stood very still. A memory black as Vel-Rauthi's heart wrapped itself around him.

The *Pegasus*—the scream of sirens—a dying man sprawled on the deck at the foot of the captain's chair. Tyr Siannas. His face was twisted with pain and some deeper torment.

Ronan crouched over him, cradling Tyr's head in his hands. Tyr coughed. Bright blood spattered Ronan's shirt.

Don't blame yourself, Cyn. It wasn't your doing. But Tyr's lips did not move. The voice was not his. It came, bodiless, from the very air. From Cynara's mind.

Ronan blocked the voice and concentrated on Tyr's face. Green eyes opened, staring at Ronan with the fury of madness.

"You," he whispered. "Little bitch. If not for you—" Tyr clawed with rigid hands, dragging Ronan down until Tyr's fading breath mingled with his own.

"You want my ship?" Tyr rasped. "You want to be captain?" He barked out a laugh. "I'm dying. Does that please you?"

Ronan shook his head wildly. "No, Tyr. You can't die."

"You were always a fraud, Cynara. A farce. Nothing. Now . . . you've betrayed Dharma, D'Accorso . . . my father . . ."

"No." But in Ronan's mind was the sure knowledge that he had brought disaster upon the *Pegasus,* upon this cousin he had always loved, because he had not been content in the life to which he had been born.

"Will you do anything . . . to save me?" Tyr croaked.

"Anything." Tears scalded Ronan's eyes. "Anything."

"Then come closer, little Cousin. Look at me. *Trust me.*" He locked his hands around Ronan's face. In that touch was nothing of tenderness, of farewell, of regret. Tyr's mind struck out, a master's thrust aimed at a novice. Ronan jerked back, but he could not escape.

He saw the truth of Tyr's character, the ambition, the willingness to sacrifice anything or anyone to win and keep power. He felt the depth of Tyr's hatred. And he knew Tyr's weakness—the mortal defect that had held him immobile with fear when he could have acted to save himself and the crew.

Tyr thrust inside Ronan's mind with groping fists, seeking the continuation of life in any way he could take it. Ronan's vision faltered. A million microscopic teeth gnawed at the space inside his skull, emptying it of thought and will and self.

You will be captain, Tyr whispered. *Your body will walk this deck. But nothing of you will be left to enjoy it.*

The blows came without ceasing, bruising phantom flesh and snapping spectral bones. Tyr drove inside him—unimaginable, excruciating violation meant to destroy utterly.

But something of Ronan remained. All the petty rebellions that changed so little, the minor revolts against tradition, everything he had fought for on Dharma came to his aid like the angels of legend. Mental abilities judged so insignificant rose to his defense. He found the strength to fight back.

Tyr was not prepared. His astonishment cut through Ronan's newfound resolve for the fraction of an instant. Tyr recovered first. He launched his final, fatal assault.

Ronan raised his shield, mirror-bright. Tyr's blow struck and rebounded onto itself, splitting Tyr's mind asunder.

Ronan's shield shattered, driving shards of glass and metal into his body. His screams mingled with Tyr's. He *was* Tyr, spinning into an abyss of his own making.

He died. A strong, slender hand grasped his collar and pulled him from the womb of darkness.

Ronan?

Cynara released him and stepped away, hands shielding her eyes. *Where is Tyr?*

He shook the veil from his face and held out his hand.
Come back with me, Cynara.

I told you to stay away.

I could not. Come with me now.

She laughed. *Not without Tyr.*

Tyr is dead. He will not return.

He lives.

This is not life, Cynara. Tyr was never with you.

We survive because of him.

Ronan knew she would not listen, here in this plane where
Tyr's presence lingered in the power she had given him. She
must come back to herself, to the doubts that had made her
deny the reality of that terrible joining.

He could not carry her across the threshold. She must
shake off the false past as he had done, or she would never be
free even if she survived the Kinsmen.

He filled his thoughts with every good moment they had
shared: Kord's rescue, the long conversations, the escape
from Dharma, their last mating.

And the love he was too great a coward to express.

You are my life, Cynara. Without you I will die.

Her confusion sucked him into a vortex of discordant
emotions. It was Tyr, not Cynara, who had suggested freely
giving up her knowledge in exchange for life and eventual
freedom; Tyr who had expressed contempt for Ronan; Tyr
who would gladly sacrifice a friend, a mate, a nation in order
to survive.

With all his will, Ronan made her see that he spoke truth,
made her accept the bond he had thrust upon her when he had
claimed the right to defend her life with his body. The lam-
bent blaze of her hair fell across her eyes. She trembled.

And took his hand.

Cynara had often dreamed of falling a great distance
and hitting the ground with shattering force, only to find
herself waking in her own bed.

She opened her eyes to the sight of bare bulkheads and
merciless light. Ronan sat cross-legged beside her, stirring
with the same sluggishness she felt in her own body. She

knew that touching him with her thoughts would be easier than reaching out with her shaking hand.

Her mind was clear. Achingly, profoundly clear.

Kinsmen. She pushed herself erect, struggling to rebuild the mental shields that surely must have failed. The ship remained silent save for the vibrations of the engines.

"I do not know," Ronan said, "how much longer my defenses will hold. Are you well?"

Well? She turned to him, and it was as if she had forgotten the look of his face, the color of his eyes, the sound of his voice.

Mother Sea . . . she had forgotten how much she loved him.

You are my life.

"Tyr," she whispered. "What did you do?"

Ronan shifted his weight but moved no closer. "You were lost, Cynara. It was necessary to bring you back if you are to escape the Kinsmen."

Back. She followed a trail of memory to Ronan's hut, Sihvaaro's warning, the challenge and its inevitable conclusion. Bitter, galling helplessness.

That was when she'd given up the battle she'd fought every day since Tyr's death. She surrendered her pride, the fierce determination to deny what her heart had always told her.

Tyr had come. Tyr had given her the dispassion to act without fear or remorse. She'd felt nothing for Ronan's grief, and only a kind of grim satisfaction when she took Lenko hostage and won freedom from their captors. She would have killed the shaaurin if necessary. All the time she and Ronan ran from the Kalevi settlement—even when they fell into Kinsman hands—she had judged every action with a calculating eye to survival.

"You believed Tyr would do what you could not," Ronan said. "I had abandoned you, and you saw no other way. But Tyr was never able to help you . . . not now, nor at any time since his death."

She could hardly endure his sadness. "I know I hurt you," she said. "You must believe . . . whatever I did or said—"

"I know." He touched her hand. "You have no cause for regret."

No cause. "You shouldn't have done it, Ronan," she said, closing her eyes to the firm belief in his. "Tyr was the one who had the power to resist the Kinsmen. *He* was the one who took Lenko hostage and got us free of the shaauri. Without him—"

"Without your mistaken beliefs of Tyr to bind you, you may have a chance of leaving this ship."

She shook her head and pressed her face to her knees. "I never told you everything about Tyr's death. I should have made you understand."

"I do understand." He unfolded his legs and leaned forward, regarding her as if she might break at a touch. "I saw it happen through your eyes, Cynara. It was not as you remember."

She bit her tongue to keep from laughing. "You weren't there."

"I know why you remember the events as you have. You changed them because they were too terrible to bear."

"I could have saved Tyr, and I killed him."

"Because he would have killed you."

"He gave me everything. He used the last of his life to transfer all his education, his skills, even his telepathic abilities. And I took them without thinking of the price. If I had refused, he might have recovered—"

"You are wrong. When he knew he was dying, he attempted to destroy your mind and take your body for his own. He would live on in any way he could, even at the cost of your life. The knowledge you received from him was only the unforeseen consequence of his attack, burned into your mind when you forced him to withdraw."

One of them must be mad. "I couldn't have. He was a thousand times more powerful than I am."

"You were made to believe this, so that you would never be tempted to defy the last bonds that held you to Dharma and offer your services to the Alliance as a free and equal *va'laik'in*. As Tyr's potential rival. But when you faced death at Tyr's hands, you fought back." He reached out, curling his fingers into a fist. "You felt him die."

Cynara's skull rang with memories as deafening as the surf at Highcliff. Sucking blackness. Blind, senseless hatred. She clutched her head between her hands, trying to shut them out.

"You blamed yourself for the circumstances of his death," Ronan continued, "but not in the way they truly occurred. You had quarreled with Tyr on the bridge when he discovered your presence as a stowaway. You were still with him when the shaauri striker appeared. You became convinced that this quarrel distracted Tyr at a moment when he should have acted to save the ship from shaauri attack. He fed your guilt. But it was his own weakness that failed him, Cynara."

The ringing in her head became klaxons of alarm. Men dashed about the bridge, stared at the screen framing the shaauri striker, called out questions that received no answer.

"Tyr's courage, his skill as a leader, masked a great flaw," Ronan said. "When the shaauri striker attacked the *Pegasus,* he was faced with a choice between capture or almost certain death. He had sworn never to let the *Pegasus* fall into enemy hands, yet he feared his own extinction too much. He froze, and thus condemned himself . . . just as your idealized memory of him almost made you lose your life."

Tyr had stood there beside the captain's chair, unmoving, ignoring the crew, ignoring the shaauri. One of the torpedoes had disabled half the bridge. Crewmen screamed in pain. Tyr fell.

"All the events that followed Tyr's critical error were lost to your memory, Cynara. No one knew what Tyr attempted to do to you. But they saw how you rose up and took command of the *Pegasus,* acting as your cousin should have, boldly winning escape."

"I couldn't have done it—"

He took her in his arms. "It was *your* courage that saved the *Pegasus,* even though you had experienced the depths of Tyr's hatred and felt his death. A lesser person would have been crippled in mind and spirit. You rose to your true nature and earned the right to become captain."

Devastating revelation. Terrible, unthinkable hope. "All these years . . . I've felt Tyr within me, reminding me of his sacrifice. Anything I did worth doing was because of him.

But I was afraid—afraid I would lose everything if I ever let him out. If I let go, even for a moment, he would . . . *become* me." She rode the edge of hysterical laughter. "They were right, the Dharmans who judged me as tainted."

"They were wrong." He tucked her head under his chin, folding himself around her. "On Aitu, you sacrificed yourself to Tyr when you believed you had no other choice—to save my life. You believed you might never return, not as you knew yourself."

"I *became* Tyr. I only returned . . . because you claimed I could save you."

"You can, Cynara. But Tyr will not help you. His influence would have led you to surrender what you most desire to protect. But he is dead. Only your erroneous guilt made him real and stronger than he ever was in life."

"I lied to myself," she said, numb with shock.

"You could not face the hatred and betrayal of a kinsman you loved and admired. You pretended that he had given you his gifts and knowledge out of that same love."

The truth of everything he had said crashed over her, filling her nose and lungs as if she were drowning.

Tyr was dead. He had never been with her at all. Now she understood why she'd always been afraid of letting him out . . . because he had tried to take her and almost succeeded. Part of her had remembered the battle for her existence even when she had forgotten how it came about. And how it ended.

Carter VelShaan had removed Cynara's memory of Tyr because she'd recognized how much it crippled her. The Kinswoman had done it out of compassion, but only Cynara had the power to banish Tyr forever.

She wrenched out of Ronan's arms and banged her fist against the bulk so hard that pain shot through to her elbow. There was no one else to receive this overwhelming rage. Tyr was dead.

Hate was the flame that would annihilate his presence even from memory. The conflagration exploded outward to consume all within the radius of its uncontrolled fury. She willed it to burn until nothing was left of the Cynara who had been.

Too late she remembered Ronan. He knelt with his hands resting on his thighs, eyes closed, accepting her rage as Tyr could not. Instinctively she tried to recall her hatred, but it had taken on a life of its own. She grabbed Ronan with both hands. His muscles were rigid, his body engulfed in agony. She plunged into his mind. His suffering became her own. Pain upon pain, the grief of unbearable loss, utter aloneness.

My father.

He held Sihvaaro in his arms and watched his dearest friend die, knowing himself the cause. He wept without ceasing, though his eyes never betrayed him. He wanted to die.

But he did not. Cynara kept him alive.

Tyr's ghost had spared her the full knowledge of Ronan's intolerable grief. Hatred was as nothing to this. Sihvaaro was dead. With him died Ronan's only true tie to the people who had taken him in, sheltering his body but denying him the right to be one of them.

Outcast. Ne'lin. Human.

Everything he had done, everything he had borne at the hands of shaauri and Kinsmen alike, had been to earn a place among his adopted people. All of it he had sacrificed for Cynara's sake. His shaauri father had died because she forced herself into Ronan's world, a life she couldn't possibly understand. In an act of desperation he had claimed her as his lifemate, perverting sacred shaauri tradition and revealing to the Ain'Kalevi just how human he was.

"Cynara."

She looked up. Ronan's eyes were remarkably clear, a facade of calm and serenity.

"They will come soon," he said. "I could not conceal your emotions, or my own."

She smiled bitterly. "And you called me strong."

"It is your strength I require now. And your trust."

"You consider my trust of value after all that's happened?"

"I will ask something you have reason to fear above any other fate."

"The fate we face now is death." She framed his cold face in her hands. "But you want to die. If not for me, you'd force them to kill you."

"Hear me, Cynara. You know I have certain skills, those the Kinsmen prepared me to use in my mission. When I entered the engineering room of the *Pegasus,* I became invisible to the eyes and minds of the crew. I made *An* Charis forget she had come to my cabin. I could influence the crew of this ship in a similar manner, though these opponents are far more formidable."

Kinsmen, not untrained nontelepaths. Cynara snatched at the scrap of hope he offered. Any plan, however desperate, would keep his mind from thoughts of death.

"What can I do, Ronan?"

"You must give me your mind. We will join, not as before in thoughts and feelings, but to the last particle of consciousness. You must surrender your very self to me."

Ronan's words swept past her rational brain and slashed at the raw wounds Tyr had left behind. *Your body will walk this deck, but nothing of you will be left to enjoy it.*

Tyr raped her mind again, taking pleasure in her helplessness, hating her because she had witnessed his downfall, his ignominious ruin. Pushing, thrusting, filling her up with himself until she struck out with the only weapon left to her: hatred. Hatred, animal instinct, the rage to kill.

Ronan had *seen* what Tyr had done. He'd made *her* see it, exposed her deepest fears. He could not be demanding this obscene perversion of what they'd once shared.

But there was no mistaking what he implied: her very being transformed to a witless extension of his, a puppet, a shadow with no self beyond what he chose to let her keep. Worse than the half-life of a Dharman woman, worse than the madness Artur Constano VelRauthi offered. Worse than death.

Surrender. Lose yourself. Nothing left . . .

She knew what she saw in Ronan's eyes. Tyr wasn't gone. He was still here, masquerading as the man she loved.

"Trust me," Tyr said, laughing at her weakness, her despicable frailty.

Never. Never again.

She lashed out, striking at Ronan with fists and the scourge of her bitterness. He took the blows without flinching. He bore the holocaust of hatred as he had borne the punishment of shaauri who rejected his very right to exist.

It could not continue. One of them must break, but Ronan simply absorbed the punishment as if it was no less than what he deserved.

He was not Tyr. He could never be. In this man was goodness, generosity, compassion checked only by his self-contempt and the certainty of his own unworthiness to exist. She gave anger and received love in return, love beyond the scope of any language.

"Scylla take you, Ronan," she whispered. "Will you never fight back?"

He smiled and lifted a damp strand of her hair. "Not you, *Aho'Va.*"

She groaned and slumped against him. "I know." Her mouth filled with the sour taste of shame. "I'm sorry, Ronan. I wasn't my—" *Tyr is gone. When have you ever been more yourself?* "I'm no better than any of them."

His hand came to rest on her hair in a kind of benediction. His gaze was quiet, wise and frighteningly detached, as if Sihvaaro had taken up residence in his body.

"Can you do what must be done?" he asked.

"Yes."

"Your mind will attempt to defend itself."

"You aren't Tyr. I won't resist you." She touched his cheek gingerly, dreading the marks her beating might have left on his flesh. "VelRauthi offered us a choice. *I* choose."

He stroked her cheek with the back of his hand. "Whatever may come, know that I honor you, Cynara D'Accorso."

Into her mind flowed the understanding of what she must do. She closed her eyes, attuning her thoughts to Ronan's, surrendering control and fear and anything that might stand between them.

His lips brushed hers. The memory of Tyr's violation faded. Gentle currents washed over her, rocking her on soothing swells that never reached a shore. Ronan made love to her without touching anything but her face, giving even as he took so that she felt as if nothing had been taken at all.

Ronan's hands grew cold. She covered them with her own to warm them, but they slipped free.

"It is done," he said.

Chapter 28

*C*ynara *opened her eyes. Ronan knelt before her, his* head resting on the deck. She pressed her temples, searching for the difference within herself, the sense of having lost something precious and unique. But her heart beat strong and sure, and her mind . . .

Her mind was full to bursting, synapses sparking with a hundred new ideas, new concepts, tools for the use of her telepathy that she had barely imagined. She sat in stunned silence while her brain struggled to make sense of the raw data, organize it, make it ready for her use.

Ronan's knowledge. Everything he had learned about wielding the mind as a subtle weapon and shielding it from attack, the varied and effective means of deceiving the lesser talents of the Concordat. And more: the focus and discipline to use it as only the most highly trained individual could hope to do.

Tyr had tried to take her life, her will, herself. Ronan had given.

"No," she said. She grabbed Ronan's shoulders and pulled him up. His eyes were glazed, unseeing. She shook him, and then in her terror she slapped him hard enough to leave an impression of her hand on his cheek.

He focused. "Do they listen to us? Can we speak freely?" Scylla's teeth. He asked *her*. He expected her to know, and she did. She knew she'd feel it in an instant if anyone tried to eavesdrop telepathically.

"Have you given it all to me," she asked, "or only shared it? Ronan!"

He drew up onto his knees with quiet dignity. "I have not lost my knowledge, or my skill. But I will not be able to use telepathy . . . for some time. You must act in my place."

It all became sickeningly clear. Ronan had exhausted the stores of his mental strength down to the last cell and synapse, just as a man might deplete his body's energy after a hard swim of many kilometers. He couldn't recover without a long rest, if he recovered at all. VelRauthi wouldn't give him the chance.

"Why?" she begged.

But she knew. Perhaps he had not intended that she realize the truth, but he couldn't give so much of himself and keep it from her.

"You do plan to die," she said. "You want revenge, but you don't want to take me down with you. So you gave me the means to protect myself while you remain vulnerable."

"Forgive the deception," he said hoarsely, "but it was necessary. When VelRauthi comes for us, which he must do very soon, you will agree to give him whatever he wants to know. You have the means and understanding to share only what you wish, and the intelligence and courage to succeed."

"Not without you."

He shook his head. "No time. Hold VelRauthi's attention and distract him from me. You know how. I will get to the communications console and send a message to those who would help you."

She cursed, and he smiled. "You will do this, *ina-ma*. If I succeed in sending the message, I will probably not survive. VelRauthi will quickly realize that I am too weak to resist him, but I will engage him long enough to allow you to escape the bridge. Make yourself unseen and find a place to hide." He stopped her protest with a twitch of his hand. "Either the ones I call will come, or VelRauthi will find you and take you to Kinsman headquarters."

"Why should they?"

"With the abilities you display, they will believe that your importance to the Concordat must surely be greater than they imagined. But your shielding is also greater than ever before. All you must do is delay them until allies come to find you."

"Allies? In the Shaauriat?"

"Yes, even here. They will hear you if you tell them you are the lifemate of Ronan Kane VelKalevi Challinor, for my parents' sake."

"But I'm not your lifemate, am I? If I were, you wouldn't leave me." Her voice broke. "What good will they do us if you're dead?"

"You will survive to return to the Concordat, and you will work for peace with shaauri-*ja*."

"Why should I?" Bitterness scorched her throat like tears. "I owe nothing to the shaauri."

"But you want peace and freedom for your own people. I know your heart, *ina-ma*."

Ina-ma. Her new Voishaaur vocabulary supplied the definition.

My breath. My soul. Beloved.

He didn't touch her, offered no caresses to prove the sincerity of the word. But he meant it. God help them both, he meant it utterly.

"It will be your vengeance against the Kinsmen for my life," he said. "You have all the knowledge you need to do this, Cynara. You already possess the courage."

"You're wrong. We're both cowards, Ronan."

"I will live on within you."

He was right. He'd live as a part of her, like Tyr, but not only in her troubled imagination. Everything he was lay encoded in her cells, never to fade or vanish until her own death.

It wasn't good enough.

"Very well," she said with a fierce new calm. "I will survive."

His jaw worked, and he whispered shaauri words like a prayer. She held up her hand to silence him.

"They're coming," she said. She couldn't hear the enemy's approach, but her brain's own proximity alarms told her that Kinsmen had sensed the mental turmoil within the cell.

Ronan lunged across the deck and pulled her close. She wrapped her fingers in his hair. They kissed with frantic urgency, but it was as if she embraced him through the unbreachable layers of an environmental suit.

The cell's door opened. Four Kinsmen entered, two aiming weapons while the others dragged Ronan and Cynara to their feet.

Artur Constano VelRauthi was waiting on the bridge. Two other high-ranking Kinsmen stood with him beside the captain's chair. A pair of the guards took posts just outside the bridge door.

"Ah, Ronan," VelRauthi said. "I hope you appreciate the privacy we granted you and Captain D'Accorso." He smiled at Cynara. "Sacred Kinsman law forbids entering an unwilling mind. Unfortunately, your shouting was impossible to ignore."

Ronan stared through the Kinsman as if he had chosen to keep silent rather than grant VelRauthi a single word in response. But he had no defense, and soon his enemy would know. He had become a hollow man, a creature stripped of the only strengths that made him VelRauthi's equal.

But he still had some small worth. Cynara's anger ate at him like the corrosive sap of a *kek* plant, but he was glad of it. Anger would keep her alive. And if hatred failed her, Sihvaaro's wisdom would teach her acceptance, as it had once taught a small and very frightened boy.

Sihvaaro would be avenged. Cynara would live.

Ronan smiled.

"I apologize for the disturbance, *Ser* Constano," Cynara said. "I agree to your terms. I'll tell you whatever you wish to know."

VelRauthi and his Kinsman aids gazed at her intently. One of the subordinates gave a stiff half nod.

"Very wise, Captain. I can see that you did not wish to surrender Ronan to our less tender ministrations, but it was inevitable. There is always a chance he may survive."

"I will not fight you," Ronan said.

"Also very wise. I misjudged your mutual affection when

we first met. Still, there was no other reasonable conclusion you could—"

"Get on with it," Cynara said coldly.

"This is hardly the place. However . . ." He conferred silently with his aides. "Very well." He signaled to the guards, who flanked Ronan to either side. "Please sit, *Mes* D'Accorso. Make yourself comfortable, and this will be far easier to endure."

Cynara sat. Ronan maintained the stance of Watchful Stillness. The silence was absolute. Ronan sensed nothing of what passed between VelRauthi and Cynara, or between the Kinsman traitor and his aides. He was deaf and nearly blind. All was in Cynara's hands.

It was a testament to her skill that he knew the precise moment when she had her Kinsman interrogators' full attention. He moved as Sihvaaro had taught him. One Kinsman guard went down with a single well-placed kick. Ronan caught his weapon in midair. The second guard turned as if in slow motion. Ronan disarmed him and clipped the base of his skull with the butt of the gun.

He knew exactly where to go. He reached the communications console and punched in the codes Sihvaaro had passed to him with his thoughts.

VelRauthi spun around. Ronan aimed both guns at the Kinsman's belly. His subordinates froze. One glance at Cynara was all Ronan dared risk.

She vanished. Ronan's keen eyes could not detect her, nor his other senses fix on her presence. The Kinsmen were equally blind. The bridge doors opened and shut again on the sight of struggling guards.

Farewell, Beloved.

Ronan laughed aloud. VelRauthi had blanched the color of bone.

"She deceived you, *kek'ko ne'lin*," Ronan said. "You thought her skills were of no consequence, but she is the strong one. You will not find her quickly."

"One woman against all of us, VelKalevi. She can't win. And you are dead."

"I know." He angled one gun toward the Kinsman Second, who seemed about to move. "I have sent a message to those who will aid Captain D'Accorso and stand against you as traitors to shaauri-*ja*."

"You're the traitor. You have nothing."

Ronan's mind sang with joyous certainty as Cynara sent him a parting gift, so strong and clear that even he could hear it. "My teacher Sihvaaro learned part of the truth, and I know the rest. You planned to use the Archon's death as a means of returning to Concordat space and regaining your power there, regardless of the consequences in shaauri-*ja*. That was always your intention—to rule humans rather than serve shaauri masters. Cynara knew the location of the world where the alien drive technology was discovered. You would steal it and keep it to yourselves." He showed his teeth. "Did you believe we would give ourselves up to you without plans of our own? Word of your treachery has already been sent to the War-Leader, *ne'lin*."

"Your claims against ours," VelRauthi said. "Even Ain'Kalevi will not speak for you."

"I will fall first, but you will fall with me. You believed the Concordat would collapse without the Archon, but your own fears set you on the wrong Path. It is your people who must decline when you are gone."

VelRauthi's expression grew blank, but not out of fear. Ronan's ravaged mind felt the attack, a barrage of mental power turned against his hands and his grip on the weapons.

He had wanted this final battle to be a true and proper challenge, but VelRauthi would never permit it.

"For Sihvaaro," he said, and squeezed the triggers. But his fingers had lost their strength. One gun clattered to the deck, and the beam of the other went wide, catching one of VelRauthi's subordinates on the shoulder. He shrieked and spun away.

VelRauthi held Ronan paralyzed while he snatched the second weapon from Ronan's hand. Immediately he aimed it at Ronan's heart.

"You've lost your power," he said, almost wonderingly. "You're completely helpless."

"Finish it."

"You do want to die, don't you? Ah, yes. I remember

Sihvaaro. He never trusted us and spoke against our plan. It's fortunate he's dead as well."

"Face me in honorable challenge, *ne'lin*."

"Oh, no. I was put in that position once before, and it did not end to my advantage." He cocked his head. "Since you have no defenses, it will be a simple matter to drain your memory of any useful knowledge."

"You may take everything," Ronan said, "but you will never use what you learn."

"Like your parents, you have a fatal tendency to underestimate your enemies." He glanced behind him. One of the guards was stirring, and the Kinsman who had been shot lay groaning on the deck in the arms of his companion. "Belloq, the man you wounded, has a peculiar fondness for the suffering of others, both mental and physical. I've found him useful in the past. I'm certain he'll be pleased to take charge of you. We may even lure the versatile captain from hiding."

"She will not come."

VelRauthi turned his back in contempt. The recovered guard attended his fallen comrade while a medic entered the bridge with another armed Kinsman, who went directly to Ronan. The medic set about treating Belloq's shoulder. As soon as she was finished, she and his comrade helped him to his feet.

Belloq came forward, clutching his shoulder. He nodded to VelRauthi. "Bind him," he commanded the guard.

For a moment Ronan was free to act. He lunged. The guard shoved his gun barrel into Ronan's stomach, forcing the air from his lungs. Someone bound his hands in steel cuffs. Belloq stared into Ronan's eyes, emotionless.

Pain. At first Ronan could not tell if it came from within or without, for it filled his skull and spilled over into his veins like liquid fire. His eyes threatened to burst from their sockets. His empty stomach attempted to turn inside out.

Then the pain stopped, and the guards picked him up from the deck. Ronan heaved and tasted blood. Belloq smiled.

"I think the captain will come," VelRauthi said.

The agony resumed, and for a time Ronan was senseless. Blurs that might have been human figures passed in and out of his vision. Sound bored into his eardrums like bone needles. Once more the pain stopped. He tried to breathe with a throat skinned raw.

The hands on his arms fell away. He became aware that the movement around him had ceased. His legs collapsed from under him. Sometime later the noises that made no sense began to take on definition, and Ronan pushed to his knees. His wrists were no longer bound. Aside from the lingering shock to his body, he could function again. He could see.

All the places where Kinsmen had stood were empty. The bridge was clear except for a lone figure bent over a monitor. A stack of weapons of various sizes lay on the workspace beside her.

Cynara abandoned the monitor and ran to Ronan's side, dropping to her knees. She embraced him gingerly, hands stroking with a healer's touch. He could not have borne any touch but hers.

"It's about time," she said. Her voice shook. "VelRauthi assured me—after some persuasion—that you would recover, and I had to leave you for a little while. I'm sorry."

"No." Ronan thought better of standing up and let Cynara support him. "You shouldn't . . . have come back."

"I could feel what they were doing to you." She seemed to have some difficulty speaking. "VelRauthi counted on that. He didn't have a very good idea of what I was capable of."

Even mild shaauri laughter hurt Ronan's throat too much. "You have suffered no ill effects from the use of your new abilities?"

"None that I'm aware of." She peered into his eyes. "It's you I'm worried about."

"I will recover. Where are the Kinsmen?"

"All confined to the briefing room, with the medic to tend the wounded, and I've sealed off all other quarters and cabins to isolate as many of the crew as possible. I've also sealed the bridge—no one else is getting in. At least not until our guests arrive."

Ronan tried to isolate the sounds in his memory: shouting, a few sharp cries, and then the wail of alarms indicating the approach of an unidentified starship.

The alarm was silent now.

"They have come," he said, sick with relief.

"They're sending a shuttle as we speak. I told them to expect resistance, but I don't think that should prove a problem for them." He thought he detected moisture in her eyes— tears from a woman who never wept. "You believed in my strength, and I had to believe in yours."

He began to rise, and she took his weight. For the first time he had a clear view of the bridge's main screen. On it was the image of a ship—a very large ship of unequivocal shaauri design. The markings painted on its hull were equally distinct.

"You never did tell me whom you intended to call," Cynara said, her lips brushing Ronan's cheek. "I trust these are the right shaauri, since they asked for you by name. They were certainly quick in getting here."

"Arhan," Ronan said. "My father's Line."

"But still shaauri. I hope—" She broke off as a new alarm sounded, indicating the shaauri shuttle's approach to the Kinsman ship.

Ronan gathered his feet under him. "I should go . . . greet them—"

"You'll stay here. We both will. They'll come to us." She steered him to the captain's chair and made him sit, then examined him minutely for injuries. Belloq had barely begun, and he hadn't bothered with mere flesh.

"I see that VelRauthi told the truth," she said. "I think I convinced him that it was a very bad idea to do otherwise."

Ronan felt such pride and awe that only the sharing of thoughts could express them. He had not regained that ability. *"Ska'eival Aho'Va,"* he said, bowing his head.

She snorted. "Save your humility. We aren't out of this storm yet." She took his hand, and they waited until a shaauri voice hailed them on the intercom. Cynara unsealed the bridge doors.

A shaaurin walked in, *va'laik'in* flanked by two Arhan warriors. He stopped, stared at Ronan and Cynara with calm curiosity, and gave a small salute.

"I greet you, *Va*-Captain Cynara D'Accorso of the Nine Worlds," he said in heavily accented Standard. His whiskers rippled with emotion. "I greet you, Ronan, son of Jonas VelArhan, kin of my kin. I am Hraan, *Aino'Ken* Arhan, brother of your father. We come to take you home."

*I*t took many hours for Hraan and Ronan, speaking in rapid-fire Voishaaur, to sort matters out between them. Cynara was able to ascertain, with her growing fluency in Voishaaur, that Hraan intended to deliver Ronan and Cynara to human space—something to do with an understandably touchy political situation among the Lines and Clans, Arhan's ambiguous position as a prohuman Line, and the need to find solid proof of the rogue Kinsmen's plots.

Cynara kept her thoughts private, but she watched Ronan come back to life and wondered if he would return with her.

That was the moment when she realized that all her resolve had been for nothing, that she had made assumptions she had no right or reason to entertain. She had sworn her love and said she expected nothing in return.

How well she had deceived herself.

She retreated to the cabin assigned to her and Ronan, sitting hard on the double-sized bunk. Coldness filled her lungs and ran in her veins. When had she learned to be so sure of the future? There had been times when any future had seemed impossible. She and Ronan had escaped death by the width of a shaauri whisker. It had been enough to survive, to feel victory within their grasp.

Enough until she faced an enemy far more subtle than destruction.

The Arhani accepted Ronan as the Kalevi could not. They welcomed him as a brother. They had known his parents. He was truly one of them. And he, among all humans, was uniquely suited to the human-shaauri negotiations that would soon become necessary.

That was the future she could not deny him.

There was no certainty. There never had been.

After a while Cynara got up and assembled the ingredients for the shaauri tea Ronan so loved. It was ready when Ronan returned. He exuded such vivid happiness that she was able to put aside her grief for his sake.

"So we've won," she said, pressing a mug into his hands.

"An Arhan skeleton crew has taken possession of the Kinsman ship," he said, grinning over the steaming *arao,* "and the Kinsmen are prisoners aboard the *Suhtaara.*" He tugged her down beside him on the bed and kissed her, filling her mouth with the taste of alien spices. "Hraan and his ship were on their way to Aitu. My message diverted them, but they had already been summoned by Sihvaaro before we arrived onworld."

"Before Sihvaaro knew we were coming?"

"He knew." Ronan smiled sadly. "I told you that Sihvaaro had certain gifts. But when he died . . ." He looked into his tea, struggling to mute his emotions. "Sihvaaro was a telepath."

Cynara nearly dropped her mug. "But there are no shaauri telepaths."

"There is much I do not understand. But it would explain a great deal about Sihvaaro . . . how well he understood me, and his readiness to accept all life as equal."

"I'm sorry, Ronan." Cynara linked her hand through his, swallowing past the constriction in her throat. "I know how much you grieve for him. I wish I could take it from you."

He kissed her knuckles. "Good has come even of this, *inama.* Hraan has heard tales of shaauri with abilities only humans are said to possess. He said that my father—before he and my mother disappeared—had been hunting legends of *ne'li* who claimed to speak without words and listen without ears." He shook his head. "If it is so, it is not an idea that will please many shaauri."

"They've allied with Kinsmen."

"But Kinsmen are human. That is the difference."

Who better than Ronan to know the truth of that. "Not all humans are alike, no more than shaauri. Not all Kinsmen are treacherous and out for power. That's what humans and shaauri must learn to accept."

"If Sihvaaro had lived, he would have had much to teach those who believe tolerance is impossible."

"But you carry his wisdom, Ronan. It isn't gone."

He met her gaze. "So do you, *Aho'Va.* And much more."

She knew he was not referring to the slingshot drive, but she felt a stab of unexpected guilt. The shaauri knew of humanity's new ship technology, and peace of any sort would be impossible in the face of such secrets.

But it wasn't her right to give them up, and she knew that Ronan wouldn't share what he knew without her permission. Their loyalty to each other was no longer in question.

"Hraan and his crew will be in danger if they enter Concordat space," she said. "If I went ahead, in a lifepod—"

"Hraan understands the risk, but this is what he wishes. He was a good friend of my father, though he was not of high position in those days. Still he blames himself for my parents' disappearance and my abduction."

"He has no idea what became of Lady Kori and VelArhan?"

"None. But he has agreed to assist me in pursuing the question with greater vigor."

"Apparently, guilt is also a shaauri emotion," she murmured.

"Arhan and certain other Lines always wished for peace with humans. Though Arhan could not stand against all the antihuman Lines, they would have protected me if they knew I survived. But they did not discover this until Sihvaaro sent word."

"Hraan would protect you now, if you remained among the Arhan."

She watched his face, deliberately dampening her mental awareness so as not to intrude. But the flicker in his eyes betrayed him.

She was right. He had not given up on the idea of becoming shaauri, finding his Path at last among those who had raised him. She was superfluous to that part of his life. The feelings they shared were irrelevant to the creation of a new world.

"Now Arhan will approach the War-Leader and speak openly of an end to war," Ronan said, as if she hadn't spoken. "You must speak to Miklos Challinor. He and the Archon might modify human opinion."

Cynara closed her eyes. "We're talking of peace, Ronan. Real peace after twenty years."

"It is possible. You and I are proof. I survived among the Kalevi, and you won their respect. It can be done."

Strangely, Cynara remembered Gunter on Bifrost, whose hatred of shaauri was absolute. And the Kalevii, most of whom would gladly see all humans dead.

Not everyone can overcome that kind of hatred, even if the Kinsmen are exposed as traitors. One man and woman against the Concordat, one Line against all shaauri . . .

"A single woman of your world once stood against a thousand shaauri and laid the Path to peace," Ronan said softly.

The mug slipped from Cynara's hands. A few brown drops of liquid spilled on the woven carpet.

"You heard me," she whispered.

He smiled. "Yes. My mind is beginning to heal. It may recover completely in time."

Cynara grabbed Ronan in a fierce embrace. He returned her kiss with a hunger she could not mistake.

There was still a little time before the *Suhtaara* reached the border. Time enough for farewells. But the shaauri used three very different phrases at parting. She didn't dare voice any of them.

Ronan threw his mug aside and fell with her onto the bunk. They were halfway undressed when a high-pitched, mechanical shriek interrupted them. Ronan released Cynara and stared at the door. A second later it opened, and a young shaaurin entered with a bob of apology.

The female—Cynara had begun to recognize such distinctions—spoke to Ronan with barely contained excitement. Ronan nodded, and she bounded away.

"Something has happened," Cynara said. "Ships—"

His expression was grim. "We are still a full day from the wormhole to Concordat territory, but a complication has arisen. Three ships stand in our path. Human ships.

"It is now a question of who will attack first."

Chapter 29

Two ve'laik'i *were waiting just outside to escort* Ronan and Cynara to the bridge. They ran most of the way, the alarm screaming in their ears, while shaauri crew went about their business with flattened ears and fur on end.

The bridge was an oasis of quiet in spite of the crisis, but the tranquility was deceptive. The smell of tension and hostility was thick on the air. The ship's Second and Third stood beside their chairs on the level below the First's station, watching the central screen with its ominous image.

Three human vessels. At the moment they were not moving, but they were deployed for battle.

Ronan went immediately to Hraan's side. The big shaaurin, who held double rank as Second of Line Arhan as well as ship's First, turned to him with an open-jawed expression of concern.

"Have you hailed them?" Ronan asked.

"I sent for you first." He glanced at Cynara. "It was my hope that you and *Va* D'Accorso might be of assistance."

"They have not attempted to communicate?"

"No." Hraan tapped his nails on the console. "They are in shaauri-*ja*. They must know we have the right and obligation to attack."

"But why are they here?" Cynara appeared at Ronan's shoulder. "Please increase magnification."

The Third complied, and the image on the screen seemed to double in size. Cynara blew out her breath.

"The *Pegasus*," Ronan said.

"And two Concordat ships—corvettes from the Royal Navy, if I'm not mistaken." She looked at Ronan. "They've come for us."

"Do you know this?"

"I can't think of a better explanation." She addressed Hraan in careful Standard. "*Aino'Ken,* one of these ships is my own, which was to continue on a different assignment while I accompanied Ronan to Aitu. I ask your patience until we can determine its purpose here."

"And the warships?" Hraan rumbled.

"I don't know. If you'll allow me to hail them, *sh'eivalin,* I will assure them that Ronan and I are safe, and advise them to withdraw."

Hraan twitched his ears in agreement. The murmur of shaauri conversation ceased. Cynara addressed the open comlink, Ronan close at her side.

"*Pegasus,*" she said, "This is Cynara D'Accorso, aboard the Arhan vessel *Suhtaara*. Ronan VelKalevi is with me. The Arhan are on a mission of peace. Stand down, *Pegasus,* and advise your escort to do the same."

Her voice echoed on the bridge. The comlink hissed. "Captain D'Accorso?" a familiar male voice said. "You are well, and not under any threat?"

"Very well. Scholar-Commander, stand down. All weapons offline, if you don't want trouble with the people who own this space."

"Acknowledged, Captain. I've advised the Persephoneans that you are not under threat."

Cynara squeezed Ronan's hand, and he returned the gentle pressure. "You have quite a bit of explaining to do, Adumbe," she said.

There was a moment of silence. "Lord Damon Challinor is with us, Captain. He wishes to speak to you. Can you come aboard?"

"Stand by." She closed the connection. "Damon?"

"I would not speculate," Ronan said, acknowledging her amazement. He looked up at Hraan. "*Sh'eivalin*, I assure you that there will be no battle. Permit me to escort Captain D'Accorso to the *Pegasus* and inform her crew of her well-being. I will return."

"It was our intention to deliver the captain to her own people," Hraan said, "but the humans regard you as outcast, kin of my kin."

"He'll be safe," Cynara said. "I give you my word as captain of the *Pegasus*. No harm will come to him among humans as long as I live."

"Then you may go."

Ronan bowed. Cynara avoided his glance, standing very stiff and straight behind the console. She opened the com-link.

"*Pegasus*, I and Ronan VelKalevi will come aboard. The situation remains delicate. Do not, I repeat, do not move from your current position or take any action that may be perceived as hostile."

"Acknowledged, Captain. Lord Damon agrees."

Cynara muttered a curse under her breath. "*Va* Hraan, we will go at once and see that the human ships leave shaauri territory."

Hraan nodded, and Ronan took Cynara's elbow. Her muscles were knotted with tension, yet even without the aid of telepathy he knew her condition had nothing to do with the present danger. It was *he* from whom she flinched, he who turned her face to stone.

Stone to bury her fear and preserve her pride. She did not wish him to leave her.

He did not wish to leave.

He released her arm and fell in step behind her. The two *ve'laik'i* escorted them by the swiftest route to a bay where a small passenger vessel was ready for departure.

Ronan took the pilot's seat, and Cynara webbed in beside him. The passage between the *Suhtaara* and the *Pegasus* was swift and brief. Kord d'Rhian O'Deira waited for them in the shuttle bay, accompanied by Healer Zheng and *An* Lizbet Montague.

Cynara was first out of the shuttle. She ran directly to

Kord, stopping just short of an embrace. Lizbet's face was flushed and smiling. Healer Zheng swept Cynara's body with her medscan. A spate of conversation reached Ronan's ears, and then all four faces turned toward the shuttle.

He placed the shuttle on standby and exited the hatch. Kord met him halfway.

"Brother," he said solemnly. "You have returned with our captain."

"Or she has returned with me." Ronan smiled and clasped forearms with the Siroccan. "You are well?"

"Yes, though the Little Mother may change that." He lowered his voice. "She's very angry."

"You took a great risk entering shaauri-*ja*."

"I didn't like leaving you and the captain on Persephone. We disobeyed orders and went back, and that was when Janek—Lord Damon—told us what you'd done."

Ronan wondered just how much Damon had revealed, and if Kord and the others knew of the assassination attempt or Cynara's plan to use herself as bait for the shaauri Kinsmen. Surely Damon would not have spared Ronan in any summary of recent events.

"Lord Damon has no love for me," he said. "Why is he here?"

Kord lifted a brow. "That's a tale you can hear on the bridge once Doctor Zheng has cleared you." He looked Ronan up and down. "A shaauri ship let you go?"

"That is a tale for you to hear." He hesitated, recognizing how much he feared losing this man's regard. "You are aware that I breached your ship's security before we arrived on Persephone, and that Lord Miklos Challinor exiled me from the Concordat?"

"You don't have to explain, Brother. I know there is good reason for everything you—"

He was interrupted when Miya Zheng appeared to scan Ronan as she had done Cynara. She frowned over the readings and pocketed the medscan.

"Ronan VelKalevi," she said. "Aside from a number of abrasions, lacerations, broken fingers, and cracked ribs, you appear to be in good health. Do you feel capable of going up to the bridge?"

"Yes. It is good to see you, *Li* Zheng."

"I look forward to hearing the entire story of your adventures, considering the many omissions in what we've been told."

"I will tell you all I can." He bowed to her, and then gave his attention to *An* Lizbet, who had come to greet him. She took his hand with remarkable boldness and grinned as wide as a *jukki.*

"Thank God," she said. "We were all so worried when we found out that you and the captain had gone alone to the Shaauriat with some dangerous plan to—"

"Montague," Cynara interrupted with affectionate severity, "this conversation can continue later. It's time to find out what in hell's going on."

The bridge was crowded with crew, as many as could fit in the limited space. Scholar-Commander Adumbe shook hands with Cynara, and Charis Antoniou in her rumpled fatigues saluted from among the ranks of her technicians. Damon Challinor stood beside the captain's chair but had not yet confiscated it for his own. His face was strangely free of hostility when he met Ronan's eyes.

After the first buzz of questions and conversation had died, Cynara went to stand before Damon.

"Lord Damon, I understand from my crew that you insisted upon accompanying the *Pegasus* in an ill-conceived scheme to 'rescue' Ronan and me from the shaauri. I assume you are aware of the risks you took, and continue to take, by entering shaauri space and confronting a shaauri warship."

Damon clasped his hands behind his back and gave her stare for stare. "I am, Captain D'Accorso. It was, however, necessary. Once your suspicious crew returned to Persephone, they refused to leave until they had spoken with you directly. By then you and Ronan had gone." He cleared his throat. "You have a very loyal crew, Captain. Once they learned that Ronan was a Challinor, and that you had accompanied him into shaauri territory hoping to . . . um . . . persuade him to join the human cause, they were unwilling to resume normal operations until they were sure you were safe.

Even if it meant penetrating the Shaauriat and courting destruction."

She glared pointedly at Adumbe and Kord. "I would have credited you with more sense than to permit this foolishness, Lord Damon, and even less desire to join them, considering your feelings about Ronan and the plan Lord Miklos approved."

Damon looked acutely uncomfortable. "I assume your memory has fully recovered? The Kinsmen took your bait?"

"Effectively, yes—after a few interesting turns of events. Ronan didn't betray the Concordat or his own people. He risked his life several times to preserve mine and thwart Kinsman plans, which were very much what we suspected."

"Where are the Kinsmen now?"

"Constano VelRauthi and his cohorts are in custody aboard the Arhan ship. I make no promises that the shaauri will let you question them. It's enough that Arhan hasn't opened fire."

"The Arhani were once human allies, the Line of Jonas Kane. Is that why they have cooperated?"

"The situation is complex and will require lengthy debriefing, Lord Damon. In the meantime, we have to get out of shaauri space. I've had some opportunity to observe their culture from very close quarters. Even the most peaceable shaaurin can be driven by perceived challenge and territorial instinct."

Damon nodded and opened the com to the corvettes. "As soon as you're ready, Captain. How do you wish to proceed?"

Cynara cast Ronan a glance of amazement. She must sense more of Damon's thoughts and feelings than Ronan could, but she was confounded by his uncharacteristic behavior.

"You still haven't told me why you came, Lord Damon," she said.

He dropped his gaze to the deck and shifted his feet. "You may recall that I had a vision of Ronan attacking our Archon," he said. "It was one of many that made me believe that he was our enemy in spite of his Challinor blood. However, during your absence there've been certain . . . alterations to my perspective." He looked directly at Ronan. "I never fully accepted my precognitive abilities. I didn't want them, even when they proved accurate. But then I *saw* Ronan giving his life for Concordat interests, abandoning what he had always wanted to serve those who'd rejected him. I saw him die."

Ronan did not look away. In Damon's eyes he saw the impossible: apology, understanding, and acceptance. Brotherhood.

"You would gladly have seen him dead on Persephone," Cynara said coldly.

"Yes. I was wrong." He lifted his head as if he could salvage some part of his pride. "I did not perceive how I could change Ronan's fate, but I realized that I had to try, even with only the most ill-conceived and superficial of plans."

"Lord Miklos agreed?"

Damon smiled, an expression both startling and sincere. "I'm also operating outside orders." He sobered and glanced at the central screen. "One other thing I saw, Captain—that both you and Ronan are essential to any future hope of peace between shaauri and humanity."

Ronan felt Cynara's gaze and the returning awareness of shared emotion. Her feelings were in turmoil, and he was afraid to seek beyond them. Afraid of the price yet to be paid.

He spoke the words Cynara would not. "Did you see what would become of me, Lord Damon?"

"I know only what I hope," Damon said. "That you will return to Persephone and rejoin your family."

"After what I have done?"

"I blamed you for what was beyond your control," Damon said. "If we had questioned the reports of our parents' deaths, if we'd looked for you, none of this would have happened."

Our parents. "Our mother and father are still missing and believed dead," he said. "I could not learn anything more."

Damon crossed the space between them. "There will be time for that, and for the forging of new bonds, even between enemies." He offered his hand.

Ronan took it slowly. Over Damon's shoulder he saw Cynara turn her head to hide her face. But she was happy—happy for Ronan as she was afraid to be happy for herself.

"Will you come back with us?" Damon asked.

"You saw that Captain D'Accorso and I were necessary for any future peace between shaauri and humans," Ronan said. "I would not see either species harmed by endless war."

"I know you're not a traitor."

"But unlike any other human, I understand shaauri ways and thought." The words dammed behind his teeth, and he forced them through. "I am accepted among the Arhani, and even by some who hate the Concordat."

"You still regard the shaauri as your people."

"I cannot escape my humanity. This Captain D'Accorso has taught me."

"Are you offering to act as a mediator and ambassador for the Concordat?"

To leave Cynara. To be parted from her for months, years, time unmeasured.

To preserve what they both loved.

"If you would trust me in such a capacity."

Damon glanced at Cynara, who was deep in conversation with Adumbe. "We would have to petition the Archon, and you'd be required to face the scrutiny of our Kinsmen. But Captain D'Accorso's recommendation would be very highly regarded." He hesitated. "You don't want to leave her."

Ronan was unable to answer. He looked around the bridge, crewmen and women busy at their stations, conversations filled with amazement and hope, Cynara in the center of it as she was meant to be. This was her world, these her true people.

Damon had not asked if Cynara would leave her ship to go with him, back to the shaauri. He understood too well.

"She is captain of the Pegasus," Ronan said at last. "Once, because of another man's madness, she doubted her right and fitness to command this vessel. Those doubts are gone." He smiled, though his face felt rigid as a mask. "This is the Path to which she was born, and the greatest wish of her heart. She has no need of assistance."

"Even though she loves you?"

He almost denied it. She had been his lifemate for a time, when necessity had compelled the bond. She had never asked that their mating of convenience be made permanent.

"Captain D'Accorso has seen the best and worst of shaauri-*ja*," he said. "She has an understanding of shaauri language and culture, and knows that there is much the two species share. She can speak for them among humans, as I can speak for humanity among shaauri."

"Will the shaauri accept such an arrangement?"

"That, too, must be presented to *A'Aho-Kei'hon-vekki* and debated among the Lines and Clans. It will not happen quickly. But shaauri admire boldness in the face of impossible odds. My presence, and that of Arhan and its allies, may smooth the path."

"And the Kinsmen?"

"Proof of Kinsman treachery against shaauri-*ja* will be, as humans say it, a 'mixed blessing.' But the Lines will know that the Concordat also wished to expose the Kinsmen as enemies to all."

"You can't do this alone, Ronan, even if they don't kill you for your trouble."

"Eventually other humans must come as negotiators, those who have properly learned shaauri ways. And only if the Concordat is willing to make concessions that may run counter to human convention and belief."

"I have some very interesting information that may incline the Concordat to set aside old grudges." Cynara joined them, resting her hands on Damon's and Ronan's shoulders as if they were old, easy companions.

But Damon could not begin to feel what Ronan felt—admiration, respect, love beyond any for teacher or friend. He understood the significance of her words. "When VelRauthi and his subordinates probed you on the bridge—"

"—I returned the favor and discovered that you weren't the only Kinsman agent in the Concordat. Your assignment to assassinate the Archon was the most formidable, but at least a dozen other agents were positioned to carry out similar political murders on other worlds as soon as word of the Archon's death reached them. All together, these would have had a profound impact on the Concordat as a whole."

"How could they have breached our security?" Damon demanded. "We took every precaution against Kinsman infiltration."

"That I don't know," Cynara said, "but I'll give their locations to you and the Archon's intelligence service so that you can arrest and question them."

Damon pulled a pocket recorder from his suit. "I must ask that you begin at once, Captain, in the event these agents decide to act on their own."

"Of course, Lord Damon. And I'm sure you'll be a most enthusiastic proponent of our new peace effort."

"Blackmail, Captain?"

"Mutual advantage. Surely your unique abilities can detect the future benefits in a permanent peace?"

"You may have noted that my abilities are not reliable," Damon said with a hint of his former rancor. "I saw Ronan dead, and he survived." He addressed Ronan with a twisted smile. "I misjudged you in every way."

"Then we know the future can change," Cynara said. "We have the power to change it."

"As people can change," Ronan said. "Human, and shaaurin."

"There's an old human saying," Damon said, " 'The enemy of my enemy is my friend.' " Let us hope that the evil these Kinsmen have done will help to bind our species."

"Captain D'Accorso said to me that not all Kinsmen are treacherous and in search of power. My father was Kinsman, and so is Brit Carter VelShaan. Someday they may serve a new and unforeseen purpose."

"Are you also precognitive, Ronan?" Damon asked half mockingly.

"No. But I have learned that there are telepaths among shaauri. I have a theory that many of these become ne'li, outcasts, because they are torn between many Paths."

Cynara lifted her brow. "That's a very radical idea, Ronan. Will shaauri even consider it?"

"Shaauri must be taught to accept this idea, if it proves valid. As humans may learn from shaauri—as I learned from Sihvaaro—so shaauri may learn from humans that some may walk between Paths for the advantage of all."

"And who better to teach them than you?"

Their gazes met. Cynara took his hand and led him to the

briefing room adjoining the bridge, sealing them away from Damon and the crew.

Ronan opened his mouth to speak, but Cynara pressed her finger to his lips.

"I know what you plan to do," she said softly. "Go back with Arhan and face the War-Leader. I never expected anything else."

He caught her hand and turned it to kiss her palm. Her skin was warm with the taste of hope and sadness.

The time they both dreaded had almost come.

"Ronan," she said, resting her hand on his cheek.

"I know you must remain in the Concordat to command the *Pegasus* and share what you have learned," he said. "You do not hate the shaauri, though their ways are strange and often terrible to you. You will speak well for them."

"I understand so much more now," she said. "Some of it is in here"—she tapped her temple—"and some here." She pressed her hand to her chest above her heart. "Because of you, there's nothing in either place binding me to the past."

She held up her hand with its golden rings. One after another she pulled the rings from her fingers and clenched them in her fist.

"Sil akai," she said, and tossed the rings in a gleaming arc across the briefing table, where they lay like a child's discarded dice.

Ronan took her naked hand between his. "You were always stronger than Tyr."

"And you were always the equal of any man or shaaurin, no matter what you believed."

She would not let him deny it, but kissed him as if they had all the time in the world to talk and make love and discover each other again. He knew how much his mind had healed by the way his need fed on hers, by the way her urgent thoughts became entangled with his.

Stay with me, her body said. *Stay.*

"You can come back to Persephone," she said, kissing the angle of his jaw, "before returning to the shaauri. Arhan will wait." She nipped his ear. "You can set things right with the Archon, and Miklos—"

"No." He set her back so that he could see her eyes.

"Arhan must take action swiftly, without hesitation, and I must go with them. It is the only way to exploit the small advantages we now possess."

"It is when you face the most difficult challenge that you must call upon all Paths."

He heard Cynara's voice as clearly as if she had spoken aloud. But he also heard Sihvaaro's voice, from the day long ago when he had first taught Ronan that profound lesson.

"Sihvaaro," he said.

"He lives in me as he lives in you. He was right, Ronan."

"He spoke of Paths, Cynara, not people."

"Yet 'all Paths are One.' If that is true, then what can stand between us?"

Ronan found it difficult to speak. " 'There is a time to battle for what must change,' " he said thickly, " 'and a time to accept what will be.' "

"Yes. But Sihvaaro said something else, when he first met me. He called me your lifemate."

Ronan looked away. "He did not understand."

"I think he did, better than either one of us. He was a remarkable person, and his gifts were great."

"As are yours. You must not waste them."

She gripped his upper arms and gave him a shake. "You swore before your Line that I was your lifemate. I didn't release you from that pledge."

"It was a deception I never expected you to honor."

"It was a little high-handed," she said with a crooked smile, "but it was the right thing to do. It still is." She compelled him to meet her gaze. "You still have some crazy idea that you're somehow unsuitable to be the lifemate of a simple Alliance captain."

"To lifemate is . . . it is—"

"I know. Sacred. Forever." She buried her fingers in the short hair at the nape of his neck. "Do you love me, Ronan?"

There could be no more deception. His mind had reawakened, and his heart lay helpless before her challenge.

All at once she opened her thoughts to him, withholding nothing. Her love was fierce and undeniable like river floods after the great Thaw, spilling down from the Semakka Mountains. It drowned him in humility and awe.

"I had something to prove to myself when I took command of the *Pegasus*," Cynara said, "a whole lifetime's worth of rebellion against my culture, realizing the fulfillment of my greatest ambitions, showing myself worthy to take Tyr's place when I was afraid I could never be. None of that is important now."

"Your captaincy is important. Your skill and ability cannot be replaced. The *Pegasus*—"

"The *Pegasus* will do very well without me. It's only a matter of time before the Concordat builds a whole fleet of the ships, and they'll need captains."

"Kord—the others—"

"—will also be perfectly fine. I have confidence that Lizbet, in particular, is ready to strike out on her own." She raised her hand. "And before you bring it up, I can give Damon all the information he needs in a few hours."

Ronan felt his temper slipping its leash, hope and denial like opposing *ve'laik'i* battling inside his skull. "You cannot be happy away from your own people, or among mine. Every day would be a struggle to win respect and acceptance."

"It sounds very familiar." She bared her teeth with something less than humor. "And I'll have a teacher of vast and varied experience."

"Even I may not survive—"

She placed her hands on her hips. "Are you finished?"

He stared at her. She laughed, pure joy.

"You know by now that I was never content to be what my birth dictated. I've always wanted to see what's around the next wormhole—and I still haven't got a proper souvenir from a shaauri world. That's why I'm going with you. And you don't have anything to say about it."

Ronan tipped back his head and hissed through his teeth. "Sihvaaro," he said, "why have you set me such a test?"

Cynara pulled his head down and rested her forehead against his. "Because he knew you could do it. Do you remember the last thing he said?"

He breathed in the scent of her hair. 'The circle will be complete.' "

"And now," she said, setting her mouth to his, "it is."

Glossary

CHARACTERS

Aarys, Tala: Third of Aarys striker

Adumbe, Scholar-Commander Taye: Pegasus second-in-command

Annukki: Ronan's childhood friend, now *ri'laik'in*

Antiniou, Charis: chief engineer on the *Pegasus*

Archimedes: mascot cat on the *Pegasus*

Ardith: medical assistant on the *Pegasus*

Basterra, Cargomaster Segar: cargomaster on the *Pegasus*

Belloq: a shaauri Kinsman

Beneviste, Magnus Egon: father of Nyle Beneviste

Beneviste, Matrona Egona: mother of Nyle Beneviste

Beneviste, Fico Nyle: Cynara's former fiancé

Bhruic: guard on the *Pegasus*

Challinor, Lord Achilles: birth name of Ronan VelKalevi

Challinor, Lord Ambros: Ronan's elder brother

Challinor, Lord Damon: aka Phineas Janek; Ronan's younger brother

Challinor, Lord Hector: Archon of Persephone, Ronan's uncle

Challinor, Lady Kori Galatéa: Ronan's mother

Challinor, Lord Miklos: Ronan's uncle

D'Accorso, Magnus Casnar: Cynara's father, leading burgherlord of Elsinore

D'Accorso, Cynara: captain of the *Pegasus*

D'Accorso, Matrona Zurine: Cynara's mother

D'Accorso-fila, Elendra: Cynara's sister

Gajda: Royal Intelligence agent assigned to Miklos's personal guard

Gunter, Sam: survivor of the abandoned mining colony on Bifrost

Hanno: Ronan's primary caregiver on Aitu, *li'laik'in*

Hraan: Aino'Ken Arhan, First of the *Suhtaara;* adopted Line-kin of Jonas VelArhan

Janek, Phineas: aka Damon Challinor; see Challinor, Lord Damon

Jauregi: second pilot of the *Pegasus*

Kane, Eeva: founder of the Kinsmen

Kane, Jonas: see VelArhan, Jonas Kane

Larsen, Magnus Vidar: member of Dharman Offworld Trade Council, powerful telepath

Lenko: First of Ain'Kalevi

Mains: Royal Intelligence agent assigned to Miklos's personal guard

Mairva: Ronan's childhood companion, now *ve'laik'in*

Montague, Lizbet: first pilot-navigator of the *Pegasus*

O'Deira, Kord d'Rhian: weapons specialist of the *Pegasus*; Ronan's blood-brother

Riko: Ronan's childhood companion now *va'laik'in*

Samit: Second of An'Kalevi

Siannas, Matrona Donata: Cynara's late aunt, married to Jesper Siannas

Siannas, Magnus Jesper: Cynara's uncle by marriage, originally of Persephone

Siannas, Tyr: Cynara's cousin, former captain of the *Pegasus*

Sihvaaro: Ronan's teacher and mentor on Aitu

Silta: male offspring of Annukki

Teklys: Persephonean agent assigned to young Achilles (Ronan)

Tesar: majordomo of *Magnus* D'Accorso

VelArhan, Jonas Kane: Ronan's father

VelKalevi, Ronan: adopted Kinsman of Line Kalevi; see Challinor, Lord Achilles

VelRauthi, Artur Constano: leader of the Kinsman rebellion

VelShaan, Brit Carter: Kinswoman employed by the Archon

Zheng, Miya: Chief Medic of the *Pegasus*

LOCATIONS

Aitu: shaauri colony world, Ronan's home for twenty-three years

Anvil: world of Concordat; Miya Zheng's homeworld

Bifrost: abandoned human colony

Concordat: federation of twenty human colony worlds, headed by Persephone

Dharma: primary planet of the Nine Worlds confederation

Elsinore: city-state of Novaterra

Eos: capital city of Persephone

Luhta: shaauri world on which Kinsmen are based

Matisse: colony world of the Nine Worlds confederation

Nemesis: colony world of the Nine Worlds confederation

Nine Worlds: confederation of human colonies separated from the Concordat by shaauri territory

Novaterra: largest island in the Dharman western hemisphere

Persephone: primary world of the Concordat

Sirocco: colony world of the Nine Worlds confederation; Kord's homeworld

VOISHAAUR PHRASES

Farewell

>   Until we are whole: *tan uri-kah*

>   With the Ancestors: *sil akai*

>   Fortunate Path: *kei'lai*

Thank-you

>   My honor to you: *Ina-sh'ei vai kana*

Oath

>   By my Path and by my soul: *ta'i'lai ta'i'ma*

Insult

>   Stinking: *kek'ko*

>   Ancestorless ghost: *n'akai ne'lin*

Body-without-fur (used for humans): *anki-ne'karo*

Endearment

My breath/my soul: *ina-ma*

Miscellaneous

One is called (male or female): *ilku se*

So be it (so say the Ancestors): *akai'po*

VOISHAAUR-STANDARD GLOSSARY

A'Aho-Kei'hon-vekki: War-Leader; First of Firsts Clan Blood
   Leader
a'amia: predatory bird; raptor
Aarys: antihuman Line, spacefaring
Aho: First; primary leader
Aho'Ah'Aarys: First of First House Aarys
Aho'Ain'Kalevi: First of Second House Kalevi
Aho'An: First of Body
Aho'Kei: First of Clan
Aho'Ken: First of Line
Aho'Kil: First of House
Aho'Va: First of Will
Ain'Kalevi: Second House of Kalevi
Ain'Kalevi-ja: Place of Second House Kalevi
Aino: Second; secondary leader
Aino'Ain'Kalevi: Second of Second House Kalevi
Aino'Arv'Darja: Second of Third House Darja
Aino'Kei: Second of Clan
Aino'Ken: Second of Line
Aino'Va: Second of Will
An: honorific for *an'laik'in*
An'lai: Path of Body
An'laik'in: of the Body Path
anki: Body
Anki-ja: Place of Body
anki-ne'karo: body-without-fur
arao: shaauri "tea"

Arban: human-allied Line, spacefaring
Arv'Darja: Third House Darja
Arv'Kalevi: Third House Kalevi
Arva'Kir: Council of Three: First, Second, and Third
Arvi: Third; tertiary leader
Arvi'Va: Third of Will
Aur: shaauri homeworld
ba'laik'in: preadolescent shaauri child
ba'ne: void
bali: childhood
be'laik'in: shaauri on Walkabout
be'rokh'-kaari'la: Walkabout; time of selection
Clan: see *Kei*
da'amera: courage
Da'amera-ja: Place of Courage or Challenge; area where challenges are fought
Darja: antihuman Line of Aitu
eival: honorable
End of Void: mythical time when all living creatures took form
he'i: yes
House: see *Kil*
Hraan: Aino'Ken of Arhan
hylpup: small mammal native to Aur
ina'sh'ei vai kana: "My honor to you"; thank you
ja: place
jukki: monkey-like mammal native to Aitu
Jyri: forest on Aitu
kai: the Ancestors
Kalevi: antihuman, conservative Line, Ronan's adopted line
Kalevi-Kai: Kalevi ancestors
karo: hair, fur
Kei: Clan: equivalent of human "nation," made up of many Lines
kek: plant native to Aitu with bitter, corrosive sap
kek'ko: stinking, disgusting
Ken: Line: all Houses of one "surname"
Ki: honorific for ki'laik'in
ki'lai: Path of Reason
ki'laik'in: One of Path of Reason

kiel: fortunate
Kil: House: extended family in one location
kio: all/every
kio'laii: of all Paths
kio'n'uri: creature of shaauri legend
kir: council
kivi: Reason
koinno: predatory mammal of Aitu
la'salo: mammal of Aur, a graceful runner
Lai: Path: one of six occupational categories in shaauri society
Lai-ilkujoi: Selection, the means by which shaauri find a Path
Lenko: First of Second House Kalevi
li'laik'in: one of Path of Heart
Line: see *Ken*
linei: Path of Heart
Linei-ja: Place of Heart
ma: breath, soul
mii'eival'kai: law; order; tradition
Moikko: Clan to which both Kalevi and Aarys belong
myl'vekk: blood-drinking "bird" of Aitu
ne: no
ne'karo: hairless, furless
ne'lin: ghost; wraith; outcast; of no path
nemii: lawless
neva: no one, nothing
OutLine: foreigner; from outside the Line
Path: see *Lai*
Pohomi: former First of Ain'Kalevi
Reckoning: see *sh'ei-lostajoi*
relka: shaauri alcoholic drink
ri'lai: Path of Spirit
ri'laik'in: of Path of Spirit
riama: Spirit
Riama-ja: Place of Spirit
rohka-toi'sun: Time of Irresponsibility; childhood
Ronan-ja: "place of Ronan"; Ronan's hut in Ain'Kalevi-*ja*
Selection: see *lai-ilkujoi*
Semakka: mountain range on Aitu

sh'ei: face; honor

sh'ei-lostajoi: Reckoning; means by which opposing shaauri "test" each other's determination and courage

sh'eivalin: general shaauri honorific

sh'kei'eivalin: Clan brother/sister

shaauri: people of Aur

shaauri-ja: shaauri territory

shaaurin: singular of shaauri

siv'alku: male reproductive organ

sivu: mate

sivu'uri: lifemate

sivuj'avar: kidnap-for-mating

ska'eival: most honorable

Soraan: Line with settlements on Aitu

striker: midsize shaauri warship

Suhtaara: Arhan ship

toi'sun: irresponsible; usually in connection with *ba'laik'i*

uri: whole

Va: honorific for va'laik'in

va'lai: Path of Will

va'laik'in: of Path of Will

vali: Will

Ve: honorific for ve'laik'in

ve'lai: Path of Blood

ve'laik'in: of Path of Blood

vek'riam: Blood/Spirit; exercises of the Eightfold Way

vekki: Blood

Vel: Voishaaur prefix for "adopted"

VelKalevi: adopted of Kalevi

VelShaan: adopted of Shaan

vil: insect found on Aitu

Voishaaur: common language of shaauri

Walkabout: see *be'rokh-kaari'la*

General Glossary

Alliance: affiliation of the Concordat and Nine Worlds

Aphrodite: Persephonean corvette

Archon: hereditary ruler of Persephone
Bolts: Cynara's nickname for Miya Zheng
burgher-lord: aristocrat of Dharma
Darter: small shaauri warship
Eightfold Way: philosophy practiced by Sihvaaro and Ronan
Elsinore: primary city-state of Novaterra; Cynara's home
Eos: capital city of Persephone
Faber: title for Dharman male of working class
fenek: Dharman slang word for buttocks
Fico: title for unmarried Dharman male of upper class
fila: Dharman suffix indicating unmarried woman
Filia: title for unmarried Dharman female
High Town: highest section of Elsinore, occupied by the
    wealthy and elite
Kinsman rebellion: unsuccessful uprising of certain Kinsmen
    against the Concordat
Kinsmen: human telepaths adopted into shaauri Lines
Little Mother: Kord's name for Cynara, used in Sirocco
Long Silence: "Dark Ages" of human colonies; time of isola-
    tion and loss of technology
Low Town: lowest section of Elsinore; occupied by "working
    poor"
Magné: plural *Magnus*
Magnus: title for mature Dharman male of upper class
Magna: "coined" title for unmarried Dharman woman of au-
    thority
Matrona: title for married Dharman woman
Matroné: plural of *Matrona*
Mes: Persphonean title for female citizen
Middleton: middle section of Elsinore, occupied by "middle
    class"
Nesté: plural of *Nestus*
Nestus: title for Dharman male of middle class
Nova: card game
Offward Trade Council: Dharman authority regulating off-
    world trade, Dharma's spacefleet, and the *Pegasus* Project
Pegasus: Alliance flagship utilizing the alien slingshot drive
Pontos: shuttle of the *Pegasus*
Royal Intelligence: Persephone's secret service
safetide: Dharman farewell

Ser: Persephonean title for male citizen
slingshot drive: nickname for the alien stardrive discovered in
    Dharma's asteroid belt
Standard: common language of Concordat
striker: midsize shaauri warship
Thalassa: shuttle of the *Pegasus*
Watergiver: Siroccan Clan Mother
wormhole: "tunnel" connecting two distant locations in space

Susan Krinard graduated from the California College of Arts and Crafts with a BFA and worked as an artist and freelance illustrator before turning to writing. An admirer of both romance and fantasy, Susan enjoys combining these elements in her books. Her first novel, *Prince of Wolves*, garnered praise and broke new ground in the genre of paranormal romance. She has won the *Romantic Times* Award for Best Contemporary Fantasy and Best Historical Fantasy, the PRISM Award for Best Dark Paranormal Fantasy, and has been a finalist for the prestigious RITA Award.

Susan loves to hear from her readers. Write to her at:

Susan Krinard
P.O. Box 51924
Albuquerque, NM 87181
(For a reply, please send a self-addressed stamped envelope.)

Or e-mail her at: sue@susankrinard.com

Her website, www.susankrinard.com, contains information on all her books and a link to receive her monthly and quarterly newsletters.